1 Nigel

'She was a very intelligent woman, in her day,' said Nigel to the fat nurse with the eating disorder.

How infuriating it was at that moment to have lost the power of speech. Kate longed to say 'What do you mean – "in her day"? I still am.'

'She was one of the most beautiful women of her generation,' continued Nigel.

Well, no, she couldn't object to the use of the past tense in that context. She'd kept her looks well into her seventies. At the time of her sudden, unexpected rise to fame she had been dubbed 'Britain's most Glamorous Gran' by the *Daily Mail* and 'The Sexy Septuagenarian' by the *South Wales Echo*. But then her beauty, like her fame, had faded.

'Sexy too.' Surely Nigel couldn't have read her thoughts? It was decidedly not one of his talents. 'Very sexy.'

She wanted to smile. She wanted to acknowledge the surprising pride in her son's voice. She wanted to exult in the memory of how sexy she had been. But she didn't. She had no idea how badly the stroke had affected her facial muscles. Her smile might be a travesty.

'She can't understand what I'm saying, can she?' asked Nigel.

'It's possible,' said the fat nurse. 'The hearing is often the last sense to go.'

The last sense to go! They think I'm on the way out, thought Kate.

'I'd hate to hurt the old trout,' continued Nigel.

The old trout!

'Well, you'd best not call her an old trout, then, had yer?' said the fat nurse, very reasonably, Kate thought. She felt, very faintly, as if from a long distance away, the grip of the nurse's plump hand, sticky like a doughnut, and she tried not to flinch. 'We aren't an old trout, are we?'

We aren't plural either, you silly cow, thought Kate uncharitably.

'She's been one hell of a mother,' said Nigel. 'She's been one hell of an act to follow.'

Kate sensed the departure of the fat nurse. She heard the scraping of a metal chair on a hard floor, and she realised that her eldest child had settled down to sit beside her. Child! He was seventy-four. She pictured him as she had last seen him. His great round face was looking too big as his body shrank. There was a large bald patch in the middle of his snow-white hair. He needed a hip replacement. And he was twenty-five years younger than her!

She longed to sleep. She wished he'd go. It had been such a shock to wake up and find that she couldn't move her legs or arms. She'd felt as if some maniac had encased her in plaster of Paris. She'd tried to cry out, but no sound had come. She'd broken out in a hot sweat which had cooled and dried disgustingly on her shrivelled old body. She had discovered, to her great relief, that she could open her eyes, and had found herself staring at a cracked and peeling ceiling, dimly lit by a barley-sugar night-light. There had been a smell of disinfectant and stale cabbage.

How had she got there, wherever she was? Her last memory had been of sounding off in the Golden Glade Retirement Home, getting worked up as usual about the state of the world. She could see them now, a circle of pale frightened old women leaning on their zimmer frames and gawping at her with their mouths open like a nest of young thrushes waiting to be fed, Dorothy Pearson because her mouth was always open, the rest because they had been astonished and terrified by her fervour. Then blankness, blackness, confusion. What had happened?

Going Gently

David Nobbs

ARROW

Published in the United Kingdom in 2001 by
Arrow Books

7 9 10 8 6

Copyright © David Nobbs 2000

First published in the United Kingdom in 2000
by William Heinemann

Arrow Books
The Random House Group Limited
20 Vauxhall Bridge Road, London SW1V 2SA

Random House Australia (Pty) Limited
20 Alfred Street, Milsons Point, Sydney
New South Wales 2061, Australia

Random House New Zealand Limited
18 Poland Road, Glenfield
Auckland 10, New Zealand

Random House (Pty) Limited
Endulini, 5a Jubilee Road, Parktown 2193, South Africa

The Random House Group Limited Reg. No. 954009

www.randomhouse.co.uk

A CIP catalogue record for this book
is available from the British Library

Papers used by Random House are natural, recyclable products
made from wood grown in sustainable forests. The manufacturing
processes conform to the environmental regulations
of the country of origin

Printed and bound in Great Britain by
Bookmarque Ltd, Croydon, Surrey

ISBN 0 09 941465 1

Going Gently

'Spellbinding... Kate is a superbly realised character: a strong passionate woman with an unquenchable thirst for life and a keen social conscience... Like Nobb's most famous creation, Reginald Perrin, she is an iconoclast and a rebel, and always heroic in her championing of the underdog. And, just like the Reginald Perrin novels, *Going Gently* is enormously entertaining and extremely funny' *Guardian*

'Ultimately most serious when making us smile, David Nobbs has written his funniest novel yet... Nobbs is wonderful [at] conjuring up the mist and salt of Swansea in just a few words, and the tang and touch of teenage passion... No writer save Waugh is so brutally explicit with dialogue... *Going Gently* stares morality in the face and howls with merriment' *The Times*

' *Going Gently,* like all the best comic novels, mixes sadness with laughter to great effect... probably Nobb's finest work' *Independent*

'There's no knocking Nobbs as a true king of comedy... We are not overendowed with comic novelists, and most of those initially hailed as the heirs to Waugh and Wodehouse have conformed to the Kingsley Amis principle of getting their funniest book out of the way first. So we should be thankful for the continuing brilliance of David Nobbs.' *Mail On Sunday*

'An unsung comedy hero, Nobbs... could probably write a guide book about Luxembourg and still have you laughing so hard you'd rupture a ligament' *Later*

'[The heroine's] refusal to deny her past lies at the heart of this elegiac novel... Nobbs celebrates the resilience and generosity of the human spirit' *Sunday Telegraph*

This is David Nobbs's thirteenth novel. His previous books include the Henry Pratt novels and the Reginald Perrin novels. He has also written many series for television, notably *The Fall and Rise of Reginald Perrin*, *A Bit of a Do*, and *Love on a Branch Line*. He lives in North Yorkshire.

A reassuring voice, disembodied, cultured, slightly stilted, had provided the answer, an answer that had not been at all reassuring. 'You've had a massive cerebro-vascular accident,' it had said. 'What you would call a stroke. You're in hospital. You're in good hands. There is nothing to fear.'

There is nothing to fear? Only boredom, discomfort, pain, humiliation, death. Hardly anything else at all. So, it had happened, the one thing she had dreaded, the stroke.

Nigel was holding her hand now. She could feel the pressure of his huge hand on hers.

'I don't know if you can understand what I'm saying, Mother,' he said, 'but I've contacted Timothy and Maurice and they're both making arrangements to fly over. Timothy's in Majorca and should be here tomorrow. Maurice has some urgent loose ends to tie up in St Petersburg, so it may be the day after. They were both coming the week after next for your hundredth anyway, so they'll just come a bit sooner.

'Elizabeth must be away, but I've left a message on her answerphone, asking her to ring me. I didn't say why. I didn't want to alarm her. I mean, there's no cause for alarm. You've survived. You'll pull through. You're going to be blowing out those hundred candles all on your own. Your will-power's legendary.'

She slept on and off after that, and only woke properly when she felt a distant squeeze of her hand, and he said, 'I'm off now, Mother dear. I'm going to the Caprice. I'm going to have the eggs Benedict and the sea bass. Timothy will come tomorrow.'

She felt his stubbly cheek against her lined old face, and was grateful, knowing how difficult physical contact was for him. She almost choked on his aftershave. For more than fifty years she'd been irritated by his aftershave. He always used too much. He floated through life in its sickly embrace, in the hope that it would hide from the world the suspected sourness of his breath. Uncharitable to think of that now. For shame, Kate Copson.

Alone at last! Oh, the relief. So alone. Oh, the fear. Come

back, Nigel darling. I'm so alone. Not really alone. There were other women in the ward. She didn't yet know how many.

She opened her right eye cautiously. She couldn't move her neck, but she could move the eye just sufficiently to catch a glimpse, to the right, of a window. There was daylight. The sky was angry. So was she. For a moment she felt relieved at this sight of the great world outside. Not for long. There was a whole universe out there, and here she was, separated from it, probably for ever. No more Venice. No more Peru. Not even Barnet High Street ever again. Impotent fury swept over her.

She closed her eye hurriedly as she heard footsteps approaching. Another nurse spoke to her, not as cockney as the first. This second nurse pulled at Kate's mouth, but not roughly, and managed to open it sufficiently to insert a cool, thin, round tube. Of course. A thermometer. Records must be kept.

'You're almost normal. Well done, Kate,' said this second nurse. Her hands were bony. Kate liked the fact that she referred to her in the singular, although she did rather spoil it by asking, 'How are you feeling?' and supplying the answer herself. 'A little better! Good!'

Almost normal. She liked the 'almost'. She wouldn't mind that on her gravestone. 'Kate Thomas, 1899–1999. She was almost normal.'

1899-1999. It came as a shock to her to realise that she didn't expect to survive to the end of the year. That wouldn't do. She wasn't ready to die yet.

She was distracted from these thoughts by the return of the nurse, with a doctor.

'Doctor Ramgobi's here to see you, Kate,' said the nurse.

'How is she?' asked Doctor Ramgobi in that cultured, slightly stilted voice that Kate recognised from earlier.

'Doing all right. Doesn't seem to respond, though.'

'I see.' Again, she could only just feel the fingers as Doctor Ramgobi prodded and probed. She hoped he'd washed his

4

hands. They were gentle fingers, though. Respectful. No more intrusive than they had to be. Then he almost repeated his earlier words. 'Well, Kate, you've had a major cerebro-vascular accident.' He spoke the medical words with precision and a dusting of pride. She noticed that he had scaled down 'massive' to 'major'. Perhaps he'd thought 'massive' tactless. 'What you would call a stroke.' There was just a faint disapproving tone in his voice, which was a bit rich, since it was he who was using the layman's term, not she. 'You're in Ward 3C of Whetstone General Hospital. You will be cared for as well here as anywhere, Kate, so you mustn't give up hope.'

As he walked away, Kate heard him say, 'She's *the* Kate Copson, you know, Helen,' and the second nurse said, 'Sorry, doctor. Not with you,' and he said, 'Ah! The fleeting quality of fame.'

The Kate Copson. Not just *a* Kate Copson. She felt absurdly pleased. And she suddenly realised, as she reflected on the doctor's visit, that her mind was working as well as ever. She'd been analysing his every sentence. Good God, she might be trapped and paralysed and helpless, but she wasn't a halfwit yet.

She opened her right eye again. The clouds in the sky in her little window on the world were turning gold and silver and pearl, great feathers of cloud lit by the setting sun. Below them were smoky, puffy, wispy, angry little clouds that the sun couldn't touch. The light was fading. The darkness was coming.

Kate closed her eye and returned to her new dark world. Was her light fading? No! It mustn't! She was a fighter. She would astonish them all. She would not go gentle into that good night, to quote a fellow child of Swansea. Not while she had her brain. She wasn't ready. She had one last task to perform. She had a murder to solve.

The boldness of this thought took her breath away. It almost killed her there and then. How could she, almost a hundred years old, solve a murder, lying in a hospital bed, unable to question anybody, unable to examine any of the evidence, unable to write anything down, almost forty years after it had happened? What hubris to think that she could succeed where Inspector Crouch, thoroughness his middle name, had failed.

But she was *the* Kate Copson, not *a* Kate Copson! She could do it. She had to do it. For almost forty years she had avoided the subject, for fear of what she might find. Now the fear of not knowing was greater than the fear of knowing. She dreaded the thought of dying without knowing which of her three sons had murdered her fifth husband. Or should that be, strictly speaking, her fourth husband? Or, to be even more strict, not a husband at all? It was a fine point of linguistics. She almost laughed. To be thinking of such linguistic distinctions now!

It wasn't so much that she needed to know which of her sons was the murderer as that she needed to know which two of them weren't. She couldn't bear to die suspecting all three.

Of course, the fact that the murderer had left a note saying 'Sorry, Ma' didn't necessarily mean that it had been one of her sons. Elizabeth could have done it, although Kate didn't seriously entertain that theory. Poor Elizabeth would never be capable of doing anything as extraordinary as murdering someone. It could even have been one of Graham's many enemies trying to implicate her sons. She had managed, long ago, to persuade herself that it was probably so. She knew now, in the intensity of her darkness, that she had been fooling herself.

She sensed, rather than heard, one of the other women in the ward walking towards her bed. The woman came up so close to her that she could smell the madness on her. 'Oh,' she said, 'he's such a pretty little baby. Oh, bless his little cotton socks.' How did anybody get as mad as that? How could you see babies where none existed? Kate shrank from her. The woman moved off, to her great relief, but the incident had brought home to her just how weak she was. She wasn't ready yet to solve a murder. She wasn't even ready yet to live in the reality of this ward.

Well, she didn't need to. Her great-grandson Ben was deeply

into virtual reality. It was the coming thing. Soon you'd be able to spend a fortnight in Majorca without leaving Basildon, or, if you were a masochist, a fortnight in Basildon without leaving Majorca.

Majorca! That was where Timothy lived. Could Timothy murder someone? No! Too soon to be thinking such thoughts! Spare yourself this pain, Kate.

Ben had been very patient with her, teaching her how to use the video machine. He'd been four at the time. She hadn't used it much. There wasn't much she wanted to watch once, let alone twice. She would use it now. She would escape from the ward, from her paralysis, from her humiliation, by replaying the video of her life. She wasn't ready yet to become the Sherlock Holmes of the Bedpan. She needed to be a child again first.

What a life she had led. Now she could lead it again, and again, and again. Play the best bits endlessly. Fast-forward through the dull bits (though there weren't many of those). Who could begrudge her her escape? And it wouldn't, perhaps, be entirely escape, for some of the clues to the identity of the murderer might lie far back in the past: a psychiatrist would expect them to, not that she trusted psychiatrists, but it was good to think that maybe she could combine an escape from reality with a confrontation of reality. It would be what Ben would call 'a double whammy'.

The thought of Ben disturbed her deeply. At sixteen he reminded her so much of Gwyn. He had those same dark, florid, jowly, sultry, sensuous good looks. Oh Lord, she was going all adjectival at the memory. He had no right to remind her of Gwyn. It wasn't as if they were related.

Gwyn! Her first love! She shuddered, inside herself, far behind her face, where there was no paralysis and therefore no protection against pain. Gwyn! The memory still hurt, eighty-three years later.

Rewind, and play.

2 Gwyn

She was born Kate Thomas, preceding her identical twin Dilys into this world by almost one and a half hours. People said later that it was typical of her to be so eager to enter into the vast excitement of life.

Her father, John Thomas Thomas, was headmaster of a small school in the poorest quarter of Swansea. Every day, he took a horse-drawn tram from their posh new home in Eaton Crescent to the school. Electric trams were introduced in 1900, the year in which Kate said her first word. It gave little indication of the originality and invention that would follow. It was Daddy.

John Thomas Thomas was a tall, handsome man with a thick but not luxuriant moustache which lent gravitas to a face that didn't need it. In his brown Celtic eyes, contradiction reigned. Severity twinkled. Humour wore a frown.

Her mother, Bronwen Thomas, née Davies, was a twinkly little pharmacist's daughter from up country, beyond Carmarthen. She had a petite beauty, a perfect complexion, a wonderful voice and inexhaustible energy, all of which she attributed to the love of a good man and the eating of laverbread every morning. She might have been a singer, if she hadn't fallen in love with John Thomas Thomas. She might have become one of the first stars of the steam radio, and been known as the Welsh Nightingale. She might have visited Venice and tasted wine and been kissed on the promenade deck of a Cunarder by a charming rotter with white whiskers, if she hadn't met John Thomas Thomas and borne him six children. But she wouldn't have been as happy.

Kate and Dilys were followed by Enid, who was timid and

frail, and by Myfanwy, who was loud and lusty. It seemed that Kate was to live in a house dominated by femininity, but then, in 1906, along came Oliver, the apple of everybody's eye. Fair, warm, extrovert, charming, life and soul of the party, more of his mother in him than his father. And then, two years later, Bernard was born, dark, intense, questing, querulous, nervous, delicate, short-sighted and shy. That completed the family. John Thomas Thomas believed that Bronwen had suffered enough.

And what a family it was. Lying in her hospital bed, eyes closed, pretending to sleep, Kate was astonished by the clarity of her memory of that delightful period in her life, her pre-war childhood in that chatty, cheery, narrow, huddled town, alive with the lilt of Welsh talk, seasoned by the tang of the sea, resonant with music, awash with cockles, a town crowded on to a piece of land a little too small for it, a town that lay between heaven and hell and introduced Kate to both those concepts. Kate's heaven was the coast, and the Mumbles train, the oldest passenger railway service in the world, which chugged hourly to Oystermouth round Swansea Bay, which has been compared, somewhat fancifully, to the Bay of Naples. Kate's hell was the valleys, the mines, the slag-heaps, the strong men and the strong drink and the bare, black, brooding hills.

What fun they had enjoyed, in their smart new three-storey gabled terraced house on the edge of the spreading town. How could they have had such fun in a house where no swear-word was ever uttered, no sexual function was ever mentioned, no naked thigh was ever seen, no alcohol was ever consumed unless you'd fainted first, no naughty joke was ever heard, no food was ever praised, and laverbread was eaten every morning? But what fun they had, except on Sundays. What charades they played, what quizzes they held in the cheery back room with the armchairs drawn up higgledy-piggledy round the cramped little coal fire, the sombre knitted texts on the walls, the shiny mahogany dining table.

When they had visitors they sat in the front room, the best room, the parlour, with its bay window, there's posh. But the room never breathed, however early you lit the fire. However hard you tried, life never came to it.

Happy innocent times. Did Kate linger on these pleasant memories? No, gentle reader, she did not. So eager was she to relive the excitements of her first love that she fast-forwarded through these happy days, the sooner to get to Gwyn, even though this would also take her all too soon to the cruel moment when her innocence was shattered for ever.

Linger a while, Kate, please. Relive again those trips on the Mumbles train, fifteen carriages on bank holidays, three thousand people clinging to it, and all of them wearing hats. The carriages on the lower decks were like cattle trucks, but the top decks were open to the soft winds and the engine's soot. Great flocks of wading birds fed on the Swansea mud at low tide. Kate remembered wondering what it would be like to be a little bird, a turnstone, perhaps, or a shy sandpiper.

Linger a while, Kate, on the walk from the terminus at Oystermouth, the painful walk in your corset, bodice and tight-fitting pleated blouses that your mother made so lovingly in imitation of the fashions of the day, so that you might hold your head up high, and the corset was so tight that you *had* to hold your head up high. Linger as you climb the hill, past the castle, and drop down into the gentle curve of Langland Bay and the long, rolling waves.

Remember Swansea beach in those days, the crowded beach by the Slip, the pretty Swansea girls with lips as soft as Welsh rain and hats with brims so wide that the sun could never spoil the milk of their complexions, the smart young men in their best jackets and their bowlers and trilbies, the little boys in sailor suits, and not a naked leg to be seen. Remember the refreshment stall under the awning, the bathing machines for the very bold, no bathing on Sundays if you please, the big striped helter-skelter, the blind men begging, the fortune-teller, the one-armed juggler, the drunk sandwichman advertising a temperance hotel in Llansamlet, the vitality of a vanished world. Ride again down the helter-skelter (you only did it once, you weren't allowed to really, you were middle class, you lived off Walter Road, in the sober suburbs on the hill, this bursting beach was almost out of bounds altogether).

But no, Kate didn't linger. She hurtled on through the barley-sugar hospital night. She barely paused to recall the excitement of the first motorised bus service to Gower, in 1910, when she was eleven and beginning to be looked at by boys. The vehicles were Dennis's, and they chugged all the way to wild Rhossili. One day, many decades and almost as many husbands later, Kate would call her home Rhossili Cottage, but now she had little interest in Rhossili, she was too eager to rush towards Gwyn.

Fast she sped past the chapel, three times a day every Sunday, the Reverend Aneurin Parkhouse sounding off in his sonorous, treacly voice, rich with intimations of impending doom, heavy with warnings about sin, warnings which Kate was not to heed. It was there that she discovered to her horror that she had no religious feelings whatsoever. The distant, almost inaccessible heaven and the ever-present, almost unavoidable hell of the Reverend Aneurin Parkhouse were as nothing compared to the heaven of Gower and the hell of the dark valleys.

At last she paused, to remember a morning in the breakfast room of 16 Eaton Crescent. It was a large, dark room with just one window near the back. There was a large table covered in a thick, dark red cloth. No breakfast was ever eaten in the breakfast room, and Kate had no idea why it was called the breakfast room. At some stage, she couldn't remember when, a portrait of Lloyd George was placed on the wall above the table. Later, when he was known to have been a womaniser, the portrait was turned to face the wall, so that its bare back could serve as an Awful Warning.

The breakfast room also contained the most lovely thing in the whole of Kate's pre-war, pre-Gwyn world, and that was the rocking chair. Kate would often sit there, rocking gently, dreaming of foreign places and dragons and princesses and untamed Arab horses which she tamed because nobody else was brave enough. But lately she had dreamt more and more about boys. She was fourteen now, after all, and her legs were developing nicely, and she had seen a boy in Walter Road, oh such a boy. She knew his name. He was Gwyn Jones, son of Bryn Jones, one of the Joneses of Jones and Jones, a Swansea department store second only to the great Ben Evans emporium itself. Ah, so that is why she has lingered on this memory, you shrewdly observe.

John Thomas Thomas came into the breakfast room as she was dreaming of Gwyn. He said, 'I want to speak with you, Kate,' in a serious but not unkind tone, but it was his headmaster voice, and so she stopped rocking. 'Mrs Evans Sunday School tells me you ask her questions. She told me some of the questions that you have asked.'

Kate had asked, 'What are people who don't believe in God called?' There had been a gasp at this boldness. 'English,' Willie Jenkins had said, and been slapped for his patriotism. 'What happens to people who don't believe in God?' she had persisted. 'They seek the consolation of the Devil and fall into Swansea Harbour in their cups and drown like Eli Watkins,' Mrs Evans had said. 'Why were all the miracles in the Holy Land and none in Swansea?' she had asked. 'Because Jesus wasn't Welsh,' had been the swift retort of Mrs Evans Sunday School.

'Why do you ask all these questions?' John Thomas Thomas asked.

In later years Kate's quick wit would be known from Penzance to Niederlander-ob-der-Kummel, but she could never have thought more quickly or more successfully than in that pre-war breakfast room in Swansea.

'I think it's our duty to ourselves to ask questions,' she said. 'I think the only way we can be certain of anything is by asking questions and getting the right answers. If we don't ask questions, we start to take our faith for granted and it becomes valueless.'

John Thomas Thomas looked at his daughter and tried to hide his amazement and pride. Just the suspicion of a smile passed across his serene face, and Kate felt awful about deceiving him.

'Good,' he said. 'Well spoken, Kate Thomas.'

Kate asked no more questions in Sunday School and a more intelligent woman than Mrs Evans would have realised the significance of this and spoken of it to John Thomas Thomas. Atheism was consigned to a secret corner of Kate's being, along with whether it was natural to grow hair at the top of your legs and bleed horribly and feel awful every month. These last points worried her so much that she plucked up courage and asked her mother about them. Bronwen Thomas explained the facts of life to her simply and without embarrassment.

It was on a Sunday, of all days, on a solemn, silent Sunday, that the greatest event in Kate's fifteen-year-old life occurred. Gwyn Jones spoke to her for the first time. It happened outside the chapel. The world was wearing its Sunday best, and the weather was fair. Gwyn's first remark, it must be admitted, wasn't one of great originality. It was, 'You're Kate Thomas, aren't you?' But it had one real virtue as an introductory remark to a girl whose knees were collapsing and whose insides were squirming like a trapped jellyfish. It was an easy remark to which to reply. 'Yes, I am,' said Kate.

Gwyn Jones's next remark again failed to ignite any conversational sparks, but had the virtue of impeccable accuracy. 'I'm Gwyn Jones,' he said.

This provided Kate with an altogether more challenging test. She almost said 'I know,' which would have mortified her, then narrowly rejected 'Are you?' which would have been very silly, since there would have been no reason for him to say 'I'm Gwyn Jones' if he wasn't, and she knew he was anyway. In the end she settled on a response that was admirably safe, while again giving no hint of the wit that was to come. 'Oh,' she said.

And then John Thomas Thomas and her mother Bronwen and all the clan were upon them, and seven-year-old Oliver said to Gwyn, 'I'm Oliver. What's your name?' and Gwyn said, 'Gwyn,' and Oliver said, 'I'm going to drive the Mumbles train when I grow up. What are you going to do?' and Gwyn Jones said, 'I am grown up, Oliver, and I'm going to work in my father's store,' and five-year-old Bernard said, 'Are you really grown up? Golly,' and Oliver said, 'What are you going to be in the store, Gwyn?' and Gwyn said, 'Oh, you know, I'm going to own it, and that sort of thing,' and John Thomas Thomas said, 'Well, we must get home. Goodbye, Gwyn Jones.'

As they walked up Walter Road, a bus passed them with a gas balloon strapped to its top. The children had never seen such a thing before. John Thomas Thomas explained that it was because of the war.

Some children didn't care about the war and it didn't seem to make much difference to your life when you were sailing your model boat on Brynmill Pond, but Kate hated the thought of it and didn't want to read about it. She knew it was all something to do with a place called Serbia, which was a very dangerous place, but however it was explained, and clever though she was, she never could grasp why it was necessary to kill so many people. Most people thought that it was a good thing, as the Hun had to be smashed.

That Christmas John Thomas Thomas got braces from Kate, and Oliver and Bernard got socks, and her mother got wool, and her sisters got gloves, and none of them suspected that the reason for Kate's choice of presents was that they enabled her to go to different departments in Jones and Jones, and gave her a chance of encountering Gwyn.

Jones and Jones was a wonderful shop, a four-storey palace where the change whizzed around on overhead wires, and porters helped ladies to step down from their carriages, very necessary, for the poor things could hardly move in all the corsets and bodices that imprisoned their straining flesh. It was a cornucopia of socks and shoes and shirts and skirts and beds and saucepans and china and beds and braces and bloomers and mirrors and sheets and pillows and beds. Kate looked at the beds and wondered what sort of bed she and Gwyn would have when they got married.

'Hello, Kate. Thinking of buying a bed, are you?'

Oh, the humiliation. The bad luck that he should come across her here. Oh, the shaming blush that set her pretty face on fire. She could feel the shame still in Ward 3C of Whetstone General Hospital.

'I'm off in ten minutes,' he said. 'Would you like to go for a walk?'

'With you?' asked our heroine, and blushed still more at this extreme stupidity.

'No,' he said. 'With the Mayor and his Corporation. Why do you sound surprised? You're the prettiest girl in Swansea.'

'What?' gasped the prettiest girl in Swansea.

'Well, are you coming or not?' asked Gwyn Jones.

'Oh yes,' said Kate hurriedly.

They walked up Walter Road to the Uplands and then to Cwmdonkin Park. Kate was terrified that she would see a member of her family. It ruined the walk. He was so good-looking, five foot ten or so and well built, dark, really you could almost have taken him for an Italian, and instead of walking proudly at his side she was scurrying along like a frightened rabbit.

When they reached the park she felt safer. They sat on a bench, near the top of the steep park, looking down over the slate roofs to the oily glistening sea.

Gwyn Jones lit a cigarette. He smoked a whole cigarette, and he was only seventeen!

'Have one,' he said.

'Oh no, I couldn't,' said Kate.

'Go on.'

'No.'

'Why not?'

'I promised my father not to.'

'Are you frightened of your father?'

'No. I respect him.'

Gwyn Jones nodded, as if taking a piece of vital information on board.

'Do you like thrushes?' he asked.

'Why do you ask that?' asked Kate.

'Because there's one over there, and I couldn't think of anything else to say,' he admitted.

Kate laughed.

'You have a lovely laugh, Kate,' he said.

'Thank you.'

The thrush flew away. A blackbird landed on the expanse of grass in front of them and held its head sideways, listening for worms. Kate expected to be asked 'Do you like blackbirds?' but Gwyn Jones was a more resourceful conversationalist than she had supposed, and he asked, 'What do you want out of life?'

'Everything,' she said.

'Oh good,' he said. 'I was terrified you'd say "I don't know".'

'I never say I don't know,' she said, 'even when I don't know.'

'Good for you,' said Gwyn Jones. 'Do you like liquorice?'

'No.'

'Pity. I've got some.'

'I could learn to like it.'

Gwyn Jones lit a second cigarette. What manliness. And Kate learned, with astonishing rapidity, to like liquorice. And the sky darkened, and the first drops of rain began to fall, and Kate shivered, and Gwyn Jones put his arm round her, and kissed her, and he smelt of cigarette smoke.

'Did you enjoy that?' he asked.

'No,' she admitted. 'You smell of smoke.'

'Have you had more enjoyable kisses?'

'Of course not, Gwyn. I would never let any boy except you kiss me.'

She blushed again, shamingly, to her roots. She felt so angry with herself that she wanted to cry. The rain began in earnest, and Gwyn Jones walked her swiftly down the hill, through the Uplands, and down the snicket that led to the back gate of her house. The gate was set in a high wall. She stood under the wall where she couldn't be seen even from an upstairs window, and let him kiss her once, then tossed her head like a thoroughbred and slipped through the gate into the little neat unlovely back garden, and was halfway along the wet red-tiled path edged with stones before she realised that she hadn't arranged to see him again.

Through the big window at the back of the dining-cum-living-room she could see the whole family at lunch. She was late. She entered the room, trying to look calm, trying not to look bedraggled. The children looked at her wide-eyed. None of them had ever been late for lunch before.

'You're late,' said her father.

'You're wet,' said her mother.

'You've been smoking,' said her father.

'No!' said Kate.

'Don't lie to me. You smell of smoke,' said her father.

'I'm not lying,' she said coldly. She could never have believed, until that moment, that she could have spoken coldly to her father.

'Why do you smell of smoke if you haven't been smoking?' asked her father.

The children stared at her, hardly daring to breathe.

She couldn't say 'Because Gwyn Jones kissed me, and he'd been smoking' or 'When Gwyn and I have children, I will never accuse them wrongly'. So she said nothing.

'Go to your room,' said John Thomas Thomas.

Her mother looked as if she wanted to intervene, but said nothing. The children's eyes grew wider. The fish-cakes (it was a Friday) grew colder.

She went to her room, her simple room on the second storey, linoleum on the floor, an iron bedstead, a stag at bay in a glen as wet as this wet Friday, and more knitted texts. She flung herself on her bed, and sobbed.

Our Heroine Wronged!

She would soon get over that, but . . .

A Hero Is Knocked Off His Pedestal!

That would take longer. Barely half an hour before his accusation she had refused to smoke because she respected him. Virtue Is Unrewarded, a sentiment which did not feature in any of the tapestry texts.

She got up off the bed, tossed her head angrily, and thought, To hell with virtue, then.

She looked at herself long and hard in the mirror. She saw high cheekbones, a straight nose with flared nostrils, a dimpled chin, big brown eyes, a fine if pale complexion and a wide mouth with full lips, and she thought, I really do believe that if I was a boy I wouldn't find it unpleasant to kiss that, and that cheered her up no end.

But she was still angry with her father, and when Enid came up to say that she could come down, she said, 'No, thank you. Tell him I prefer my own company,' and Enid almost fainted.

Later that day, when she did at last come down to an unusually silent house, she sought confirmation of her beauty. She sought it wisely. She didn't ask her parents, who might have wondered why she was asking. She didn't ask her sisters, who might have been beastly. She didn't ask Bernard, who might have been honest. She asked Oliver. She cornered him in the front hall, by the grandfather clock, and she summoned him into the cold parlour. He followed eagerly, tickled pink by her secretiveness.

'Oliver,' she breathed. 'Am I the prettiest girl in Swansea?'

'You're the prettiest girl in the whole wide world,' replied that charmer with a blush.

This was beyond her wildest dreams. She'd have been satisfied by 'Swansea', and thrilled by 'Glamorgan', but 'in the whole wide world'!

It was amazing how resourceful she was in meeting Gwyn Jones and what lies she was able to tell now that she no longer respected her father. Gwyn never smoked in her presence again after she asked him not to. 'Thank you, Gwyn,' she said, and he replied, with that disarming frankness that made him stand out from all the other boys, 'Well, I don't particularly enjoy it. I only do it out of bravado.'

Yes, he did stand out from all the other boys. There was a seriousness about him, deep down inside him, that turned Kate to jelly, and the looks he gave her were so serious, without being solemn, that she was almost sure that she stood out for him from all the other girls. Sometimes he seemed to look beyond her towards something he didn't much like, and then his eyes would return to her and he would smile. That look frightened her. That smile undid her altogether.

The other children in Kate's class talked foolishly about the boys they liked. Kate didn't speak of Gwyn at all. He was too precious to be shared. She was sure that it would be the same for him.

She knew that it was serious. Each of their brief shared moments seemed better than the last. Each parting seemed the most painful yet.

She knew, too, that he was bold, but even so, the suggestion, when it came, knocked her breathless. They were sitting on the beach, near the Slip, on a late spring morning only just warm enough. The sun was shining on the great bay that swept from the high hills round past the town to the Mumbles Lighthouse. The beach was almost deserted. The tide was out. Turnstones were turning stones. Oystercatchers were catching oysters. In the marshalling yards, shunting engines were shunting and marshalling. All was as it should be in this corner of the world. There was nothing to show that this was the twentieth month of a terrible war that everyone had expected to end in weeks. Gwyn Jones looked at Kate with that unusually grave face of his and spoke the words that turned her world upside down.

'My parents are away on Saturday night,' he said, and he gently kissed her right knee and then rolled over in the sand and didn't look at her.

She gasped.

'They're leaving you on your own!' she exclaimed.

'They trust me.'

She couldn't believe it.

'How incredible,' she said.

'They made me promise.'

'Promise what?'

Far above them gulls were wheeling. Poor things. They would never have conversations as momentous as this.

'Promise not to do anything naughty.'

Her whole body was tingling. Her breasts were heaving. Her insides were seething. It was awful. It was wonderful. She felt sick. She felt terrified. She felt happy.

'Making love to you wouldn't be naughty, Kate. Making love to you would be the best thing ever.'

He ran his fingers up her thigh. It was excruciating. The Mumbles train whistled. She would never forget that whistle.

'How can I make love to you, Gwyn?' she asked.

'Creep out of your house when everyone's asleep.'

The enormity of it! The utter and total impossibility of it!

'But it'd be, it'd be almost midnight by then,' she said. 'That means it'd be . . .'

She couldn't say it.

'Sunday,' he said.

She nodded. She couldn't speak. She couldn't swallow. There was a lump like an oyster shell in her throat. Am I sure about being an atheist, she wondered. Supposing I'm wrong. I'd be struck down by a thunderbolt. Supposing I was caught. It would kill them.

But then again there was that intense longing inside her, that emptiness waiting to be filled.

'I'll do it,' she said.

'I never doubted you, Kate,' he said. 'I'll come and fetch you. I'll stand at the end of the crescent.'

'No!' she exclaimed. 'You mustn't.'

'I can't let you walk the streets alone at night.'

'It isn't the streets. It's Walter Road. It's respectable. I won't be frightened. I'd be far more frightened that someone I knew might see us.'

He gave in reluctantly. His tongue forced her lips apart, their tongues felt each other like affectionate snakes, she ran her tongue over his teeth – his teeth were the equal of any in Glamorgan – and then he let go of her and said 'Saturday' and hurried off before she could change her mind.

As she walked home, in a fervour of fear and sexual stimulation, Kate looked in astonishment at people going about their everyday business and thought, Don't they know this is the most astonishing, memorable day in the history of the world?

The rest of the week seemed an eternity to her. She was, after all, only sixteen. She tried so hard to be normal that she ended up worrying that she would be so normal as to be abnormal, so she tried to be a bit abnormal, and then worried that she was being abnormally abnormal, and hurriedly became abnormally normal again. The excitement never left her genitalia, and her stomach ached, and she felt weak at the knees and was terrified that she'd get so anxious that she'd start her period two days early and ruin the whole thing.

She tried hard to be nice and helpful, praising the sausage meat at breakfast, which drew an odd look from her mother, because it was the same sawdusty sausage meat they had throughout the Great War. Her father frowned. Food was a necessity, not a pleasure, although he lapped up his Welsh cake and bara brith as enthusiastically as anybody. Blind in his righteousness, John Thomas Thomas noticed nothing odd in her behaviour. Nor did her brothers and sisters, cocooned in their childish egotism, although Bernard did once say, 'What are you thinking about, Kate?' and to her horror she blushed as she said, 'Nothing,' and even John Thomas Thomas gave her a brief questioning look, while Bronwen's blue eyes rested on her momentarily with keen speculation and compassion. And the horrible thing was that Kate wished that she wasn't there, wished that she wasn't still part of this close-knit family, and hated herself for thinking so.

Saturday seemed to go on for ever. The pain in her insides intensified. She was sure she'd be sick. How she managed to eat her thin slices of tongue at tea she would never know.

She went to bed at the usual time, even kneeling at the side of her bed and pretending to say her prayers as usual.

Almost as soon as she had got into bed she got out of it again and knelt to pray once more.

'Almighty God,' she prayed. 'I realise that I'm not an atheist. I'm an agnostic. If You do exist, forgive me for doubting You, and I'm sorry if You think I'm going to sin tonight, I don't think I am, because I love Gwyn so very much, but I know it's naughty to creep out of my home in the middle of the night, but there's no other way, so I'm sorry. Amen.'

She felt better after that. She also felt sleepy. How on earth was she going to keep awake?

She would count sheep. No, that was so boring that people used it to get to sleep. She began to count how many letters there were in the names of the girls in her class at school. Arbel Meredith thirteen. Glenys Edwards thirteen that makes twenty-six. Caitlin Price-Evans, there's pretentious, that double barrel, they were only glorified grocers, oh Lord, that sounded snobbish, seventeen or eighteen if you counted the hyphen, which you should because it took up as much space as a letter eighteen plus twenty-six makes forty-four Sheila Proctor thirteen so many thirteens that makes . . . that makes . . . start again . . . Arbel Meredith thirteen Glenys . . . suddenly she knew that she'd been asleep. How long had she been asleep? She was wide awake now, no risk of further sleep. Had she nodded off for a moment or for several hours? How did you tell? There were footsteps in the street and the faint clip-clop of the cabs in Walter Road. She strained to hear the grandfather clock in the hall but it was two storeys away, and quite faint.

It struck quarter past. Quarter past what?

What I Will Do With My Life, by Kate Thomas. I will marry Gwyn Jones and have three children and an old house and lots of money, enough to have holidays abroad *and* be good to the poor.

Half past. Half past what?

What will actually happen tonight? Caitlin Price-Evans claims to have had sex and said it was all grunting and wet beds, which doesn't sound immensely appealing, but my body tells me otherwise, and what sort of man would want sex with Caitlin Price-Evans and her fat legs anyway, some grunting farmer who narrowly preferred her to sheep on a casting vote, Gwyn won't be a grunter. Gwyn! His lips. Can I really picture them? How much hair will there be on his body?

Quarter to. Quarter to what?

The mournful hoot of a distant tram. The bark of a dog. The whining of the wind. The clip-clop of the late-night horses. The roar of a car. Oh please, please, let there be no noise as the clock strikes the hour.

Bong. Oh, let it not be one o'clock already. Bong. Or even two. Bong. Three in the morning? Bong. Four, had she slept for hours? Bong. Or even five. Bong. It can't be six. Bong. It couldn't be seven, or it'd be getting light. Bong. Waves of relief. It's still evening. Bong. Great neighing of a startled horse. Silence. Bong. Silence.

Ten bongs. Was there a bong during the neigh? There must have been. Eleven o'clock. Could there have been two bongs during the neigh? She considered the neigh carefully, tried to time it from memory, felt it had been a one-bong neigh.

Eleven o'clock. What time could she safely get up? Supposing John Thomas Thomas was doing to her mother what Gwyn Jones would soon be doing to her. Unlikely as it seemed, her parents had had sex in the past, because you couldn't have children without sex. Unlikely as it seemed, John Thomas Thomas had said to Bronwen whatever it was that Welsh chapelgoers said to their wives when they wanted to make love, and he'd said it at least five times. Almost certainly much more, because you didn't have children every time you did it. And at that the awful thought struck her that maybe she'd have a child by Gwyn Jones, and this terrified her so much that she missed the ding-dong ding-dong of the quarter, and the clock didn't seem to ding or dong for ages and then suddenly she heard the ding-dong ding-dong ding-dong ding-dong of the half-hour, and she couldn't move, she was petrified, she'd be heard, she'd be caught, she wouldn't be caught but she'd have twins, it ran in the family, she daren't go, but the room was filled with the waiting presence of Gwyn Jones, expecting her, wanting her.

Ding-dong ding-dong ding-dong ding-dong ding-dong ding-dong oh oh oh oh!! A quarter to twelve. Now or never, Kate Thomas.

Never.

A life lived in fear? Never.

Never say never.

Now.

Move, legs, move, damn you. For a moment she thought she was paralysed with fear and then she was moving, slowly, agonisingly slowly, she was out of bed, she was feeling for her clothes, she daren't put the light on, somebody might see.

She got dressed slowly, awkwardly, in the dark. She carried her shoes, and crept to the bedroom door, closed the door with great care, crept past the bedroom where Oliver and Bernard were sleeping, crept down the narrow stairs to the first-floor landing, past the door of her parents' room, heart hammering in her ribcage, down the wide main staircase, feeling the banisters, round the two corners counting the steps.

In the hall she realised the enormity of the task that still awaited her. The front-door key was kept on the ledge round the bottom of the face of the grandfather clock. She daren't light a gas lamp or a candle. There was just enough moonlight coming through the frosted glass pane in the front door to show her the bulk of the clock.

She fetched a chair from the dining-room, climbed up on to the chair, felt along the ledge for the key, and, just as she was picking it up, the clock terrified her by striking next to her ear, she dropped the key, lunged, caught it by sheer good luck, felt herself falling off the chair, jumped, landed with a thud, saw the chair toppling, caught the chair, leant on the chair, panting with fear, and listened. The clock finished its twelve bongs and there was silence. The Welsh Sunday had begun! There was no noise. Utter silence, deep as a grave. No one had heard the thud of the chair or the thudding of her heart.

She put the chair back in the dining-room, sat on the bottom stair while she put on her shoes, crept across the hall, turned the key with infinite care. The door opened without a squeak, she locked it no less carefully, and emerged from the porch into a night which smelt gorgeously of horse manure and hydrangeas, but was far too bright for comfort.

She scurried to the end of Eaton Crescent, eager to get out of sight of her house. She forced herself to walk calmly down Walter Road. There were few people about. The suburbs slept self-righteously. Only the wicked were abroad. Kate was wicked.

A man in a long dark overcoat bid her good-night and looked at her inquisitively. She tried to look older than sixteen and hoped that her answered good-night was sufficiently worldly.

A horse-drawn carriage strained up the long straight hill from the town centre. The horse looked at her and deposited a heap of manure in the road. Had it recognised a sinner?

Control yourself, Kate. That sort of thought is stupid.

She turned left into St James's Crescent. The moon had gone behind clouds. There was a smell of approaching rain. The wind was getting up. Soon Kate would be going to bed.

The bulk of St James's Church loomed like a rebuke. She tried to ignore it.

Lovely St James's Crescent. Lovely sober three-storey end-terrace house of lovely Gwyn Jones. Bay windows to each side of the pillared entrance. There's stately. Suddenly Kate felt daunted, and an awful thought struck her. Supposing his parents had come back unexpectedly.

They hadn't. There he was, filling the doorway, more handsome even than in her memory, smiling, hungry.

'I knew you'd come, My Kate,' he said.

She was quick to reply, 'My Gwyn.' This was a meeting of equals.

This was a night of lovers. Luckily Gwyn's bedroom was on the detached side of the house, or the neighbours might have complained about the noise. This was a night of beautiful young bodies thrilled by the completeness of their love. At first, yes, she was awed, Kate the chapel girl, Kate the virgin. She was awed at their nakedness, at his gasp when he saw her full beauty for the first time, awed at the size of his erect penis, for which nothing in her education or her reading of literature had prepared her. But soon she was awed no longer, and soon after that she was a virgin no longer, she was bursting and exploding with razor-sharp ecstasy. She thought for a moment that it was their lovemaking that was rattling the windows on this wild, wet, Welsh night.

Just once Kate imagined her father looking down at her sorrowfully from a framed photograph on the mantelpiece, but then she looked down at Gwyn, the bedclothes humped over his bouncing bottom as he thrust himself into her so ardently and yet, as it only occurred to her years later, with rare gentleness. She cried out again at the joy of orgasm and wanted to cry out to her father and to all fathers, 'There can be nothing shameful in this glory.' She lost count of the number of times he entered her. She lost count of the number of times she lay back exhausted and fulfilled and so . . . complete, only to be roused to further ecstasy even deeper within herself. Gwyn seemed to put his whole life into that night, and Kate responded with a sustained ardour beyond her wildest imaginings.

In the middle of all this she had an image of poor Caitlin Price-Evans desperately avoiding the wet bits in some farmer's bed, and asked Gwyn what he was going to do about the sheets. He hadn't thought. 'My poor baby,' she said. 'You haven't thought about that, have you?' 'I'll wash them and dry them before they come back,' he said. 'I'll have to.'

Mundane thoughts about laundry put a full stop on the purple passage of the night. Entwined together, they drifted into sleep. And then suddenly it was getting light, it was gone half-past six, Kate leapt up, she had to get home, oh how she had to get home. She rammed her clothes on, kissed Gwyn briefly, and was gone.

She longed to run through that wet and gloomy dawn. How could the world be so gloomy after such a night? The hydrangeas drank the rain greedily, the slate roofs glistened gloomily, the light grew stronger with terrifying speed.

Kate let herself into the house as carefully as she had left it, locked the door, fetched the chair from the dining-room, put the key back on the ledge beneath the clock face, which stood at five to seven, not as bad as she'd feared but dangerous enough, took the chair back to the dining-room and crept up the stairs, heart hammering again. The house remained silent. The door to her parents' bedroom was still the same. The narrow stairs to the second floor were still the same. Her cold bedroom was still the same. The linoleum under her feet was still the same. The samplers with their warnings about sin were still the same. The sad stag and the wet glen were still the same. Only Kate was not the same. Only Kate, lover of her king, was utterly changed for ever. She got into bed, pulled the bedclothes over her head, smelt the rich odour of the king's semen still upon her, and fell into a deep, deep sleep.

She was so tired that morning that she had to pretend to be ill. Her temperature was normal and she was declared fit for church. Did nobody suspect?

The Reverend Aneurin Parkhouse preached on the subject of sin that morning and, just once, seemed to look straight into her eyes. Did he suspect? No. He preached about sin because he always preached about sin, and he looked straight into her eyes because he always looked straight into her eyes, because he longed to sin with her and knew he never would, which was why he was so aware of the frailty of human nature that he always preached about sin.

That evening, at tea, Bernard, that irritatingly perceptive

28

child, said, 'Kate's trying not to yawn. I don't think Kate slept very well last night.'

Oliver, who, if he'd been a medieval king, would have been known as Oliver the Oblivious, said, 'I dreamt of dragons last night.'

'What did they do?' asked Kate eagerly, welcoming the distraction.

'Drank lemonade,' said Oliver.

'I slept like a log,' said Myfanwy. 'I always do.'

'I didn't,' said Enid. 'I had dreams too. I dreamt there was someone moving about upstairs.'

Kate's heart almost stopped.

Somehow Sunday passed, and of course nobody suspected, Kate was protected by the enormity of it all, it was hard to believe in anything of such enormity now, and especially the enormity of that, and it was hard to believe that you could feel such a stranger in your own family, sitting round your own cheerful little fire, with people who were your brothers and sisters yesterday and today were as distant from you as creatures from outer space.

Soon Kate was to feel even more distant from her family. That was after Gwyn had told her that he was going to the war. He told her the very next time they met. She shuddered with joy at the sight of him walking towards her past the floral clock. He avoided meeting her eye as he destroyed her world. She screamed at him for having fooled her. He held her very tight and said that he'd wanted to tell her, but hadn't wanted anything to spoil that wonderful night. She calmed down then. She had no alternative. She dared not ruin their parting.

They met just twice more but his parents were back now, and there wasn't time to find anywhere else to make love. Sandy fumblings in the dunes would have been unbearable after that night. They would have become children again.

They never did make love again. Gwyn died, along with

twelve thousand other wasted patriots, on the first day of the Battle of the Somme. Maybe he'd had a premonition. Maybe that had been what he'd been seeing when he looked past her in that way she feared. Maybe that was why he'd seemed to have put the whole of his life into that night.

3 Timothy

She opened her eyes just a fraction, very cautiously, and was amazed to see that daylight was streaming brightly into Ward 3C of Whetstone General Hospital. White clouds were scudding past, innocent little clouds riding boldly on the gale. Her memories of her night with Gwyn had taken all night. She must have played them in real time.

The realisation that he was dead was almost as great a shock as it had been at the time. She closed her eyes, as if to escape from it and, because she wasn't trying to sleep, fell asleep instantly. She was awakened by the clanking of a trolley.

'There you go, Mrs Critchley,' said a cheery voice. 'Nice poached egg for you today.'

'I didn't order a poached egg,' said another voice, presumably Mrs Critchley's. 'I ordered continental.'

'No, I've got the chitty here, love. You ticked poached egg.'

'I did not and I am not your love,' said Mrs Critchley stuffily.

'Aren't you? Sorry about that, ducks.' The breakfast lady didn't seem to have taken offence. 'But I've got poached egg down and poached egg you'll have to have.'

Mrs Critchley mumbled something.

'What's that, sweetheart?' asked the breakfast lady.

'I can't afford a cooked breakfast,' hissed Mrs Critchley.

'Bless you, dear, you don't have to pay. You're in hospital.'

'Oh. Am I? Sorry.'

The breakfast trolley clanked across the hard floor.

'Bacon and sausage for you, Glenda,' said the breakfast lady breezily. 'There you go.'

'That's right. I've got to build my strength up,' said a weak voice, presumably Glenda's.

'Good for you,' said the breakfast lady.

The trolley clanked again.

'Nice poached egg for you, Hilda,' said the breakfast lady. 'There you go.'

'I couldn't eat a poached egg,' said an indignant Hilda.

'Well, why did you order one then?'

Kate found, to her surprise, that she was getting quite interested in the saga of the breakfasts. Well, anything was better than the pain of Gwyn's death.

'I must have ticked the wrong item,' said Hilda. 'I've never been good with forms.'

'Well, it says poached egg, and I've got nuffink for you but poached egg, so poached egg it's going to have to be, I'm afraid, Hilda.'

'I don't like the look of it,' said Hilda. 'It looks as if it's got a great big eye and it's staring at me.'

'Don't be silly. Got to keep your strength up. That'll slip down the red lane somethink lovely. Now, you just eat that up for me.'

The trolley clanked away. Kate could hear it disappearing down the corridor. No breakfast for her, evidently. Well, she didn't know how she'd eat it if there was any.

So it seemed that there were just three other women in Ward 3C. Kate pictured Ward 3 as a long corridor with a series of small side wards off it. Ward 3C, she imagined, had four beds, two against each side wall. Of course she could be wrong. There might be empty beds which would be filled at some later stage. But she doubted it. Beds were at a premium in the NHS. She could imagine poor Elizabeth's indignant voice. 'Why on earth won't you go private, Mum? Where's the sense of it?'

Kate had identified the voice of the woman called Mrs Critchley as being that of the mad woman who thought she'd given birth to a baby boy. She imagined her as quite tall, very pale, and painfully thin, with bruised arms. Glenda and Hilda remained shadowy figures as yet, but seemed to have some potential as a double act.

She tried to sleep, but, because she was trying, sleep wouldn't come. For just a moment she felt so full of self-pity that she didn't want to live. That wouldn't do.

She tried to begin to think of the task that she had set herself. It had been a bizarre murder. What was significant about the torn-off list of double-glazing salesmen? Who but Maurice would have had access to a name board from Leningrad railway station? Or could the name board have been fabricated? Oh Lord, she was tired. It was a hopeless task. How would she succeed where Inspector Crouch, thoroughness his middle name, had failed? She'd been a fool to even think she could do it. Oh Gwyn, were you really killed on the first day of the Battle of the Somme?

Not necessarily! He didn't have to be. Her body was imprisoned, but her mind was free and felt all the more free because her body was imprisoned. And the thought of her mind as a video had amused her because she knew how surprised young Ben would be that she'd understood the principle of the video machine at last. Come on, then, Kate, what are you waiting for? Rewind. Stop at the beginning of that night, *the* night. And play.

But before she could even begin to relive that night, the nurse called Helen brought her back to reality.

'Well, have you had a good night?' she asked, in tones that suggested that she didn't think Kate a complete idiot. But again she spoilt this favourable impression by inventing the reply that she wanted to hear. 'Oh, good. That's good, Kate.'

Helen forced Kate's mouth open as gently as she could and slid the thermometer in, and Kate had a fleeting vision of Walter and something larger and warmer than a thermometer sliding into her mouth, but that was far into the future, well, no, it was far in the past but it was far into the future of her journey through the past, well, she knew what she meant, and the memory of it had quite shocked her, recollected in cold blood at ninety-nine years of age.

Helen slid the thermometer out of her mouth. 'Still up a bit, not quite there yet,' she said.

And then Kate heard the voice of Doctor Ramgobi. 'Well, Kate, and how are we this morning?' He didn't wait for a reply, but spoke to Helen. 'Difficult to tell if there's much going on in her brain. Far too early to give her an ECG or anything like that. What are we feeding her through these drips? Let's have a look again.'

Of course. She was on drips. Maybe, in view of all the recent food scares, that was how the world would end up being fed. A lot of fun would have gone out of life, but at least we'd be spared all those celebrity chefs on television.

Doctor Ramgobi had moved on. She heard him ask, 'How are we today, Mrs Critchley?'

Why did so many of them have to use the plural? But Mrs Critchley accepted it as natural and said, 'We're very well, doctor. He's just had his first feed of the day, and he's such a bonny little thing.'

'Jolly good,' said Doctor Ramgobi. 'That's what we want to hear. Good morning, Glenda, and how are we today?'

'Very well indeed, doctor. I feel ready to go home.'

'Not just yet, Glenda. Not just yet. We've got to build up your strength first.'

'But it's the ironing, Doctor Rambogi.'

'Ramgobi. The ironing?'

'He doesn't know one end of the iron from the other.'

'Ah, we're speaking of Douglas, are we? I spoke to Douglas when he was here yesterday and he's doing just fine.'

'He thinks he is, but he won't care if his cuffs are creased. I always iron his underpants, doctor. He can never see the point. "Nobody's going to see them," he says. "You never know," I say. "I've seen you looking at that schoolmistress at number seven." Many's the laugh we've had over that.'

'I see, yes, jolly good, most droll. Ah, Hilda, and how are we today?'

'Not so good, doctor, I'm afraid. I couldn't swallow my egg.'

'Dear dear. Think of all the pain that hen went through, and you so scornful of its end product!'

'It's my digestion, doctor. It's worn out.'

'Nonsense, Hilda. Fresh air is what you need. It's a lovely day – for Whetstone. Nurse'll take you twice round the block, and you'll be attacking your lunch with gusto.'

Soon after that Kate fell asleep. She slept until lunch-time when she woke just enough to realise that Doctor Ramgobi had been wrong about one thing. Hilda was not attacking her lunch with gusto. 'Mince and I have never really hit it off. I get so confused. I'm sure I meant to tick the cod.' Kate drifted off again, woke up again, opened one eye, and saw Timothy standing there, looking down at her with concern and love, looking every inch the distinguished novelist that he wasn't. She closed her eye again hurriedly. She hoped Timothy hadn't seen. She didn't want him to know how alert she was. Not yet, anyway. 'Always keep your powder dry,' Heinz had once said. An absurd phrase, but in his delicate, precise German accent it had sounded rather charming.

For a moment she wondered if she had really seen Timothy. Perhaps she'd started hallucinating. Old people did. But no, the other nurse, the one with the plump hands, was speaking. 'Guess who's here, Kate. It's our son. He's come all the way from Majorca to see us.'

'Hello, Mum,' said Timothy. He always called her Mum and he always wanted her to call him Tim. She thought it indicative of his intellectual laziness. All that intelligence, all that ingenuity, which could have been of such use to the world, wasted on writing those second-rate detective novels. Not that they sold badly. Once he'd got readers hooked, he wasn't likely to lose them, since in essence he wrote the same book over and over again. 'You know where you are with a Rand.' 'I always get Auntie Lizzie the latest Inspector Trouble for Christmas.'

But how fine he had looked in that moment when she had glimpsed him at the side of her bed. He was tall and, at seventy-two, still held himself quite erect. He had a good head of hair, even though he wore it too long, but its streaks of grey were quite dramatic and distinguished, some people thought he'd paid a lot to have them put in. He had a comfortable white beard which made him look like a cross between a philosopher and Father Christmas. He was wearing one of his usual lightweight denim suits. He had no spare flesh on his body at all. And the look on his face! She had never seen him looking as loving as that. She realised that he hadn't noticed her looking at him, because, if he had, he'd have hidden his emotion.

He clasped her hand, she could still only just feel it, and said, 'I don't know if you can understand what I'm saying, Mum, but I'll talk to you anyway. Nigel rang me and told me the bad news, and of course I flew over as soon as I could. Carrie wanted to come, but I said best not. You're wrong about Carrie, you know. You aren't often wrong, but you are about her.'

He suddenly let go of her hand and she thought, the nurse is back. He can't let her see how fond of me he is. You'd never think he'd lived in Majorca for some thirty years. Nothing Spanish seems to have rubbed off.

She was right about the nurse's return. 'I'm just going to take our temperature, Kate.' She was right about Carrie too. She wished she wasn't. There were some very nice Australians. 'Won't be a jiffy,' said the nurse. 'And then I'll leave you and Tim together. Isn't he a nice son to come all the way from Majorca?'

36

'Least I could do,' mumbled Timothy.

The nurse slipped the thermometer out of Kate's mouth and said, 'Much the same. Nothing to worry about,' and Kate expected her to go, but she didn't, she said, 'I've been to Majorca.'

'Oh?' Timothy wasn't really interested, and Kate thought, You'd be a better writer, Timothy, if you were more interested in people.

'Magaluf. It's nice there, isn't it?'

'Oh, I've never been to Magaluf!' The scorn in his voice was only just held back by good manners.

'What?? And you live there! That's amazing. No, it was really great. I hardly went to bed all week.'

'Ah, well, I live in Deya, which is in the North. It's very pretty and very quiet.'

'Oh, well, you can't have everything, can you?'

'Erm, could I have a word?'

They moved away from the bed towards the door, and Timothy said, in a low voice, 'Is this what my mother's usually like?' but she had very good hearing and could still hear every word.

'Well, yeah, I mean, she hasn't been in long, know what I mean?' said the nurse. 'She *has* had . . .' She lowered her voice even more, but Kate could still hear. '. . . a massive stroke. It'll take time. It's bound to, know what I mean? Tell yer one thing, though. There's something going on. She was dreaming a hell of a lot last night.' The nurse returned to the bedside, perhaps to cover herself in case Kate had heard. 'I was just telling Tim you was dreaming a lot last night. Good dreams they was too, from the sound of them.'

It was odious to hear the nurse talk like that about her night with Gwyn. Why couldn't Timothy say, 'Nurse, my mother is a woman of great sensitivity, delicacy and style. For her, sex is a matter of private passion and public discretion.' Why couldn't he show some of his mother's famous spunk? She had once heard a man say, of her, at a party, 'That is one spunky lady, or I'm the Nawab of Pataudi.' She couldn't remember who had said it, but it hadn't been the Nawab of Pataudi.

'Yeah,' continued the nurse. 'It sounded as though wherever she was she was having a good time, know what I mean?'

'Er . . . yes. I wonder which of them you've been thinking about, Mum.'

Colluding with the nurse! How could he? And only a minute ago she'd been thinking how snobbish he sounded about Majorca. Maybe she'd become a snob too. Maybe she'd always been one. Maybe he'd got it off her. She hated the thought.

The nurse departed at last, and he felt free to hold her hand again.

'Mum?' he said. 'If you can understand me, give me a sign.'

She realised immediately that this was the defining moment of her time in hospital. She realised that she didn't want to relate to people any more. Not yet, anyway. She could respond to her children so inadequately that it was better not to respond to them at all. She realised that she didn't want to have to care about the other women in the ward. She realised that she didn't want to have any kind of relationship with either of the nurses. She realised too, and surprised herself with the speed of the thought and its calculating nature, that, if she was serious about solving the murder, it might be useful if the suspects were off their guard with her. She gave no answering sign, therefore, to the second of her sons. He sighed.

Then, sitting on what she assumed to be an inelegant and uncomfortable hospital chair – what a shock that would be to his fastidious backside – he said things to his mother that he would never have been able to say if she had had her eyes open, perhaps couldn't even have said if he believed that she understood them.

'I love you, Mum. I love you more than I can say. Nobody could have had a lovelier, prettier, more stimulating mother. It took me a long time to forgive you for Dad, but I did in the end, and later I think I came to believe that there was nothing to forgive. Well, I have to assume that you can't understand this, but I think you're terrific.'

She wanted to cry. She was human, after all. She longed to give him a sign, to squeeze his hand, if of course she was able to move her hand, she didn't know about that. She gave no sign, and she suspected that he'd have been embarrassed if she had. But what an effort of will-power it was.

'I know I'm not a priest,' he said, to her astonishment, 'but I absolve you utterly,' and then he added, with that oh-so-British embarrassment which hadn't faded even under the sun of Deya, 'Oh, not that you need the last rites or anything like that. I've spoken to the nurse. The doctor's very hopeful.'

She wanted to laugh, and to cry. She loved him when he was embarrassed, and it was so absurd of him to be embarrassed even when he'd become convinced that she couldn't understand.

'I've spoken to Nigel,' he said. 'He told me that you looked surprisingly good.'

Oh good. Maybe she did, though she doubted it.

'As of course you do,' he added a little too late. 'I gather Nigel has spoken to Maurice and he's on his way back from St Petersburg.' Oh heavens, that sign from Leningrad station. 'Oh, and I've left a message on Elizabeth's answerphone. We think she must be away.'

He sat beside her in silence after that, for a long time. At first she wanted him to go, but then she got used to his presence. She was very fond of him, after all. He'd always done his best to be a good son, 'within the context of ploughing my own furrow', as he'd put it, though she'd thought that a rather wistful and self-deceiving description of his less-than-agricultural life.

And then she found that she was so frail that just knowing that he was there tired her out, and she longed for him to go.

At last he did.

39

'About tomorrow,' he said, still not entirely sure, it seemed, that she couldn't understand. 'If Maurice is back we'll leave the field clear for him. If not, one or other of us will be here. We'll have to play it a bit by ear.' He squeezed her hand. 'Goodbye, Mum.'

'How's the baby?' Mrs Critchley asked him as he set off.

'Er . . . what? Ah. Doing well. Mother and child doing well,' he said.

'I'd booked a single room,' she said, 'so I have to say I'm very surprised, but you can't say much when a little child is involved, can you, but I'll tell you something. Next time I come to Buxton, I won't be staying here.'

'No. Absolutely. Quite,' he said, and Kate could just imagine how quickly he fled.

When he'd gone, she thought, You absolved me. Can I absolve you? Oh, Timothy, I do love you. I don't want to die without knowing that you are innocent of murdering my fifth husband (or my fourth, or not a husband at all, but we can leave the linguistics till later).

She wanted to go back and relive her night with Gwyn again, but she knew, in her heart, that it wouldn't work. There was a limit to this seeing your life as a video. When she was eight, she'd eaten so much chocolate that she'd been sick and hadn't fancied chocolate again for months. 'Let that be a lesson to you,' her mother had said. It had been. Gwyn must wait, lest the emotion be dissipated by repetition.

She must move on, on inexorably towards that far-off murder.

But now the video image proved useful again. She would fast-forward through her last two years at school, in a Swansea made hateful to her by grief. Fast-forward through teacher-training college, where she began to rebuild her life. Fast-forward through the lonely hours in which she had studied the causes of the Great War, because it might help her if she could find out why he had died, and because she felt ashamed of herself and for the great mass of humanity for not caring about the causes while they were happening, because, if they had all cared enough, it might not have happened, and Gwyn might have lived to marry her, and then of course neither Nigel nor Timothy would ever have existed.

She fast-forwarded through all that because it hadn't helped, and it hadn't helped because her conclusion had been that Gwyn need not have died. She came to the conclusion that a limited war in the Balkans had turned into Armageddon because there were so many people in so many countries who for so many reasons wanted it to be so. In Germany, in France, in Italy, in Russia, in Austria, in Hungary, and in Great Britain there were many people who believed in peace, but there were also many who believed in war, and the many who believed in war were usually in more powerful positions than the many who believed in peace, since greed, ambition and the lust for power were powerful motives for war, almost more powerful than the desire to teach a bloody lesson to the peoples one didn't like. There had been an arms race in Europe for decades. Many people believed that arms races made the world safer. It had not proved to be so.

Kate came across two telling passages of prose during her studies. In the Jungdeutschlandbund impressionable young Germans had read, 'It will be more beautiful and wonderful to live for ever among the heroes on a war memorial in a church than to die an empty death in bed, nameless . . . let that be heaven for young Germany. Thus we wish to knock on God's door.' In *Scouting For Boys*, impressionable young Britons were urged to avoid the example of the Romans who lost their empire because they became 'wishy-washy slackers without any go or patriotism in them'. Lord Baden-Powell exhorted members to 'be prepared to die for your country . . . so that when the times come you may charge home with confidence, not caring whether you are to be killed or not'. Many men in many countries, Kate read, welcomed war as a possible solution to the economic and social evils in the big industrial cities.

'War,' said Kate to her assembled children many years later, 'is old men sending young men to die.' Shame on you, all you old men, that you didn't let my young man live.

So she believed that Gwyn had died in vain. There was no cure in that direction. The cure came, as it usually does, from the slow, slow drip of time, and now that her food was dripping into her, drip drip drip, and her life was dripping out of her, drip drip drip, there was no point in dwelling on the lost years, the long sleep of her soul. Fast-forward with our blessing, Kate dear, to the day, long ago, when you met, for the first time, the man who would father Nigel and Timothy, that absurd figure who ceased to be absurd in the only way he could, by becoming tragic.

4 Arturo

She'd thought him absurd at their first meeting, on the train taking her back to Penzance. She was on her way from London, where she'd been visiting Myfanwy with her mother. Myfanwy was a nurse at Charing Cross Hospital. She'd found digs with a Mrs Lewis, in Willesden. Mrs Lewis was Welsh, so it was probably all right, but Bronwen was pleased to go to London just to make sure.

He got on the train at Newbury, making a dramatic entry on a wave of autumnal air. He had a cape and a blackthorn stick. His hair was fair, and his eyes a piercing blue, but his nose was too small for the rest of his face.

The train set off with a jolt, and he fell into his seat in an ungainly manner, which made her want to laugh.

'Manners,' he said, 'are the curse of the middle classes.'

'I'm sure you avoid them very nicely,' she said.

'Manners, or the middle classes?'

'Both, from the look of you.'

'You sound intelligent,' he said. 'I must say that surprises me.'

She raised her fine eyebrows questioningly. Several men had already praised her eyebrows. Mr Wilkins, who lived next door to her lodgings, had called them evocative. He hadn't told her of what they were evocative.

'Why should I not be intelligent?' she enquired.

'Because you're beautiful,' he said. 'You are very beautiful, you know.'

'You put me in a difficult position there,' she said. 'If I say "Yes" you'll think me conceited. If I say "No" you'll think me stupid. If I say "Am I?" you'll think me arch.'

The suburbs of Newbury slipped past unnoticed, which was a blessing.

'Why did you say what you said about manners?' she asked.

'Because you didn't laugh at me when the train deposited me in my seat so rudely. You wanted to. I saw that.'

'Yes,' she said gravely. 'I plead guilty to having good manners.'

He smiled, then, and she felt the first faint flicker of excitement.

They were steaming through a river valley. Cows were munching in meadows green from the recent rains. Some of the trees were just beginning to turn. From time to time the view was obscured by the smoke from the engine.

'I shall try to be intelligent, to justify your good opinion of me,' she said. 'You're an artist, aren't you?'

'My disguise is penetrated,' he exclaimed with delight. 'Allow me to introduce myself. Arturo Rand, painter and poseur.'

'Arturo! That's an unusual name.'

'My parents christened me Arthur. I wasn't having that.'

He produced a silver flask, unscrewed the top and poured amber liquid into it.

'Whisky. The purest spirit in the world. I drink too much of it,' he said complacently.

He held the metal top out to her. She accepted it and drank cautiously. It set her throat on fire. She coughed, and took another sip.

'It's wonderful,' she said. 'I didn't know that anything so fiery could be so subtle. I didn't know that anything so concentrated could taste so pure.'

'That's single malts for you,' he said. He smiled again, and said, 'Luckily, however much a person knows, there's always more to teach them.'

'That's certainly lucky for me,' she said.

It was his turn to raise his eyebrows, which were bushy.

'I'm a teacher,' she said. 'My name is Kate Thomas. I'm Welsh.'

'I know that,' he said. 'You have a Celtic lilt. Your voice is as soft as the western rain, and I daresay your lips are softer.'

She looked at him in astonishment, and felt her heart racing.

'Nobody speaks like that,' she said.

'I am not nobody.'

He came across the compartment, and kissed her lips, very softly. Then he sat down again and made no comment. He looked out of the window at the beginnings of a town. She looked too, but the town was commonplace. Their eyes met. He looked very solemn, but she couldn't tell whether he was really solemn or pretending to be solemn.

The train stopped, and a fat woman got in, and she stank.

Neither Kate nor Arturo felt able to continue their conversation in the presence of the fat woman. The train set off with a burst of chuffing and skidding, as if the engine was trying to be more magnificent than it was. An Arturo of an engine, Kate thought.

She couldn't believe that she'd allowed herself to be kissed by this absurd stranger. She thought about Gwyn and the pain still threatened to crack her heart open.

The worst thing had been not being able to tell anyone. She'd longed to tell her father, but he'd have thought it wicked. She'd longed to tell Dilys – what was the point of having an identical twin if you couldn't confide your innermost thoughts – but she hadn't been able to. As for the others, Enid would have been jealous, Myfanwy contemptuous, Bernard inquisitive, Oliver thrilled, and they would all have been security risks. And her mother, how she had longed to open her grieving heart to her.

She closed her eyes and tried to conjure up again the sweet smell of that Swansea night, rain, horse manure and hydrangeas, but it came now polluted by the sour stink of the fat woman.

She opened her eyes again and found Arturo staring straight

at her. He held his nose and raised his eyes and she began to giggle. She laughed until the tears ran down her face and suddenly they were tears of grief. Never to be able to touch him again ever, even once. Never to see his unnaturally grave but kindly face. Oh, Gwyn, I hardly ever saw you laugh. Already I have seen this idiot . . . no, not fair . . . this fool laugh more than I ever saw you laugh. She looked across at Arturo and realised that he was busying himself with looking at the gentle hills of Somerset. He wasn't intruding on her private grief. She felt surprised by his sensitivity, and grateful for it. She longed to talk to him, and hoped that the smelly woman would get off at Taunton.

She did. Lucky Kate. Unlucky Taunton. Arturo opened the window, grinned, and began to speak very excitedly and angrily in a wild foreign tongue. For just a moment she was alarmed, and then she understood. He was making sure that they had the compartment to themselves. She laughed in delight, and he laughed too.

The train set off with a jerk. An awkward silence fell between them as they clattered through the rich Somerset country, the soil getting redder all the time.

Kate sensed that Arturo wanted to say something sincere and unaffected, but wasn't quite confident enough to do so. She decided to help him out.

'It's my turn to put you in a difficult position,' she said.

'Oh?'

'Are you a good artist?'

'That doesn't put me in a difficult position at all,' he said. 'Yes, I am a good artist.' Suddenly he looked boyish, younger than his twenty-four years. 'Whether I'm quite good enough remains to be seen.'

'Is that why you adopt so many props?' she asked.

'Props?'

'The whisky, the name, the stick, the cape, the moustache.'

46

He fell silent, and she knew that she had gone too far. Oh Kate and your impulsive tongue, you have hit upon the one thing that is not permissible – the truth.

She attempted to make amends.

'Can I see some of your work?' she asked. 'I'd very much like to.'

'All in good time, Kate.'

She got out her sandwiches, and offered him one. They'd been made by her mother. They were neat and thin, with the crusts cut off. They were little square rebukes against the pleasures of the flesh. They were reminders of the poverty of the great mass of humanity. They were sermons in bread. She was ashamed of them.

He produced his sandwiches, and she realised that he was ashamed of them. They were great doorsteps, rough-hewn, oozing their innards like dead animals.

They ate both lots of sandwiches without comment. It was a time for avoiding controversy.

After Exeter the train ran down the estuary of the Exe. They tide was out. Great flocks of migrating waders were feeding in the mud. Some, nearest to the tracks, flew glistening into the air at the approach of the roaring engine. The train ran along the coast, plunging in and out of short tunnels, steaming cheerfully past shingly bays and sandy bays and a sullen, swollen, pearl sea.

'I love the sea,' said Arturo. 'I can't paint except by the sea. I can't breathe except by the sea. I'm a dry man. I need watering.'

'I grew up with water too,' said Kate. 'I was offered several jobs. I thought Penzance was a brave choice. The end of the earth. I think now it's just another version of home.'

'Tregarryn is like nobody's home,' he said. 'Tregarryn is wild.'

'Tregarryn?'

'Where we live.'

She should have asked him straight away, but didn't dare.

47

That little 'we' sat there between them, tiny word but vast obstacle. It sat between them in Teignmouth station and all the way up the lovely estuary of the Teign. As the train drew in to Newton Abbot, she plucked up courage and asked about it, blushing, to her horror, as she hadn't blushed for years.

'You said "we",' she said, and she knew that it was coming out in a horrible little voice, which she despised. 'Who would that "we" be exactly?'

He grinned. The beast had known what she was thinking, and said nothing. She couldn't believe that she cared about him at all. But it was a nice grin, almost irresistible, and he had good teeth.

'That "we" would be a little community of artists,' he said. 'Me, two other painters, the wife of one of the painters, and a sculptor. It's not a large community yet, but we hope it will get bigger.'

The train stopped, and he began to jabber away in a foreign tongue again, fending off the good people of Newton Abbot. She found herself laughing joyously at the success of his antics.

The train set off again with another of the jolts that seemed to be the speciality of the driver.

'And who is your particular partner?' she asked, managing not to blush this time. 'Or are you the one with the wife?'

'No, I'm not the one with the wife,' he said, 'and I have no particular partner. I have been to bed with one of the painters, but she doesn't love me and I don't love her. And I had the sculptor once, but I didn't enjoy it and neither did he, it was just an experiment.'

Our Heroine is Struck Dumb at the Thought of Bohemia.

He asked her about her family, and she talked about them with great affection and at excessive length, being Welsh.

She asked him about his family, and he talked about them with great reserve and excessive brevity, being English.

And then they were at Bodmin Road and he said, 'I change

here,' and he gathered his things together, waved his blackthorn stick at her, tossed his cape over his shoulder imperiously, said, 'Goodbye, Kate,' and was gone. She wanted to open the window and cry, 'But you haven't given me your address. When will I see you?' but of course she didn't.

Next morning, when she awoke in her lodgings, in beautiful Regent Square, she felt, as she felt every morning, the awful emptiness of her world. But it wasn't of Gwyn that she was thinking. It was of Arturo Rand.

Three weeks passed, and Kate didn't hear from Arturo. The charming little house where she lodged, in an exquisite diminutive square of two-storey Georgian cottages, on the slope between the main street and the promenade, no longer seemed charming. The pastel colours of the houses, so pretty in the spring, seemed wishy-washy now. The autumn wind tore the leaves off the cherry trees, tossed the palms, battered the houses. She found it difficult to concentrate on teaching history to the daughters of people prosperous enough to pay for this doubtful privilege. She must see Arturo. If he would not go to her, then she must go to him.

As the bus drew nearer to the lane that led from the main road to Tregarryn, Kate began to feel a knotted sickness in her stomach. This was ridiculous. It was no problem, surely, to wander down the lane and say, calmly, 'Hello there. Your community intrigued me. I thought I'd pop down and take a look'?

She couldn't do it. She couldn't look remotely calm as she walked down that lane. Her voice would come out little and breathless. She hated herself for her nervousness. It was pathetic. Arturo was a silly little man, five foot six, compensating for his feelings of inferiority with all his show of boldness. To compare him with Gwyn! To have abandoned you, my darling, for this. She persuaded herself into believing that it was noble of her not to get off the bus, but she still had a wild hope that he would be there, at the end of the lane, waiting for the bus to Bude, and she would say, 'Well, this is a surprise. I'm just on my way to Bude, heard it's nice, thought I'd have a look at it. We could have tea somewhere.'

She hated Bude that day. She loathed its Arturoless streets. She felt angry with life, with the world, with the history of the human race. Unable to do much about that, she kicked a lamppost instead, and bruised a toe quite badly.

On the bus back, she dreaded that he would be standing there with one of the artists, the sculptor with whom he had spent a disappointing night, or the painter whom he didn't love, a haughty great woman in scarlet who would think her incorrigibly provincial. So her disappointment at finding nobody at all at the end of the lane was tinged with relief.

She felt about her attempted visit to Tregarryn much as she felt later about the Anglo-French invasion of the Suez Canal. It was an expedition that should not have been begun in the first place, but that, having been begun, should not have been aborted.

When she got home she wrote a letter to her identical twin.

Dear Dilys,

How awful it is that we see so little of each other. I'm so pleased that you're happy in Macclesfield. It sounds such fun. I was so happy to read about your dream semi. John sounds to be a peach and as for little Tom, what a treasure he must be. I wish I wasn't so ambitious. Oh dear, that sounds as though I regard your horizons as limited. I don't mean it that way. I know that geographically you are limited, but your hikes on the Derbyshire moors sound very enjoyable and your half-day outing to Congleton sounded stimulating. I should love to see Macclesfield and Congleton and hope to do so next hols.

Dilys dear, I have a dreadful secret which I have never told anyone and I can't even tell the rest of the family, but I must tell you. I don't know whether after we have been apart for so long you are still able to leap across the miles and share experiences with me, but there has been a man in my life too.

She went on to tell the story of Gwyn. She cried as she wrote it. She thought she had stopped crying over it, but the humiliating day had worn down her resistance.

Three days later, she came out of the school with Miss Langan and Miss Carter, and THERE HE WAS.

It hadn't been a good day. She'd waxed lyrical about the Tolpuddle Martyrs, and Lily Gardner had said, 'Is it true Tolpuddle's on the River Piddle, Miss?' and all the girls had giggled, and she had said, 'How can I teach you the vast sweep of history when you have such tiny minds?' But now the day was a good day. Lily Gardner was forgotten. THERE HE WAS.

He was dressed entirely in purple – purple shoes, purple socks, purple trousers, purple shirt, purple jacket, purple cravat, purple cape. He waved his blackthorn stick at her, and she felt like going back to Bude and apologising to the lamppost.

Miss Carter, who was walking out with an insurance salesman, was horrified. Miss Langan, at whom no one would ever wave a blackthorn stick, was mortified.

'I see I have company,' said Kate, knowing that nothing would ever be quite the same in the common room again.

She didn't want to kiss him, he didn't deserve to be kissed, he was an irresponsible young man who trifled with a young woman's affections, but Miss Carter and Miss Langan were watching and it would be quite nice for them to see her kissing him, and it wouldn't be very Bohemian to bear a grudge, and that settled it, so she kissed him. He smelt of pipe tobacco and whisky.

'Come and meet my friends,' he said.

She recognised Arturo's friends the moment she entered ye

olde tea shoppe. They were sitting at an olde table at the foot of ye olde stairs. She particularly noticed a tall woman with a heavy bust, green eyes and a scarlet gash of a mouth, who wasn't at all pleased to see her. Then there was a small, solemn young man with receding hair, a worried frown and a very pale face, dominated by a long, severe nose. And there was a great big bear of a man who unrolled himself endlessly from a dwarfed Windsor chair and said, 'Never been so delighted to lose a bet.'

Kate, determined not to be abashed by these people, stared him in the face and said, 'I dread to think what you were betting about.'

'I bet Daniel there'd be nothing sexy in the whole of Penzance.'

Indignant shoppers turned to stare at this big, loud man.

'You're offending people,' Kate said, in a low voice, 'either because they don't like the word "sexy" or because they thought you'd already lost your bet because they thought they were sexy.'

The woman with the green eyes looked more sour than ever.

'Aren't you going to introduce me?' Kate asked.

'No,' said Arturo.

'I suppose introductions are dreadfully middle class,' said Kate.

The man called Daniel smiled at her, indicated to her to sit beside him, and said, 'I'm Daniel Begelman. I'm a painter. This is Stanley Wainwright.' He indicated the bear-like man. 'He's a sculptor.'

Stanley Wainwright held his hand out across the table. Kate almost scalded her arm in the steam from a jug of hot water as she held, and survived, his iron grip, and met his hungry eyes without flinching.

'And the lady is another painter, Daphne Stoneyhurst.'

Kate looked Daphne Stoneyhurst straight in the eyes and said, 'I'm delighted to meet you.'

'Well, I'm so glad one of us is,' said Daphne Stoneyhurst.

'Daphne!' said Arturo. 'That's no way to speak to the woman I'm going to marry.'

Kate tried not to gasp, tried not to look provincial, hoped against hope that she wouldn't blush, attempted to look as though this sort of thing was said to her every day. But she was glad she was sitting down. Her knees might have buckled if she'd been standing.

Daphne Stoneyhurst went pale, Daniel Begelman frowned, Stanley Wainwright smiled as enigmatically as the Mona Lisa, but on a larger scale.

'Don't worry, Daphne,' said Kate. 'This is news to me, and I'm certainly not going to marry Arturo.'

'I should hope not,' said Daniel. 'You hardly know him.'

'But that isn't why I'm not going to marry him,' said Kate. 'I'm not going to marry him because I know him only too well.'

Daphne smiled maliciously, and Kate realised that Daphne was even more angry with Arturo for bringing her than she was with her for allowing herself to be brought.

The waitress came to take Kate's order. She walked as if she had corns. Kate plumped for toast and butter, and gave the waitress a big smile. She thought the artists were rather offhand with the waitress.

'I must say it's very stimulating to meet artists,' she said, getting into her stride now, and absolutely refusing to be the provincial schoolmistress. 'I've only met one before. He was a post-Raphaelite.'

There was a horrified silence.

'You mean a pre-Raphaelite, dear,' said Arturo.

'You haven't seen his work,' said Kate sweetly.

Daniel, Stanley and Arturo laughed. Daphne didn't.

After tea, they walked along the promenade, beside a gently heaving, deceptively quiet, soupy, oily sea. The Atlantic was biding its time, gathering its strength for the winter. They were an odd sight, Arturo all in purple, Stanley in corduroys with no hat, Daniel in a loose smock, Daphne in a long thing more like a sack than a dress, and Kate in the sensible skirt and blouse of the history teacher. Around them, fashionable Penzance swirled and stared, the men in their dark suits and coats and bowlers and top hats, the ladies in their cloche hats and long straight dresses, all the corsets and bodices blown away with the war.

'Is the sea difficult to paint?' asked Kate.

'Nothing is difficult to paint,' said Arturo, 'and everything is difficult to paint.'

'I see,' said Kate. 'I'm sorry I asked.'

'To sculpt the sea is the challenge,' said Stanley. 'One day I will. In the meantime, I could gaze at its immensity, its omnipotence, its magnificence . . .'

'Until we reach the nearest pub.' Daniel said with affection what other people said with malice.

Soon they did reach the nearest pub, and Kate realised that Daniel had spoken the truth. Suddenly the sea lost its magic for Stanley. He marched towards the pub.

Daphne linked arms with Kate, and Kate tried, unsuccessfully, not to stiffen. She felt that there were elements of her native puritanism in her antipathy to touching Daphne, so she gave Daphne's arm a squeeze. Daphne looked straight into her face, and smiled with everything except her eyes. 'I have the funniest feeling, Kate, that you and I are to be great friends,' she said.

Kate had never been in a pub before, but that evening she went into the Cornish Arms, the Duke of Cumberland, the Golden Lion, the Farmers' Arms, the Prince of Wales, the Union, the Turk's Head and the Seven Stars. Some of the pubs were clean and some of them weren't. Some of them were noisy, and others were even noisier. Most of them were dark, secretive places, places of shadow. She saw men playing games she had never heard of before – cribbage and shove-halfpenny and euchre. She saw loose women and loose teeth and she heard loose talk. She had never tasted beer before, and when she took her first sip she thought she would never dare to take another, but she was riding on a tide of Bohemianism, she'd been told it was an acquired taste, and she was determined to acquire it. By the time she had acquired it she was so full of liquid that she had to go on to whisky.

They talked about art, and then about sex, and then about sex in art, and then, as they got drunker, about art in sex. The next morning, Kate could remember very little of their conversation. Now, seventy-seven years later, she could remember even less.

But she did recall that at one stage she asked them if they were members of any artistic movement, and Arturo said, grandly, 'I am a Randist. I am the only Randist, but, when I'm famous, there will be others.'

She remembered Daniel attempting to talk seriously, saying that no artists could be unaware of movements in art, and that in 1922 no artist could say that he was unaffected by cubism, even if it was to react against it. 'None of us would call ourselves cubists, but there is the knowledge of the existence of cubism in everything we paint. We can never unknow what we know.'

She remembered Stanley saying, 'Daphne is in crisis. She doesn't know whether she's a neo-vorticist or a post-vorticist or a neo-post-vorticist.' He also spoke passionately, at one stage – in the Farmers' Arms she thought it was – about the purity of art.

She found herself being asked to join them, give up her job, move to Tregarryn. She felt flattered and astonished and excited. 'We need outside blood,' Daniel said. 'We need an injection of common sense,' said Stanley. Kate wasn't too pleased by that. Was that what they saw her potential as – an injection of common sense? So, when Daphne said, petulantly, 'I don't know why you should think of Kate as having common sense,' Kate smiled sweetly at her and said, 'Thank you, Daphne. I'm glad someone appreciates me.' Daphne tossed her head like a wilful carthorse.

Later – in the Turk's Head, she thought – she commented to Stanley that, since Daphne obviously resented her, there must be more than she'd thought going on between Daphne and Arturo.

'Not really,' Stanley said. 'Daphne's mainly lesbian.'

Mainly lesbian! What Bohemianism! Kate felt shocked, but she also felt shocked that she didn't feel more shocked.

'Well, why does she resent me so much, then?' she asked.

'It's nothing to do with sex,' said Stanley. 'It's because she likes being the only woman around.'

'But there's Daniel's wife.'

'Ah. Olga. Olga isn't really a woman in her own right. She's an appendage of Daniel.'

At some stage Arturo joined in the attempts to get Kate to join them. 'Please come,' he implored. 'Please come and be my lover.'

A lover! That would be a wonderful thing to be. How angry Enid and Myfanwy would be if they knew she was a lover. But of course she couldn't be.

'I can't,' she said. 'I have a job.'

'You're so delightfully old-fashioned, Kate,' said Daphne. 'It really is heart-warming to see such old-fashioned dedication to duty.'

They discussed Picasso and Braque and Kate noticed that the more drunk Stanley grew, the more nonsense he talked, whereas the more drunk Arturo grew, the more sense he talked. Daniel drank carefully, and Daphne drank an enormous amount without it seeming to have any effect on her at all.

In the Golden Lion they played darts with great excitement and lots of cries of 'Mugs away' and 'Nice arrows, Daphne'. The artists imagined that they were cutting a great dash as people of the people, utterly unaware that all the other people in the pub, who were people of the people, were looking on them with utter scorn. Kate was aware of this, but couldn't have cared less. These people were fun to be with.

Kate just couldn't get interested in the darts. She didn't care whether she won or not. She realised that Daniel was the same. He seemed to have no competitive spirit. They stood together, a little apart from the game, watching Arturo and Stanley in fierce battle for the title of Tregarryn Darts Champion of Penzance.

'It would be nice if you did join us,' said Daniel. 'You'll like Olga.'

'Why is she not here?'

'She's sick today. She's pregnant.' He looked so proud and so boyish. Kate longed to hug him, but there was a reserve about him, an awkwardness about him, which made such intimacy difficult. 'Don't be frightened of Arturo. His . . .'

'Please don't say his bark is worse than his bite,' said Kate. 'You're far too good an artist to resort to cliché.'

'You know my work?' Daniel was thrilled.

'No, but I know the sort of man you are.'

'Oh.' Daniel was flattered but disappointed. He gave her hand a little squeeze and eased himself out of his embarrassment by changing the subject. 'Look at Arturo,' he said. 'He's a little dog, always lifting his leg against the lampposts of the world.' Kate told him about kicking the lamppost in Bude. He looked at her gravely, and said, 'Try not to be too serious about Arturo.'

Stanley won the match, and Kate realised that Stanley would always win, Arturo would always lose, and Daniel would always watch. Three men fulfilling their allotted roles.

Her head was swimming now. She could hardly stand. They were in . . . probably it was the Union. It seemed a bit more respectable than the other pubs, and its respectability drove Stanley to behave outrageously.

'You're all peasants,' he shouted at the patrons. 'You're dead from the neck up.'

'You'll be dead from the neck down tonight,' retorted a ship's chandler, and everybody laughed.

The cold night air sent them spiralling into extreme

drunkenness. Kate remembered Stanley saying 'Look at all those stars. Look how many there are. There are hundreds', as if he was being a truly perceptive observer of the night scene.

They couldn't find Stanley's car. Up and down the wind-swept streets they lurched. Kate fell and crashed into a lamp-post. She remembered thinking that Cornish lampposts just didn't get on with her.

Arturo tried to support her, but when she leant against him he fell too, and she fell on top of him, and he kissed her.

They found the car at last. What a little car it was. Kate realised later that it was a rusting old Austin Seven. She found herself lifted up, bundled into the back seat, wedged uncomfortably between Arturo's slimness and Daphne's big thighs.

'I really mean it,' said Stanley. 'I've never seen so many stars. There were literally hundreds of them, all over the sky. How do you start this thing?'

'You have to crank it, you fool,' said Daniel.

How they laughed!

'Let me out,' cried Kate. 'I'll walk home.'

The car sprang into noisy, bone-crunching life. Stanley got back in and drove off, jerkily. Kate could hardly have been more frightened if she was being abducted to join the white slave traffic.

She was being abducted! Stanley lurched down Market Jew Street and out towards the countryside.

'Not this way!' she shouted. 'I live back there.'

'You live with us now,' said Stanley. 'You live at Tregarryn.'

'No!'

'Oh come on, darling,' pleaded Arturo. 'Away with dull care and convention. Break free of your bonds. You can do it.'

'You're coming with us,' said Stanley. 'Welcome to the real world, little chapel girl.'

'Real?' screamed Kate. 'You call this real?'

'Let her out, for God's sake,' said Daphne.

'Daphne doesn't want me,' said Kate. 'I almost want to come, because of that.'

Daphne raised her arm to hit Kate, but only succeeded in bruising it on the roof of the car.

'Shit!' she said.

'Let me out,' screamed Kate. 'I have girls to teach.'

Daniel shouted, 'Stop the car!' not loudly, but with such authority that Stanley obeyed. At the time Kate thought nothing of this, but the next day, thinking back and trying to piece together what had happened, she was astonished at the force of Daniel's personality.

'Stop this fooling,' he said. 'Take the girl home.'

Nobody spoke on the way back. Daphne was sulking, Arturo was running his hand imploringly over Kate's body, Stanley was concentrating on his driving, and Daniel and Kate were hoping that Stanley wouldn't change his mind.

He didn't. He pulled up in Regent Square outside Mrs Finicky's. That wasn't her real name. It was Kate's nickname for her.

Arturo kissed Kate very gently and whispered, 'Please come.' Just for a moment it was very tempting, but she had no idea how sincere he was, and reason and duty prevailed.

They all shouted 'Good-night', then they all went 'Sssh!' loudly, then they all laughed loudly, then Stanley drove off loudly with a crash of gears, and Kate was alone in the silent town. She looked up at the vast constellations of the heavens and felt very tiny indeed.

She lurched up the drive and took so long to unlock the door that Mrs Finicky came down in her dressing-gown to see what was going on.

'What time do you call this?' demanded Mrs Finicky.

'I call it Gladys,' said Kate, 'or possibly five past Gladys. What time do you call it, Mrs Finicky?'

In the morning, when she crawled out of bed and looked out of her room across the graveyard to the great bulk of the Church of St Mary the Virgin – oh Lord, the last thing she needed that morning was a church to remind her of her sins, why did she always seem to be near a church? – eleven things worried Kate the Not Virgin.

It worried her that she had a violent headache. It worried her that she felt sick. It worried her that she had a black eye. It worried her that she'd overslept. It worried her that she'd been drunk. It worried her that it didn't worry her more than it did that she had been drunk. It worried her that she had said, 'I call it Gladys,' thereby making it unlikely that she would be able to persuade Mrs Finicky that she hadn't been drunk. It worried her that she had called Mrs Finicky Mrs Finicky to her face, because it wasn't Mrs Finicky's fault that she was finicky, she was a war widow with a lot of love to give and no man left to give it to, so she gave it to her china dogs and shepherdesses instead. It worried her that Mrs Finicky might get in touch with her parents to warn them of her behaviour. It worried her that the car in which Arturo had been travelling had been driven across Cornwall the previous night by a very drunk sculptor, and she had no way of knowing whether they had arrived at Tregarryn safely. But above all it worried her that, after being worried that she would never be able to fall in love again, she had fallen at least half in love with an impoverished artist who called himself a Randist, drank too much, dressed entirely in purple, and sulked when he lost at darts.

The moment her head hit the pillow, Kate was awake. For two hours she had longed for sleep, she had had a battle to keep her eyes open. Now she knew immediately that sleep wouldn't come. Daphne's macaroni cheese lay too heavily on her stomach.

As she listened to the wind rattling the shutters, she reflected on her first evening at Tregarryn. Arturo had met her off the bus. He'd been standing there at the end of the lane, grinning happily, all pretension gone, save for the fact that he was dressed entirely in mauve. He even carried her bag! She tried not to let her astonishment show.

A loud, staccato fart disturbed her thought. For a moment she thought that she must have farted herself, but then she realised that the noise had come from the other side of the room. There was somebody else in the bedroom, some unknown person, some windy intruder. She tried to sit up, and found that she couldn't, she was paralysed, a sharp pain ran through her body inside where the paralysis didn't reach, and she remembered that she was in Ward 3C of Whetstone General Hospital. One of the patients had farted in her sleep. If she had got the geography right, the noise had come from the opposite corner of the ward. It must be Glenda.

What a complicated journey back to the past I'm making, she thought. Here I am lying in bed in hospital in the middle of the night remembering the time I lay in bed at Tregarryn in the middle of the night remembering my arrival and first evening in Tregarryn. Away with sleeping patients and farting Glendas, I will banish them from my thoughts. Back to Tregarryn. My arrival. Will-power.

The lane down to Tregarryn was unlike any road that Kate had seen. Over the centuries it had sunk deeper and deeper beneath banks of earth. There was a bank as tall as her on either side. Out of the tops of the banks, trees were growing. Their contorted roots formed the top part of each bank. Their branches met overhead in an almost perfect canopy. Just a few tiny rays of sunshine penetrated this natural roof. There was the sound of running water, and the ever-present wail of whirling seagulls. The lane made two sharp hairpin bends before emerging from the trees on to the side of a steep hill yellow with gorse and purple with heather, and there below them was a steep narrow valley, little more than a gash in the hostile cliffs, with a tiny shingle beach on which a few very small boats were drawn up. There were some slate-boarded cottages, with slate roofs, and, to the right, the chimneys of a larger house peeped shyly over an unkempt blackthorn hedge. Tregarryn.

The lane led down to the village, and a path led off to the right to Tregarryn House. Arturo opened a white gate in the hedge, made a gesture like a magician, and led Kate into the garden as if it was his invention.

The house was long and low, stone built, with a roof of large, heavy slates. A simple two-pillared portico lent just a touch of splendour to its simple rows of windows.

In front of the house there was a formal garden, in three terraces of gravel studded with little square flower-beds and grand Victorian stone urns. Wide steps led from one terrace to the next, past astonishing *objets d'art* such as Kate had never seen. A Burmese Buddha. An Inca sun god. An Egyptian king. A Javanese coriander press. A Maori war god. A Perseus by a student of Cellini. A sacrificial milk churn from the Yemen. A gilt-encrusted totem pole from North Dakota.

Kate stared in astonished silence. Arturo told her where they had all come from with such pride that it was as if he had collected them himself.

'The house was built by an eccentric explorer,' he explained. 'Sir Tristram de Vere Boddington. He retired here, and lived a life of complete isolation, surrounded by his collection. He left the house to his great-niece Isobel, on condition that she either lived in it or rented it out to artists who would appreciate the beauty of his collection and be its custodians. She's seventy-seven, and nobody knows what will happen when she dies, but, in the meantime, here we are.'

'It's incredible.'

'Yes.'

They stood and watched as the sun slid down behind the hill opposite. Suddenly the valley was a gloomy place. Arturo put his arm round her waist, traced the curve of her hips with his fingers, and said, 'Shall we see how it goes and take your bag up later?'

'See how it goes?'

'You can sleep with me or you can sleep alone. There's no pressure on you.'

'I'm glad of that. I'll sleep alone.'

'Kate! Don't be like that. Let's see how it goes.'

'I know how it'll go. I won't sleep with you yet.'

'What am I to read into "yet"?'

'I'm not sure, yet.'

'You don't mean you won't sleep with me until we're married?'

'I didn't know you were serious about us getting married.'

'I would be if you were.'

'Well, we'll have to see, won't we? Would it worry you if I wouldn't sleep with you until we were married, if we were going to get married?'

'It wouldn't worry me. It'd be highly embarrassing, but I'd brave it out.'

'Why would it be embarrassing?'

'We're an artists' colony, Kate. It'd seem desperately conventional.'

'It's nothing to do with getting married, anyway. It's to do with commitment. I don't really know you yet, whatever I may have said in Penzance. I've never even seen your work.'

Arturo led her into the house, up a wide bare wooden staircase, flanked at the top by a pair of huge ivory chessmen.

'From Bengal,' he said proudly.

On the wooden boards of the corridor that ran the length of the first floor there were two charming brightly coloured rugs.

'Bolivian,' said Arturo, as if hoping that all this detail would impress Kate into sleeping with him.

He opened the end door to reveal a small bedroom, very

simply furnished with a bed, a chair and a small pine wardrobe with one drawer. There were no lovely artefacts here.

'The guest room,' he said. 'Oh, Kate, it seems such a shame. Supposing I die young. Every night lost will have been such a waste.'

'Why on earth should you die young?'

'I'm an artist. I don't look after myself.'

'You're absurd.'

'Do you love me?'

'I think I do.'

'Oh God! I'm on probation.'

'We're all on probation, Arturo,' she said grandly. 'It's called life.'

Supper was taken at a large pine table in a huge kitchen furnished with bulky pine cupboards. The plainness of all the pine contrasted rather sadly, Kate felt, with the glory of the collected artefacts.

She sat next to Arturo. She felt uncomfortable, exposed. She wasn't used to eating in kitchens. She certainly wasn't used to having wine with meals. And she had never tasted anything like Daphne's macaroni cheese before. It was gooey, almost tasteless, and very difficult to swallow. The wine was thin and acid and she wondered if she would ever learn to like it. She tried desperately to relax and not look middle class, but when Daphne, at the head of the table as duty chef, asked her, 'Well, Kate, what do you think of my macaroni cheese?' she heard a polite little voice, the voice of a stranger, saying, from deep inside herself, 'It's very nice, thank you,' and felt shamingly wet.

'That is too too wet,' said Daphne.

Unlike the macaroni cheese, thought Kate. A bit of sauce would have done wonders. She took a draught of her red wine, and shivered in revulsion against its sharp, raw taste.

'Cold?' asked Stanley Wainwright, and she had the uncomfortable feeling that he was watching her all the time.

'This house is cold,' said Olga, who had a round, pale face and looked sickly and had said nothing except 'Hello, Kate.' 'I'm so worried about the baby's first winter. Snug as a bug in my tum-tum this winter. What about next winter?'

'We'll have repairs done,' said Daniel.

'If we can afford to,' said Stanley. 'That will be a decision for the management committee.'

'If it's as cold in the house next winter,' warned Daniel, 'we'll have to leave.'

'It's intolerable that you keep holding this threat to our heads,' snapped Daphne.

'Please,' implored Arturo. 'We have a guest. Let's not argue.'

Olga stood up and said, 'I'm leaving the room because I feel sick, everybody, not out of protest. And it's no reflection on your macaroni cheese, Daphne.'

Daniel managed a couple more mouthfuls and then he stood up.

'Best go and see how she is,' he said.

'He always goes to her!' hissed Daphne, the moment he had gone. 'He always bloody goes to her to stroke her tum-tum.'

'Is it a crime to care for your wife?' asked Kate.

'Oh God!' Daphne cried. 'We've got another one here. She's going to tend to his every fucking need.'

Kate smiled stoically, but she couldn't hide her shock. She wasn't used to women swearing. Well, she wasn't used to anyone swearing.

'I've shocked our little chapel girl,' said Daphne.

'How dare you talk like that to my guest?' shouted Arturo. He pushed his plate away. 'Sorry, Daphne, I'm not very hungry tonight.'

'Right. That's it,' said Daphne, standing up so violently that her chair slid back, scraping agonisingly across the tiled floor. She glared at them and said, 'I'm never going to cook my macaroni cheese again,' and with that devastating news she flounced out, slamming the door. There was silence, save for the rattling of the windows, the squeaking of the shutters and the sighing of the wind, saying 'Seen it all before'.

The silence was broken at last by Stanley.

'Welcome to Tregarryn,' he said.

Kate tried to smile, but a great weariness swept over her. It had been a long day and her first evening at Tregarryn had been traumatic. She ached in every limb. She longed for sleep.

Arturo reached across, clasped her hand, and said rather shyly, 'Would you like to see some of my work?'

Kate knew that you cannot say to an artist, 'I'm sorry. I'm too tired. Some other time,' so she said, 'I'd love to.'

Behind the house, tucked into the hill, a long, low studio block had been built. It was a very basic structure, but slate hung to fit in with the rest of the hamlet.

Almost every available space in Arturo's studio was hung with his pictures. Their colours were bright, verging on the simplistic. Their shapes were violent. They were full of swirling movement. The paint was applied thickly, aggressively. Nothing in Kate's experience had qualified her to judge them. And there he was, standing there, looking at her looking at them, waiting for her comments, no, waiting for her compliments. She found his presence deeply unnerving. She sensed that, although the pictures seemed close to abstraction, they were not entirely abstract. She felt that they must be landscapes, but landscapes seen through a distorting mirror. Even if she hadn't been so exhausted, she wouldn't have known what to say. A little imp almost persuaded her to say, 'They're very nice.' She could imagine the eruption that would follow.

The silence went on and on. It became dreadful. She longed for sleep.

'Well?' he said at last.

'Oh, Arturo, they're overwhelming.'

'Ah!'

He seemed pleased, but not pleased enough.

'But do you like them?'

It was an inexcusable question, she thought.

'Oh yes,' she said, but her natural honesty forced her to qualify it. 'I'm almost certain that I shall like them.'

'What on earth do you mean?'

'Oh, Arturo. There are so many of them, and I'm so tired, and you're standing right beside me, unnerving me, and I don't want to say the wrong thing.'

'Oh no! Heavens, no! Mustn't say the wrong thing.'

'I didn't mean it like that. I meant, a body of work like this demands very careful consideration. You put a lot of painting into them. I need to put a lot of looking into them. They deserve that. You deserve that.'

'I suppose so,' he admitted, slightly mollified.

'It's clear to me that they're forceful, colourful, energetic, complex and daring,' she said. 'To my untutored eye they look almost, but not quite, abstract. As I look more, I begin to understand more.'

'Well, yes,' he said. 'That's the intention.'

If only she'd left it there. Whether you're a salesman, an after-dinner speaker or a lover, stop when you're winning.

'That one, for instance,' she said, indicating a large and particularly swirly picture in the middle of the wall to the right of the door. 'At first it was a mass of jumbled colour, of aggression and even anger. Now I can see that it's the cliffs at the end of the little valley, to the end of the beach, with just the suggestion of shingle, and the little boats drawn up there, very subtle.'

'It's a portrait of Daphne in the nude,' he said. He didn't seem angry, just slightly disillusioned. He escorted her up the wide stairs in silence, and then, at the door to her room, he made one last try.

'Are you sure you won't reconsider?' he said.

'Sorry. I'm too tired, anyway.'

'That's my room over there if you change your mind. Any time, I'll be there.'

'Thanks.'

'I'm sorry you copped for the macaroni cheese.'

'Thank you.' She wanted to say something amusing to end the evening. 'It's a pity we didn't supply the Germans with Daphne's macaroni cheese. It might have shortened the war.'

He laughed, kissed her, sighed, and was gone. She stood there, in the corridor, shocked and upset with herself for making any kind of joke about the war. It seemed so disloyal to Gwyn.

Now the wind howled and it wasn't hard to imagine that it was Gwyn's voice wailing to her from the heavens. That was ridiculous. She didn't believe in that sort of thing.

She pulled the bedclothes over her head and snuggled deep into the resultant womb. But sleep wouldn't come.

Her door was opening. She sat bolt upright as it creaked.

'Don't be alarmed, my darling. It's only me.'

She felt for her candle and matches, and lit the candle.

'Oh, Arturo,' she said. 'Won't you ever take "no" for an answer?'

'Of course. Of course, darling, but we do live in a democracy, and I do have my views.'

'In sex, the person who says "no" always has to win.'

'Don't you think one day you might say "yes"?'

'Very probably.'

'Well, why not say "yes" tonight, then?'

So she told him. He sat on the bed and she told him about Gwyn. She didn't want to, she didn't know whether it was right to, but she had to. He sat there, in his mauve pyjamas, holding her very tight, and out it all poured, the tale she had longed to tell her sisters and her mother, but had only been able to tell once before, in a letter to her twin. He sat very still. She cried a little. He licked her tears, licked her salt tears, kissed her gently on the forehead and left the room very quietly, without another word, shutting the door so gently that it was like another kiss.

The moment he'd gone, the tears stopped and she wished that he was still there, she had got Gwyn off her chest, he had been so sensitive, they had been so close, she longed for him to return and hold her. She dried her face and blew her nose and blew out the candle and lay listening to the wind. She thought it was raining, but it might have been a stream running down from the cliffs. She thought about Arturo's paintings. She began to feel drowsy. She gave herself a wry smile at the thought that his paintings could send her to sleep.

Her door was opening! He'd come back. Her heart began to beat very fast. She made up her mind in a flash, lowered her nightshirt off her breasts, lit the candle at the side of the bed, and turned towards him, holding out her arms, feeling her nipples rise.

'Good God!' said Stanley Wainwright. 'I hoped I might not be entirely unwelcome, but this is ridiculous.'

She gasped and struggled desperately to pull the nightshirt back over her breasts.

'What the hell do you want?' she snapped.

'I had thought you intelligent,' he said. 'That is the least intelligent question I have ever been asked. You know what I want.'

'Get out of my room.'

'Kate! Please! Be fair. I didn't know you'd be baring your breasts and welcoming me with open arms. Talking about welcoming me with open arms . . .' He approached the bed, smiling, and pointed to the flies of his pale green pyjamas. '. . . How about opening me with welcoming arms?'

'Stanley! Get out!'

'All too much for our little chapel girl?'

'How do I know? It might all be too little for me,' she retorted. 'And don't you dare ever patronise me again. I'm fed up with being referred to as the little chapel girl. Now get out, please.'

'I'm sorry,' said Stanley. 'Kate, I'm sorry. I don't know what's wrong with me.'

'Oh come on, Stanley, don't give me a performance. I'm not that naïve.'

'Listen, Kate, I could tell you weren't sleeping. I just wanted to see you. I didn't want to embarrass you. I never dreamt you'd be . . . you're very beautiful, Kate, and I think maybe I love you, and I thought I'd tell you, think carefully, take your time, you've seen me at my worst tonight, but I'm worth ten Arturos. He's as big a fraud as his name. He can't paint, you know.'

'Why don't you get a girl of your own?'

'I'm picky. I'm very picky. Good-night, Kate. I'm sorry.'

'I suppose I have to admit it wasn't entirely your fault,' she said. 'Good-night, Stanley.'

He closed the door as gently as Arturo. She blew out the candle and thought again about Arturo's paintings. Could he paint? How could she ever know? Did it matter to their relationship?

The door was opening! Which one of them was it? She pulled the nightshirt tight round her throat and lit the candle.

Daphne came towards her slowly and solemnly, like a ghost. She was stark naked. She had rolls of fat on her stomach and a huge bush of pubic hair. She was stroking her nipples gently. She didn't look a bit like Arturo's painting of her. 'I'm sorry about this evening,' she said. 'I still think we can be friends.'

Whether Kate would ever have joined the Tregarryn community but for Miss Penkridge cannot be certain. Nor can it be certain whether she would have married Arturo if she hadn't joined the community. The whole course of her life might have been different but for this formidable lady, with her close-cropped mannish hair, her complete lack of make-up or artifice, her sombre black clothes.

'You have been seen in what even at my most charitable I can only describe as extremely doubtful company, Miss Thomas,' said Miss Penkridge, seated behind a desk bare save for an inkwell, a fountain pen, a blotter, an indiarubber, a box of pencils, a bible and a volume of Lamb's *Essays*.

Who had sneaked on her, wondered Kate. Miss Carter or Miss Langan? Miss Carter had never referred to the man she had seen Kate kiss. Miss Langan had said, 'Did that man who kissed you give you the black eye? Was he a Spaniard?' Kate had replied, 'Nobody gave me a black eye. I fell into a lamppost in a drunken stupor.' Miss Langan had gone pink with excitement at the thought of a drunken stupor. 'Why should you think he was a Spaniard?' Kate had asked. 'Spaniards are animals,' Miss Langan had replied. 'Have you ever been to Spain?' 'No,' Miss Langan had replied, 'but I'm going next month.'

Kate realised that she could muse no longer. Miss Penkridge was waiting for a reply.

'Oh?' said Kate.

'Yes. Unfortunately the brother of one of the parents frequents the Turk's Head. Not a place in which one would expect to find the brother of a parent, but he's a fisherman.'

'Are you suggesting that he is therefore beyond the rules of decent society?' asked Kate.

Miss Penkridge gasped at this boldness. She picked up the copy of Lamb's *Essays* and clutched it to what would have been her bosom, had she had one, as if she hoped it might afford her moral protection against this difficult young lady.

'I know the degree of your sympathy for the lower orders, Miss Thomas,' she said. 'I was not being patronising to fishermen. I merely meant that they face more hazards than most, so they need more comforts than most. I daresay I would need the occasional sherry if I braved the Atlantic in a small boat.'

There was a moment's silence in the sombre study, with its oak-panelled walls. Both women were listening to the gale, and thinking of the perils of the sea. And neither wished to be the next to speak.

Kate was the first to crack.

'I'm sorry if I was outspoken,' she said.

'Don't be. It's one of your virtues.' Kate was astonished by this, and even Miss Penkridge seemed surprised by her generosity, and went slightly pink.

'A parent, who is a corn chandler, is an occasional customer in the Turk's Head. No doubt he has to go there to conduct business. He also has seen you in that hostelry, the worse for drink, in the company of people who use bad language, and lack decorum.'

'They're artists,' explained Kate.

'Well, that is certainly better than criminals,' said Miss Penkridge, 'but does it excuse such behaviour?'

'No, I don't think it does. They're good friends, but I don't always like the way they carry on. I've remonstrated with them about it.'

'Good.' Miss Penkridge was sufficiently reassured to put down the volume of Lamb's *Essays*.

'May I ask, Miss Penkridge, what all this has to do with my teaching?' enquired Kate.

'It's a bad example to the girls.'

'Surely none of my girls frequent the Turk's Head?'

'Of course not. Maybe I was a little devious. It is not the way the parents expect the teachers of their children to behave.'

'I teach the children, Miss Penkridge. I don't teach their parents.'

Miss Penkridge gasped. A pink spot appeared on each of her cheeks. She looked at the volume of Lamb's *Essays* and decided that it was no longer a strong enough crutch. She picked up the bible.

'I will point out that you have been seen with these unsuitable genii three times,' she said. 'I would not have brought an isolated lapse to your attention. Miss Thomas, now that you are here, perhaps we should also discuss something more important.

Your teaching methods. How do you think you are doing?'

'Well,' said Kate, 'I think the children like me.'

Miss Penkridge snorted.

'They adore you!' she exclaimed. 'They liked you even before the black eye. Now they adore you.' She looked embarrassed. 'Three of them have a crush on you to my knowledge.'

'I'm sorry to hear that,' said Kate. 'It doesn't . . . I can't . . . I don't give them any encouragement.'

'You can't help being beautiful,' said Miss Penkridge, who could never be beautiful but need not have been plain. 'It's a rod you have to bear, and I'm sorry for you, but that isn't the point and being liked isn't the point either, is it?'

'Well, in my desire to teach through collaboration and not confrontation it's a good first step,' said Kate. 'It's all I feel qualified to claim, which is why I started with it.'

'I see.' Miss Penkridge looked out over the playing fields. Herring gulls, tossed inland by the gale, had given up their search for herrings and settled on a safer diet of worms. Their perpetual clamour provided a dismal background to the interview. 'I see. Do you feel that you are giving the children the facts that they need to pass their exams?'

'I hope so. I don't believe history should be taught as an unrelated series of dates and facts, but I realise that it's my duty to include these within the overall framework of my teaching, and I hope they will be remembered more easily because they're taught in context. Oh dear, that sounds pompous.'

'No, it sounds fair. Let's discuss this framework, shall we? Because you teach in a stimulating manner, because you interest the children, which is, Kate Thomas, little short of a miracle, they discuss their history lessons at home. Even Lily Gardner.'

'Well, I'm pleased.'

'Mr and Mrs Gardner aren't. It seems that you regard history as a great confrontation between the rich and the poor, the powerful and the powerless, an endless battle in which all the improvements that have taken place in the world have been the result of actions and policies carried out by people on the Left of the political spectrum.'

'I believe that to be largely so. It's a simplification, of course.'

'Of course. A dangerous simplification for the Lily Gardners of this world. Not, one would say, a dispassionate view. Wouldn't you say that as a teacher, Kate, as a teacher of young people, you have a duty to be dispassionate?'

'Yes, but I hope I have a duty to be passionate also.'

'Let's turn to something even more serious. Religion.' Miss Penkridge gripped the bible more tightly. 'You seem to have a prejudice against religion.'

'Not against religion, Miss Penkridge. Against the use that is made of religion. A vast amount of the world's ills is caused by religious intolerance.'

A herring gull squawked loudly, just outside the window. Miss Penkridge permitted herself a rare, brief smile.

'Even the herring gull protests at your extremism, Miss Thomas.'

'I don't believe it is extremism.'

'I would not expect the Lily Gardners and Margaret Penhaligons of this world to make the distinction, at their tender age, between religion and man's use of it. This is not a view of history, however many grains of truth it might possibly contain, that the Governors would wish our pupils to be learning.'

'I love my pupils, Miss Penkridge. I don't give a fig for the Governors.'

Miss Penkridge gasped. Even the herring gulls fell silent.

'I'm sorry,' said Kate. 'I shouldn't have put it so strongly, but I can't help my feelings.'

'Yes, you can,' said Miss Penkridge. 'You can and you must. I don't want to lose you, Miss Thomas.'

'Is that a threat?'

'No. A fear. I hope you will accept this as a warning, and

74

season your fervour with the salt of common sense, not the pepper of revolution.'

'You've left out the mustard of my hot passion,' said Kate. 'I resign. I wish you the condiments of the season.'

A herring gull protested loudly at this cheap crack. Kate half wished that she hadn't said it, but it was too late.

The wedding took place on a fine May Saturday, in 1924.

Kate spent her wedding eve in the warmth of her family, in the crowded dining-room-cum-sitting-room, the throbbing engine room of the house. They had kippers for tea, with bread and butter and Welsh cakes and bara brith. Bernard, almost sixteen now, quizzed her about Arturo, questions that she didn't want. Oliver, nearing eighteen and as handsome as a cherub, shone with pleasure at the prospect of her joy. Enid was very quiet, claiming to be fighting the onset of a migraine, but Kate suspected that she was just eaten up with jealousy. Myfanwy laughed and joked lustily, trying to wind Kate into gaiety, and not succeeding. Annie, the orphaned cousin from Llanelli who had come to live with them in 1921, after her mother died, laughed her infectious laugh, and her coarse red cheeks sparkled with excitement. If only Dilys could have been there to complete the family, but of course that was impossible. She would write to Dilys, tell her every little detail, imagine her eyes eagerly devouring her letter in exile in Macclesfield, not a place famous for exile. It had been difficult to tell Arturo about Dilys, she'd been worried that he'd ask too many questions, but she needn't have worried, he'd been too wrapped up in himself to care much about a twin he'd never met, and accepted her explanation of a family quarrel that 'we don't talk about. Her name is not to be mentioned in this house again.'

Arturo had visited the family twice, and had played his part nobly. He had presented himself as a sober young man utterly dedicated to his muse. He had allowed John Thomas Thomas to believe that he created his art in the service of God. But he wasn't there that wedding eve. Kate wouldn't see him on her wedding day until the ceremony. Everything was to be done properly, on her day of days.

She didn't sleep much that night. How could she, when she was sleeping in the same bed, in the same bedroom, watched over by the same damp stag and the same frowning texts, listening to the same chimes of the grandfather clock as on that night? When the clock struck a quarter to twelve, the urge to get up and go and see Gwyn was almost irresistible.

She tossed and turned a great deal that night, trying not to think of Gwyn, trying to think about Arturo, trying to love him as much as she should.

In the morning she had bacon and sausage meat and laver-bread and it was as if she'd never been away. Then she sat in the rocking chair in the dark breakfast womb and wished that she could go back, back into her childhood, into her infancy, into her mother's womb, into a foetus, into an egg, into a nothing.

Bernard looked at her quizzically, and said, 'Are you all right?' and she began the long job of pulling herself together.

'Oh yes,' she said. 'Everything's going to be fine. This is just the storm before the calm.'

Oliver blushed and said, 'I tell everyone how beautiful my sister is.'

Myfanwy said, 'Come on. Don't just sit there. You're getting married.'

Enid said, 'If I'm a bit quiet today, Kate darling, it won't be because I don't want you to be happy. It'll be because of my migraine.'

Annie said, 'I'm lucky just to be part of this family, but to be sitting in the family pew on this day of all days, I just can't thank you enough for inviting me.'

John Thomas Thomas said, 'We will all pray for your happiness, Kate,' in a tone of voice which made her feel more like a serious outbreak of flooding than a human being.

Kate wondered how happy her father was that morning. She knew that he believed that artists drank. He had asked her if she drank and she hadn't dared say 'Yes. Quite a lot', and she hadn't been brazen enough to say 'No, never', so she'd said 'A bit', which was a pathetic compromise and useless too, because her father had been just as hurt as he'd have been if she'd said 'Every night, and to excess'.

'Come on, then, Kate,' said her mother, helping her up from the chair and her childhood. 'Let's get you looking your loveliest. You're going to be the toast of Swansea today.' She looked at her eldest daughter gravely, and said, 'You are happy, aren't you?'

Kate had to say something, so she said, 'I was thinking about Dilys,' despising herself for saying it, because it wasn't true, but she couldn't say, 'I may be making the greatest mistake of my life.'

'I didn't know if you still miss her,' said her mother.

'Oh yes,' said Kate. 'I still miss her.'

Her mother kissed her then. How lovely to be kissed by her mother. Her mother had never kissed her as much as she'd wanted her to, or, she suspected, as much as her mother wanted to. John Thomas Thomas frowned on outward displays of emotion.

The fashion in the early 1920s was for straight women. Curves were regarded as fat. Kate insisted on wearing as straight a dress as possible, though it was difficult and, her mother thought, very sad that she should want to hide her lovely curves. But she must be a modern girl and there must be something of the look of the flapper in her long wedding dress. She wore white, of course, for only Arturo among those present knew that she was not a virgin.

She was driven to the chapel by horse and carriage, her father stiff and solemn beside her, handsome in his morning dress. People stood at their doors to wave and smile, and Kate waved and smiled back, feeling sick.

The chapel was crowded. All the family were there from all over South Wales, uncles and aunts and nieces and nephews; the two cousins called Herbert Herbert, who were always known as Herbert Herbert Cricket and Herbert Herbert Politics, so that there could be no doubt to which of them one was referring; Cousin Nancy from the Vale of Towy, as warm as a new-laid egg; and the great-aunts, who always wore black and were tiny and sat shivering beside black ranges with not enough fuel on the fire in tiny houses in Pontardulais and Ammanford, and Kate had to visit them every Christmas, and they gave her a penny, and she was made to kiss them, and their cheeks were as cold as marble.

Miss Penkridge was there, astounded to be invited, but surely delighted? Miss Carter was there with the insurance salesman to whom she had still not got engaged. Miss Langan was there, on her own. She had been to Spain and nobody had behaved like an animal towards her, although she had given them every encouragement.

Several girls from Kate's childhood were there, Arbel Meredith and Glenys Edwards whom she liked, and Caitlin Price-Evans, whom she didn't like, but she had a hyphen and would add tone and so Kate had invited her to please the family. Tone was important at a wedding in Wales. Kate could still remember the devastating comment of Mrs Herbert Herbert Politics on returning from an obscure family wedding in Tony-pandy. 'There wasn't a single pair of gloves on the bride's side.'

No boys from Kate's childhood were there. She had only known one boy, and he was dead.

All the faces turned to look at her as her father led her down the aisle. His face was stern and grim, she hoped her smile didn't look set in concrete.

In her high heels she seemed at least four inches taller than Arturo. She hadn't wanted to wear high heels, but had bowed to the inevitable. A queen has her responsibilities.

She squeezed Arturo's arm and hoped he wasn't feeling as awful as she was. He must be finding the massed ranks of the Welsh daunting. He had brought so few people of his own. The members of the community, of course, Stanley Wainwright, who was his best man; solemn Daniel Begelman, who was truly happy for them both; pale frail devoted Olga who was absolutely miserable because she'd left Ruth with friends and it was her very first time without her; and rouged, outrageous Daphne Stoneyhurst. Apart from that there were just six assorted relatives from the Fens, to none of whom he was particularly close, and his sister Cicely, whose only consolation for having a streaming cold on this great day could be that her nose matched her red outfit perfectly. His parents were dead. He'd been an orphan since the age of eleven.

Kate had an awful fear that she wouldn't be able to survive the ceremony without fainting, that she would suddenly go clattering to the unyielding floor of the chapel.

Swansea was Gwyn's town still. Kate willed herself back to Tregarryn, the terraced garden, the narrow valley, the great gull-wheeled cliffs and the long Atlantic breakers. And it worked. There was just one bad moment, when she feared that someone might object to the wedding, and that it might be her. How easy it would be to say 'I object. I don't love him quite enough', but then she thought of him as he had been when she had kissed him outside the school, dressed all in purple and waving his blackthorn stick, and she thought, Yes, I can love him enough.

The reception was simple, but she didn't feel ashamed. Why should she? They were simple people at Tregarryn. It was held in the Temperance Hall, so that there should be no doubt about the matter, because John Thomas Thomas knew that not all the family were teetotal: Nancy and the country cousins had been known to lash into their elderberry and parsnip wines, Uncle Evan from Llansamlet had been seen coming out of the Uplands

Hotel, it was even rumoured that Herbert Herbert drank (Herbert Herbert Cricket, not Herbert Herbert Politics, let there be no calumny).

There were sausage rolls and ham and tongue and cold sewin, which, as every Welshman knows, is finer than salmon. There were boiled potatoes and there were tomatoes and cucumbers in profusion. There was junket and blancmange and stewed apples with cloves, and Welsh cakes and bara brith and scones with jam *and* cream, and to wash it all down there were three kinds of fruit juice and a choice of tea or coffee.

The artists, who had never been to anything where there was no alcohol, listened to the tide of talk, a great wall of bilingual chatter that you could cut with a knife, and they were astonished that a whole room could get drunk on gossip, and the gorgeous galleon that was Kate in full sail rode proudly on the waves and hove to, safe against all storms, in the Bay of Admiration.

Stanley kissed her and said, 'I know you can't understand why he chose me as best man, when I've spent a whole year trying to bed his fiancée, rather than Daniel, who'd be loyal to the ends of the earth, but that is Dame Life, Kate, in all her rich absurdity,' and Kate said, 'Please, Stanley, promise not to try it on now I'm married,' and Stanley said, 'I promise to try not to try it on, but I can't promise to succeed, because I can't begin to understand why you prefer him to me.'

Daphne kissed her and said, 'You look ravishing. Will you never ravish me?' and Kate said, 'Daphne! This is a temperance hall,' and Daphne said, 'Don't be silly. No one can hear us in this racket.'

Arturo kissed her and said, 'Oh, if only it was over and we were in bed. Oh, Kate, I think I'll come in my trousers,' and Kate said, 'I'm pleased you did come in your trousers,' but she was shocked to the core to hear him say such a rude thing in public. He had accepted with reluctance her refusal to have sex before they were married, once she explained that it wasn't on moral grounds but because she didn't want to get pregnant and hurt her parents. He had said, 'It didn't stop you with Gwyn,' and she had said, 'I was sixteen then,' and he had accepted that.

Her father said, 'I'm very proud of you, Kate, and how you've carried yourself this day,' which would have been a rare piece of unqualified praise if he hadn't gone on to say, 'but I wish you were still a schoolmistress and not a cook.'

'I don't like the way you denigrate cooks, Father,' she said, 'but, yes, sometimes I do too, but what does it matter now, we'll be having children soon.'

Her mother said, 'I cannot believe I have produced anything as wonderful as you,' but Kate knew that, if her mother had felt the need to qualify compliments, as her father did, she would have gone on to say, 'but couldn't you have found somebody more worthy of you?'

Oliver said, 'I wish all the fellows could see you today. You're a goddess.' Later she heard him say, to Arturo, 'You mean you don't do another job? You paint *all day*?'

Bernard said, in tones of awe at his proximity to such wickedness, 'Are they all communists?' to which she replied, 'They profess to be. There isn't a great deal of evidence of it in their actions.'

Enid said, 'Be careful on the ferry. Mansel Phillips whose mother isn't quite right drowned when a ferry sank under him in the Malay Straits,' and Kate said, 'Enid! We're going to Brittany!'

Myfanwy said, 'Are you a virgin?' and Kate said, 'Myfanwy! What a question,' and Myfanwy said, 'Kate! You aren't!'

Arturo's sister said, 'I can't believe I've got a streaming cold today. I look a frightful mess and I wanted to do him proud. We're so outnumbered,' and Kate said, 'it isn't supposed to be a competition, Cicely.'

Olga said, 'Are you looking forward to having children?' and Kate said, 'Yes, I am,' and Olga said, 'Take it from me, it's worth it. I felt sick every day for seven and a half months, I was hot all the time, I couldn't sleep, I still can't because Ruth never sleeps through and she cries half the night, but it's worth it.'

Annie said, 'Getting married's the last thing I'd want, but if it's the right thing for you I hope you'll be very happy.'

Daniel said, 'I don't want to worry you, Kate, and I didn't know if I should tell you, but I thought I'd better because you might be able to do something about it, but Arturo and Stanley and Daphne keep going out into the yard at the back and mixing gin with their fruit juices.'

She touched his shoulder gently, and went in search of Arturo. Her heart was leaden.

She looked into his eyes, and she could see that they were glazed.

'How could you do this to me today of all days?' she said.

'Sorry,' he said. 'I'm nervous.'

'You think I'm not? No more – please.'

She approached Stanley and said, 'Please, Stanley, don't drink any more gin and try to stop Arturo,' and he said, 'For you, Kate, and for nobody else, I'll do it.'

She had a quiet word with Daphne, but Daphne's reply was less quiet. 'That little shit Daniel told you, didn't he? God, I hate prigs and sneaks.'

'I know very few people who are less shits than Daniel,' said Kate. 'And he told me because he's brave and he cares,' and Daphne said, 'It seems to me you should have married him,' and Kate said, 'I should be so lucky,' and Daphne said, 'I hate you. Do you know that?' and Kate said, 'Thank you for being so charming on my wedding day. I shall never forget it.'

Kate turned away and strode off. Uncles from the valleys parted before her like the waters of the Red Sea and she found herself facing Daniel, who said, 'What did she say?' and Kate said, 'She said I should have married you,' and Daniel looked her straight in the eyes and said, 'I should be so lucky.'

To her horror, Kate's eyes filled with tears. She turned away and burst into sobs. Silence fell on the Temperance Hall, and she had a vision of all the faces turned to her in horror, John Thomas Thomas and her mother and Daniel and Miss Penkridge and Caitlin Price-Evans and everyone.

'I'm sorry,' she said. 'I'm sorry. It's all been too much for me. I'm so happy. So very, very happy. And all of you here, it makes me so happy, so very very happy. But all the emotion, and the heat and everything, it . . . it makes me so happy.'

Her father came to the rescue, and Daniel pushed Arturo forward and hissed 'For God's sake' at him, and to do Arturo fair, he made a supreme effort and managed to grab Kate's right arm and her father grabbed her left arm and they marched her out together, her puritan father and her drunk husband.

A taxi took them to the station, a train took them to Cardiff, and another taxi took them to the hotel which was the chosen venue for the first night of the honeymoon.

Later, Kate would be glad that the first night of her married life was such a fiasco, because, even if it had not been, it could not have compared with her night of love with Gwyn. Now, there could be no comparison.

But she didn't feel that way as she watched two porters carry her husband into the bridal suite and lay him senseless on the marital bed.

Dear Dilys,

I have such lovely news. I'm pregnant. I was so pleased to hear that you are pregnant again too. I feel so close to you even though we're so far apart. It's a great comfort to me to know that you are there in Macclesfield, after all, you could be overseas.

I still can't quite believe that you weren't at my wedding. I sometimes play it back in my mind and set you in there with all the other guests. You behave terribly well and look wonderful and are reconciled to Father. I even see a tear running down his cheek. As you can see, I have a strong imagination.

Arturo is well and sends his best wishes. Of course he hopes it'll be a boy, you know what men are like. I don't care what sex the child is, provided it's healthy.

Every morning when I wake up I feel privileged to be carrying a living growing thing, which will become a child. I'm so very careful. I wonder if you're the same. I drink a bottle of stout every day, as this is supposed to make the baby grow strong. I hate it, but I hate our cheap red wine too, so I endure it.

I'm sorry I burdened you with all those doubts about my marriage, Dil. I have been working hard to make it a success, and I think it will be. Arturo can be childish and selfish and absurd, but he's fun and he's never cruel and I like him so very much that I think it could be said that I love him!

He sold a painting the other day. I didn't think it one of his best, and nor did he, but a Miss Freeth from St Ives thought it a dear little thing – not how Arturo likes to hear his pictures described, he thinks they're harrowing, but you can't insult a buyer. You can insult a non-buyer, though. He was very rude to an American lady who said of a picture, 'I like it, but it wouldn't go with my wallpaper.' He drew himself up to his full height – probably a mistake, as he's only five foot six – and said, 'Madam, I am a painter, not an interior designer.'

It *is* a great problem with painting, though. Some of Daniel Begelman's pictures are really good, I think, but disturbing. To look at them for an hour is stimulating and exciting, but to have them on your wall for ever is just not on. Daphne's just the opposite. To look at one of her paintings for an hour would be to waste fifty-nine and a half minutes, but if you had one in your drawing-room it would look pleasant for ever.

People admire but don't like Daniel's work, and like but don't admire Daphne's.

Stanley is almost a very good sculptor. There's just something a little unwieldy, a little heavy, about his figures. They're grandiose. Everything he does he regards as great art. You should have seen his face the day he was offered a commission to make a mermaid for the entrance to Truro Fish Market. 'Who do they think I am?' he thundered. 'Hans Christian Andersen?'

Oh, this'll make you laugh. I hope. Maybe it'll just seem too rude in Macclesfield. Stanley has produced a huge figure, about twice life size, looking out over the sea from our bottom terrace. He calls it *The Dreamer*. It's a slight case of hubris when you think of all the great art on the terrace, but the face is good, and I said so. 'I think it's brilliant to be able to make granite wistful,' I said. But I was standing right by the genitalia, and I said, 'Stanley, from my admittedly very limited experience I don't find the testicles very convincing.' Imagine our father hearing me say that! What a dreadful woman I am. He flushed, he hates criticism of any kind, and said, 'You're talking balls, Kate.' I said, 'Exactly.' He didn't get it, he has very little humour, and none about himself. 'Just how many testicles have you seen, Kate?' he said, and I said, 'Four.' He said, 'Let's make it the round half-dozen, then,' and dropped his trousers right there in the afternoon sun. I examined his very closely, determined not to be embarrassed, and said, 'Thank you. Very nice, but I still don't think you've quite got the hang of them.' He didn't get that, either. I feel I can never drop my guard with Stanley. There's something dirty about the way he looks at me. He's actually not unattractive. He has a girlfriend in London and goes up there twice a month, but won't let us meet her. Something strangely coy at the heart of his masculinity.

Daniel and Olga's little girl Ruth cries a lot, but then they give in to her every whim, they're besotted, and I think that's no good, much as I like them for it.

My role is chief cook and bottle-washer. Correction. Only cook and bottle-washer. I love it, though. I feel at peace cooking in our great pine kitchen, Dil, but I just wish the sun streamed into it of an evening. The hills don't give us our sun till mid-morning and they take it away again in late afternoon, and then we are a gloomy place.

I've had no sickness yet with my pregnancy. I just hope you are feeling the same utter contentment in Macclesfield. I do hope John is keeping well. He must be so delighted that you are going to have another child to keep Tom company.

With much love,
    Your affectionate twin
    Kate
XXXXXXXXXXXXXXXXXXXX

On fine mornings Arturo had developed the habit of working, fuelled by black coffee, until the sun came up over the hilltop, and then taking breakfast on the terrace.

One golden morning in late September, he sat with Kate on the bottom terrace, eating bread and marmalade and sipping tea. There was the sound of wood being chopped in the hamlet below, and the faint chugging of a distant motor boat. Otherwise, silence. Daniel, Stanley and Daphne were hard at work in their studios. They all did work extremely hard. It was the best thing about them.

Arturo seemed preoccupied, grave, intense.

'I had a letter from Dilys this morning,' she said.

'Oh?' he said from afar. At the last moment he decided to have only butter and no marmalade on his third slice of bread.

There was silence then, save for his irritating munching and the gentle mewing of a kittiwake and the chugging of the boat.

'Aren't you going to ask me what it says?'

'What does it say?'

'Arturo! Take an interest sometimes, please.'

'I am taking an interest. I asked, didn't I?'

The chugging boat revealed itself as a little red fishing smack. For a few seconds its noise still came muffled by the cliffs, then the chug came loud and clear, as if from about thirty yards behind the boat. The pale blue sky, the golden haze, the bright red boat alone on a silver, shimmering sea made a scene like a child's painting. They stared at it in silence for a moment, so peacefully that a stranger might have thought that they were very close to each other.

'Sorry,' said Arturo at last. 'I've been thinking. I've had rather an amazing idea.'

'Oh?'

Ruth began to scream from somewhere inside the house, but the screaming soon stopped. Olga had probably picked her up.

'You're as bad as I am,' said Arturo. 'You haven't asked me what my amazing idea is.'

'Right. Forget Dilys. What's your amazing idea?'

'No, no, if that's your attitude. Fair's fair. You think all artists are egotists, but we aren't.' He took a pear and gazed at it as if he had never seen a pear before, the way he did, the way she liked. 'Tell me what Dilys has to say. My great idea can wait.'

'Oh, all right. Our visit to Macclesfield is off. They're emigrating to Canada next week.'

'Bit sudden, isn't it?'

'John's got a long-term contract doing the plumbing for government buildings. They have to go.'

'So I'll never meet this mysterious twin.'

'Not until we go to Canada.'

'It's a bit selfish, isn't it, going off without seeing us?'

'Circumstances have given Dilys a low opinion of family life.'

'No, but, identical twins, this must be hurtful for you.'

He came over and put his arms round her and kissed her lips.

It seemed as though he really cared, but when she said, 'Now, what's your great idea?' his eyes shone with excitement. He forgot all about Dilys in an instant.

'You know my painting of Port Isaac?'

She did. She didn't like it. His paintings were growing steadily less abstract, and, as they did so, she found that she was liking them less. The abstraction had hidden the shallowness.

'Yes,' she said cautiously.

'I took it down to look at it last night. I think I must have had a bit too much wine. I hung it upside down by mistake. It looked better that way!'

She refrained from saying, 'I'm not surprised.'

'I thought I might exhibit it upside down.'

'Why not?'

Later, Kate wished that she had tried to dissuade him. But how could she have known how momentous the consequences would be?

The funeral took place on the first day of the General Strike, in 1926. Luckily, the grave had already been dug.

Kate and Arturo and their one-year-old son Nigel were accompanied on their sad journey by Daniel and Olga Begelman and their two little girls, Ruth and Barbara. Olga and Kate were both pregnant again. This time Olga was flourishing, 'so it's a boy. I know it', and this time Kate was feeling sick a lot of the time. It had been Daniel's idea that he and Olga should come. 'All religions are the same in the face of death,' he had said, 'and Olga'll be able to look after Nigel during the service.'

Stanley was the only one of them with a car, and he was touring Scotland, so there was nothing for it but to go by train. The journey would have proved trying at the best of times. The eve of the General Strike was not the best of times. They had to change trains at Bodmin Road, Taunton, Bristol Temple Meads and Newport. One train was cancelled, and by the time they got to Newport trains were ending their journey wherever the driver lived. Their driver lived in Bridgend.

There were thirty or so passengers waiting to go to points further west. They huddled together on the platform at Bridgend, as the train steamed off to the sidings without them. A cold wind blew. A kindly porter told them that there was the possibility of a bus.

They stood at a windy bus-stop. The children were tired and querulous. One child ran off, and a black-shawled Swansea woman yelled out in a voice as Welsh as a Penclawdd cockle, 'Come over from by there to by 'ere, Nerys, or it's taking you home lost I will be.' There's Welsh, thought Kate. It's grey and cold and we're burying my sister, but I'm coming home. Her eyes filled with tears.

A bus roared up towards them. It said 'Swansea' on the front. Thirty people held their hands out, for fear that it would go roaring past.

But it did stop, and there were seats for everyone, and suddenly they were all more cheery, until Daniel asked for tickets to Swansea, and the conductor said, 'We're only going as far as Neath.'

'The board says "Swansea",' Daniel wasn't one to give in easily.

'Yes, because it's the Swansea service, see, but we're only going as far as Neath, because we lives in Neath, see.'

'I still don't understand,' said Daniel, who understood perfectly, but wanted to make things at least slightly awkward.

'Well, it's like this, see. The service is the Swansea service. It will cease at Neath. Disruption due to strike. If the board said "Neath" that would mean we were stopping at Neath because we stopped at Neath, not because we were stopping at Neath because we weren't going on to Swansea because we're disrupting it, see.'

'Well, I must say, I have a great deal of sympathy for the strike,' admitted Daniel.

'We all do. We're communists,' said Kate. 'We're in sympathy with the oppressed throughout the world.'

'Well, there's nice,' said the conductor. 'That's very touching, that is. Thank you. I'm only sorry, speaking personally, like, that all that sympathy won't get you to Swansea.'

But it did. As they got off in Neath the conductor whispered to Daniel, 'Follow me.' He led the small group of communists and their children through the deserted streets of Neath. 'Our Kerry'll take you,' he said. 'Only drawback will be his load, that's the snag, but you can't have everything in this life, and possibly not in the next life either.'

And with that philosophical thrust he left them at the end of a row of low terraced houses.

Kate had become aware, from the smell as she carried Nigel, that he needed changing. She changed him now. Daniel had brought a torch. Arturo pointed the torch towards little Nigel's backside while Kate changed the nappy, and thought himself quite a hero for doing so.

They had to stand at the end of the road for about twenty minutes. They began to feel foolish as well as cold and sad. Then a small, noisy lorry drew up, its back covered by a flapping tarpaulin.

'Sorry to be so long,' said the conductor. 'I had to wake our Kerry up. He was travelling to Carmarthen tomorrow. I said, "Better go tonight under cover of darkness, Kerry. Go tomorrow you'll be branded a strike-breaker. You'll get stones thrown. You'll get your tyres let down. I persuaded him to go tonight. He'll drop you off in Swansea en route, like.'

'Are we prepared to go in a strike-breaking van?' asked Arturo.

'Of course we are,' snapped Kate. 'We have children.'

There was room for Olga and the three children in the driver's cab with the strike-breaking Kerry. Kate, Arturo and Daniel sat in the back, on the load, which turned out to be onions, and which wobbled beneath them disconcertingly as Kerry drove through Skewen.

Everyone was sad at the tragic premature death of Myfanwy Thomas. When Kerry pulled up outside 16 Eaton Crescent, Oliver and Bernard came out to meet them. Oliver was at the University of Wales in Aberystwyth, and more handsome at twenty than ever. Bernard was a solemn earnest sixth-form boy. Both boys had been crying. They both had red eyes, and Bernard's bulbous nose was also red. But neither of them had cried as much as Kate.

'It's the onions,' she said. 'Onions always make me cry.'

They all knew that onions only make you cry when they're cut, but none of them said anything. If Kate needed to hide the depth of her grief, they respected that.

Next day they buried Myfanwy Thomas, who put the care of her patients before her own safety and died of a rare tropical disease at the age of twenty-three. The chapel, more suited to funerals than to weddings, was crowded. The Reverend Aneurin Parkhouse chose sin as the subject of his sermon. Myfanwy had been taken by God because she was good, and we would not be taken by him if we sinned unless we redeemed ourselves, that was his gist. God would not want us if we were evil, he would send us to hell. If Kate had been back at school and this had been a lesson, not a sermon, she would have put her hand up, leader of the awkward squad, and asked, 'Are you suggesting, sir, that while we may have to face hell, we'll have a much longer life on this earth if we sin?'

After the service and the burial, many of the mourners crowded into the front parlour. A fire burnt quietly in the genteel marble fireplace, the grate so far back that all the heat went up the chimney. On the mantelpiece a Georgian clock ticked discreetly. The white fluffy carpet was thick enough to muffle the sound of feet. The heavy cream curtains hung lifelessly in the bay window. Thick lace curtains kept the sun and prying eyes at bay.

At first, the chatter in the room was muted. John Thomas Thomas was gaunt with grief. Bronwen's eyes gave the lie to her smiles. Kate, going to the scullery for more tea, met Bernard coming from the scullery with more bara brith. She hugged him impulsively. Poor Bernard, he had never been hugged like that by a woman before, and he blushed. Poor Bernard, little did he know it, but he would never be hugged like that by a woman again. He never cleaned his teeth properly, and he always had skid marks on his underpants, what woman would fancy him?

'The sad thing is, none of us really knew her, I beg your pardon?' said Bernard.

Kate had noticed that he had developed a habit of saying 'I beg your pardon' after he'd stuck his neck out and said something that he regarded as controversial. He didn't lack moral courage, so he did come out with things, but he lacked confidence, so he anticipated the objection that he expected. He had no idea, of course, that he was doing it. She found it immensely endearing and it made her long to protect him.

'What on earth do you mean?' she asked, fulfilling her expected role as an objector.

'Well, she was a nurse. She never let us see her caring side.'

'That's very perceptive,' she said, and almost added, 'for eighteen.' She hoped she hadn't sounded patronising.

As well as bara brith, that rather less than exciting Welsh fruit loaf, there were bloater-paste sandwiches and potted-meat sandwiches and Welsh cakes and scones and three different kinds of cake. And the tea people drank!

In the breakfast room, on her way back from the scullery with yet another pot of tea, Kate met Enid going to the scullery for more bloater-paste sandwiches. Enid looked very pale, and shocked Kate by saying, 'Everyone thinks it should be me that's dead. Wishy-washy Enid with her infected tonsils and her migraines. Boring Enid, who hasn't a thought in her head.'

'Oh, Enid,' said Kate. 'How can you think that? If those are the sort of thoughts you have in your head you'd be better off having none.'

Arturo didn't lift a finger to help, but Daniel handed round the cakes with the best of them. He might have been born to shine at Welsh funerals. Kate knew that everyone was thinking, 'I know he's Jewish, but what a pity Kate didn't marry him.'

Herbert Herbert (Herbert Herbert Cricket, not Herbert Herbert Politics) told Kate that Oliver was the golden boy of the University of Wales. He represented the university at cricket, rugger, hockey and croquet. When she put it to Oliver that he was the golden boy, he said, 'Fiddlesticks.'

'We've a wonderful family, you know,' said Kate.

'Oh, I know. I wish they weren't so narrow, but . . .'

'They wouldn't be our wonderful family if they weren't.'

'Exactly.'

Annie scurried inelegantly backwards and forwards, replenishing plates, refilling cups, so privileged to be allowed to be one of this wonderful family that she showed it at all times, to Kate's irritation, which was really irritation with herself for allowing herself to be irritated.

She couldn't talk to her mother or they would both burst into tears. She couldn't even meet her mother's eyes.

Her father said to her, 'I've been speaking to your friend Mr Begelman. He's very suitable.'

'What for, father?'

'For a friend. I congratulate you. He's . . . serious.'

The conversation began to get more animated, more cheerful, as if people had forgotten that they were at a funeral. Kate felt upset about this, for Myfanwy, but even as she felt it she knew that it was silly. The service had been their expression of their loss. This gathering was their affirmation, uncertain though it was as yet, that life must go on.

She mustn't be angry with Arturo, or regard him as

egotistical, because she overheard him talking about his work to Bernard. No, that didn't anger her. What angered her was that he was telling Bernard things he hadn't told her.

'I'm planning an exhibition in which all the pictures will be hung upside down,' he was saying.

'Good Lord,' said Bernard.

Kate pretended to be examining a rather anaemic watercolour of Snowdon.

'I intend to paint all my pictures upside down,' continued Arturo, delighted to lord it over a younger man.

'Good Lord. You or the pictures?'

'What?'

'Are the canvases going to be upside down, or are you?'

'Oh, the canvases. If I was upside down all the blood would go to my head. I'd pass out.'

'Ah. So what's the point?'

'The point? What isn't the point? The point is, we look at people in a preconceived way, we look at the world in a preconceived way, we bring to our study of it a whole range of assumptions, a whole visual language of satisfied expectations, which prevent us seeing anything as it really is. To see anything as it really is we have to start to look at it as it really isn't, in order to reassemble it as it really is. That's the whole point of art.'

'It seems rather a simplistic way of attempting to achieve anything as grandiose as that, I beg your pardon?' said Bernard.

Arturo went back with the Begelmans on the day after the funeral. He needed to get back to work. There were still no trains, but they managed to borrow an Alvis 12/50 Tourer through the good offices of Herbert Herbert (Herbert Herbert Politics, not Herbert Herbert Cricket). Arturo had driven Stanley's car occasionally, so he was confident that he'd be all right, and, somewhat to Kate's surprise, he was. He would bring the car back when the strike was over, and take Kate and Nigel home by train.

Kate was very happy to stay with her dear parents and try to help them come to terms with their grief. She spent long hours talking with her mother, often in the great master bedroom past which she had crept on that night. Annie jumped at the chance of taking Nigel for walks. She told Kate how much she loved children. When Kate asked her if she'd like children of her own, she said, 'Certainly not. I couldn't imagine letting a man do the awful things he has to do to you before you can have them. I can't think how you can endure it.'

Kate followed the progress of the General Strike closely. She wanted it to succeed. She longed to see better conditions for the workers. She would never be on the side of the Establishment. But she didn't want it to succeed too quickly. It was so lovely to be at home again for a few days.

The strike collapsed, disappointing her both politically and personally. On the day of its collapse she walked all the way back from town with Enid. Both of them felt low. Enid didn't want Kate to go home, and Kate didn't want to go.

As they climbed the long, gentle slope of Walter Road, that artery of respectability in the less than respectable town, two schoolgirls passed by and said, 'Good afternoon, Miss Thomas.'

'Your pupils seem to like you,' said Kate.

'Oh, I get on all right with them,' said Enid.

'They respect you too.'

'Oh yes. They aren't the problem.'

'Who are the problem?'

'Adults. I have nothing to say to them. I have no small talk. I'm not original. I'm never funny. I'm never exciting. I'm not pretty like you, so I'll never find a man.'

'Oh, Enid! You are pretty.' A slight exaggeration, but only slight, and permissible between sisters.

'The men I might have married are lying in Flanders Field.'

Enid said this just as they were passing uncomfortably close to Gwyn's house. There, on the right, was the bulk of St James's Church. There it was, behind the church, the window of what had been his bedroom. Kate couldn't help glancing at it, and she couldn't help wondering if Enid had brought the subject up because she knew. She longed to talk to Enid about Gwyn. She couldn't.

'Oh, Enid,' she said, 'come and see me at Tregarryn in the holidays. Please!'

She tried not to speed up, but she longed to put the road to Gwyn's house behind her.

'I'd be in the way. I'd have nothing to say to artists.'

'Oh, Enid. To hell with artists.'

This cheery profanity shocked Enid deeply and brought home to Kate the gulf that now separated them.

'To hell with the artists. I want you. I need you.' And then Kate admitted to Enid what she had barely admitted to herself. 'I'm so very unhappy.'

Enid arrived on a bad day. Kate had had a bad morning, shopping in Wadebridge. Arturo, to give him credit, had pushed Nigel's pram up the steep lane, dank under its canopy of trees, but he'd drawn the line at coming to Wadebridge with her, and in some ways it was even harder taking the pram down the hill, there was always the fear of its running away, and that was without the shopping bags piled high all round the poor boy. Luckily Nigel had been in placid mood, but she was seven months pregnant and by the time she got home she was utterly worn out.

Arturo would have gone shopping with her if she'd insisted, but he would have been so sulky, impatient and long-suffering that she would have wished he wasn't there.

Twice she had asked Stanley. 'Shopping?' he'd said on the first occasion. 'Where?' 'Wadebridge.' 'Wadebridge??' He'd made it sound like a cross between Swindon and the Tower of Babel. 'Kate, I would come normally but not today,' he'd said. 'I'm at an absolutely vital stage with *Liberty*.' He'd been commissioned to create a large figure called Liberty which would grace the portals of Redruth Library. 'I see,' Kate had said, 'your Liberty is my slavery.'

But she'd tried once more, and on the second occasion he had agreed too readily. There must be a snag. There was. He'd pulled into a farm track, just beyond Delapole, and tried to persuade her to make love to him, on the grass verge, under the stunted hawthorn hedge. She'd had to punch him, and had given him a nosebleed, and he'd been very, very cross. The arrogance of it, the unbelievable arrogance.

Daniel would have come, of course, and Olga would have looked after Nigel, but Daniel and Olga had left the community almost as soon as they had got back from Myfanwy's funeral. They had gone to Russia. 'They'll respect us there,' Daniel had said. 'We talk about being communists. We aren't. We don't share our earnings. We aren't a community in the true sense.'

'Artists have to be individuals first and foremost,' Stanley had said.

'The strong should support the weak,' Daniel had insisted.

'Quite right,' Arturo had said. 'We have to be responsible members of society as well as individuals.'

'I think the idea of the strong supporting the weak is insufferably patronising,' Daphne had said.

'It's funny how the two of you who make money don't want to share it and the two who don't do,' Kate had said.

None of them had liked this remark.

'Why don't you go and finish that fish stew?' Arturo had said, and Kate hadn't liked that remark.

Kate missed them badly. Well, she missed Daniel badly.

It was no use asking Daphne to go shopping. 'Listen, darling,' she would say, 'You can do the fucking women's jobs if you like, but don't expect me to collaborate in your humiliation of your sex. If we have a rota, and the men do their first turn first, because I don't trust the bastards, yes, I'll do it. Not before.'

And when she got back from her shopping trip that day, with

an hour to put everything away, snatch a brief rest and traipse up the hill again to meet Enid's bus, Arturo wasn't painting at all. He was sunbathing on the top terrace, naked except for a plaster cast round his private parts.

'What the hell are you doing?' she asked.

'Modelling my private parts for Stanley. He says he can't do genitals properly. He says you told him that, so it's your fault. I hope he can get the cast off or you're in trouble.'

'I'm seven months pregnant, Arturo. I've lugged this pram almost two miles.'

'Downhill.'

'It's just as hard downhill, and here you are sunning yourself.'

'The sun is incidental. You always say I'm an egotist. I'm enduring the agony of itchy and extremely painful private parts in order to help a fellow artist and I get criticised. You're never satisfied, Kate.'

'I won't be if you can't get that cast off.'

'That isn't funny.'

'Not to you, no. You've no sense of humour.'

'You aren't exactly being hilarious, you bitch.'

He'd never called her anything like that before. She was absolutely furious. Stanley came out at that moment, all innocent smiles, and said, 'Hello, Kate,' with a casual cheeriness that infuriated her, and she said, 'You've chosen the wrong man, Stanley. You'll have to make adjustments in scale.'

Arturo didn't speak to her again all day. All through supper he chatted to Enid, who grew more and more embarrassed, but not a word did he utter to his wife. Stanley tried to joke about the difficulty he'd had in getting the cast off Arturo. 'I nearly ruined his Saturday nights for ever,' he said, and that infuriated Kate and Arturo and embarrassed Enid still more. Only Daphne behaved well that night. She was charming to Enid and resisted several chances of making the kind of rude crack at which she would usually jump.

The next morning, Kate went down to breakfast to find Enid sitting all alone at the great kitchen table, as white as a sheet.

'What on earth's the matter?' Kate asked.

Enid was so upset she could hardly speak.

'Daphne!' she spluttered. 'Daphne . . .'

Daphne entered at that moment.

'Daphne!' said Kate.

Enid rushed out on to the terrace, oblivious of the fact that it was raining hard.

'Daphne!' said Kate again.

Daphne spread her arms wide in a gesture of helplessness. How can I resist my feelings, her gesture seemed to imply.

'I only stood at the door,' she said. 'I left the moment she screamed.'

'Were you naked?'

'Well, yes. I wasn't sure how quick on the uptake she'd be.'

'Oh, Daphne!'

Kate rushed out and put her arms round her sister. Tears streamed down their faces. So did the rain.

'Well, there's one thing,' said Kate. 'You think you aren't attractive. This shows you are.'

'Kate!' said Enid. 'Is that all you can think of? Aren't you shocked? You're wicked!'

There's gratitude, thought Kate.

Kate and Arturo hardly spoke now, even after Timothy was born. He painted all day and all evening, she cooked the meals and watched the sea. Black, petrol, aquamarine, purple, blue, midnight blue, turquoise, green, grey, silver, pearl, white, she watched the sea in all its colours and wished that she could paint.

Arturo sometimes drew and made sketches, but he didn't paint from life any more, he went into the studio and locked the door and drew a blind across the window 'so that the light is constant, and my paintings are timeless and not influenced by the moment. My art is more condensed than the real world. It's more real than the real world can ever be. I leave the illusion that the real world is real to Daphne, with my blessing.'

Daphne and Stanley were scornful of Arturo. They were certain that he painted the canvas the right way up, and just turned it upside down when he'd finished. He claimed that the whole point lay in the technical challenge posed by painting the scene upside down. Kate wanted to believe him. She needed to believe him. It would have been easier to believe him if he had let her in, just once, to see him painting upside down.

'No!' he said. 'I expect faith from my wife. I need faith from my wife. Without that faith, you and I are nothing.'

Daniel and Olga came to stay for a weekend, with the children. They were off to Palestine the next week. 'I have to be a Jew first and an artist second,' Daniel said. 'Without my acknowledgement of my Jewishness, my work is meaningless.' He was evasive about his experiences in Russia.

It was a busy weekend, with Ruth and Barbara to entertain and little Reuben to be looked after too. Kate managed just one very brief talk with Daniel, on the middle terrace.

'Why didn't Russia work, Daniel?' she asked.

He looked away. He was embarrassed.

'We were naïve,' he said. 'I feel ashamed of having been so naïve. I can't talk about it. And you, Kate, how are things with Arturo?'

'I can't talk about that,' she said. 'I think he must be my Russia.'

'I miss you,' he said.

'I miss you.'

He ran one finger down her arm, and went back into the house.

Timothy was only five weeks old when Stanley left. 'It's been a good place for me,' he said, 'but it couldn't stand still, it could only go up or down, and unfortunately it's gone down. I'm leaving straight away, because I hate endings. I like to get them over with.'

Daphne was more succinct. 'Rats leave sinking ships,' she said. 'This is a sinking ship and I'm a rat.'

So Kate and Arturo were left alone in the creaking house with the two small children. Arturo painted all day. They had no means of paying the rent. There was barely enough money for food, and none for anything else. Then one day Arturo opened an envelope and beamed at Kate and said, 'I have an exhibition in St Ives. We're saved.'

And they were. The exhibition was a big success. His upside-down paintings went like hot cakes, or upside-down cakes, as Kate said. A London dealer saw it and advised Arturo not to sell the few paintings that were left, but to save them for a London show, at which they would fetch London prices.

He swaggered more and more. He twirled his blackthorn stick. He hammered the single malts. He bought an Alvis 12/50 Tourer, the very model that he had borrowed. This struck Kate as symbolic of his lack of inventive powers. Sometimes he took Kate and the children for rides. More often he went alone, with his easel and paints and brushes, his stick and his flask. Kate wondered if he was seeing another woman. Certainly he took less and less notice of her.

He did work hard, though, that was one of his virtues. Sometimes he stayed in his studio all night. He rarely kissed Kate now, almost never showed any gentleness. Occasionally he would take her, swiftly and noisily, at unexpected moments. There was no cruelty in it, but no warmth either. She didn't like it, but felt that if she refused him there would be nothing. Once she took the children to Swansea for a week. They chugged around Swansea Bay on the Mumbles train, soon to be replaced by trams. Sometimes they caught a bus to bold, breezy, masculine Rhossili, or soft, gentle, feminine Oxwich, or the windswept cliffs of Pennard. Kate realised how much she loved

Gower, its bleak moors and miniature valleys studded with gorse and old whitewashed farms, and the glorious bays never far away. How silly she had been, as a child, to be so eager to grow up. How overrated being grown up was.

She dreaded their return to Tregarryn, but hoped against hope that Arturo would have missed her, that her absence would have rekindled at least some of his love, that she would be able to see, in this self-obsessed egotist, at least something of the amusing charmer who had laughed with her on the Penzance train, and had seemed to stand for a freer, bolder, more generous life than the one she had known.

But no, he was just the same. How acutely she missed the ordered warmth of her family life in Wales. That was where she now felt that the true generosity was. Sometimes she thought that her iconoclasm had been no more than a youthful fancy. At times she almost hated Arturo for making her think like that. She fought her hostility desperately.

At the private view of his London collection in the small but elegant Winchester Gallery there were pictures of North Cornwall, of the children, of Kate, of Arturo, of Tregarryn, of flowers, of his dentist and of horses, and all of them were upside down, and Arturo spoke very pompously about them.

When the overweight daughter of one of Portugal's leading gynaecologists asked him what would happen if she bought one of his pictures and hung it the right way up, rather than upside down, he said, 'Why, nothing, charming creature. You would still have a beautiful picture, but you would have cheated yourself enormously of its value.'

Overhearing this exchange, a society masseur with a place in Jermyn Street said, 'So the value of your picture lies not in its intrinsic merit but in its upside downness, does it?'

'It lies in both,' said Arturo. 'If it lay only in the upside downness, then the picture itself would be valueless, and a valueless picture would still be valueless upside down. Since my pictures are not valueless, the value cannot therefore lie solely in their upside downness. It lies partly in the fact that they were painted upside down and party in the fact that they are to be seen upside down, that is their unity, every work of art must have a unity. The artist, I, and the viewer, you, share a distorting vision, experience the distortion together, and are enriched.'

'You are enriched. I am poorer, if I buy the picture.'

'No, I am the poorer. I have only your money. You have my genius.'

Every word that Arturo spoke embarrassed Kate and drove him further from her. She drank glass after glass of wine in the hope that it would dull her pain. Her aching legs screamed to leave the room. Her head throbbed with tension. When a very well-spoken young man with the face of an angel and incredibly curly hair smiled devastatingly upon her and asked her if Arturo really painted everything upside down, she said, 'Of course he doesn't. Would you? And as for his philosophy, nuts. It all began when he hung a picture upside down when he was drunk.'

She shouldn't have said it, and she wished that she hadn't even before she discovered that the gorgeous young man, whose name was Oswald Philliskirk, was an art critic. His savage attack on Arturo's integrity in *The Times* did much to burst his brief bubble.

'You watched me!' Arturo said in their hotel room, after he'd read the article. He was white with anger. 'You spied on me.'

'I didn't,' said Kate. 'I wasn't even sure until this moment, when you didn't deny it. You're a fraud.'

'Of course I am,' said Arturo. 'I've always known it. You've always known it. Now the whole world knows it. You silly bloody bitch.'

He raised his arm as if to hit her. For a moment she thought he was going to hit her. She didn't flinch, and, maybe because she didn't flinch, or because there was no actual violence in him, whatever his other faults, he didn't hit her. She might have preferred it if he had. It might have eased her guilt. Guilt and shame were all she felt now. Guilt and shame at her actions. She felt nothing whatsoever for Arturo.

He walked to the door of their hotel room, turned to look back at her, and said, 'You are so beautiful, Kate.' Tears streamed down his face. 'I loved you so much,' he said. 'So much.'

She looked at him in horror. She was numb. His tears didn't move her. She felt only that she was seeing a performance, a very good performance, from a fraud who had never felt a genuine emotion in his life.

She caught the twelve o'clock train from Paddington to Swansea, where she had left the children. They were pleased to see her. So were her family.

On the third day of her visit, after the boys had been put to bed, she said, 'I'll go back tomorrow. I'll go, but I think it's over.'

The next day she knew it was over. A farmer had come across Arturo in an old barn three miles from Tregarryn. He had hanged himself, and, an artistic touch, he had hanged himself upside down.

5 Maurice

'Who's a lucky lady?'

The words seemed to come from a very long way away and barely registered on Kate's consciousness. She was still in a state of shock after reliving the tragic end of her life with Arturo. She was remembering the shock and the guilt and the sorrow that had swept over her more than seventy years ago. She was asking herself now, in Ward 3C, the same questions that she had asked a thousand times before. Could she have saved Arturo if she'd behaved differently? Should she have behaved differently? Had the Arturo she had loved disappeared beyond recall? Could she have made him feel that he was not a fraud?

'Who's a lucky lady?'

Luckily, the fat nurse with the eating disorder repeated the words. Her name, Kate now knew, was Janet, and her downfall was the doughnut. She had also deduced, from remarks and insinuations overheard, that Helen, the nurse with the bony hands, also suffered from an eating disorder.

'We are!' said Janet triumphantly, answering her own repeated question. 'We're a lucky lady. Who's come all the way from Russia because he loves us?'

'You shouldn't call her "us", nurse,' said Maurice. 'Nobody could be less plural than her.'

'What?'

'My mother is a very singular lady.'

Dear dear Maurice. She felt his lips on her cheek and she very nearly opened her eyes and tried to smile at him. She wanted to run her long fingers over his dear, smooth-shaven face. In all probability she wouldn't be able to, she hadn't managed to move them yet in the limited trials she had made. In any case it would have given the show away. She would have had to start reacting to fat Janet with the eating disorder, thin Helen with the eating disorder, mad Mrs Critchley, lonely Hilda, farting Glenda, smiling Doctor Ramgobi (she assumed that he smiled, he often sounded as though he was smiling). And for what purpose? She wouldn't be able to save Janet and Hilda from their eating disorders. She wouldn't be able to restore Mrs Critchley's sanity or ease Hilda's loneliness or make Glenda less windy. She wouldn't be able to tell Maurice that she loved him.

'I know you, don't I?' Janet asked Maurice. 'I've seen you on the telly.'

'Very possibly,' admitted Maurice.

'*Coronation Street*?'

'No.'

'Give us a clue.'

'Maurice Copson, BBC News, Moscow.'

'Oh yeah. You're the bloke they sent to trouble spots when Kate Adie was already somewhere else.'

He laughed. No stuffiness about him, despite his high opinion of himself.

'That's right,' he said.

'Say it for me now. Say it about this place.'

'Sorry?'

'Say, "Maurice Copson, Ward 3C, Whetstone General Hospital, BBC News." I got that the wrong way round, didn't I? Say it and then I can tell my mum. She thinks you've got ever such a lovely voice.'

'Right. For your mum. "Maurice Copson, BBC News, Ward 3C, Whetstone General Hospital."'

'Lovely. Ta very much.'

'No problem.'

His hand was clasping hers. His skin was rough. Probably he

kept losing his gloves in the cold Russian winter. He lost most things. She remembered shocking a nun on the three o'clock from Paddington to Swansea in 1948, when she'd asked Kate about her children. 'My youngest son is seventeen, idealistic, utterly impractical. Last Saturday he went to a party and lost his front-door key, his wallet and his virginity.' The nun had gone pink. They'd been passing through Maidenhead at the time. It had shut the nun up, which had been the general idea. She'd made Maurice laugh with her tale of the pink nun in Maidenhead. She'd always loved making Maurice laugh. She wondered if she'd ever make him laugh again.

'Well, Ma dear,' he said, as if he could read her thoughts, and she often felt that he did have psychic powers, 'I don't know whether you want to recover or not. I gather from Doctor Ramgobi that it's by no means out of the question that you can make quite a dramatic recovery, if you still have the desire to do so. You have an amazing constitution still, and it's very much down to you. I like that man.'

Yes, she thought, only you have the compassion and the strength to be so honest with me. I love you so much. I wish you'd married. Old age can be so lonely, without children. My children have been a joy to me, on the whole. They say that the hair of sexy men falls out, so I'm hoping that you've been sexy even though you haven't married. I suspect none of my other children have been very sexy. I can't have had no sexy children, can I? Am I rambling?

'I wish I could have come straight away,' he said, 'but I had a job to finish. I hope you can understand me. You always tried to get me to talk about my doings. Things are very bad in Russia now. The state's assessment of a person's needs is a bath towel every twenty-three years, and even that's too ambitious a target for modern Russia to deliver. I have to report these things, Ma. The Mafia are very powerful, the communists are waiting in the wings, chaos is their breeding ground. I have to keep the pressure on our government to give Russia the help it needs. I am the conscience of the West.'

Yes, well, I think you have begun to believe your own publicity, Maurice, she thought. The historical irony didn't escape her, of course. The same idealism, the same love of social justice, that had made her profess to be a communist in the 1920s had made him a passionate opponent of communism in the 1990s.

'Nigel rang and told me,' he said. 'It surprised me how emotional he was. I'd never realised how much he bottles up. Then of course Timothy rang. Floods of tears. I can't get hold of Elizabeth, but I've left a message on her answer machine. She must be away. If you can understand all this. I'm probably tiring you. I'll just sit in silence for a while.'

But she couldn't rest. Her mind was churning. Every reference to Russia reminded her of the name board of Leningrad railway station. The murderer had left a note saying 'Sorry, Ma'. Only Maurice called her 'Ma'. He couldn't have murdered Graham. Not Maurice. Could he? He knew the truth about Graham. Could he have murdered for that? Surely not? He'd known she'd loved Graham. Surely he wouldn't have killed the man she loved, however disapproving he was?

These thoughts exhausted her. She nodded off, and only woke up when the food trolley clanked down the corridor towards the ward.

'Toad-in-the-hold, Mrs Critchley? There you go.'

'Take it away!'

'You ordered it.'

'Take it away. I don't want any.' She lowered her voice. 'I can't afford to pay.'

'You don't have to pay, Mrs Critchley. It's free.'

'Free? How can it be free?'

'Because I'm paying for it today!' Maurice! Good old Maurice.

'Oh, that's very kind of you. Thank you very much.'

'No problem.'

'This hotel used to be the best in Buxton. People were impressed when you said you were staying at the Spa. Fillet steak. Artichoke mousse. *Magret de canard*. Look what we're reduced to now. Toad-in-the-hole. How's the little one?'

'She's doing very well,' said Maurice without hesitation. 'She's put on two pounds.'

'Oh, bless her. And there was me thinking it was a boy. Oh, bless her little cotton socks.'

'Toad-in-the-hole, Glenda?'

'Oh, yes, please. Must keep my strength up.'

'There you go. Plum pie and custard?'

'Oh, yes, please.'

'There you go.'

Maurice's gnarled hand in hers. She believed that she could feel his hand a bit more than the others. Maybe her feeling was beginning to come back, or maybe it was just because it was so gnarled.

'Prawn salad, Hilda?'

'Oh, no, thank you. I'm allergic to prawns.'

'Well, why have you ticked them, then?'

'I can't have. I'd have ticked toad-in-the-hole if there was toad-in-the-hole. I'm very partial to toad-in-the-hole. Well, never mind, I'm not hungry.'

'Well, I've a spare toad-in-the-hole, as it happens. Mr Watson in 3A is with us no more.'

'Oh, but I couldn't. I couldn't take advantage under those circumstances. You know what they say about a dead man's shoes. Well, a dead man's toad-in-the-hole, it wouldn't be right. I just couldn't stomach it, knowing.'

'Mr Watson isn't dead, Hilda. He's gone home.'

'Oh. Oh, well, I suppose that's all right, then.'

'That's the ticket. There you go.'

What other nation, thought Kate, could have invented sausage in a batter pudding? What other nation, having invented it, could have called it toad-in-the-hole? What other nation, having invented it and called it toad-in-the-hole, could have eaten it?

'Your condition has certain advantages, Ma,' said Maurice. 'You are spared toad-in-the-hole. What other nation could have invented toad-in-the-hole, and Little Chefs, and Marmite?'

They'd always been on the same wavelength.

Surely if Maurice had murdered Graham, he wouldn't have drawn attention to himself by writing 'Sorry, Ma' and leaving a name plate from Leningrad railway station?

She wished she could ask him how Clare was.

'Clare sends her love. She's very well.'

It was uncanny.

Shortly after supper, Mrs Critchley had a visitor. As ill luck would have it, he came just after Mrs Critchley had been escorted to the lavvy, as she called it. This gave him an opportunity of explaining himself to a ward that wasn't remotely interested. 'My name is Pilchard. I also live in Orchard Close. Mrs Critchley lives in number 33 and I live in number 12, but due to a certain irregularity in the numbers in the cul-de-sac, I am actually opposite her. I don't get much sense out of her, but it cheers her up to see me.'

Mr Pilchard's theory was not borne out by Mrs Critchley's first remark on her return from the lavvy, which was, 'Get out of here! You took my Jennifer from me and I never want to see you again.'

'I've never heard of her Jennifer,' Mr Pilchard told the ward. 'Not one of her better days. A strategic withdrawal is indicated.'

Glenda's husband arrived shortly afterwards, and Glenda told him he looked thin.

'You aren't getting enough to eat, are you?' she said.

'Yes, I am. I made myself a steak-and-kidney pie.'

'Since when could you make pastry?'

'You don't need to make pastry these days. You buy it.'

When it was Glenda's turn to be helped to the facilities, as she called them, her husband offered to take her.

'No,' explained Janet. 'She may need help, know what I mean?'

'Who better than me to help her? I'm her husband,' said her husband.

'Sorry. It's a ladies. I have to do it. Besides,' she added rather grandly, 'she might need professional assistance.'

When Janet had taken Glenda on the long trip down the corridor to the facilities, Glenda's husband Douglas told the ward, 'She thinks I can't look after myself. I can. I made a soufflé yesterday. It didn't rise, but it was tasty. Can't tell her that, she'd go up in smoke.'

Maurice joined in the discussion of the techniques of making soufflés rise.

'Mine never rise very much,' admitted Douglas, 'and it's the same difference with cakes. There's nothing I can do about it. The gaskets have gone on the oven.'

Hilda had no visitors, she never did, and there were no other visitors for Kate. 'Nigel and Timothy have left the field clear for me,' explained Maurice.

Shortly before nine o'clock, a time which seems like three in the morning in hospitals, Glenda's husband took his leave of her, and Maurice squeezed his mother's hand in farewell.

By ten o'clock the other three patients in the ward were asleep. Mrs Critchley was snoring loudly, Hilda was emitting whistles which reminded Kate of shepherds training dogs in the Welsh hills, and Glenda was giving short rasping breaths accompanied by occasional low moans and staccato farts which would have shocked her gentility to the core, had she known about them. Kate was now able to allow herself the luxury of opening her eyes for whole minutes at a time.

There, in that small, square ward, lit by the barley-sugar night-light, Kate took up her time travels again. The barley-sugar night-light became the Cotswold sun, and, just after a fart from Glenda so loud that it almost woke her, Kate met Maurice's father for the first time.

6 Walter

He turned and looked at her, as if prompted by some sixth sense, just as she walked down the aisle of the magnificent, airy, Perpendicular church. Her immediate impression was of his great size and of the luxuriant anarchy of his jet-black hair. He smiled at her, and she found herself smiling back. Well, why not smile? It *was* a wedding.

He sat on the bride's side, she of course on the groom's. She knelt, in imitation of a woman at prayer, feeling ashamed but knowing that she'd have felt even more ashamed if she'd shocked her parents by not kneeling. Her mother, radiant in a black dress of Welsh lace embroidered with curling Celtic patterns, turned and smiled at her, and Kate turned, as if to look at the fifteenth-century stained glass for which Fairford Church is justly famed, and whose importance the golden boy had explained. 'They're all very proud of the glass, for goodness' sake swot up on it, so you can hold your own,' he'd urged, more keyed up than she had ever seen him, though that wasn't surprising.

Yes, the windows were beautiful, but it wasn't because of them that she turned round. She turned to see if she could meet the big man's eyes again. She did. An uncharacteristically coy impulse made her slide her eyes past him and up to the great west window, then she looked back at him and grinned in admission of the deception. He grinned back. There was nothing classically good-looking about him, he was too ungainly, his shoulders were too bulky, he seemed slightly hunched, as if embarrassed by his size. But Kate thought him the second most handsome man that she had seen that day.

The most handsome, of course, was her brother. The luxuriance of Oliver's childish curls had gone, but he still had a delightful curliness which managed to avoid any suggestion of effeminacy. He was exactly six foot tall, almost slim, always elegantly dressed. His smile was warm. His teeth were perfect. Nobody was surprised when the younger of the Pelt-Wallaby girls fell for him. He was the golden boy, the most popular house surgeon in the hospital, charming, dashing, deft, quick-witted, athletic, humorous, generous, judged even at twenty-three to be certain to go far, and seemingly never troubled by thoughts beyond the range with which he was comfortable. He stood there, in front of the glittering congregation, at the side of his best man, Gareth Herbert, son of Herbert Herbert (Herbert Herbert Cricket, not Herbert Herbert Politics), in all his afternoon glory in his morning suit, top hat in his left hand, right hand fiddling with his private parts through his pocket, somebody should stop him, nervous as any young man would be who was marrying the younger of the Pelt-Wallaby girls.

Kate met Enid's eyes, and smiled. Enid had a headache, which might or might not develop into a full-blown migraine, and her answering smile was tense. At her other side Bernard shifted uneasily in his ill-fitting morning suit. He'd nicked himself shaving. A tiny sliver of cotton wool still adhered to his cheek.

The Pelt-Wallaby side of the church was crowded with men whose morning suits fitted like gloves, and elegant women whose gloves fitted like morning suits and whose simple but expensive knee-length ensembles had the somewhat fuller figure that was coming back after the straight look of the mid-twenties.

There were far fewer people on the Thomas side, and the man's hired morning suits didn't quite fit, and the women's dresses were too straight, in the fashion of the previous year, and they'd tried too hard, they had too many accessories, and Kate's heart went out to them. She thought up a silly little jingle about it.

> There is no compassion in fashion
> There is no forgiveness in dress.
> The more that you wore, the more people saw
> That you hadn't got more, you'd got less.

This made her feel better, and she was pleased to realise that she didn't feel the least bit embarrassed, she just felt full of love that day for all her relations. Nevertheless, she was delighted when a contingent from the hospital, good-looking young doctors and pretty young nurses, came in at the last moment to swell the groom's ranks.

She saw her mother touch John Thomas Thomas's arm. There was no answering touch. John Thomas Thomas was communing with his Maker.

There was a rustle of excitement, a turning of heads, she was able to look backwards and to her joy saw the big man wait until he'd smiled at her before he turned to gaze at Fenella Pelt-Wallaby, sliding along as if on castors on the arm of her father Horace. Fenella seemed in a trance of ecstasy, looking neither to left nor right, smiling distantly. She was actually short-sighted and terrified of tripping. Her nose was too long, and her forehead too wide and her mouth too narrow, but her family was rich, and everyone agreed that she was a great beauty.

The service was impressive and elegant. Oliver spoke the responses with just the right degree of hesitation. The sermon was impeccably brief, the singing of the last hymn brought tears to the eyes of all except those whose make-up was liable to be ruined by crying.

As they made their stuttering way back up the aisle, behind the happy couple, towards the great west window with its vivid and imaginative depiction of the Damned in Hell, Kate felt uneasy, not because of the window, she didn't believe in Hell, she didn't believe she was Damned, she didn't believe in Things with Capital Letters, but she had felt very exposed, very self-conscious since Arturo's suicide. Whenever she met people, she wondered if they were thinking, behind their polite faces, was it her fault, was she responsible for his death? She'd wondered if the pain of Gwyn's death would ever go away, and in the end, to her great relief and regret, it had. Now she wondered if her feeling of guilt would ever go. She had to brace herself to face the rigours of the reception.

Outside the church, they stood around in a great throng, and watched the taking of photographs. She even appeared in one of them, standing between Enid and Bernard in a family ensemble. Bernard said, 'It all seems vaguely indecent, somehow, all this show in the middle of a depression, I beg your pardon?'

Enid said, 'Oh no, I think it's wonderful,' but she looked small and bleak, her dress hadn't worked, she looked far too old in it. 'I think it's all utterly lovely.'

'Oh yes, Enid,' said Kate impulsively. 'But, oh Enid, if only Dilys and Myfanwy could be here,' and Enid's eyes filled with tears, which might have been tears of joy for Oliver and Fenella, though they didn't look like tears of joy, or they might have been for the sad absence of Myfanwy and Dilys, or they might have been, Kate felt herself ungenerous for thinking, tears shed for herself and for her fear that no man would ever stand at the altar in his morning suit fiddling with his balls through his pocket because of her.

The reception took place in a marquee in the box-hedged garden of the Pelt-Wallaby home, a mellow, honey-gold Cotswold manor house. Smart waitresses held trays of orange juice, elderflower cordial and champagne.

Alcohol had been a major issue. Kate still had vivid memories of the evening on which the thorny question had been raised. She'd had nowhere to live after the shock and, yes, the disgrace of Arturo's suicide. She'd had no money and precious little chance of earning any with two small children to bring up. So she had moved back with the children into the family home, into her old room. There, watched by the *Stag at Bay*, warned by the strict messages on the samplers, chilled by the linoleum, with a view over the slate roofs towards the new houses being built high above them on Town Hill, she had slowly rebuilt her confidence and her nerve.

One weekend, all the family had been present. Oliver had come from the hospital to discuss the wedding. Bernard, a trainee accountant in London with Simms Fordingbridge, had come because he adored and worshipped Oliver. After they'd finished their Saturday tea – tinned salmon and salad, with tinned pears to follow, and as much bread and butter as you could eat, and Welsh cakes and bara brith – and after they'd made light work of the washing-up, and after Kate had put the boys to bed, they had all gathered round the fire, even though it wasn't lit. Annie had been knitting. Bronwen had been embroidering. Enid had been marking homework. John Thomas Thomas had been reading his Welsh religious newspaper, *Y Tyst* (*The Truth*). Bernard had been studying an accountancy manual. Kate had been reading *Middlemarch*. Oliver had cleared his throat and said, 'Father, Mother,' so gravely that John Thomas Thomas had lowered his newspaper, and Bronwen had gone quite white. Kate had never seen Oliver look so nervous. He'd been terrified.

'Father, Mother,' he had repeated. 'I . . . I have to tell you that there will be alcohol at the wedding. There will be champagne and wine.'

John Thomas Thomas had folded his newspaper and placed it neatly on his lap.

'Oh dear,' he had said.

'The Pelt-Wallabies would find it very odd not to have alcohol at a wedding.'

'We understand, dear,' her mother had said, looking

116

anxiously at John Thomas Thomas. 'It's their daughter. It's their wedding. They must do as they please.'

'We would be considered a very narrow family, in London, I beg your pardon?' Bernard had said. He had told Kate that he went to pubs with his friends from Simms Fordingbridge and drank hock with his Wienerschnitzel when he dined at Schmidt's in Charlotte Street.

'Narrow, is it?' John Thomas Thomas had replied. 'I think, Bernard, I would be happy to be called narrow, in London. Well, thank you for telling us, Oliver. We don't need to drink any of it.'

'I will drink it, Father, in moderation,' Oliver had said. 'I have no wish to offend my new relatives.'

'And what about your old relatives?' John Thomas Thomas had asked very quietly.

'Hush, dear,' Bronwen had said. 'He must do as he thinks fit.'

'Well, be very moderate. You aren't used to it.'

Oliver had met Kate's eyes. She had known that he was very used to it.

'The rest of you are not to touch a drop,' John Thomas Thomas had commanded.

'Oh, Father, I'm thirty,' Kate had said. 'I think I can be trusted to lead my life the way I think fit.'

'I haven't seen much sign of it,' John Thomas Thomas had said, and Annie had choked, and Kate had seen her mother angry with John Thomas Thomas for the first time.

'For shame, John Thomas,' Bronwen had said. 'For shame. That was not a Christian way to speak.'

'I'm sorry,' John Thomas Thomas had said. 'I apologise, Kate. I'm upset, but that is no excuse. Drink alcohol if you must.'

'I don't pretend that I must,' Kate had said. 'But I will. I like it. In moderation. I see no harm in anything in moderation.'

'Really?' Bernard had said. 'Do you see no harm in poverty in moderation? Do you see no harm in murder and starvation, in moderation, I beg your pardon?'

'I spoke foolishly,' Kate had said. 'I'm upset too. I love this family. I hate quarrels.'

'Well, I shan't drink alcohol,' Enid had said smugly. 'It gives me migraines.'

'How do you know?' John Thomas Thomas had thundered.

Enid had gone bright red. All her smugness had vanished in an instant.

'I . . . er . . .' she had floundered, 'I had it once at a party. It was put in my orange juice. I didn't know.'

'Good. If that is the truth you are not to blame, though I hope you'll learn not to go to parties where there are wicked unprincipled people present,' John Thomas Thomas had said.

'That would cut out most of Swansea, I beg your pardon?' Bernard had said.

'Well, I shan't touch alcohol,' Annie had said. 'I'm so fortunate to be going to this wedding at all. I have to pinch myself sometimes, to believe it's true.'

Kate smiled to herself, standing near the doorway of the marquee, remembering that conversation. She had a glass of champagne, so did Oliver, and she had seen Bernard take one when he thought no one was looking, sip a little, and pour the rest into his orange juice.

She sailed across to a group of assorted Pelt-Wallabys, who welcomed her with broad smiles, although the smile of the elder of the Pelt-Wallaby girls was just a little forced, since Kate was so very much prettier than her.

'Your house is so beautiful,' said Kate. 'In Wales we don't have architecture. We only have buildings.'

They laughed, as if Kate had said something very witty, and she began the serious business of charming them for Wales. Enid was so quiet and wan, Bernard so unkempt and serious, John Thomas Thomas so stiff and stern, Annie so red and coarse and Bronwen too loyal to John Thomas Thomas to even attempt to shine. Kate kept her end up, for Oliver, lest the smooth, suave Pelt-Wallabys and their county friends thought him an escapee from a tribe of uncouth Celts.

All the time she was talking, Kate was aware of the broad-shouldered man with the jet-black hair, standing in a group to her right. She had looked at the seating plan. She was sitting between Doctor Ian Pelt-Wallaby and Mr Walter Copson. Her heart sank at the prospect. She wanted to sit next to the big man. But she showed none of this. She continued to charm the Pelt-Wallabys, but it was a performance, given for her brother's benefit to an audience who, she hoped, knew nothing about her part in Arturo's death. Out of the corner of her eye she saw her mother all alone for a moment and her heart went out to her. She excused herself from the Pelt-Wallabys and went over to Bronwen.

'Happy?' she asked.

'Very.'

'Proud?'

'Extremely.'

'Me too. Oliver is wonderful. Aren't you having any champagne, Mother?'

'Of course not.'

'It seems such a shame. Wouldn't you like to?'

'Of course not, Kate. Do you think a drink can compare with the love of a good man?'

They were summoned to the wedding breakfast, and Kate forgot all self-consciousness, all past worries, when she discovered that Mr Walter Copson was none other than the huge man with the jet-black hair. She had just not expected that he would have so blunt a name.

'I'm Kate Thomas,' she told him. 'I'm Oliver's sister.'

'Walter Copson,' he said. 'I was at Cambridge with Jonathan Pelt-Wallaby.'

They stood for the grace, which was spoken by John Thomas Thomas.

'Oh Lord,' said John Thomas Thomas in his rich, resonant Welsh tones – he could have been a preacher if he hadn't been a headmaster – 'make us truly thankful for what we are about to receive. Oh Lord, on this day of joy for these two young people, help us to remember the many millions in this world who are less fortunate than ourselves. Help mankind find the energy and vision to conquer this great depression. Lead us to a greater understanding of the causes of poverty and help us to fight the iniquities and inequalities that contribute to it, so that, when the suffering is over, the world may be a better place. Amen.'

As they sat down, Walter said, 'Bit heavy, wasn't it? Bit preachy? Likes the sound of his own voice, I think.'

'Not really,' said Kate very sweetly. Not many opportunities on this scale fall into one's lap. 'My father is a very sincere and modest man.'

Walter was, for a moment, devastated. Even his broad shoulders sagged at the immensity of his gaffe. Kate looked over his back to the top table, and saw Fenella's mother congratulating John Thomas Thomas and pretending to have been delighted with the text of his grace.

'I'm so sorry, Kate,' said Walter. 'We're off on the wrong foot.'

'Well, that's good,' said Kate. 'It means things can only get better.'

'I noticed you in the church,' said Walter. 'I hardly dared hope that I'd have the good fortune to sit next to you.'

'I think it's a stroke of good fortune for me too,' said Kate.

The wedding breakfast began gently, with melon. Its arrival gave Ian Pelt-Wallaby a chance to break in on Kate and Walter.

'Ian Pelt-Wallaby,' he announced.

Kate introduced herself and Walter.

'I was at Cambridge with Jonathan Pelt-Wallaby,' said Walter.

'Ah yes. I don't know him awfully well. I'm actually one of the Shropshire Pelt-Wallabys,' said Ian Pelt-Wallaby. 'Despite which my father sent me to Winchester, not Shrewsbury. Some idea of making me stand on my own two feet, I believe.'

The young lady on his left spoke to Ian Pelt-Wallaby about the melon, and Walter took the opportunity to whisper to Kate, 'Frightful family, the Pelt-Wallabys. Apart from Jonathan, and Fenella, who's actually quite a sweetie. The rest of them won't give me house room.'

'Why ever not?'

'Trade. They regard me as new money, even though we were founded in 1808.'

'Who's we?'

'Boothroyd and Copson.'

'Boothroyd and Copson! That sounds so solid. What do Boothroyd and Copson do?'

'Make pistons.'

Kate had never thought that pistons sounded sexy before. The trouble was that she could think of nothing to say about them.

'Oh,' she said.

'The lady says, "Oh,"' said Walter. 'If I'd said I was a solicitor, she'd have said, "Really? What's your speciality? Divorce?" If I'd said I was a doctor, she'd have said, "Really? Are you a surgeon or a specialist or a GP or what?" But I say, "We make pistons," and the lady says, "Oh."'

'I think your pistons sound utterly enchanting,' said Kate. 'Instinct tells me that they're probably the most marvellous pistons in the whole world. But I don't know anything about pistons. I feel as the poor King must feel when he's being shown around a steelworks.'

'You must come up and see my pistons some time,' said Walter.

'I'd love that.'

'Do you play gofe, Kate?' asked Ian Pelt-Wallaby.

'No.'

'Pity. It's such a lovely game.'

'I don't like games,' said Kate.

'What do you like?' asked Walter.

'Conversation. Laughter. People. South Wales. Mid Wales. North Wales. Food. Wine. Animals. Birds. Theatre. Music. Books. Wit. Style. Trust. Love. Gardens. Walking. Pistons.'

Walter's eyes held hers. She felt quite excited. She had never felt quite like this with Arturo, she realised now. Oh Lord, don't start thinking about Arturo, Kate Thomas.

'Do *you* play gofe, Walter?'

'I'm moderately keen on gofe, Ian, yes,' said Walter, smiling at Kate to show that he didn't really pronounce it 'gofe'.

'Have you ever played the fifteenth on the West Course at Wentworth?' asked Ian Pelt-Wallaby.

'No.'

'Oh. It's a par four dogleg. You have to keep the ball down the left-hand side of the fairway. I was lucky enough to birdie it yesterday.'

Kate looked round the room, while Ian talked to Walter about such diverse subjects as the seventh at Sandwich, the sixteenth at Troon and the fourteenth at Carnoustie. She could see that things were a little forced on the top table. She felt such love and compassion for her parents as they ate their sole-and-asparagus tartlets and didn't touch their elderflower cordial. Horace Pelt-Wallaby looked quite shifty, sipping his Chablis, and Oliver was trying hard to look as if he wasn't really enjoying the wine. She looked round the great tent, throbbing with charm and conversation. Things seemed to be going with a swing at almost all of the fifteen round tables. But she caught sight of Enid making heavy weather of a man with a handlebar moustache, Enid pale and struggling in the midst of all this vitality. Oh, Enid, she thought, oh my dear dear Enid, if only you had some gumption.

It was quite a shock to Kate to remember at this point that she was a mother. Nigel and Timothy at the tender ages of five and three had been judged too young for bliss. Well, she hadn't exactly forgotten their existence. She had forgotten that she hadn't told Walter of their existence. Here they were, getting on like a house on fire – he had just rested his great, piston maker's hand briefly on her soft thigh, to let her know that he wasn't really thinking about gofe – and she hadn't told him that she had children. If she didn't tell him, he'd show her his pistons, one thing would lead to another, they'd end up going to bed together and going at it like pistons and afterwards she'd say, 'Well, I must say that beat childbirth into a cocked hat. Oh, did I tell you, incidentally, that I have two small boys by my first husband, who hanged himself? Oh, didn't I? Sorry.'

She had shocked herself with the thought of going at it like pistons with Walter. She looked across at the top table and wondered if Oliver and Fenella were still virgins. She looked at her dear parents making excruciating polite conversation and thought how lucky it was that they couldn't see into her mind. She would have no compunction about sleeping with Walter. She knew that already. No compunction, and no guilt.

In the meantime, she must address this question of the boys. How should she do it? 'I suppose you don't have any children, unlike me'? 'I hope the boys are behaving themselves with our friends'? 'We didn't have alcohol at my wedding'?

Anyway, she needed to tell him, so she turned to Ian and said, 'Ian, the young lady on your left has nobody to talk to at the moment.'

'Oh Lord,' said Ian Pelt-Wallaby. 'Do you think I should mount a rescue operation?'

'Yes, I do.' She turned to Walter, and was just about to speak, when he said, 'Do your boys like games?'

'Timothy doesn't much, but . . .' Only then did she realise the implications of his remark. 'You know about the boys!'

He smiled into her eyes. 'I've been asking around during the champagne. I know a lot about you. I get the impression you're a rather extraordinary lady.' He rested his great horny hand on her slim, delicate one, very gently, just for an instant. An electric instant. 'I must talk to the lady on my right now,' he said. 'Social duty calls.'

The lamb *en croute* arrived and proved as palatable as the sole-and-asparagus tartlets. Margaux succeeded the Chablis. The moment Walter turned away from Kate, Ian steamed in like a dish of boiled potatoes.

'Of course I don't get as much time to play gofe as I would like,' he said. 'I'm on call a lot of the time.'

'On call?'

'I'm an anaesthetist.'

'I can't say that surprises me.'

'Why on earth do you say that?'

'Because I think you're probably very good at putting people to sleep.'

Ian Pelt-Wallaby went as pink as his lamb. His mouth opened and shut like a bemused haddock's.

'That really is a most astonishingly rude thing to say,' he said.

'Isn't it?' agreed Kate, and she gave him a really sweet smile, which confused him totally. 'But you see you're being pretty rude yourself. You can't wait to talk to me because I'm pretty and you're desperately trying not to talk to the young lady on your left because she has a squint. You're wasting your time with me because I am immensely attracted to the man on my right, who is talking to the matronly lady on his right because he has good manners, as you should have, having been to Winchester. Mind you, your school motto sums up everything I find repellent about the public school system. "Manners maketh man"! Manners hideth man. Your motto is a recipe for the creation of confidence tricksters.'

Kate enjoyed that moment. She really felt that Ian Pelt-

Wallaby deserved it. More than thirty years later her words would come back to haunt her. Lying in a hospital bed, sixty-eight years later, she felt sorry for Doctor Ian Pelt-Wallaby, anaesthetist and golfer and long since dead, no doubt, who might have felt better about his encounter with Kate if he'd known that the last laugh would be on her.

The Pelt-Wallabys dropped the Thomases entirely after the tragic death of Fenella Pelt-Wallaby in childbirth just before Christmas, in 1932. That Christmas a card winged its way to the family home in Swansea. After that, nothing. The anger that the Thomases felt towards the Pelt-Wallabys was muted only by the fact that they had no more wish to see the Pelt-Wallabys than the Pelt-Wallabys had to see them, but Kate, that proud and snorting thoroughbred, had felt the humiliation more than most and felt it even now, lying in Ward 3C, remembering that Christmas of 1932, in that substantial gabled terraced house in Swansea.

Kate was almost eight months pregnant, and her swollen stomach seemed a gross piece of tactlessness. She knew it was absurd to think like that, she didn't believe that Oliver thought it so.

If it hadn't been for Nigel and Timothy they might have dispensed with family celebrations altogether, but the boys were unaware of the screaming silence of the absent child, of the cot that had been bought and sold.

Nigel, old enough at seven to sense that something untoward was happening that Christmas, responded by behaving badly. Not only did he reduce Timothy to tears by telling him that Father Christmas was really his new father Walter, but he stole the orange from Timothy's stocking. Later Timothy saw the swelling in Annie's thick left stocking and said, 'Is that an orange in your stocking, Annie?' and Annie said, 'No, Timothy, it's a bunion,' and Timothy said, 'I like bunions fried,' and Nigel said, 'Not onions, frogface. Bunions,' so that was all rather amusing, and even Oliver had to smile, Lord knew what was really going through his mind. His eyes were deep set and there were dark bags under them, and the sorrow made him look more handsome than ever. He remained his usual affable, charming self and didn't allow even Kate close enough to discuss his tragedy. To be a surgeon and to be helpless, as you lose your wife and child in the act of birth, that must have been particularly hard to bear, thought Kate. To be the golden boy, the charmed one, and find that it counted for nothing, that was hard. Kate wondered what John Thomas Thomas said to God about that in his prayers. John Thomas Thomas's presence in the house that Christmas was a bit like that of a God. He was a kindly figure, but an aloof one. He sat, silent and magisterial at the festive table, joining in and yet apart, and, for the first time, Kate found something rather pathetic in him.

Walter praised the stuffing, and Annie went even redder than usual and said that she had made it. Kate could see that Annie was in love with Walter. Probably Enid was in love with him too. He was a deeply lovable man.

They had planned to have their first Christmas Day at home, in the large house of the heir apparent to the kingdom of the pistons, in the rolling land to the south-west of Birmingham, where the leaders of industry lived. They would have given Nigel and Timothy a day to remember, and on Boxing Day they would have entertained Walter's parents. Walter would have produced fine bottles of wine from his cellar, and crusted port. The Thomases drank nothing with their meal, not even water. But Walter was the first to say, after the tragedy, that they must rally round. They had got married very quietly, as they had wanted. Now it was the time to think of other people.

The Christmas pudding didn't come in flaming, brandy was not allowed even for that purpose. It was rich and sticky and gastronomically absurd when everybody was already full to bursting, but it was tradition and everybody tucked in enthusiastically and pretended that they enjoyed it. Nigel got a penny in his portion, and Timothy got a penny in his portion, and Annie got a penny in her portion and said, 'Aren't I just the luckiest person in the whole world?' and then she went red as she realised that the pudding had been made just before the tragedy, and the third penny had been for the baby, even though the baby could not have understood. Kate wondered whether the baby had had any consciousness as it died in the act of being born, and the thought terrified her, and she because acutely conscious of the living being inside her, which she was sure would be a girl. How could she endure the tension of childbirth now? She gripped the table, sweat poured down her back, she thought she would pass out, she was chewing a particularly recalcitrant mouthful of pudding, it would never go down, her throat had closed, her mouth was too full, somebody asked if she was all right and she tried to say, 'I feel as though I've got claustrophobia of the mouth,' but she couldn't speak for pudding, so she made a little pantomime of that, and people laughed, and the moment passed. She felt dizzy and weak, but immensely relieved. She wasn't going to faint. She wasn't going to need to be rescued. Walter, her rock, leant across and touched her hand and smiled, then fetched a jug of water. She drank two glasses, and it tasted sweeter than any wine.

Light relief was provided, inadvertently, by Nigel.

'What are husbands for, Mummy?'

Everybody laughed. It sounded so funny. Timothy laughed especially loudly, because everyone else was laughing, but he had no idea what he was laughing at. Nigel flushed sullenly.

'Don't laugh at me!' he shouted, and rushed out of the room, slamming the door.

Walter hurried after him, and in a couple of minutes they came back. Nigel looked very awkward and abashed.

'I explained that we were laughing with him, not at him,' said Walter.

'Husbands are daddies, aren't they?' asked Nigel.

'Yes, dear. Some husbands are daddies,' said Kate. She looked uneasily at Oliver, so cruelly denied the pleasure of being a daddy. His face was a stone.

'Your husband isn't my daddy, is he?' persisted Nigel.

'I'll tell you all about it later,' said Kate. 'This isn't really a suitable time for it.'

Bernard asked if anyone thought that the formation of a National Government to deal with the economic crisis could be the first rung on a very slippery ladder which might lead eventually to the destruction of our democratic traditions. Poor Bernard, thought Kate, it was his way of trying to lighten the conversation.

On Boxing Day they had a run out in two cars. Walter drove in front in his brand-new 3 litre Lagonda. Oliver followed in his Riley 9 Monaco. Walter took John Thomas Thomas and Bronwen and Enid and Nigel. Oliver took Bernard and Annie and Kate and Timothy. Annie had never been in a car before, and she was terrified. She gave instructions to Oliver in the guise of a monologue to Timothy. 'Uncle Oliver's coming to a steep corner in a minute, Timothy. Watch Uncle Oliver slow down quite a lot.'

They drove up out of the town on to the hills and moors of a bare Gower. Over barren moorland, through stunted skeletal winter woodlands they drove in their splendid, gleaming cars. They turned left by Oxwich Castle. 'Watch Uncle Oliver go very slowly, because it's a very steep hill, Timothy.' They crossed a vale of marsh and reeds and lurking birds, and then they were at Oxwich. There were only a few people on the beautiful long beach that curved beneath the bare winter hills. One or two boys, wearing Christmas presents, were playing ducks and drakes, skimming flat stones across the water, bouncing them over the low breakers. The wind ruffled their hair, Kate touched Oliver's hand just once but didn't meet his eyes. Nigel and Timothy galumphed on the great sands that stretched for miles, and Nigel hit Timothy, and Enid said, 'Tell them to be careful, Kate. Glandon Llewellyn, whose father paved Cousin Nancy's garden, fell in three inches of water, knocked himself out and drowned.' Nobody drowned on this occasion. They went home and had cold ham and Welsh cakes and bara brith.

The next day they visited the cold aunts in their cold houses. That evening Herbert Herbert Cricket and Herbert Herbert Politics called with their respective spouses, Mrs Herbert Herbert Cricket and Mrs Herbert Herbert Politics. They sat in the front room, and talked about the Irish Question, and whether the League of Nations had the will-power to stand up to Japan, and poverty, and pistons, and the price of laverbread, and hasn't Jones and Jones gone down, used to be such a fine store, they're missing that son of theirs who was killed.

On the 28th Oliver set off to rebuild his life, Bernard went back to London and Simms Fordingbridge, and Walter and Kate and the boys left for the Midlands.

'Next Christmas you'll all come to us,' called out Kate, as Walter cranked the Lagonda, proving that, whatever talents she had in other directions, she had precious little as a prophet.

'I'm sorry,' he said.

'I wish you hadn't said that,' she said. 'I think they must be the two most pathetic, overused words in the English language. "I'm sorry." You will be sorry, Walter.'

It was a statement, not a threat.

'I'll never do such a thing again,' he said.

'Too right you won't,' she said, 'because I won't be here. I'm leaving you.'

That really shook him. He hadn't expected that. He came towards her over the thick carpet.

'Don't touch me,' she screamed.

He shrank back from her hostility. He'd gone white, absolutely white.

'How did you find out?' he croaked.

'Len Goldstone told me.'

Maurice began to cry. Kate hurried across the huge expanse of the drawing-room, up the wide impressive staircase of the pseudo-medieval, post-Lutyens house, along the suburban imitation of a feudal corridor, into Maurice's bedroom.

Walter followed her. He wasn't a maker of pistons now. He was a lap-dog.

She whipped out her left breast and began to feed the scrawny infant. He gurgled with pleasure at the beginning of the milk.

Walter stood there, silent, watching. Nigel and Timothy were sleeping soundly, in the huge bedrooms. The house was silent.

'This is what my breasts are for now, Walter,' she said. 'From now on they will be put to good use. Practical use. You must approve of that. You're a practical man.'

'I suppose it didn't occur to you that Len Goldstone might be lying,' said Walter.

'I don't want to speak about it while I'm feeding Maurice,' she said. 'It'll be a miracle if my milk hasn't gone sour already.'

But Kate's milk had not gone sour. Maurice drank appreciatively then fell fast asleep. Kate kissed his forehead, wiped the tears from her eyes, blew her nose, and went slowly downstairs into what she called the drawing-room and Walter called the lounge because he thought drawing-room was pretentious, as if the great thick fabric of the curtains and settees and chairs wasn't pretentious, being the nearest thing to the Bayeux Tapestry that you could buy without leaving Solihull.

He was drinking whisky.

'Decanter in extremis,' she said.

'Is that Latin?'

'No. It's Kate. It means, "When in trouble, hit the bottle".'

He pushed the decanter towards her. She shook her head.

'You asked me if I thought Len Goldstone might be lying,' she said. 'Yes, I did. I knew you'd sacked him. I knew he'd be bitter and resentful.'

'I don't see why. I had to do it. We aren't out of the depression yet.'

'I don't see much sign of it in this room. Sorry. We don't need to debate the ethics of management now. You'll be spared all that.'

'I don't want to be spared all that, Kate. I don't want you to go. I love you.'

'You've a funny way of showing it. I need tea. I need tea desperately.'

She went into the kitchen. It was a room on a scale that could have provided a banquet for the court of Henry VIII. He followed her. He was looking a little more relaxed. He believed that she was softening. Let him believe. Let him dream.

They sat at the kitchen table, she with her tea in a Wedgwood mug, he with his whisky in a cut glass. The table was too large. Everything in the house was too large.

'Yes,' said Kate, 'I did think Len Goldstone might be lying.'

'Then why did you tell me you knew I'd been sleeping with Helen Winch?'

'To hear you say, "Darling! Of course I haven't!" But you didn't, did you? You went as white as a sheet, went down on your knees, and said, "I'm sorry."'

She saw him thinking, If only I'd bluffed it out. She hated him at that moment.

She let the silence last for quite a while. He didn't dare interrupt it. He felt, she knew, that time was on his side.

'I'll leave in the morning,' she said.

'Oh, Kate, don't be silly. Please. We can work this thing through.'

'You went from the maternity ward, to be with her!'

'I've said I'm sorry.'

'That doesn't make much difference.'

'It would never have happened if you hadn't been pregnant, Kate.'

'I can't believe that remark. It's like saying that you wouldn't have looted the shop if all the glass hadn't blown out of the windows.'

'I know it sounds awful, Kate, but the truth is I'm a highly sexed man.'

'Well, I know that, but I did think that it was me that aroused you to those heights. I didn't think a secretary from Head Office would do the same thing for you. Did *she* wrap her legs round your face in the early hours? Did your tongue stimulate *her* clitoris?'

'Kate!' He was very shocked.

'Doing it's all right but talking about it is dirty, is that it?' she asked.

'No, but . . . I don't like talking about it like that in cold blood. These things are personal.'

'I had hoped so,' she said icily, and paused to let him realise just how comprehensively he was being outmanoeuvred. 'You don't know about such things when you're a chapel girl from Wales. Arturo didn't do such things. You don't read about such things. I found it extraordinary, wonderful, because it seemed such an intimate thing to do. If I thought you'd done those things to her I'd kill you. No, I wouldn't. Let's not be silly.'

'You can't leave,' he said. He waved his arms at the magnificence of the house. 'You can't lose all this.'

'All this? Do you think I care about all this? This isn't a home. It's a statement.'

'Do you think I don't know that? Do you think I don't feel crude and ignorant in your presence?'

'I didn't want you to feel those things. I never thought you crude or ignorant. I thought you wonderful. I thought you wonderful, Walter. My wonderful, wonderful Walter. That's what you've destroyed.'

She banged her empty cup on the draining board and strode back into the drawing-room.

'All this!' she said, waving her arms scornfully. 'I never liked it. I only liked you.'

'But how will you live?'

'Splendidly. Proudly. Richly.'

'But what on?'

'That's right. Reduce it to money. Everything boils down to money in the end with you, doesn't it?'

'Yes, yes, crude materialistic, uncultured Walter, we all know that, but you have three children, you have to have money.'

'You'll offer me what I need. You aren't mean.'

'That's true.' He sounded crestfallen. 'Yes, I'll support you.'

Kate went over to the great windows and pulled back the thick curtains. She wanted to look at the night, even though there was nothing to see. She felt at one with the darkness. She wanted to wrap herself in it, and never be seen again.

'I said you'd offer me what I need,' she said. 'I didn't say I'd take it.'

'Oh, Kate. No false pride, please.'

'*False* pride? You think it *false* pride to believe that what I have given to you doesn't deserve betrayal?'

She could feel him behind her. For one awful moment she thought he was going to attempt to achieve reconciliation in sex. Then she realised that he didn't even dare touch her. When she turned to face him, he flinched.

She walked past him and sank into the larger of the two settees. It would be an exaggeration to say that he joined her on it. True, he did sit on the same settee, but it was so vast that if they'd stretched out their arms to each other, their fingers wouldn't have touched.

She realised that he was winding himself up for one last appeal. She tried to pre-empt it.

'If you sold one of the settees you could reinstate Len Goldstone,' she said.

He waved away this irritating irrelevance.

'Kate!' he implored. 'I know what I did was wrong, but . . . you've told me yourself you've been a naughty lady.'

'No, Walter,' she said. She leapt to her feet angrily and stood over him. He seemed to have shrunk and shrivelled, as if he'd been left out in the rain overnight. The last time they had been to the theatre had been to see *The Importance of Being Earnest* in Birmingham. He'd marvelled at its wit and elegance. He'd told her that she could have played the part of Lady Bracknell. Well, she would play it now. Her last performance for him would be her finest. 'No, Walter,' she said. 'I am not a naughty lady. I am a sexy lady. The two are very different. I am aware of the difference. That is my tragedy. You are not aware of the difference. That is yours.'

She strode from the room.

'I can change,' he mumbled to her wake.

'No, Walter, you will never change,' she told him scornfully.

In that, she did him a grave injustice. Once again she had proved an incompetent prophet.

But that's another story.

7 Elizabeth

A small luncheon party was held in Ward 3C of Whetstone General Hospital on Friday 15 October 1999. Present were Mrs Kate Copson (paralysed), Mrs Glenda Harrington (dying), Miss Hilda Mandrake (lonely) and Mrs Angela Critchley (mad as a hatter).

Mrs Angela Critchley, née Wilmot, had chosen ham salad (wet ham, undressed salad) followed by fruit salad (tinned). Presented with this salad spectacular, she refused to take any of it. She believed that she was in the Spa Hotel, Buxton, and she was frightened because she couldn't afford to pay.

The thoughts of Mrs Glenda Harrington, née Barker, had turned to the cottage pie (freeze-dried and sent from Cardiff), followed by the sponge pudding with custard (tinned). She was anxious to be seen to eat a hearty meal, in order to persuade Doctor Ramgobi that she was fit to return home. She found the cottage pie delicious but too rich, and could only manage five mouthfuls. She found the sponge pudding delicious, but too heavy. She could only manage two mouthfuls. She covered the remainder of the sponge pudding with the custard in order to make it look as if she had eaten more than she had.

Miss Hilda Mandrake, née Mandrake, had plumped for the parsnip bake, followed by the cheese (processed) and biscuits (stale and limp). On being presented with these delicacies, she denied having chosen them, intimating to fat Janet, née thin Janet, that parsnips gave her wind, they always had, even in her palmier days, and cheese gave her nightmares. If she had ticked these items, it was in error. She couldn't vouch for the consequences if she ate them in her present circumstances. A mixture of dreams and dyspepsia might make it a disturbed afternoon for the rest of the ward. On being told that there was no alternative, she ate just enough to keep alive, but not sufficient to suggest, she hoped, even to Doctor Ramgobi, that she was fit enough to go home. Janet removed the remains of Hilda's meal, and scoffed the lot in the office.

Kate Copson, née Thomas, had been spared the difficulty of choosing between all these mouth-watering offerings, as she was on drips and had no idea what was being fed into her.

Mrs Glenda Harrington rebuked Miss Hilda Mandrake for referring to the subject of wind. It was not a suitable subject for ladies at any time, she intimated, let alone during luncheon.

Miss Hilda Mandrake, to her eternal credit, refrained from pointing out to Mrs Glenda Harrington that she was a fine one to talk, since she broke wind regularly and noisily during the long reaches of the night.

Mrs Angela Critchley informed them that she had not thought much of the menu. The Spa Hotel had gone down and she would complain to the manager. She had booked a single room, and she had had to share it with three other women, one of whom broke wind, another of whom talked about breaking wind, while the third had given birth to a baby boy who would soon, no doubt, be breaking wind himself. It was inexplicable, unless the hotel had recently become a Moat House.

Mrs Kate Copson said nothing. She listened, made a few deductions and a few guesses, and compiled the above report in her head. It amused her, and helped her to forget the agonising break-up of her marriage to Mr Walter Copson.

At 1.25 p.m. Mrs Kate Copson finished her report and settled down to go to sleep.

When she woke up, she had no idea where she was. Somebody was holding her hand, and she didn't know who it was. She was on the point of opening her eyes, to see where she was and who it was, when the clank of a trolley in the corridor and a stirring of the ward's fetid breath reminded her that she was in hospital, reminded her not to reveal that she could understand what was going on.

Whose hand was it? She found herself thinking about what it must be like to be blind, to see only blackness every second of every moment of every day of your life, and a great thrill of thankfulness swept through her body. The unidentified owner of the hand must have felt this tremor and misunderstood it, for the hand gripped Kate's hand more tightly.

'Ah! You're awake,' said Elizabeth.

Elizabeth! Her little girl! The apple of her eye! The disappointment of her life! How she longed to open her eyes just for a moment and gaze at that beloved face, lined now but still attractive, 'pretty, but not as pretty as her mother'. Where was the harm? Did it really make sense to carry on with this enormous pretence? Yes. She hadn't the energy to relate to people any more. Have you ever tried, gentle reader, to keep your eyes closed for any length of time? It becomes more and more difficult. The feeling of pressure mounts. To open them, even if only for a second, becomes irresistible. Kate was prepared to keep her eyes closed all day. What will-power, in a lady of ninety-nine. What strength. What weakness, too. Two parts strength, one part weakness, and just a dash of whatever she was getting through her drips. The cocktail of Kate's hospital life.

'We were in Spain,' said Elizabeth. 'The phone was on the blink. We thought we'd told Nigel. Obviously we hadn't. We've grown a bit careless about things. We've come to think of you as immortal, you see.'

Kate felt a little tremor run through Elizabeth's hand as she realised that she had made a bit of a faux pas in speaking on the assumption that Kate was dying. She was grateful to Elizabeth for not continuing, not saying, 'Oh, not that you're dying, of course!', as Timothy would have. That was Elizabeth for you.

Not intelligent enough to avoid the faux pas, but intelligent enough not to make things worse by continuing. 'Bright, but not as bright as her mother.' Poor Elizabeth. You never stood a chance. Elizabeth had inherited Heinz's sandy hair, and her mother's brown eyes. Nobody knew where her comfortable chunkiness had come from.

Heinz had chosen the name. 'It's quintessentially English,' he had said. He loved England, even after what England did to him. 'Our English rose,' he'd called Elizabeth. 'Our princess.' Strictly speaking, of course, he should have said 'Our German–Welsh rose', but it wouldn't have had the same ring.

The English rose, still flowering though in need of careful pruning and watering, squeezed Kate's hand. Kate decided that the feeling was coming back to her hands. It didn't seem as though Elizabeth was on the far side of the room, as it had when Nigel had visited.

'The boys tell me that they don't think you can understand what we say,' she said. The boys! They were seventy-four, seventy-two and sixty-seven! 'But I'm not prepared to take that risk. I'd hate you to be waiting for me to say I love you, and me never to say it. So I'll say it, Mum. I love you. I love you so much. Terence sends his love too, incidentally.'

Terence was Elizabeth's second husband. He had two grown-up children. So did she. He was slightly pompous, somewhat dull, aware of it, sorry about it, but unable to do anything about it. 'Every other Terence I know gets called Terry,' he'd said once. 'I can't seem to break the Terry barrier.' 'You don't want to,' Kate had said. 'You'd be horrified to be a Terry.'

Terence had taken early retirement from his business as a designer of fitted kitchens, though he still did the occasional job for somebody rich enough to be worth giving up golf for. He was sixty-three. Elizabeth was sixty-one. And she still referred to her brothers as 'the boys'! That made Kate want to smile. Elizabeth wouldn't see anything funny in it. She hadn't much sense of humour. 'It's the German in her,' people said, and that infuriated Kate, because Heinz had had a dry, wry wit of a continental kind. He used to say things like 'I sued the travel agent last year. Well, I saw Naples and didn't die', which amused some people and left others cold.

Kate's pleasant memories of her third husband were rudely interrupted when Hilda farted loudly.

'Hilda!' said Glenda.

Again, Hilda resisted the temptation to turn on Glenda and point out that she regularly farted through the night. All she said was, 'I knew I shouldn't have had the parsnip bake.' Kate thought that Hilda would be desperate not to fall out with Glenda, because Glenda was the nearest thing to a friend that she'd got.

'You are stubborn, Mother,' said Elizabeth.

Kate understood the thought process that had led Elizabeth to say this. She had thought, Good God, after all you've lived through and achieved, surely you needn't be stuck here in this fetid ward with these windy women when you could have gone private, if it hadn't been for those damned principles of yours, which are stupid anyway, because you'd help the NHS more by paying than by using up their resources.

I got my principles from my father, replied Kate silently to what Elizabeth hadn't said, even though my life has been so different from his and if he knew the half of what I've got up to he'd be turning in his grave, so I can't do anything about my principles, thank you very much.

A wave of love for her father consumed Kate. Elizabeth's strong golfing hand clasped her frail one more tightly, too tightly.

'Oh, am I hurting?' said Elizabeth, loosening her grip.

Elizabeth remained silent for a while after that. Kate wished that she'd go, so that she could begin to think about her time with Heinz.

Kate drifted in and out of sleep after that, and backwards and forwards in time. She recalled, with pleasure and amazement, the intensity and variety of her lovemaking with Walter. It was odd that she could remember so little about her second wedding day. It had been such a quiet wedding that there shouldn't have been much to forget. She remembered that she'd refused to wear white, on the grounds that she wasn't a virgin because she'd been married before. She hadn't told anyone that she'd been going to bed with Walter regularly for more than three months.

Poor Elizabeth, sitting there utterly unaware of what her mother was thinking. Kate found herself in 1994, an old woman refusing to behave as she should, irritated that Elizabeth was going on a golfing honeymoon, saying, at Elizabeth's second wedding, 'Don't you want to see the Andean altiplano, the Welsh community in Patagonia, the Spice Islands, the Great Barrier Reef, San Francisco, Seville, Siena, Istanbul and Trebizond? Don't you want to see the Sacred Valley of the Incas and the Temple of Karnak at Luxor and Mount Olympus? Don't you want to see the Blue Danube, the Black Sea and the Rose-Red City of Petra? Don't you long to stand where Socrates stood?' and Elizabeth had shrugged and said, 'Well, you know how it is. Terence loves his golf and I go along with it.' 'Is that what it'll say on your gravestone?' Kate had retorted. 'Here lies Elizabeth Simpson. She went along with it'? Elizabeth had said, in that irritating way she had of missing the main point, 'I'm not going to be buried. I'm going to be cremated. I've given instructions.' People had said, 'Elizabeth's very nice, but she has no imagination. It's the German in her coming out.' This had angered Kate even more than the attribution to Heinz of the responsibility for her lack of humour. No imagination! Heinz had had the imagination to see what was going to happen in Hitler's Germany long before it happened. He had had the imagination to see into children's minds and create wonderful toys for them. He'd said, of Elizabeth, 'So, my princess doesn't want a throne. She prefers a typewriter.'

At last, at long last, Elizabeth left. Kate was ready now, for a rerun of her life with Heinz.

But first she had to endure a visit from Doctor Hallam. She had been surprised to discover, from a remark of one of the nurses, that she was 'under Doctor Hallam'. She had assumed that, if she was under anybody, she was under Doctor Ramgobi. The phrase struck her as absurd, anyway. The days of being under men were long gone.

'This is Kate Copson, Doctor Hallam,' said Helen.

'Ah. Yes,' said a rather posh, supercilious, youthful voice. 'Yes. Stroke? Yes? Severe? Yes? OK.'

Kate had thought thin Helen pretty good at answering her own questions. She was a novice compared to Doctor Hallam.

'Temperature? Nearly normal. OK. Blood pressure? No problem. Good. Good. Much activity? Almost none, right. Any sign of *mental* activity?'

Doctor Hallam paused for a reply, to Kate's surprise and, evidently, to the surprise of Helen, who suddenly realised that she was expected to speak, and said, 'Not really, doctor, but . . .'

'OK. Looks a pretty classical cerebral infarction. Dysphonia, probably dysphasia too. Any problems?'

'Not really, doctor.'

'OK. Good. Fine. Now what have we got being fed into her? Let's have a little looksie here. M'm. M'm. Right. Right. OK.' He paused, presumably to think. 'OK. Right. Erm . . . well, I think old Ramgobi's got this one about right. No change needed. Good.'

Doctor Hallam moved on, and Kate thought, If my condition is what you think of as OK, good and fine, I'd hate to be your mother.

It was still not quite time for Kate to have an uninterrupted life with Heinz. First, after Doctor Hallam's flying visit, she had to be settled down for the night by thin Helen with the eating disorder. This involved, gentle reader, humiliations that were not entertaining for Kate, or indeed for Helen, and would not be entertaining for you. These humiliations were frequent and prolonged, night and morning. They were terrible for Kate. Realism is all very well, up to a certain point, but I think, after the life that she has led, this lady deserves better than to have these dreadful processes spelt out to the world.

'Have a good night, Kate dear. Sleep well for me,' said thin Helen, and, to Kate's astonishment, she kissed her on the forehead. Kate's defences weren't ready, and she almost cried.

Kate wanted to say two things to Helen. She wanted to say, 'Helen, sweet dear Helen. Eat. Please, please eat, for me,' and she wanted to say, 'I will have a good night, don't you worry. I'm going to spend it with Heinz. Dear, kind, imaginative Heinz, whom I wronged so dreadfully.'

8 Heinz

Dear Dilys,

Here's a bit of news to brighten up the cold winter days. I've met a new man, and I think I'm in love. My new man is a gentleman, and a gentle man (I've learnt that the two are not always the same). By profession he's a designer of toys, and he loves children. He's so good with the boys, it's a pleasure to see him with them. He's courteous and well-mannered and kind, so in many ways he's the ideal catch. There is a snag, though. Heinz is German.

Does that sound awful? I don't mean that I'm prejudiced against foreigners. But it does mean that he's struggling to make a living here. Aren't we all? (Walter sends me a cheque every month. Every month I tear it up. Some people think this is very unfair on the children, but it cannot be otherwise. I will not take money from the man. Secretarial work is not so awful, and I make enough for us to survive, since dear Olga looks after the children when I'm out and will take no money for it.) Also, with the threat of war hanging over Europe we have to expect to face prejudices and I'm not sure how strong I am any more. And how will I tell Mother and Father? I know that neither of them would say anything. Father's too good a man to rebuke me for loving a foreigner. Mother loves me so much, she loves us all – yes, you also, Dil, despite 'the event' – that she would never criticise me. But they'll see complications ahead and it'll worry them. They'll think, 'Why can't things ever be simple, for Kate?' and, yes, I suppose I sometimes think that too.

You're the one we should envy, Dilys. You have your formidably wonderful John, your rock, and your two lovely children, one of each, somehow typical of the magnificent simplicity of your life. And with you, of course, as with everything else in my life, there's the fly in the ointment. Horrid fly. Nasty, smelly ointment. I'm referring, of course, to your being so far away. I can never afford to visit Canada now. Is there no hope of your visiting Europe?

I realise that I haven't told you how I met Heinz. It's very simple. He lives in a bedsitter opposite us. I met him at the baker's.

Why should a German toy designer be living in a mean street in West Hampstead? Because, dear Dilys, he's that great rarity, a man of principle. He walked out on his job with the Nordrheinmechanischemetalwerkenspielwarengesellschaft on principle because they're introducing Nazi toys to corrupt the minds of little children. He also fled the country because he's convinced that the fight is lost there and the peril can only be countered from outside. Having decided, he worries about it no more. He is a very logical man, yet if that suggests that he's dull and humourless, nothing could be further from the truth. His eyes are a light and piercing blue, which could be as cold as an Arctic dawn, but they are warmed by a sparkle of humour that is not like anything we usually describe as Teutonic.

I hope John and the children are well and that Gladstone has recovered from his worms. I still can't get over your naming a poodle after a Prime Minister!

Dear Dilys, I miss you so. Write at length, and soon – please.

With more love than I can say.

Kate

One morning in March that year, Heinz met Walter for the first time. Walter was collecting Maurice, and arrived almost at the same moment as Heinz, who had called to ask Kate to go to a concert that evening. Kate offered them coffee, and the two men eyed each other cautiously from their battered old leather armchairs. What a contrast they made. Both men were tall, but there the resemblance ended. Walter was thickset, powerful, clumsy, his hair still jet black and a dark growth on his chin and cheeks even when he had just shaved. Heinz was slim, slight, neat, with sandy hair, a shy moustache and a small, immaculately trimmed goatee beard. Outside, beyond the shabby French windows, the children were playing with Ruth, Barbara and Reuben in the shared garden.

'Why don't I treat you two young lovers to dinner?' asked Walter. 'You are lovers, aren't you?'

Neither Kate nor Heinz replied to his second question, but Kate replied to the first.

'Thank you, Walter, it's kind of you, but I'd rather not,' she said.

'Pride, Heinz,' said Walter. 'She has too much pride.'

'I think so,' said Heinz quietly, looking at Kate searchingly.

'Oh, you think so, do you, Heinz?' said Kate.

'Yes, I think so, Kate,' said Heinz.

'The standard of the repartee's gone down since my day,' said Walter.

'I know that you send Kate a cheque every month, Walter,' said Heinz. 'M'm, good coffee, Kate. I know that she tears them up. I admire her for this, as for much else. I think that to refuse the offer of a meal is perhaps to turn pride into churlishness.'

'You speak excellent English, Heinz,' commented Walter.

'Oh, do you think so?' said Heinz, pleased. 'Thank you. I think it is quite correct if a trifle stilted due to lack of familiarity with the vernacular.'

'I know why Kate is so anxious not to accept help from me,

Heinz,' said Walter. 'Yes, Kate, this coffee is good.'

'Why is Kate so anxious not to accept help from you?' asked Heinz.

'Because she still has strong feelings for me,' said Walter.

'Is that so?' asked Heinz.

'Yes, Heinz, it is so,' said Walter.

'The standard of the repartee's gone down since your day,' said Kate, and then she sighed. 'All right, Walter. I don't wish to be churlish. I accept your offer of dinner.'

'Splendid,' said Walter. 'What time shall we say? Eight o'clock?'

'That should be all right,' said Kate. 'The children will go upstairs to Daniel and Olga's and sleep on the floor. They like that. They think they're camping.'

When Kate went up to the first-floor flat, she saw Olga alone. Daniel was painting in his little studio at the back. Olga was even paler than in the Tregarryn days, so that, with her round face and long nose, she looked like a Jewish barn owl. The Begelmans' living-room was very bare, as if they were flaunting their poverty. The only richness was on the walls, which were like a museum of Daniel's paintings. Kate became more and more certain of their high quality every time she saw them.

Olga readily agreed that the children should stay the night, then she hesitated for just a moment.

'What is it, Olga?' prompted Kate.

'I don't know if I can ask this. Well, I can ask, I suppose. It's Daniel.' Kate had known that it would be. She had realised, over the years, that gentle, frail Olga would fight like a ferret for Daniel. 'He's so depressed. So . . . convoluted. So . . . knotted up in himself. A night out with the boys would do him so much good.'

'It isn't actually a night out with the boys, Olga. I'll be there.'

'Yes, I know, but . . . don't take this the wrong way, Kate, but, beautiful though you are, feminine though you are, to me you are one of the boys.'

'Is there a *right* way to take that?'

'Oh yes. I mean that you are always game for some fun.'

'It's not easy to ask, Olga. Walter, whom I'm divorcing, is paying.'

'We can pay. We're not quite on the breadline yet. But Daniel is so isolated here, Kate. He's stranded here in West Hampstead.'

'In your own words,' said Kate, ' "I can ask, I suppose." '

Kate didn't want to ask Walter, she didn't want any more favours from him, but it would be good to have Daniel with them, and so, when Walter brought Maurice back from the zoo, she did ask.

'I've arranged about the children,' she said, 'and that's all fine, but . . . you know who Daniel Begelman is? The Jewish painter who was with us at Tregarryn. He's a very nice man, he's a very good painter, he can't sell his work, he's pretty depressed, he'd be so grateful, so, I wondered, could we invite him along?'

'He sounds riveting company.'

'Well, no, that he isn't. But he'd enjoy it, and I don't think Olga'd mind too much.' Her instinct was that Walter would be less likely to agree if he knew that Daniel's wife had made the request.

'Why can't he sell his work if he's good?'

'Too unfashionable to sell to galleries. Too uncomfortable to hang in private homes. There are no roses and honeysuckles on the cottage wall of his art.'

'Is that a crack at my lowly tastes?'

'Yes. Did Maurice enjoy the zoo?'

'No. He wanted to free all the animals.'

'The darling! Can we invite Daniel, then?'

'Did you ever fancy him?'

Kate's instinct told her to be honest.

'Yes.'

'Did he fancy you?'

'Yes.'

'Do you still fancy him?'

'Yes.'

'Does he still fancy you?'

'Yes.'

'Well, you should definitely ask him. A friend of your first husband, whom you still fancy, your second husband, whom you still fancy, and the man who will in all probability soon be your third husband, and all of them lusting after you like mad. It should be quite an evening in the old Bandalero tonight.'

Walter came in a taxi, to pick them up. 'The rich man entertains the paupers in style,' he announced.

On the way to the Bandalero, the cab was held up in traffic. This gave them the opportunity of studying two large sculptures, one of God and the other of Mammon, which stood above the flamboyant pillared porch of a particularly megalomanic bank. They stared at the statues in silence for a moment.

'Impressive,' said Walter.

'Or perhaps merely eager to impress,' said Daniel.

'I hesitate to mention it in front of a lady,' said Heinz, 'but the private parts are curiously clumsy.'

'Oh no!' said Kate.

'Oh yes!' said Daniel. 'Yes, they're Wainwrights.'

They drank their aperitifs at a corner table in the crowded bar. Fashionable London swirled around them, many of the men in evening dress, and the influence of Schiaparelli prominent in the heavily padded shoulders and great bulbous sleeves of many of the women.

'Poor dears,' said Kate, 'they think they're so chic, and they look as if they're getting ready for baseball or for war.'

'The latter is, sadly, the more likely,' said Heinz.

'I only mock the fashions because I can't afford them,' admitted Kate cheerfully.

148

Kate and Heinz drank dry Martinis, Walter and Daniel had whiskies. They talked at first about Tregarryn and its inmates.

'Stanley used to spout about the purity of art,' said Kate. 'Now he's prepared to take commissions from banks.'

'He only adopted such an idealistic pose because he wasn't sure if he was marketable,' said Daniel.

'Well, you've never sold out,' said Kate.

'I've never sold anything. I can afford to be idealistic. I can't afford anything else.'

'I don't really believe that,' said Kate. 'I believe you're a man of principle.'

Her eyes held Daniel's for just a moment, and a faint flush came to his pale cheeks. Walter gave a little grin, but his eyes didn't smile. There was a faint flush on Heinz's cheeks too.

'What about the woman?' Walter asked. 'What was her name? Daphne? What became of her?'

'Can't paint her stuff quickly enough,' said Kate. 'Sold out in a different sense.'

'Daphne is so pleased by her painting that she paints the same one over and over again,' said Daniel. 'The galleries know what they're getting – a ready sale. The public know what they're getting – a charming, undemanding picture. Daphne knows what she's getting – a good living.'

'Are you bitter?' asked Walter bluntly.

'Not with her. I never resent other artists' successes. I only resent my failure.'

'I wonder if the people who snap up her stuff realise she's a lesbian,' said Kate.

'I wouldn't call her a lesbian,' said Daniel. 'I'd call her a bisexual.'

'Well, I know she had a bit of a fling with Arturo before I met him.'

'There was a bit more than that,' said Daniel.

'She had a fling with him after I met him? After I married him?'

'That wasn't what I meant.'

Daniel looked uncomfortable. So did Heinz. Walter seemed to be enjoying himself.

'Did she go to bed with Arturo after I'd married him, Daniel? I want to know.'

'Well, if you must know, yes. Once or twice. When you were shopping, usually.'

'No wonder nobody would come shopping with me. That riles me almost as much as the sex.'

'Sorry.'

'No. I'm glad you've told me. It releases a bit more of my guilt. But if you didn't mean that, what did you mean?'

'When Olga's parents were ill, and she had to go away, Daphne came to my bed more than once.'

Kate's heart began to pound. Heinz was giving her a very concentrated, quizzical look. The question had to be asked. She just hoped her voice wouldn't sound strained.

'What happened when Daphne came to your bed?'

'Oh, I threw her out, of course.' Daniel tried to make his smile insouciant. He couldn't. He'd never been insouciant in his life.

Kate went weak at the knees. She began to shake with relief. She wished Heinz wasn't staring at her. He seemed to realise that he was being less than his usual courteous self, and tried to smile. The smile didn't work. There was great tension round the table.

Daniel's eyes met Kate's and she knew that he was wondering just how much she wanted him. He had no idea that she was in the process of rejecting the possibility of an affair with him. She had been amazed at the extent of her relief when she'd discovered that he hadn't been unfaithful to Olga with Daphne. She would have liked herself more if the relief had been because of her feelings for Olga, but she had to admit that she'd never liked Olga very much. She had realised in a flash that her desire for Daniel, a desire considerably greater than she had ever admitted to herself, was inextricably bound up with her admiration of him. If she tried to make him unfaithful to Olga, and failed, she would be disappointed. But if she tried to make him unfaithful, and succeeded, she would be devastated. She began to feel much calmer, almost happy. She began to think that now she would be free to like Olga more.

She gave Heinz a really affectionate smile. He opened his eyes wide as if to say that he hadn't a clue what was going on, then he smiled rather uncertainly.

'Tell them about your travels, Daniel. It makes a good story,' she said.

'Does it? Oh.' Daniel accepted, wryly, that he had been relegated, for reasons he probably didn't yet understand, from potential lover to comic turn. Well, never mind. He would oblige. He was an obliging sort of chap. 'Well, in Tregarryn I found it all, ultimately, pointless. I went to Russia. I felt it was the obvious thing for an idealistic communist to do. It turned out to be the worst thing for an idealistic communist to do, especially a Jewish one. I decided that I needed to be a Jew first and a painter second. I went to Palestine. But in Palestine my work became dull and didactic. It became political and vulgar. I returned to Europe.'

'And when Daniel says "I",' interrupted Kate, 'he means his entourage. The ever-loyal Olga, and Ruth, Barbara and Reuben, whose education has been unconventional, to say the least.'

'Quite so,' said Daniel. 'We went to Greece. Olga taught the children, I painted. I painted the classical landscapes in modern style. No longer didactic. So little didactic that they became meaningless.'

'You thought they were,' said Kate. 'They aren't.'

'I decided to abandon painting as thoroughly as I'd abandoned Judaism. I sought the physical life. You don't see me as a man of the soil? I'm sorry. Anyway it wasn't the soil. We went to Lincolnshire. After the Peloponnese, Grimsby.'

He paused, for dramatic effect. Kate, who knew the story, waited, wondering which of the two men would need to say 'Grimsby?' first.

It was Walter, of course. Heinz had never heard of Grimsby and couldn't realise its strangeness in that context.

'Grimsby?' asked Walter.

'Grimsby. I decided to become a fisherman.'

'Good Lord. And how did you like being a fisherman?'

'Oh, I never became one. I looked at the sea, and it was too rough.'

He laughed his surprising, high-pitched laugh. His laugh was irresistible, and they all laughed. Stimulated by the strength of their drinks, and excited by the sexual tension and the subsequent release from it, and roused by the glamour of the occasion, and picturing pale Daniel staring at the waves in horror, they got the giggles. Tears streamed down their eyes. Once they'd started, they couldn't stop. Bertrand, the supercilious Parisian maître d', approached them with the air of a man investigating a problem with the drains.

'Your table is ready,' he said in such strangulated vowels that he set them off into fits once more.

Bertrand led them across the great art deco restaurant, which looked like a cross between an Odeon cinema and the restaurant of a great ocean liner. Heads turned to look at the strange group – a beautiful lady in her mid-thirties, wearing an excessively plain dress; a tall, ungainly man in evening dress with riotous black hair; a very erect, precise man in an expensive but old-fashioned suit; and a funny little Jewish figure in a smock and wearing a flat cap, his secular yarmulke, and all of them giggling uncontrollably. Bertrand looked fixedly ahead, as if disassociating himself from them, and led them to the worst table in the room, right by the door to the kitchens, and, to his fury, none of them minded a bit.

The laughter soon ended after they'd sat down, and they

settled to the serious business of eating. The food at the Bandalero, if hardly innovative, was classical and delicious. Kate's galantine of chicken *en chaud-froid* was exquisite, Walter's pheasant pâté was coarse and full of flavour, Daniel fell upon his smoked salmon roulade with the air of a man who expects to be banished to the wilderness before breakfast, and Heinz ate his *jambon persillé* with an intensity of concentration that made him seem oblivious to the rest of the world. Lying in hospital, sixty-three years later, being fed intravenously, Kate could still salivate at the memory of the galantine.

Their hunger somewhat assuaged, they began to talk seriously during the fish course. Daniel recalled overhearing someone saying, at an exhibition, 'That little Jew-boy's pictures are quite striking,' and being chilled to the marrow. 'I would rather be described as a little shit,' he said.

'Daphne referred to you as a little shit on my wedding day,' said Kate.

Walter frowned.

'I should have said "On my first wedding day",' amended Kate hastily. 'Don't look like that, Walter. I haven't forgotten ours.'

'Did she?' said Daniel. 'Well, there you are, you see. Not upsetting in the least.'

Heinz put down his knife and fork, and said, 'Let me tell you why I left the Nordrheinmechanischemetalwerkenspielwaren-gesellschaft. It was because of the toys that were planned. One of them was a clockwork Nazi which goose-steps across the carpet and salutes. They were attempting to get it to say "Heil Hitler", but they had trouble with the technology. When I left it was still saying "Shit heiler". The other is a little Jewish corner shop. It comes with a little window and a little hammer and the child can smash the window with the hammer. The window is immediately replaced, a new window pops up and, lo and behold, the happy child can smash the window again. Fifty times he can experience this joy, and even then the little chap won't need to worry, his proud father will buy him refills. That is how it is now, Kate, in the land of *my* fathers.'

He gave them all a faint smile that had no humour in it, and resumed his slow, careful, precise exploration of his sole *Véronique*. Kate reached across and touched his arm.

Daniel gave a crooked little smile that had only sadness in it – it seemed an evening for strange smiles – and said, 'So maybe I have to become a Jewish painter again. Can art stand by?'

'Sometimes art has to stand by,' said Kate. 'It's too important to be sucked into the maelstrom. Mothers have to remain mothers, children children, artists artists. We cannot allow politics to destroy our innocence. Ideals have to be preserved. They'll be needed when the nightmare's over.'

The great room throbbed and buzzed with laughter and vitality. Only at the table by the entrance to the kitchens, it seemed, was there concern for the state of the world.

Kate looked across at Walter and wondered. He was being uncharacteristically quiet. Perhaps he felt out of his depth. He had never been comfortable with abstract ideas. But it wasn't like him to be so silent. In the old days he would have barged in and changed the subject to something that interested him. Perhaps he really was a changed man, as he claimed.

Shortly after the arrival of their main course, Walter looked up from his entrecôte *marchand du vin*, and asked, 'Have you approached English toy firms, Heinz?'

'Oh yes,' said Heinz. 'I have put out what I think you might call – excuse my poor English – exploratory feelers. It's not easy, though. I am not yet *au fait* with the tastes of English children.' He smiled at Kate. 'Sorry, Kate. British children. And these firms have their own men. Good men. Why should they employ an alien?'

It was the first time Kate had heard Heinz described as an alien. It wouldn't be the last.

'Would you say you have engineering skills?' persisted Walter.

Heinz examined the remark as if it was one of Daniel's paintings. He thought as he ate, with care and thoroughness, as if his mother had made him chew every suggestion thirty-two times before swallowing it.

'I would say I have quite considerable skills,' he said at last. 'My toys are very precise. Some of them are very small. Many of them are extremely . . . er . . . oh, my poor stumbling English . . . intricate. Yes, I think I can say I am a thoroughly accomplished precision engineer.'

'And you are a skilled draughtsman?'

'Of course.' There was no suggestion in Heinz's tone that this was a boast. It was a statement of fact. 'I am an inventor and a draughtsman. I do not make the things, I design them.'

'Very precise draughtsmanship and very precise physics are what I'm going to need in the years to come,' said Walter. 'How would you like to come and work for me?'

'I don't want charity through the back door,' said Kate. The moment she had said it, she realised how stupid she had been. It mortified her still, in her hospital bed, to recall how stupid she had been. She had blushed. Thirty-six years old, and still blushing.

Walter was merciless. 'What on earth's it got to do with you?' he asked, in mock astonishment. 'I'm offering Heinz a job, not you. Oh! I see! You think you're going to marry him! Well well! Well, if you do, I hope you'll be very happy.' He smiled, adding his tenpenn'orth to the night of the strange smiles, for this was a smile conceived in pain and delivered in anger. Kate was shocked at the depth of his emotion.

'Your remark does not please me either, Kate, I am sorry to say,' said Heinz, picking his words out in that careful, precise way of his, like the prancing steps of a horse in dressage. 'I am not happy to hear the offer of a job described as charity. I hope it does not sound immodest to suggest that I just might be of more value to Walter than the money he proposes to pay me. That is, after all, the principle on which businessmen offer jobs.'

'I wish I hadn't spoken,' said Kate. 'I wish all of you and all these diners and tables and waiters and chandeliers and all the dreadful magnificence of this place would disappear and leave me to my shame.'

Daniel reached across and touched Kate's arm.

'Please, Daniel,' said Heinz. 'My turn!' He turned to Kate and offered yet another variant to this night of smiles – a smile of shy love. 'Please don't feel shame, my darling. Only my innate shyness, my clumsiness with the English language and my inability to support you and your family has prevented me from asking you for your hand.' A waiter approached. 'Go away!' Heinz told him. 'Learn to intrude at suitable moments only.' The waiter departed hurriedly. 'Well, Kate, in broaching the subject at all I have conquered my shyness, and my clumsy English may perchance help to emphasise the depth of my feelings.' He turned to Walter. 'Walter, do you still want to remove a major obstacle to my marrying Kate?'

'That's irrelevant,' said Walter. 'We mustn't overestimate Kate's importance in this. I have a job, a most important job, for which I think you may be admirably suited. God, I'm catching your impeccable English. I sound so bloody formal.'

The waiter hovered again.

'Oh, come on,' said Daniel. 'Let the poor fellow clear away.'

They remained silent while the waiter cleared the plates, and then there were desserts to choose. They chose them out of habit rather than hunger. You are in a restaurant, you don't dare not to order a dessert, so you eat a dessert you don't want. And all the while, as they chose their desserts, Kate look at Heinz, and he at her, and they exchanged smiles that were rather timid but had a touch of glory in them.

When at last the waiter had gone, Walter said, 'Mind you, it'll be a bonus if Kate starts to think well of me again. I love her so much, you see, that, now that I've accepted that I can never have her love again, I need to win her admiration.'

'You have it, Walter dear,' she said. 'I think perhaps we can be friends again.'

Daniel turned to Heinz and said, in a low voice, 'I think in all the excitement you may actually have forgotten to pop the question. The lady wishes to say "yes". Give her something to say "yes" to.'

'Will you marry me, Kate?' asked Heinz.

'Yes, please,' said Kate.

'Thank you, Daniel,' said Heinz.

'My pleasure,' said Daniel. 'It frees me from a dangerous fantasy.'

Happiness fluttered over their table, as frail and as fleeting as a butterfly.

Then Heinz said, 'You haven't told me what this job entails, Walter.'

'I haven't, have I?' said Walter. 'I'll be converting all my factories to make weapons of war against Germany. The demands of the armed forces will be very precise indeed. It will entail a lot of work, and no glory.'

The arrival of the desserts at that moment seemed tactless, but they wouldn't have helped the cause of peace by refusing to eat their peach melba or pear *belle Hélène*, so they tucked in.

The cadaverous Bertrand approached the table with the air of a man spreading a dust-sheet over the victims of a traffic accident.

'Is everything all right?' he asked, in a tone that indicated that his real meaning was, 'Have your English palates proved adequate for the formidable task of appreciating our delicious and subtle French food?'

'No, everything is bloody well not all right,' said Walter.

Bertrand reeled. He went pale. 'I'm so sorry, sir,' he said.

'What is the problem, sir?'

'We're rushing headlong towards another disastrous world war, that's the bloody problem,' said Walter.

The maître d' sighed. His sigh might have been a sigh of sadness for the destructive folly of man, but to Kate it sounded like a sigh of relief, as of a man saying, 'Oh, is that all?'

Sometimes, as she sailed through the stormy reaches of her life, Kate forgot that she was an old woman in a hospital ward, so that it would come as a great shock when Janet said, 'Well, and how are we this morning?' or Helen said, 'Good morning, Kate. How have you slept? Like a log. Good, that's marvellous news.' That night, her fifth in hospital, she remained conscious of her surroundings but seemed to float above them, in air kissed by the sweet breath of Wales. It was strange to look down on herself, in bed, while walking with Heinz on the gorse-clad cliffs of Pennard, listening to the wailing chorus of the gulls while also hearing mad Mrs Critchley crying out 'Rodney! Rodney!' which was a new one. It occurred to Kate that maybe she was dying, maybe she wouldn't live long enough to find the murderer of her fifth husband (or her fourth, or not a husband at all, according to . . . well, we've been through that).

She was tempted to speed up her journey through her past. Couldn't do that! It wouldn't be fair on Heinz, or indeed on herself. She needed these memories. They had been difficult years at the time, her years with Heinz, lived out as they were under the shadow of war. Now, in retrospect, they were lived out under another shadow as well, the shadow of guilt.

She couldn't hurry through his first meeting with the family, and the inevitable warning about Dilys that had preceded it. She squirmed, up there above her bed, as she watched herself travelling with Heinz on the three o'clock from Paddington. Walter had the boys for the weekend. They liked being with Walter. He was kind and he was rich and he behaved towards them as if they were little adults.

She'd delayed telling Heinz about Dilys until the train emerged from the Severn tunnel and they were in Wales. It was, after all, a Welsh story.

'There's something I have to tell you, Heinz,' she said, as they steamed towards Newport between the hills and the dunes.

'Oh?'

'I have an identical twin sister.'

'Good Lord! And you never mentioned her!'

'No, well, it's a painful subject. I miss her so much.'

'Is she . . . dead?'

Heinz gripped her hand firmly, but tenderly. The two ladies in the compartment were riveted.

'No. She's in Canada. Happy with a nice husband I've never met and two lovely children I've never seen.'

The train began to slow. The slate roofs of Newport were beginning to dry after the rain. A watery sun shone fitfully.

'Why no mention of her before, Kate? It isn't like you. We have no secrets.'

'Don't be cross, Heinz. It's difficult.'

The two women began to gather together their shopping bags. The one with the Swan and Edgar bags cast a baleful look at Kate, as if rebuking her for not starting her story earlier. The one whose bags all had Welsh names – John Lewis, Peter Jones, D. H. Evans – hesitated at the door of the compartment, as if contemplating staying on till Cardiff to hear the end of the story. But she didn't.

Nobody got in the compartment, but Kate didn't resume the story until the train was moving again. She needed the protection of the monotonous clatter of the wheels.

As the train slid out of the station they passed a herd of men, all writing down the number of the Castle Class engine that was pulling the train.

'Train spotters,' she said apologetically.

'We have them in Germany too. You were saying it was difficult about Dilys.'

'Yes. My family don't speak about her. I must ask you never to mention her name.'

'Kate! What happened?'

'An incident. I call it "the event". I can't speak of it.'

A train rushed past them in the opposite direction, rocking their carriage. When it had gone, Heinz spoke very quietly. 'You must tell me, Kate. What happened?'

Kate didn't reply.

'If you don't tell me, I'll ask Walter.'

'Walter doesn't know. I never told him. I never told Arturo either.'

'They didn't mind? They didn't need to know?'

'Arturo was wrapped up in himself. He wasn't interested. Walter respected my wishes.' Heinz raised his eyebrows. 'Yes, Heinz. He could be very considerate over small matters.'

'I hope I can be very considerate too, but this is not a small matter, Kate. To have a secret, on a matter of such importance, is not, I think . . . how would you say? My English is so bad . . . a propitious start.'

So, as the train snaked into the suburbs of Cardiff, Kate told the tale that she had never before told anybody.

'She crept out of the house at midnight one Saturday night, for a night of love with a boy. She was sixteen. My father found out. He called her wicked and banished her from the house. She was sent to a fierce aunt in mid-Wales. She ran away to London. She might have met anyone. She met a nice plumber called John, and married him. They live in Vancouver.'

'We'll go to Canada, to see them.'

'I hope so, one day.'

'I shall insist. I shall take you there.'

'Thank you.'

She squeezed his hand, but she didn't meet his eyes.

'This is the posh end,' she said, as the taxi purred up the long hill of Walter Road. 'People have grapes in the house here when nobody's ill.'

Her attempt at idle chatter didn't fool Heinz. He knew how nervous she was. He wasn't sure which was the greater of her anxieties, that her family wouldn't like him, or that he wouldn't like them. She need have no anxiety on the latter score. She had talked about her family with such affection that he liked them before he had met them. She'd told him that Bernard would make challenging statements and tack 'I beg your pardon?' on to the end. She'd told him that Enid would remind them about someone who married a German and fell into a vat of moselle wine and drowned. She'd told him that little orphan Annie, who so resented the existence of that other, more famous little orphan Annie, would tell him how fortunate she was to be a part of such a family. She'd told him that John Thomas Thomas would weigh him up gravely, and address him as Heinz Wasserhof if he liked him. She'd told him that Bronwen would adore him if Kate looked happy. She'd told him that Oliver would be very, very charming.

And that was what Heinz would be too. As the taxi turned left into Eaton Crescent, he prepared himself for being very, very charming indeed.

Kate couldn't help feeling a little awkward, bringing home a third fiancé, when Enid, Annie and Bernard hadn't managed one between them, and Oliver had been so unlucky in love. It didn't occur to her that it hadn't exactly been a bed of roses for her – one hanging and one divorce for adultery – but she knew that maturity and laugh lines had only added to the beauty of her warm, liquid, sensual face, and she felt extremely fortunate in life and love that night.

To her relief, they didn't take Heinz into the front room, with its smell of disuse, but straight into the cheery dining-cum-sitting-room with the French windows. A large reproduction of one of Cézanne's many paintings of Mont Sainte-Victoire now hung over the dining table. There were herrings wrapped in laverbread for tea, and as much bread and butter as you could want, and Welsh cakes and bara brith.

It was much as Kate had promised, and she could have cried for joy.

Bernard said, 'There isn't going to be a war, Heinz, Hitler isn't such a fool, I beg your pardon?' Kate avoided Heinz's eye for fear that she would giggle.

Enid was worried about Heinz going to work for Walter. 'You be careful with those machines,' she told him. 'A cousin twice removed from Llandovery worked as a compositor on the *South Wales Echo* and fell into the presses and was printed to death.' Kate had to make absolutely certain not to look into Heinz's eyes then, and she also had to resist the temptation to add, 'Thereby becoming, at a stroke, a cousin three times removed.'

Annie went even redder than her normal coarse colour before saying, bravely, 'A friend of mine who has visited Germany tells me it's very heavily wooded.'

'Well, yes, some parts are,' said Heinz. 'You haven't been?'

'Oh, no!' Annie seemed shocked at the suggestion of anything so exotic. 'I've never been abroad. Oh, not that I'm complaining. I've nothing to complain about. I'm so fortunate to be a part of this kind, loving family. I never forget it.'

No, nor do we, thought Kate, but of course she didn't say it, nor did she meet Heinz's eyes.

'Do people ever suggest that in leaving Germany you're running away?' asked Oliver, to Kate's astonishment, because it was so unlike him to put anyone on the spot like that, it was more typical of Bernard. She wondered if Oliver had been soured by his tragedy.

Heinz paused, partly to measure his words, in that way he had, and partly to empty his mouth of bara brith.

'I would have stayed to help stop Hitler, had I believed him stoppable,' he said.

'What you have done is the right thing, Heinz Wasserhof,' said John Thomas Thomas. 'You don't fight a volcano by standing in the crater.'

A lump came to Kate's throat, and she almost burst into tears. Her father liked him. She looked across at her mother, who gave her a very quick smile and looked away hurriedly, so she knew that her mother was on the point of tears as well.

Later that evening, they sat round the fire, with John Thomas Thomas buried in a book of Welsh essays, and Enid doing her marking, and Annie knitting with her legs akimbo and a ladder on the inside of her left stocking, revealing a stretch of pink thigh for all the world to see, should any of the world want to see it, which none of the world did, and Kate could see that Oliver was wondering whether to warn Annie about the ladder, and Bernard was quizzing Heinz about Hitler.

'So, what is he, Heinz, this Hitler? Is he a Fascist? It seems to me that he draws his ideas from the Left as much as from the Right, I beg your pardon?'

'No, I agree,' said Heinz. 'He needs supporters from the Left as well as the Right, so he needs ideas from the Left and Right. He is an opportunist as well as a fanatic, and all the more dangerous because he genuinely believes in at least half of what he preaches. If he succeeds, the hands of the Left as well as the Right will be stained with blood.'

Bernard started on another question, but Bronwen said, 'Leave the poor man alone, Bernard. He's had a long journey.'

'It's all right, Mrs Thomas, I'm not tired,' Heinz said, but, to Kate's regret, the discussion of political ideas was over almost before it had begun, as was so often the case in Britain, where to care about political issues seemed to be a social embarrassment.

'Please call me Bronwen, Heinz,' said Bronwen.

'Mother!' said Enid. 'I nearly forgot. I saw Mrs Humpries in

the Uplands this afternoon. Her mother has a lump in her left
. . . *bron*.'

'You don't need to say it in Welsh,' said Kate. 'They have
breasts in Germany too, and Heinz is thirty-seven.'

'I'm sorry,' said Enid, 'but there are words I don't like using
in front of strangers.'

'Heinz isn't a stranger,' said Bronwen. 'He's part of the family
already.'

John Thomas Thomas looked up from his book and began to
smile, then remembered that he wasn't supposed to be listening,
it was assumed that he was far away in his essays, so he gave a
little, half-guilty, rather boyish smile and went back to his book.
But the conversation became a little more circumspect after that,
because everyone knew that he was listening.

As the long hospital night dragged on, Kate drifted between
sleep and memory, between present and past, between bed and
levitation, between Mrs Critchley's snoring and her third
wedding day. Months passed in minutes. Recollection had
strange gaps. Of that wedding she remembered little except for
her father's support, for he was certain that Heinz was a good
man, and the sadness in Oliver's face, for, deep down, he had
never truly recovered his old joy in living.

She found that her memories of her lovemaking with Heinz
had faded also. As one may remember that one enjoyed a book,
even when one has completely forgotten the plot, or remark that
the food in a restaurant was excellent long after one has
forgotten what one ate, so Kate had precious few memories of
the many precious private moments she had spent with this
precious man. It had all been very straightforward. A hot flush
of shame brought her whole body out in another sweat as she
recalled a remark she had made to Nigel many years later. She
had been provoked into being indiscreet by her irritation with
him over the complete secrecy in which he cloaked his personal

life, and she had been led astray, not for the first time, not for the last time either, by her desire to live up to her reputation for being amusing. 'It's odd,' she'd said, 'that the fifty-seven varieties were with Walter, and not with Heinz.' Nigel had, rightly, been embarrassed. It had been so wrong of her to breech the code of confidentiality in which the civilised world hides these matters. It had been unfair to Heinz and to Walter and indeed to Nigel, who had always been such a thoughtful and attentive son – oh Lord, let it not be Nigel who murdered Graham. She uttered a low moan as she remembered the great task that lay ahead, the task that it was at last safe to undertake, and it so happened that Hilda also moaned at that moment, and Glenda, disturbed deep in her disturbed sleep, turned and farted, and Mrs Critchley, far away in her dreams, cried, 'Rodney! Not in the foyer!' and the night nurse came in to see if everything was all right, and Kate thought, She'll see that I'm levitating, that'll give the show away, and she tried hard to slip back into the bed below, but she couldn't.

Luckily the night nurse didn't notice her, and it occurred to her that perhaps her body was still in the bed and only her consciousness was floating. Perhaps she was already dead! Perhaps there *was* a God, after all, and this was heaven, not as high as she'd expected, or perhaps it was hell, not as low as she'd expected. Perhaps there was an afterlife but no God. She couldn't see any reason why the soul shouldn't live on even if there was no God.

She slept for a while, and when she awoke the sweat had gone cold on her body and she was shivering, and it seemed to her that the levitation had been an illusion. She knew straight away that she wasn't dead, which was such a relief that she didn't even mind about the cold sweat.

She returned to her life with Heinz. They bought a pleasant Edwardian house called the Gables in a quiet, shady road called Dollery Road in the pleasant Warwickshire village of East

Munton. When they first saw it, in the spring of 1937, the pink snow of blossom was falling. Heinz only had a fifteen-minute drive to work at the head office in Coventry.

Nigel and Timothy settled well in their new school, where Nigel shone at physics and chemistry and Timothy at English and Latin. Nigel did quite well at games and Timothy very badly. Maurice started school and liked it from the start. All her children liked Heinz and Walter. Kate thought that she was very fortunate in her boys. She was surprised when Heinz and Walter both told her how much it was all down to her, for being such a good mother. It seemed to her that she struggled as a mother.

How could any of them have murdered Graham?

Nigel came home from school one day in a very serious mood, leading a tearful Timothy.

'He got beaten up because you're married to a German,' he said. 'Morris Major says he's probably a fifth-columnist.'

'Oh dear,' said Kate. 'I am sorry.'

Normally beans on toast would be sufficient to dry Timothy's tears, but that day he refused to eat them. 'They're Heinz,' he said, his eleven-year-old face twisted with suspicion. 'They're probably poisoned.'

'That Heinz has nothing to do with our Heinz,' said Kate. 'They aren't German beans.' But she gave him boiled eggs instead, and made soldiers out of the bread, and he said he didn't want to eat soldiers unless they were German soldiers. 'They are,' said Nigel, so Timothy ate them, chopping off their heads quite fiercely, and Nigel, being very grown up at thirteen, winked at Kate, and she felt very uneasy about letting Timothy get away with such hostility to the bread soldiers.

Later, Nigel asked Kate if he could have a word in private.

'Mother?' he said. 'I know I'm only thirteen, but I think I'm pretty worldly. Do you think Heinz *could* be a fifth-columnist?'

'Do you know what a fifth-columnist is?'

'Not exactly. Morris Major says they're infiltrators, whatever that is. Spies, I suppose.'

When Heinz got home, Kate told him what had happened. They sat the boys down and Heinz told them all about what was happening in Germany and why he had come to Britain. He said that in the holidays they could tour the works and have a look at all his blueprints and how they were getting ready to convert all Walter's production to weaponry, to use against the Germans.

'You will get ridiculed at school,' Kate said. 'You're just going to have to be strong. Show it doesn't upset you, or pretend it doesn't upset you. If they don't see you suffering, the boys'll get bored. You mentioned Morris Major. Is there a boy called Morris Minor?'

'Yes,' said Timothy. 'He gets beaten up even more than I do.'

When the boys went to see Walter's works, Kate didn't go with them. 'I just can't face the thought of guns and tanks,' she said. 'I know we need them. I know Hitler has to be stopped. I can't bear to look at them.'

She knew that if she went she would think of Gwyn, but she didn't tell Heinz that.

Kate only saw Heinz get really angry once. It was on the day Elizabeth was born. It was also the day on which Neville Chamberlain came back from Munich and waved a piece of paper.

'How can anyone be so naive?' he said. 'Especially a politician. It's a contradiction in terms. Look at her, Kate, so helpless in your arms. Do the silly bastards think they've made the world any safer for her?'

He looked at his three-hour-old baby and made a face at her, as if to say, 'Sorry, my little darling, you're in this world of ours now, whether you like it or not.'

Then he looked at the tired, strained face of his wife and said, 'Oh, darling, I'm sorry. It isn't the time to say it. I shouldn't be worrying you with these things now.'

He kissed her forehead and sat stroking her hand very gently. Elizabeth fell asleep. It was very peaceful in the maternity ward, less peaceful in Heinz's brain.

'Half of the people in Walter's world think he's overreacting,' he said. 'Don't they realise, evil never goes away of its own accord?'

The weather was perfect on that June day in 1940. A modest sun shone out of a pale blue, misty sky. The dew still glistened on the lawn, where a blackbird listened happily for worms. A song thrush was singing joyously from the topmost branch of the hazel tree. The police officer was in a good mood too.

'Am I being interned?' Heinz asked.

'No, sir. We're just asking you to come to the station and answer a few questions.'

Kate thought that she wasn't going to be able to continue breathing. Fear grabbed her throat.

'I'll get you some overnight things, just in case,' she said.

'I'm sure that won't be necessary, madam,' said the officer confidently, soothingly.

'May I say cheery-bye to my daughter?' asked Heinz.

'Of course, sir.'

The policeman was a family man, and he gave a kindly smile and a wink to Elizabeth, who was almost two.

Heinz kissed Elizabeth and hugged Kate and turned and waved and said, 'See you soon. Bye-bye, Kate. Bye-bye, princess.'

'Bye-bye, Daddy,' said his princess.

'Bye-bye,' said the nice policeman, and he grinned and waved.

'It's absolutely bloody ridiculous,' said Walter. 'I need him, for God's sake. He's doing essential war work, for God's sake. We're making guns, not Dinky Toys.'

'I'll get him back,' said Kate.

Walter smiled. 'If anyone can, it'll be you.'

'I bloody will. It's so stupid. Oh, how I loathe stupidity.'

They were standing in the front garden of the Wasserhof house. Elizabeth was asleep in her pram. The boys were at school. A lawnmower was droning across the road, for all the world as if there was no war.

'I told him he should have taken British citizenship,' said Walter.

'He doesn't want to. He wants to be in there, after the victory, building a better Germany.'

'He thinks they'll win, then?'

'After *our* victory.'

'It's hard just now to believe we'll win. Oh, Kate, why didn't he apply for a permit from the Aliens War Service Department? Anyone engaged in work of national importance can get one.'

'He believes in Britain. He didn't think we'd ever do anything so stupid.'

'Doesn't he realise that war is chaotic, that the fear of invasion is in every street, that fear drives out reason?'

'Well, you didn't either, Walter. You should have made him go for a permit.'

'Get him out, Kate. I need him.'

'Well, I do miss him too.'

'Yes, yes, for sure, and I'm sorry, but I'm sure he's safe, and your conjugal rights aren't exactly of top importance just now, but providing weapons for our boys is and every day counts.'

A bullfinch, overdressed for war in his black hat and pink-red waistcoat, scolded them from a pear tree.

'I could almost wish I was that bullfinch,' said Kate. 'Life would be simpler.'

'I can't see you as a bullfinch,' said Walter. 'You wouldn't be able to stand the monotonous diet or the brevity of the sex.'

Their eyes met for just a moment.

'Right,' said Kate. 'I think I'd better go and find my husband.'

But this proved easier said than done. He had been taken from the police station to a camp somewhere. Nobody knew where. Time passed, as it does. Hitler continued to rampage through Europe, and Kate looked after Elizabeth. She knew that Heinz was safer than if he was fighting, safer than if he'd been bobbing across the English Channel in a small boat, but where was he? Day after day, and no news. She knew that the horror of war had engulfed the greater part of the Continent, she felt ashamed of herself for being so weak, but where was he? Not to know, not to be able to imagine what he was going through, in this land that he loved. How could they intern this fierce hater of Nazism?

She went with Walter to protest. She enlisted the aid of the Aliens War Service Department. She got an appointment with a Home Office official for her and Walter. They explained the important nature of Heinz's work.

'It's ridiculous to keep him behind barbed wire,' said Kate. 'It's bloody ridiculous.'

'Yes,' said the official. 'That is exactly what it is. We'll send out an order releasing him.'

'Oh, thank you,' exclaimed Kate.

'Good. That's that. Thank you,' said Walter.

'Exactly where is he?' asked the official.

They stared at him, open-mouthed.

'Which camp is he in? Where do we send the order releasing him?'

Five days later, Walter called round, and Kate could see, from the gravity of his expression, that he had bad news. Her heart raced. She put Elizabeth in her play-pen rather more curtly than she had intended. Elizabeth bawled. She led Walter into the kitchen and collapsed into a rough pine chair, which snagged her stocking, as if that mattered, but the stupid little setback made her want to cry.

'What's happened?' she asked.

'He's fine,' said Walter. 'I should have started with that.'

The relief was so intense that it hurt. Kate let out a great sigh.

'You know where he is?'

'I know where he is.'

'Thank goodness. Oh, Walter, well done. Where is he?'

'He's on His Majesty's Troop-ship *Dunera*.'

'On a ship? Where's he going?'

'Australia.'

Walter offered to continue to pay Heinz's salary, but he knew that Kate would refuse. She took a job as an ambulance driver instead.

Her parents offered to have the children for August. Kate felt that Elizabeth was too young, but she took the boys. Her neighbours in Dollery Road had young children, and would help to look after Elizabeth when Kate was working.

The boys loved the cheery house in Eaton Crescent. They loved the bays of Gower. They loved the red Mumbles trams. They loved their grandparents, and Enid and Annie.

Kate took them by train. She was almost hurt that they were so excited.

She took them to Langland Bay and they played cricket on the hard sand left by the receding tide. Nigel liked to bat and always batted a long time because he rarely got out. Timothy liked to bat and always batted a short time because he often got out. Maurice didn't want to play at all, he joined in for the sake of family unity. Elizabeth bawled because she was too young to play.

The next day they went to Bracelet Bay instead. There wasn't so much sand there, but there were lovely rocks to climb and rock pools to explore. Nigel was happy damming streams, diverting water courses, and making scientific notes about the content of the rock pools. He even tried to measure the salinity of the water. Timothy bought a notebook with his pocket money and began to write. He was writing a novel. It was about stoats. Later he would tear it up because it was uncommercial. Later still, when *Watership Down* came out, he regretted that he had torn it up. Maurice built huge sandcastles and stood beside them, rather listlessly, watching the tide come in and demolish them. He would stand there until the very last traces had disappeared. Kate sensed that he longed to grow up and found this activity a suitable symbol for childhood.

Nigel almost caused an incident when he insisted to three nuns that they were German parachutists in disguise. Kate had to intervene and mollify them. They waddled off like terrified penguins.

Every night Kate dreamt that Heinz had been torpedoed. Every night she dreaded going to sleep.

Enid was still teaching at the High School. Kate listened to her tales about the children and wondered what had happened to all the children in her class in Penzance, Lily Gardner and Margaret Penhaligon and the rest. She felt sorry for Enid and asked her if she'd ever thought of leaving Swansea. 'Somebody's going to have to look after Mother and Father, Kate,' she replied. 'They're growing old, you know.'

Kate hadn't really noticed, but she did now. Her father had retired, but still looked a fine figure of a man. He was getting very deaf though, and a little absent-minded. Bronwen's hair had gone grey, it looked as if a fine dust had settled on it, and her face had become very lined, but the lines were a map of kindness, they were the contours of generosity.

Walter came to fetch Kate and Elizabeth. Kate answered the door to him, and he said he didn't want to come in.

'That's silly,' said Kate.

'Your father's eyes will bore right through me. I'm an adulterer. I was unfaithful to their daughter.'

'That was years ago. He knows how supportive you've been. All that's forgotten now that I'm married again.'

'I'm using black-market petrol.'

'That's more serious. But he won't realise it. He isn't worldly.'

So Walter came in and stood there, uncomfortably, like a little boy, this powerful maker of armaments.

'How are you, sir?' he said.

'Very well, Walter, very well, on the whole,' said John Thomas Thomas. 'How are you?'

'Very well,' said Walter. 'Well, we'd better be getting along. We need to beat the blackout, and of course there are no signposts anywhere.'

As they drove off, Walter said, 'Well, that was hardly a conversation worth going in for.'

'I'm pleased you did, though,' said Kate, and Walter gave her a look.

A couple of days later, he telephoned her.

'I'm just ringing to see if you're all right,' he said. 'I thought you might be feeling lonely.'

'I am. Elizabeth's very sweet, but at two she's hardly what you'd call company. I'm clattering around a house that suddenly seems very big.'

'Are you working this evening?' he asked, trying very hard to sound casual.

'Not this evening, no.' She tried hard to sound casual too.

'Would you like to come over for the night? With Elizabeth, of course. The spare bedrooms are aired.'

She smiled at his tactfulness. She had to admit he was learning.

'All right. We'll come.'

'Good.'

So Kate returned to the second of her marital homes, but this time as a guest. The house seemed even larger than she had remembered.

'I may move out for the duration,' Walter said. 'They could billet half a regiment in here.'

After Elizabeth had gone to bed, Walter cooked a chicken. Kate was astounded to find that he could. It wasn't brilliant, and it was probably black market, but it was good.

He produced some 1926 Gevrey-Chambertin. Kate drank sparingly, which was a shame as it was excellent, but she wasn't entirely sure of his intentions.

'I suppose you haven't heard from Heinz,' he said, as they ate and drank at opposite ends of the long table.

'No.'

'Well, I suppose you wouldn't have. He'll still be on the ship.'

'Yes.'

'Sunning himself in southern seas.'

'Yes.'

'You're very monosyllabic.'

'Sorry.'

'Wishing you hadn't come?'

'No.'

'Good. Chicken all right?'

'Fine.'

'Good.'

'I'm sorry if I'm not more sparkling, Walter. It's a compliment really.'

'Oh?'

'I'm relaxing. I don't relax very often.'

'Good. I thought you might find it difficult, being back here.'

'I thought I might. I don't.'

'Good. Stuffing up to scratch?'

'Very creditable.'

'Surprised?'

'Very. Sorry.'

'I'm a changed man, Kate.'

'Are you, Walter?'

'Yes.'

'Oh. Good.'

'I see.'

'I didn't mean that to seem awful, Walter. You've been very kind and very supportive. Is there . . .?'

'No.'

'How did you know what I was going to say?'

'Change of tone. You put on an "Is there anyone in your life?" voice. No, there isn't. Never.'

'Oh.'

'I imagine when Heinz gets to Australia they'll get the message to release him and send him straight back again.'

'Yes.'

'Good.'

'Yes.'

'Silly business.'

'Yes.'

They went back into the lounge for their coffee. Kate hated the word 'lounge' and hated herself for hating it.

They sat at opposite ends of the larger of the settees. It could hardly be described as dangerous proximity.

Kate wasn't absolutely sure why she began to cry. Perhaps it wasn't surprising. To be back here in her old marital home, with her ex-husband being so polite, and her present husband on his way to Australia, and the thought of the horrid war and the ever-present possibility of invasion, and Nigel going to be old enough to fight in less than three years, no, it wasn't surprising.

'How long do you think the war will last?' she asked, just managing to keep the crying under control.

'Difficult to say. Quite a long time, I hope.'

'You hope?'

'Kate, we're losing. If it ends within the next year, we'll be Germans. We have a lot of tables to turn. We can do it, but it'll take time.'

'I hope Nigel doesn't have to go and fight. Oh, Walter, it will be over by 1943, won't it?'

She began to cry uncontrollably. He came over to her and put his arm round her and hugged her. Her tears flowed on to his face.

'Oh, Kate,' he said. 'Oh, Kate.'

His lips were on hers. She could feel his hard penis. Then he broke away, and stood up.

'Damn,' he said. 'Damn damn damn and blast. I didn't mean to do that.'

She gave her nose a long blow.

He sat down again, on the settee, near her, but not touching her.

'I promise you, Kate,' he said. 'I solemnly promise you, that will never happen again.'

Kate was more than somewhat disappointed to find that she felt more than somewhat disappointed.

Kate continued to see Walter during the long months that followed, and it never did happen again, and she really began to think that he was a changed man. Although he had little time, he did what he could to get Heinz back. When Kate expressed her gratitude, he said that he wasn't doing it for her but for himself, he needed Heinz, but it was Kate's belief that Heinz had done his job, and the rest was relatively routine, and Walter was either punishing himself or being genuinely unselfish. As she grew older, she felt more and more that it was better to treat people according to their actions and not their motives.

Walter was always happy to help Kate out by having the children. They brought some life to his great mausoleum of a house. So Kate was free, on her days off from her ambulance driving, to make trips. On one of these she went to West Hampstead, to see Daniel and Olga, who had refused to be evacuated to the country. 'Jews are urban people. That's why I couldn't paint well at Tregarryn.' They both looked paler than ever. Their faces were pinched. They didn't get enough to eat, though their children did. After the night at the Bandalero, Kate had made a conscious decision to like Olga more. Being a woman of considerable will-power, she did.

They had another visitor. Daphne Stoneyhurst didn't look pale or pinched. She was a mature, successful woman. Her hair was streaked with grey, which made her look more formidable than ever. She had taken to smoking cigars, and drank only whisky. Her voice had an ever more masculine timbre. Kate found herself thinking that it was a shame that such superb child-bearing hips should be wasted on a lesbian.

'Daniel and I have been working hard on the Home Office over this ridiculous internment of aliens,' Daphne told her, to her amazement.

'Well, I have a lot of Jewish friends who're interned, mainly on the Isle of Man,' said Daniel. 'Artists of every kind, gentle people fleeing Nazi persecution, imprisoned as Nazi spies. I can't stand by.'

'It gives me a feeling that maybe my life isn't utterly pointless after all,' said Daphne.

'When this battle's over, we'll all enlist as war artists,' said Daniel.

Daniel had opened a bottle of cheap wine which Kate could hardly drink. He'd never had any idea about wine, and now he couldn't afford anything decent anyway. They'd already drunk the bottle that Kate had brought. She'd have to go on to whisky. Daphne had brought plenty of that, and Daniel and Olga weren't really drinkers.

The children drifted in and out of the room. The Begelman children didn't seem like children. They seemed like small adults, tough and mature, testimony to Olga's iron will.

Kate and Daphne grew drunk slowly. Daniel returned to the subject of internment. 'It's wicked morally,' he said. 'It undermines the whole reason for which we're fighting. It's stupid practically. It denies us the aid of some of our finest minds and most gifted scientists.'

That evening in West Hampstead Kate learnt for the first time of the scale of the internment. Many years later, she met the Amadeus String Quartet after a recital and learnt that they had all first met in the internment camps in the Isle of Man. She looked at those gentle, musical men and wondered what kind of person would consider them a security risk and waste valuable manpower guarding them. That night, in West Hampstead, she felt reassured at discovering how many other deported and interned people there were but also alarmed by it. Her dear Heinz would be lost in its immensity, become just a number.

'I feel as though he's slipping through my fingers,' she said. Only her pride and her will-power kept her from crying.

'You can't go home tonight, either of you,' said Olga. 'You're too drunk.'

'Have you room?' asked Kate.

'The children will sleep on the floor,' said Daniel. 'You and Daphne can share a bed.'

Daphne looked at Kate and smiled ironically.

'Don't look so alarmed,' she said. 'I won't eat you.'

Kate thanked the children for agreeing to sleep on the floor. Reuben, thirteen years old, sallow and solemn, educated in Palestine, the Peloponnese, Salamanca and West Hampstead, said gravely, 'Our home is your home.'

And so Kate and Daphne shared a bed. It was a very large bed. Normally, all three children slept in it, the girls on the two outsides.

There was no need to feel awkward. There was plenty of space between her and Daphne. But it was one of those beds that sag in the middle, and every now and then they rolled towards each other and touched accidentally. At first Kate thought it was accidental that Daphne's hand was touching her bottom, but as it crept gently over her buttocks she realised that this time it was no accident.

She removed the hand and gave it a tiny smack.

'Sorry, Daphne,' she said.

'Are you still our little chapel girl deep down?' whispered Daphne. 'I believe you are.'

'Not at all,' whispered Kate. 'I have my code of honour, that's all. I wouldn't be unfaithful to my dear Heinz ever, be it with a woman, a child, a hermaphrodite, a transvestite, a goat or the best-looking man in the whole world, not ever. Good-night, dear Daphne. Sleep well.'

Many people worked for the release of the aliens. Notable among them were Angela Rathbone, Colonel Josiah Wedgwood and George Bell, Bishop of Chichester. There were several debates in Parliament on the issue, and the case for their release eventually prevailed. It cheered Kate to find that the British sense of justice had not been entirely destroyed by the chaos and panic of war, and that common sense did eventually prevail, in the end. But it didn't do Heinz any good. Everyone acknowledged that a mistake had been made, but rectifying it was another matter. There simply wasn't the transport available from Australia. The troop-ships were needed for the troops.

Every now and then a letter arrived from him. He was in a vast camp in the vast interior now, living in dry, dusty heat. He was being well treated. He was healthy. His letters should have cheered her up, but they were curious, cautious affairs. Perhaps he felt that a censor might read them, and so, being a particularly private man, he avoided anything too personal. Or maybe he was censoring himself, so as not to make her too emotional. Or maybe, in his situation, he didn't feel able to be emotional.

She wrote to him, and her letters were equally impersonal, partly because his letters were so impersonal that it seemed inappropriate to reply in any other way, but also because she found that she just couldn't bring herself to write the words that she wanted to write.

She drove her ambulance determinedly, never fearlessly, never recklessly. She drove with the sound of sirens and bombs outside, and the sounds of human agony inside. She drove along roads carpeted with broken glass and rubble. Searchlights picked out the skeletons of buildings. Walls hung loose from buildings like severed thighs. She thought of her children, who might become orphans, and of Heinz, who might find nobody to welcome him when at last he returned. You could not allow such things to affect you, in war. War was total. War consumed you. Kate did her bit, and was consumed.

Other people did their bit in Swansea, when three nights of bombing destroyed almost all of the huddled, muddled centre of the town. Kate grieved, bitterly, for her home town.

War was total, up to a point, but nobody would have expected Kate to drive her ambulance on the day of Heinz's return. For return he did, in 1942. At last a place had been found for him on a troop-ship. As the day of his return drew nearer, Kate grew more and more nervous. Losses at sea were heavy. He could still be torpedoed. Every night now, as before, she dreamt that he had been torpedoed. She dreaded going to bed.

On the eve of his arrival she didn't dare go to bed at all. The previous night she'd dreamt that she'd been taking part in an orgy in a bombed building in Swansea. It was the shell of Jones and Jones, still smouldering, and she'd been making love to Walter, with Gwyn watching, Gwyn still eighteen. Herbert Herbert Cricket had been having it off with Mrs Herbert Herbert Politics, and Mrs Herbert Herbert Cricket had been unbuttoning the flies of Herbert Herbert Politics, and Gwyn had laughed lecherously, and then a naked postman had arrived, tripping though the wreckage with a telegram, and Kate had known what the telegram contained. Heinz had been torpedoed. And Walter had said, 'Thank God for that.' It had been a dreadful dream. She couldn't have faced another dream like that. She sat up with endless cups of coffee, and read Proust.

Walter insisted on driving her to Liverpool. He could always get petrol. Big houses were requisitioned, but not Walter's. People had to accept evacuees. Not Walter. He had ways and means.

The boys were staying with Walter that night. They were happy enough. Maurice was very close to his father, and Nigel and Timothy had no father but Walter. Nigel was bursting with patriotism. He couldn't wait to become eighteen and dreaded that the war would end before he was. Timothy was terrified of being eighteen, and dreaded that the war wouldn't end before he was. Maurice knew that the war would end before he was eighteen, but he was still very anxious to grow up. He just hadn't much talent for childhood.

Until she saw the great ship sliding slowly, agonisingly slowly, towards the dockside, Kate had assumed that her nervousness would cease when she knew that Heinz was safe. But it didn't cease. It grew worse. She began to shake. A cold wind was blowing up the Mersey. Occasional spots of rain were being released, a few at a time, by a miserly, gun-metal sky. Walter took off his topcoat and put it round Kate's shoulders. She tried to smile.

Walter touched her arm and said, 'I'll wait in the car.' He had grown less and less tactile of late, more and more impersonal, almost distant. Kate no longer knew what he was thinking, which was a bit of a problem. She no longer knew what she was thinking either, which was a greater problem.

The ship eased her massive way in. The decks were crowded. People were waving all over the ship and all over the dockside. People were crying. Kate thought she saw Heinz, and waved at him frantically.

Seamen shouted. Ropes snaked across from the ship to the dockside. Kate shivered and shivered, and realised that the man she'd been waving to wasn't Heinz.

At last they began to stream down the gangways, laden with kitbags and luggage. And then she saw him, tripping down the gangway with those little steps of his. He looked so lean, so brown, so vulnerable, so dishevelled; she had never seen him untidy before, but his hair was long and straggly, and the sun had bleached it a very pale blond. His moustache and beard were flecked with grey, but there wasn't a single grey hair on his head. Around his eyes there were hard lines that had come from screwing his face up against the sun. He was a creature of the sun, a gnarled tree from the Australian outback. He carried only a small canvas bag. He saw her, and his face lit up, he waved excitedly, he seemed so simple and direct. There was pure joy in his face, the purest that Kate had ever seen. She knew, in that moment, that he loved her more than ever, and that she didn't love him at all.

Terrible to her were the hugs and kisses and his tears of joy. It wasn't hard for her to conjure up some tears as well, but hers were not tears of joy. They were tears of sorrow at the dying of her love and of pity for this dear, dear man. She smiled broadly, determinedly, incessantly, but she felt that her smile was frozen and utterly without warmth. However, he didn't seem to notice.

She insisted on carrying his bag, a pointless gesture, since it was so light.

'Walter's brought the car,' she said.

'Good old Walter.'

'Yes.'

'Have you seen much of him?'

'Yes. He's been wonderful.'

'Good.'

Was he sincere? Was he naive? Thank goodness she'd been blameless.

Terrible for her was the drive down to the Midlands in Walter's 4½ litre Daimler Straight 8. Heinz sat with her in the back, and held her hand, and kept shaking his head and saying,

'It's so green', 'It's so crowded,' 'It's so grey,' 'It's so cold.'

Terrible for her were the little strokes that Heinz gave her hand as they sped smoothly past Chester and Shrewsbury and Kidderminster and Redditch on that seemingly endless, all too short journey. She gave him little answering strokes. She had decided that she would never leave him, that she could never leave him, could never say, 'Heinz, I don't love you any more.' There was too much of her mother and father in her for that to be possible. She would never be able to look her mother and father in the face again if she did. That might not be the purest motive, but had she not already decided to judge people by their actions, not their motives? She need not be harder on herself than on anybody else.

She had sometimes thought that she would like to be an actress. She had the looks for it, and it had been suggested to her more than once. Daniel had urged her. Stanley had urged her. Many men who fancied her and had no hope of her had urged her. Well, she had become an actress now. She had landed her first leading role. She would play the loving wife of Heinz Wasserhof.

Her decision gave her a modicum of peace, but it didn't make the day a great deal easier. She had to make some attempt at conversation, so she asked him about his experiences.

'Later,' he said.

He asked her about Elizabeth, about the boys, about her ambulance driving, about her family, about the bombing of Swansea. She was pleased to talk.

'The signposts are back,' said Heinz suddenly.

'The fear of invasion is over,' said Walter, and his voice sounded strained to Kate, as she felt hers must, 'but that's very different from thinking we'll win the war.'

The sun came out as they approached East Munton. It shone on the fourteenth-century church, the village hall with its tin roof, the scattered old houses, the new bungalows. It shone on the tidiness of Dollery Road, on the mellow sobriety of the Gables, on the freshly mown lawn, even on a robin redbreast with an overdeveloped sense of cliché. The sun made it even more difficult for Kate. It made happiness compulsory.

'It's still there,' breathed Heinz with a sigh. 'It's all still there. I knew it was, of course, but it's still a surprise.'

The car crunched gently to a halt in the drive. There was a deep silence, and Kate sensed that none of them wanted to get out of the car.

'Where's Lizzy-Wizzy?' asked Heinz in a hoarse croak, and Kate realised how nervous he was about seeing his daughter, who was five now.

'With the Penfolds. They're our new neighbours.'

'I'll fetch her,' said Walter.

They got out of the car at last. Kate fumbled with the lock, and Heinz looked at her gravely.

'As you remembered?' she said, to say something.

'Smaller,' said Heinz. 'Everything in England is small. Oh, but lovely. Lovely.'

'I'll make a cup of tea.'

Heinz shook his head and laughed.

'What?' asked Kate.

'You're being so British, I didn't remember you as so British.'

'Sorry.'

'No. It wasn't a criticism. It was an observation.'

Walter came back with Elizabeth before Kate could make the tea. They went out on to the porch, and Heinz opened his arms as if expecting her to run into his arms.

'My, she's grown,' he whispered. 'My, she's pretty.'

Yes, she was pretty, in a very traditional, rosy English way, thought Kate, and yes, of course she's grown. Her heart wept for Heinz in his disappointment as Elizabeth stood and stared at him stolidly.

'Hello, Lizzy-Wizzy,' said Heinz. 'Do you know who I am?'

'My name's called Elizabeth,' said Elizabeth. 'That's what my name's called.'

She put her finger in her mouth, and clutched Walter's hand. Oh innocent little girl, thought Kate, how devastatingly you mirror my heart.

Walter smiled apologetically.

'It's been a long time, Heinz,' he said.

In the end, bed could be delayed no longer. They'd explored the garden, Kate had cooked a meal, they'd eaten it, and they'd talked, talked about the same things as in the car – the boys, Elizabeth, the war, Walter, Swansea, ambulance driving – and they'd broached some new subjects – the garden, the village, Daniel, Olga, Daphne. He'd laughed when she'd told him about sharing a bed with Daphne.

He'd talked too about Australia, the camp, his journey home, his youth in Germany. He hadn't talked about his journey to Australia on the SS *Dunera*. This he had shunned.

Kate had talked again, then, about her father and mother, about Bernard and Oliver and Enid and Annie and Dilys, about Myfanwy, about Tregarryn and her youth, leaving out only the subject of Gwyn.

And now it was time for bed. The thought of bed had hung over Kate since the moment when Walter had said, 'I'll have Elizabeth for the night, if you like, so that you can be on your own tonight,' and Heinz had said, 'I think you may as well. That's very kind,' and Kate had said, 'We need to give her time and space to get used to you again, Heinz,' and Kate had met Walter's eyes and she had had no idea what he was thinking.

Kate thought that perhaps when they got into bed she would feel sexy and everything would pass off satisfactorily. She was, after all, a very sexy lady, and she hadn't had intercourse for over two years. But she knew, in her heart, that it didn't work like that for her, and that an acting performance of considerable power was going to be needed.

All her linen had begun to develop that greyish tinge that white clothes get when they've been washed too often. She changed into the least grey of them, with her back to Heinz. Unlike Walter, he had never shown much interest in her backside. She slipped quickly into bed, and waited for him. He put on his rust-coloured pyjamas, which he hadn't seen for more than two years.

'Pyjamas!' he exclaimed. 'What luxury!'

He slid into bed beside her and began to lift the nightshirt off her. She fumbled with his pyjama cord, all thumbs again. Eventually, despite her clumsiness and his shyness, they were naked.

'Linen!' he enthused. 'Now that *is* a luxury.'

She tried one last time.

'Was it really awful on that boat?' she asked.

'Some of it was so awful that I feel ashamed to share it with you.'

'I'd like you to share it with me. I think you'll feel better after you've shared it with me. I know I will. It'll be a barrier between us till you have.'

She hoped that, if he had felt a barrier between them, this might convince him of the reason for it.

He switched off the light, and began to talk. There, in the darkness, in the privacy of their bedroom, in the comfy warmth of the marital bed, he felt able to talk about it.

'The ship was pretty terrible in itself,' he said. 'There were nearly three thousand people on board, and it should never have had more than two thousand, and even that would have been crowded. There were no bunks. We slept on the decks, hard, unyielding, throbbing to the movement of the ship, agonising. All our stuff was stolen from us, and never given back. I was lucky there. I didn't have anything in the first place.'

As he talked, Kate stroked his body gently, taking great care to avoid his private parts. The only thrust she wanted was the thrust of his narrative.

He talked of the stench of vomit in the foul holds of the ship, of the inadequacy of the lavatories, of the awful black depths of the stinking ship. Vomit and human sewage and sweat. People with foul breath. Smells, smells, smells.

She asked him what sort of people they had been.

'I suppose the words "a motley crew" have rarely been so accurate, except that we weren't the crew, we were the passengers. There were several hundred people who had originally been being taken to Canada on the *Arandora Star* and had sunk and been rescued. They had an added reason to be afraid. There were captured German seamen who just wanted to get back to the war, captured Nazi fanatics, bewildered Italian waiters, Poles whose misfortune it was to come to Britain before Poland was Poland and so were arrested as aliens when if they'd arrived in some cases only a week later they'd have joined the RAF as Free Poles. There were even two Scots whose parents had been living in Berlin when the war began so they were classified as Germans.'

'Hadn't they told anybody they were Scottish?'

'Yes, but they came from Glasgow, and nobody understood a word they said. Farce and tragedy clutched hands, Kate, above those stinking bilges. Then of course there were people like me, Germans who had seen what was coming, who had fled and were desperate to help defeat Germany. But the largest group consisted of the Jews, and what a band they were, what talents there were on that ship. Physicists, chemists, nuclear scientists, mechanics, inventors, novelists, poets, cubists, surrealists, composers, flautists, oboists, harpists, doctors, dentists, psychiatrists, psychologists, philosophers, all cheek to jowl and despised by British oafs. Two months it took us to get to Fremantle. The stench of that floating cesspit will never leave my nostrils.'

Kate tightened her hand on his. Describe it in more detail, her hand implored, and maybe pity will achieve what love can't.

But he began to talk about the brighter side.

'We survived,' he said, 'and this is what also will never leave me. The wonderful nature of the human spirit in adversity. If man ever learns to have the same spirit when not in adversity, what a world we could have, Kate.' He gripped her fiercely for a moment. 'What a world we could have!' She felt his body relax. 'People formed small orchestras, Hebrew choirs, concert parties, craft clubs, bridge clubs. They gave lectures. We had lectures on literature and music and mathematics and science and on all the places we were passing, for all the world as if we were a cruise ship and people would go ashore and take excursions.'

'And what did you do?'

'Me? Very little, Kate.'

'Heinz!'

'What?'

' "Very little"! I know you.'

'Oh good. I was beginning to fear you didn't know me very well any more.'

'Heinz! I'm . . . I'm feeling shy. It's natural, surely?'

'Yes. Yes. Yes, of course.'

'So what did you do? Come on.'

'Well, I tried to be quite useful. I tried to use my background as a maker of toys. I made musical instruments out of lavatory paper.'

Wind instruments, I suppose, she thought, but did not say. It was a very silly joke, a childish joke, but she would have made it to Walter and to Arturo. She couldn't make it to Heinz.

'Were the instruments good? I'm sure they were.'

'They were very good. Good music was played on them, Kate. I fear, though, that it turned out to be a pyrrhic victory.'

'A pyrrhic victory?'

'We ended up with lots of musical instruments and no

lavatory paper. I asked one of our guards for lavatory paper and he said . . . no, it's crude.'

'Heinz! We're living through a war and I'm nearly forty-three and I don't need protecting. I think you should get the whole thing out of your system now you've started.'

'He said, "You shouldn't have used so much making musical instruments. Wipe your arse on a fucking flute, you Kraut bastard."'

She could feel the tension that was still in him, as much as ever, perhaps more. She curved her body into his and said, very gently, 'Weren't the crew kind, then?'

Heinz paused a while before replying. They lay in silence, in each other's arms, immobile in the warm bed. A tawny owl whooped.

'What a European sound,' said Heinz. 'No, Kate, this is what I find so difficult to talk about.'

'Try.'

'They were not kind at all.' He went silent again, thinking thoughts he would rather not have had. Kate ran her fingers over his smooth, hairless chest, very gently, very patiently. 'We were threatened and beaten and humiliated in every way possible.'

'But didn't they realise they weren't dealing with a nest of spies? I mean, with so many being Jews I'd have thought it was obvious.'

'It didn't seem obvious. In two months our guards didn't seem to realise what it took the Australians about an hour to work out. Most of our guards, to excuse them a little, were very stupid, of course. Low types. The dregs. They don't say to crack troops, "We have a dangerous mission for you, you will guard a lot of German expatriates, Italian waiters and Jewish musicians."'

'Was nobody kind?'

'One or two. A couple of the chefs when no one was looking. A good-hearted sailor from Tynemouth. One nice Scottish person. A junior officer who whispered that he was sorry for what they were doing, but they were under orders.'

'Under orders?'

'Oh yes. It came from the top, you see. That's the awful thing, Kate. When it comes from the top, there's no stopping people.'

'I suppose being German you got the brunt of it?' She stroked his arm.

'Oh, Kate, I think that's the most awful thing of it all. It wasn't as bad for people like me. We were treated better than the Jews. Irony of ironies.'

'Yes.'

'The way those talented Jews brought the worst out of those English oafs, Kate . . . without doing anything to provoke. I found it curiously humiliating and shaming to witness. And then again, you see, it was exactly like what I had seen happening in Germany before I left. A mirror of the rise of Nazism. Anti-Semitism, thuggery, decent people doing things under orders, other decent people looking the other way. It takes a giant man not to look the other way, Kate, and I'm afraid I found . . . I found I was not a giant.'

She put her arms round him and hugged him. That much was easy.

'So this country is as bad!' she said.

'Oh, Kate! No! This was one ship, the other is a nation. It was all sorted out, in the end. I am home. Others are home. Others are coming home. People were court-martialled. No, Kate, Britain isn't what I hoped it would be, but it isn't Nazi Germany, my shamed land. But I was not as brave as I would have liked to have been. Not as good a man as I had hoped.'

They lay in silence then. Kate drew a deep breath and pressed her lips against his. Now that the moment had come, she flung herself into it, she took the lead. He responded swiftly, hungrily, desperately. He moaned and groaned and gasped. Kate had been thinking back, trying to recall the noises and movements that she made when aroused. She made them now. She put everything into it. He gasped with pleasure, cried with ecstasy. The timing was perfect. It's easy to get the timing right when you're faking it.

He fell asleep very quickly afterwards, which was hardly surprising, he must have been very tired. She was very tired too, having not gone to bed the previous night. But sleep wouldn't come. She lay on her side listening to his regular breathing, and thought, If that's as bad as it gets, I can cope. He's a decent man and a kind man and we can have all sorts of happy times together.

She had once promised her father never to tell a lie. She had told so many lies and she had learnt that sometimes it is good to lie. This night had been the biggest lie of all. She felt no guilt about it. She also felt that, on her first night as an actress, she had given a good performance.

In the morning she wasn't so sure. She did fall asleep eventually, and, when she awoke, the bed was empty, the bedroom was empty, the house was empty. She found the note on the kitchen table:

I know that you don't love me any more. Thank you for pretending that you do. I know that, if it is over, it must be over before Elizabeth gets used to me again. I think she looks on Walter as her daddy, and I think perhaps you do too. You have been blameless and so have I. Only history has been an adulterer. I have survived the *Dunera*. I shall survive this. With deepest love, your ex-husband, Heinz.

Kate's eyes filled with tears. They streamed down her face, and, since she was paralysed, she could do nothing about it. She was terrified that her tears would reveal how active her mind still was, would blow her cover sky-high.

'My word!' said fat Janet with the eating disorder. 'We *have* been crying. Why have we been crying? There there. We'll soon wipe those tears away, and then we'll be as snug as a bug in a rug again, won't we?'

9 Doctor Ramgobi

Kate awoke, after a long sleep, with a feeling of alarm. She felt surrounded. There were hands, more than one person's, clutching both her hands. What was going on?

Glenda provided the answer.

'Are you all her children?' she asked in her carefully enunciated attempt at a posh voice.

'Yes. We're all her children,' said Nigel.

'She must be frightfully old. Oh Lord, I didn't mean . . . did that sound rude? I only meant . . .'

'. . . that we're none of us exactly spring chickens,' said Timothy.

So they were all there, with their combined age of two hundred and seventy-five, two at each side of her bed, holding her hands, none of them wanting to lose out in the Show of Affection stakes.

Kate felt thoroughly alarmed. If they'd all come together, they must think she was on the way out.

'You're right about her being old,' said Elizabeth. 'She'll be a hundred in eight days' time.'

'Really? Oh, that's marvellous.' This was Hilda. Kate imagined Hilda as small, pasty, podgy, with thick legs. 'Are we going to have a party?'

'We hadn't thought,' said Maurice. 'I mean, I'm not sure if it'd be appropriate.'

'Best not to plan ahead, really,' said Nigel. 'Best to take it one day at a time.'

All that expense and I might die before the party! Good old Nigel! The richest are always the most careful with their money.

Still, they don't sound dreadfully upset. Maybe it was a false alarm. It has to be a false alarm.

'Well, I think we should have a party, if she makes it,' said Timothy.

'We should do what she'd have wanted, if she could have told us,' said Maurice.

'Well, she'd have wanted a party,' said Elizabeth. 'She loved parties.'

Yes, but not parties at which I'm paralysed and unable to speak or eat or drink, thought Kate.

'Oh yes, I think we must have a party,' said Hilda. 'Oh! And there'll be a card from . . .' Her voice simpered. '. . . Her Majesty. She sends cards now. So much nicer than tele-messages.'

Oh my God, thought Kate. How deeply embarrassing. I've never exactly been a Royalist.

'I probably won't be here,' said Glenda. 'Doctor Rambogi thinks I'm ready to go home.'

'I think it's wonderful of the Queen to remember to send all those messages, when she has such trouble with her own family,' said Hilda.

Kate began to drift back to sleep. Even the thought of this party embarrassed her. Balloons, and a cake, and a banner saying 'Well done, Kate. 100 not out'. Bad enough without congratulations from the Queen.

She heard snatches of conversation, though. She heard Maurice saying how boring he thought rambling was, and Nigel saying, 'There's no need to go on at me. I only do it to keep fit. I go on walks to keep my body fit and I compile crosswords to keep my mind fit.'

'I thought you'd been replaced by a computer,' said Elizabeth.

'You're missing the point as usual, Elizabeth,' said Nigel. So he'd noticed it too! 'I'm not talking about getting paid. I'm not talking about doing a job. Poor old Parsifal was shown the door long ago, but I still do it, for the same reason that I always did it. For fun. Fun, Elizabeth.'

'And exercise,' said Elizabeth doggedly.

'Yes, yes, and exercise,' said Nigel, brushing Elizabeth off as if she was an irritating gnat.

Kate thought, I didn't know Nigel compiled crosswords and called himself Parsifal, though that does ring a bell, but I can't remember which bell. Fancy his not telling me. Knew I wouldn't approve, of course. He told me he did crosswords and I told him it was a waste of his mental powers. Such a puritan I was, in some ways. Not in others! Oh dearie me! I'm thinking of myself in the past tense now. This won't do.

'How's Carrie?' she heard Elizabeth ask. Kate found the thought of Carrie exhausting and she gave a low moan which startled her, it was the first time she'd managed to make a noise, and Timothy said, 'Oh God, she dislikes her even in her sleep.'

'She doesn't dislike her,' Elizabeth said. 'Mum never dislikes people. She sees through them, because she's perceptive, but she doesn't dislike them.'

'Are you suggesting she sees through Carrie?'

'Oh, don't be so touchy. How is she, anyway?'

'Perfectly all right, as far as I know.'

There was the clank of a trolley. Lunch? Tea? Supper?

'Tea, Hilda?'

'Please. Half a spoonful.'

'There you go.'

Tea-time. Three o'clock. Everything so early in hospitals.

'Glenda?'

'Please. No sugar.'

'No, you're sweet enough already.'

Hilda laughed at this. She laughed at it every day! Glenda never laughed at it. Kate sensed that she pursed her lips in disapproval of such intimacy from the staff. She wasn't sweet at all, making the daily joke even more pointless.

'Mrs Critchley?'

The tea lady's voice was always cheerful. It was a rich and loud voice. Kate imagined her as big and black and a singer of gospel songs.

'Oh no, thank you, not today, thank you,' said Mrs Critchley.

'Oh go on, have a cup on me,' said Maurice. Good old Maurice.

'Oh thank you,' said Mrs Critchley. 'You're a real gent.'

'Any chance of a cup of tea for us?' asked Nigel.

'No, sir. Not for four of you. If I had the tea, I wouldn't have the cups. Sorry, sir.'

'But my mother isn't having a cup. Her cup's going begging. One of us could have a cup.'

'Elizabeth,' said Timothy.

'That's sexist,' said Elizabeth.

'Oh God,' said Timothy.

'I was joking,' said Elizabeth, to Kate's astonishment.

'Anyway, there isn't a cup going begging,' said the tea lady. 'The system knows your mother doesn't have a cup. The computer will come up "Nil by mouth". So, no cup.'

It was an unpleasant feeling to know that there was no cup for her in the system, that she was in the records as 'Nil by Mouth'. It sounded depressingly final. She'd show them. She'd get back on tea one day, and where would their fine computer be then?

The tea lady clanked off down the corridor, and Elizabeth resumed the conversation at exactly the point at which it had been broken off. 'What do you mean, Timothy, "Perfectly all right, as far as I know"?' Kate found that depressingly thorough of Elizabeth. People said she got her thoroughness from her German side. Perhaps there was some truth in that, though Heinz had never been *depressingly* thorough.

'She hasn't phoned,' said Timothy, 'and she isn't answering the phone. I rang one of the restaurants in Deya and told them I thought our phone was out of order and they got a bit embarrassed and said they thought she'd gone away.'

'I'm sorry.'

'What do you mean, "I'm sorry"? Nothing to be sorry for. I'm not there. She goes away. I go back. She'll be back. Why assume the worst?'

Nobody replied. Nobody said, 'Because it so often happens, Timothy.' But the remark was there, in the air, and all the more potent because nobody had said it.

Timothy broke the silence himself.

'Well,' he said, 'I'm off to the loo. Perfect chance to discuss me behind my back.'

When Timothy had gone there was another silence for a moment, but Kate knew, with a feeling of weary dread, that they would discuss him behind his back. She just hadn't expected Maurice to start. Oh dear, she was thoroughly awake again now.

'Poor Timothy,' he said. 'I do try, but I can't get more than about ten pages into his books.'

'Oh God, can't you?' Nigel sounded horrified.

'Why does that horrify you?' asked Maurice, echoing Kate's thought, as so often.

'He's our brother,' said Nigel. 'I'd like to think we all admired him. I like his books.'

'They appeal to your crossword mind,' said Elizabeth. Typically, she didn't say whether she liked the books or not.

'I don't like their kind,' said Maurice, 'and I don't even think they're very good of their kind. They're technically inept. Most of the clues are just slightly wrong.'

'You seem to know a surprising amount about them if you've only read the first ten pages,' said Nigel.

'I did finish one of them,' admitted Maurice.

'Which one?'

'*Trouble at the Double*. Why?'

'Well, that's his worst. If you've only read *Trouble at the Double* you must try at least one more.'

'I don't like his prose style,' said Maurice. 'People keep going very silent. How much more silent than silent can silent be?'

Kate wanted to cheer, which was disloyal to poor Timothy.

'His people are anatomically unusual,' continued Maurice. 'Their jaws keep dropping open. Their sinews keep stiffening.'

'S'sh! Here he comes,' warned Elizabeth anxiously.

'So, what have you been saying about me?' asked Timothy.

'Haven't mentioned you once,' said Maurice. 'We have more important things to talk about.'

'Children!' implored Elizabeth.

Their conversation was interrupted by the arrival of Doctor Ramgobi.

'Ah! We have the full team in today,' he said.

'Yes,' said Nigel. 'We were given to understand that . . .' He lowered his voice. '. . . something might happen.'

'Your mother was unusually distressed this morning. She was crying. Her temperature was up. Her pulse rate was up. The nurse thought it safest to inform you.' She felt the doctor's slightly podgy hand lift her arm and take her pulse. 'I believe that, if there was a crisis, and I'm not saying there was, it has passed.'

'She moaned a few minutes ago,' said Nigel.

'Did she indeed? Maybe she's getting a little more active. Maybe her distress was a sign of recovery, not relapse.'

'Waiter!' called out Mrs Critchley.

'Excuse me,' said Doctor Ramgobi.

'Bring me some coffee and biscuits,' commanded Mrs Critchley.

'What's the magic word?' asked Doctor Ramgobi.

'Young man,' said Mrs Critchley, 'I have been coming to this hotel for twenty-seven years and no member of staff has ever spoken to me like that.'

'They can't get the staff these days,' said Doctor Ramgobi.

'I demand to see the manager.'

'I am the manager. That's how bad things are. Coffee and

biscuits will be served in the lounge after luncheon.' He must have moved on then, because the next time he spoke it was to say, 'Now then, Hilda. I'm sending you home.'

'Doctor,' wailed Hilda, 'you can't. I feel terrible today. I have such pain.'

'You are better, Hilda. There's nothing wrong with you any more. It's time to go home.'

'Oh but, doctor, I'll miss the party.'

'The party?'

'Mrs Whatsit's hundredth birthday party. We're having a cake and there'll be a birthday card from . . .' Hilda's voice curtseyed. '. . . Her Majesty.'

I don't want a birthday party, thought Kate, and if I have one I don't want a card from the Queen, and if I do have a birthday party and I do get a card from the Queen, I don't want Hilda Mandrake to be there.

'I'll see what I can do,' said Doctor Ramgobi. Kate heard him ask her children, in a low voice, 'Would it be possible to invite this lady to the hundredth birthday party, if there is one?'

'Well, I think it would be a family occasion, actually,' said Timothy.

'Yes, of course. I think it very unlikely that she'd come, but . . . well, she doesn't want to go home because *she prefers it here*. I think that says it all, don't you? She probably wouldn't come, but an invitation would be a highlight.'

'I think we can agree to that, personally,' said Nigel. 'I don't think it would be much of a hardship to any of us. If we have a party. Always that proviso.'

'Of course. Thank you. Thank you very much.' The next time Doctor Ramgobi spoke it was to Hilda. 'You won't be left out, if there's a party.'

'Thank you, doctor.' She called out her thanks to the family and then she spoke to the doctor again. 'But I still don't think I'm fit to go home.'

'No, well, unfortunately I do, and I'm the doctor, and I need the bed.'

'Doctor Rambogi!' called out Glenda urgently.

'Ramgobi. What is it, Glenda?'

'You missed me out. You went straight from Mrs Critchley to Hilda.'

'I had some news for Hilda. I didn't have anything I needed to say to you.'

'Well, this is what I want to speak to you about, doctor. You say you need Hilda's bed. What about my bed? I can go home.'

'Glenda, you are not yet ready to go home.'

'But it's the house, doctor. Douglas can't manage.'

'I had the impression he's managing pretty well, Glenda.'

'He thinks he is. You mustn't listen to him. He won't ewbank under the beds. Oh listen to me, ewbank, that dates me. Hoover, I mean. He won't . . .'

'Glenda, I am rather busy.'

'He won't take the knick-knacks off the whatnot to clean under them. He'll dust round them.'

'Glenda . . .'

'I'm sorry, but his family just don't have our standards, and that's all there is to it.'

'Glenda, I am not sending you home.'

'But I want to go, and she doesn't, so what do you do? You send her and not me. You're perverse.'

'Glenda, whether a person is discharged from hospital or not is not a matter of the preference of the patient. Nor do you get remission for good behaviour. In my judgement, Hilda is fit to go home, and you are not, and I am the doctor.'

'Doctor!' quivered Mrs Critchley. 'Doctor! A few minutes ago you told me you were the manager.'

'You're not writing all this down, Timothy!' said Maurice in a low voice.

'I want to see the manager,' said Mrs Critchley. 'I remember the days when we had a palm court orchestra. Deirdre Pinkerton and the Palm Court Players. The muffins were legendary. Now the tea comes on a trolley, there's no music except through headphones and we have bogus doctors running around the bedrooms. It's a disgrace.'

'I'll fetch the manager,' said Doctor Ramgobi wearily.

When Mrs Critchley spoke again it was towards Kate's bed. 'I don't want you to think I'm putting you on the spot, not when you've a baby,' she said. 'How's the little mite doing?'

'He's very well, thank you,' said Elizabeth.

' "He". And there was I thinking it was a girl! Silly me. I'll be forgetting my own name next.'

She began to laugh, and stopped so abruptly that Kate was convinced that she had forgotten her own name.

'I can't believe you intend to exploit all this human misery, Timothy!' hissed Nigel.

'I won't be exploiting it,' said Timothy. 'I'll handle it with tact and sympathy. And I don't need lectures on morality from a man who gives wombats nervous breakdowns in the interest of medical science.'

'I have never experimented on animals,' said Nigel.

'You use the results of experiments, though, and knowingly,' said Maurice.

'Please, children, this is hardly the time,' said Elizabeth.

'You never like discussing major issues, do you?' said Maurice.

'Well, I'm sorry,' said Elizabeth. 'But is it? Is it the time?'

'No,' said Timothy, 'but if it was, you still wouldn't want to discuss it.'

'Come on,' said Nigel. 'Don't let's let our tensions get the better of us.'

A rather brusque nurse prised Kate's lips open roughly and slid in the cold, thin thermometer. Records must be kept. Kate was always very disappointed when it was a new nurse. She relied on fat Janet and thin Helen. She repented of all her unspoken criticisms of them. And she particularly disliked this brusque nurse, who said, 'Come on, Hilda. Get dressed for me. You're going home!' with no sensitivity at all.

Hilda didn't reply, but she must have begun to get dressed, because when Doctor Ramgobi returned he said, 'Getting dressed, Hilda? That's the ticket.'

'Doctor,' said Glenda, 'I want a second opinion.'

'I wish there was somebody here to give you one,' said Doctor Ramgobi. 'I wish I had the help I should have. I wish it wasn't Doctor Hallam's day for the clinic. I wish Doctor Stringfellow wasn't off sick. I wish I hadn't had to work seventy-eight hours last week. I'm afraid you'll have to take my opinion, Glenda, however much you distrust me.'

'It's not that I distrust you exactly, doctor,' said Glenda, 'but, let's face it, you are ethnic.'

'Oh, look here,' said Maurice. 'This is ridiculous. I can't have her saying that. Madam, you're being racist.'

'Thank you, sir, much appreciated, but I can fight my own battles,' said Doctor Ramgobi.

'I see nothing racist in saying you're ethnic,' said Glenda. 'Anyone can see you are. They only have to look at you. You're as ethnic as the ace of spades. It's a fact, not a criticism. I only meant, you probably don't have health like we do where you come from.'

'Sadly, I think that's very probably true,' said Doctor Ramgobi. 'I come from Huddersfield.'

When he spoke next he was close to Kate's bed and he spoke very quietly.

'Thank you, sir, but the lady is dying and deep down she probably knows it, so I make allowances,' he said. 'Now, your mother. Her temperature is down again, her pulse is normal, there are signs, minuscule perhaps but still possibly significant, of increased activity. We must be hopeful. In any case I am confident that there is no immediate crisis.'

'Thank you, doctor. I'm sorry I was so impulsive,' said Maurice. 'I can't bear racism.'

'I'm not too keen on it myself,' said Doctor Ramgobi. 'Now, a word of warning. I am, I believe, a good, experienced and competent doctor. However, no doctor is right all the time. Despite what I've said, your mother may not last the night.'

Oh yes, I bloody well will, thought Kate. I have a piece of unfinished business to complete.

10 Dilys

Before she married Walter for the second time, Kate had another piece of unfinished business to complete. It would be a difficult task, at the best of times, and this was not the best of times. But he telephoned, and she seized the moment.

She hadn't had a good night. She rarely did, at that time. She had slept fitfully, drifting in and out of anxious dreams, not quite sure whether the mournful cries of the tawny owls were in the wooded gardens of Dollery Road or in her dreams. Perhaps there were two owls, and one of them was in the wooded gardens, and the other was in her dreams, and that was why they were so mournful.

Dawn came slowly to the Gables. The day peeped shyly out from its blankets, rubbed its eyes, grew a little lighter and then retreated again. A song thrush sang majestically, clear liquid trills, cascades of joy. Surely this beautiful bird wasn't just saying, 'This tree's mine. Keep off, you bastards.' Surely it was saying, 'The sun's shining, the dew's glistening, the sky's blue, the lawn's green, the world is sometimes breathtakingly beautiful. Oh, and incidentally, this tree's mine, so keep off, you bastards.'

Kate felt a deep pit of knotted anxiety in her stomach. She padded naked along the corridor and was just about to put on her dressing-gown to enter Elizabeth's room when she remembered that all the children had gone to Walter for the night, as they so often did.

She went back to her bedroom and pulled back the curtains, revealing her naked body in all its splendour to the song thrush, should the song thrush be interested, which it wasn't. Mist was rising from the lawn as from a drying shirt. She heard the faint metallic clang of letters coming through the front door. She hurried downstairs, forgetting that she was naked, rushed into the hall, grabbed the letters, turned and gave a little scream of shock as she saw the postman peering in through the window in the side of the hall, nose pressed to the glass, eyes wide and hungry, lapping up what the song thrush had not appreciated. They stared at each other in shock for a moment, then she covered her pubic hair with her gas bill; this seemed to release him from his trance, and he disappeared. A moment later, while she was still examining her mail, she heard a mighty crash. She couldn't worry about that for the moment. There was one suspect envelope. She ripped it open and felt swamped by relief. It didn't begin 'We are very sorry to have to tell you that your son has given his life for his country. We are sure it will be a consolation to you to know that he died bravely.'

As she hurried upstairs to get her slippers and dressing-gown she wondered if they did send letters, or if they called round. She didn't think that she could bear it if they called round and saw her face crumple up.

She hurried downstairs again, thinking about how proudly, how eagerly, Nigel had gone off to fight for his country. He was big and strong and she knew that he had felt that his arrival in the war, coming so soon after that of the United States of America, would be the grain of sand that tipped the scales.

She hurried down the path in her slippers and dressing-gown. The postman was sitting at the side of the bright red letter-box which stood halfway down Dollery Road.

'Set off too fast, didn't I?' he said. 'Fell off my bike. Must have crashed into the letter-box.'

'Ironic.'

'What?'

'Never mind. Are you badly hurt?'

'Don't think so.'

'Pity.'

He looked at her beseechingly. He really did cut a pathetic figure. She could lose him his job. That would be a very middle-class thing to do. So what? He deserved it. She wondered how often he had stared at her.

She couldn't report him. After all, he hadn't brought a letter saying Nigel was dead. Probably he was very unhappy at home.

She had power over him. She was frightening him. He deserved it, but she didn't like doing it. She decided to put him out of his misery.

'If you ever do that again, I'll report you,' she said.

He couldn't speak. She held his bike out to him and he got on. He set off down Dollery Road.

'There is one thing,' she called out.

He wobbled and almost fell off again.

'Don't bother to call for a Christmas box this year.'

She walked up the tiled path. A wren scolded her. Her phone was ringing, shrill, sinister, bringing bad news.

'Hello.' She could hardly speak for nerves.

'It's me. Walter.'

Relief. Blessed relief.

'Darling! Are you naked?'

'Walter! Of course I'm not. I haven't been naked since the postman left.'

'What?'

'Tell you later.'

'The children send their love, Kate. Shall we see you for lunch?'

This was the moment. She had to tell him today. It had gone on far too long. It was ridiculous.

'Walter? Is there someone who can look after them?'

'Well, for goodness sake, Kate. Timothy's almost seventeen. I can leave them with him. But why?'

'There's . . . there's something I've got to tell you.'

*

'So, what is it you have to tell me?' he said as he entered the house.

'Let's have some coffee and go into the drawing-room,' she said.

'You can sit in the drawing-room. I'll sit in the lounge.'

She began to make the coffee and didn't respond.

'I'm sorry,' he said. 'It's just that . . . I'm a plain man.'

She snorted.

'You drink plain champagne and eat plain caviare,' she said. 'You're as plain as Croesus.'

'No, but I mean, I'm not artistic. I'd like to be, but I'm not.'

'What's being artistic got to do with it?'

'The drawing-room. I don't draw. I'm lazy, and I lounge.'

'You are as aware as I am that drawing-room is short for withdrawing-room.'

'Talking of withdrawing,' he said, 'any chance of a fuck?'

'Walter!'

'Sorry. I can't resist seeing that shocked chapel-girl look you still get, and I do want you most awfully.'

'One lump of arsenic or two?'

'Seriously, though, Kate. We were married. We are engaged. I know it's usually the other way round, but couldn't we . . . "resume conjugal relations"?'

'After what I've told you today, you may not want to.'

He walked up to her, put his arms on her shoulders, and pressed his body against her back. She poured the coffee and didn't look at him.

'It's serious, then, this thing that you have to tell me?'

'You know it is. That's why you're being so jokey. Come on. Let's go into the . . . well, as we're going to sit, how about compromising and calling it the sitting-room?'

The sitting-room was pale and restful, with splashes of bold pink and red from the curtains and lampshades. They sat on the settee. It was half the size of one of Walter's. He looked far too large for the room. Kate felt full of love for him, and very nervous. He was nervous too. His knuckles were white.

'So,' he said with a sigh, 'spill.'

'It's about . . . it's about Dilys.'

'Dilys??' His incredulity was swamped by his relief. 'I thought . . .' He stopped.

'You thought?'

'I thought . . . I thought you were going to tell me you had some fatal disease.'

'Oh, Walter!'

'I thought I was going to lose you.'

'No. I may lose you. You won't lose me. Well, you may lose your idea of me.'

'What is all this?'

She couldn't look at him, so she looked at the thrush. It was standing on the lawn, pulling at a long, wriggling worm. How horrid to be eaten alive.

'You probably think of me as a mature woman, Walter.'

'Positively elderly.' He was frisky with relief.

'Shut up. I've done something very silly that isn't mature at all.'

She paused. He waited.

'Dilys is dead.'

'Oh, Kate, I'm so sorry. My poor darling.'

He tried to kiss her, but she pushed him away.

'Oh, I've had plenty of time to get over it,' she said. 'It happened a long while ago.'

'When?'

'1905.'

'1905??'

'She was five.'

'But . . . your letters to her!'

'I didn't post them. There wasn't a lot of point.'

'But . . . that's crazy.'

'Yes.'

'But . . . you're not crazy!'

'Aren't I?'

'But . . .'

'But me no buts.'

'What?'

'Shakespeare.'

'Ah. Well, I wouldn't . . .'

'If you say you wouldn't understand because you're only a plain man, all you understand is pistons, I'll hit you.'

'But . . . sorry, but I have to say "but" . . . well . . . how did she die?'

'She was a spastic. Every day, Walter, I watched my twin sister get a little more ill. Every day I grew a little stronger. Every day she grew a little weaker.'

'And you wished the two of you could change places.'

'No, of course I didn't. I was so thankful it was her and not me.'

Walter didn't say anything. The thrush flew away, as if the garden of the Gables was no longer a wholesome place to be.

'Oh, I cried for her, Walter. I grieved for her. I loved her. I longed for her to be well. I prayed for her to be well. I am human. I also . . . because I'm human . . . resented her sometimes. All the attention. I knew it wasn't her fault, but . . . I felt she was letting me down. The wonderful closeness of identical twins. Inseparable emotionally. Always understanding what the other was thinking. One of them in Vancouver and the other in Llandrindrod Wells and they both bought identical hats at exactly the same time. The Thomas twins. Uncanny. All that was denied me. So, ever since then, Walter, I've tried to escape the grief, the loss, the guilt.'

'There's never any escape from guilt except by facing it.'

'There speaks the blunt piston manufacturer.'

'No! There speaks a man more intelligent and sensitive than you will ever allow, you snob you.'

Kate gasped. Walter held her by the shoulders again, and let her head rest on his great barrel of a chest.

'I could never face up to Dilys's death. I could never have talked to Arturo about it, or Heinz, or you till now, when I'm forty-four. I felt such pain about it, such guilt about it, about being the one who lived, about wanting to be the one who lived, about stealing her life from her, as it sometimes seemed even though I know that's ridiculous. So, I invented a life for her, to escape the truth. The awful thing is that I invented such a dull life. I wasn't going to have her upstage me.'

'I must say I'm relieved I'm never going to have to meet that plumber of hers. I've nothing against plumbers, but he did seem dreadfully dull. Wouldn't even have wanted to pop over to Congleton for a pint. Oh, Kate, how could you have needed to do all that?'

She shrugged.

'Fantasy is a very important part of reality,' she said.

'But . . . I thought you were so strong.'

'Isn't everybody racked by self-doubt? Except megalo-maniacs, of course, and I wouldn't want to be one of them.'

'But . . . sorry, this will be the last "but", I promise. But . . . your family! You told me never to mention Dilys to them. How did you get them never to mention her to me?'

'They never mentioned her again to me after she died,' she said. 'Never ever. Not one mention. I suppose they thought I'd be too upset. Maybe they wonder if I've forgotten. Or maybe they just didn't know what to say. Not one word.'

'I think that may have contributed to your need for a fantasy.'

Walter drew her face to his, and licked her tears.

'I don't know how you could have thought you'd lose me because of that,' he mumbled into her blouse. 'You can't have a very high opinion of me.'

She drew away from him, laughing now.

'I didn't hear a word of that,' she said.

He repeated it.

'Oh, Walter,' she said, 'I'm not a very nice person, am I?'

'You're beautiful though.'

He raised his eyes towards her bedroom, questioningly.

'Yes,' she said. 'I'm ready now. I'm certain of us now, Walter. You do understand that I had to tell you first, don't you?'

He picked her up as though she was made of feathers, and carried her to bed. Kate felt that the force of his love would break her in two. Their love that afternoon had an intensity to silence thrushes. Afterwards they lay in silence, looking at the gentle April clouds, had a bath together, feeling that that was really rather daring, in Dollery Road, in 1944, and then Kate made a pot of tea. Walter took great gulps – he was always thirsty, but especially so after sex – and then Kate went to the door to see him off, and he thought she had forgotten all about Dilys for the time being, but at the door she said, 'It's funny to think that if she'd lived she'd be forty-four.'

'Well, of course she would,' he said, slightly irritated that she had gone back to the subject.

'She'd have been a middle-aged woman.'

'Not if she was still identical.'

Again they married very quietly. It seemed the only appropriate way, the second time around. The children came, of course, including the newly demobbed Nigel, who had just won the Second World War, with a bit of help from his friends. There were no other guests. They didn't invite Kate's parents because they had been shocked by her divorce, and they didn't invite Walter's parents because they hadn't invited Kate's.

They didn't expect any wedding presents, but Walter's father gave them an amazing gift. He retired and left Walter in sole charge of the firm, the Boothroyd side having given up its interest long ago. Walter was an only child, and the apple of his father's eye. His father, Harold, had an even bigger house than Walter's. It looked like a cross between a minor château of the Loire and the clapboard Georgian mansion of a Kentucky horse trainer.

After the wedding they went to Swansea to make their peace with John Thomas Thomas and his beloved Bronwen. Kate's second divorce seemed to have shaken them even more than the first. That had been an aberration. This looked suspiciously like a habit. That had been Walter's fault. This time the fault seemed to be Kate's.

The situation was not made easier, for Kate, by the ironic fact that Maurice, Walter's only child, wasn't with them, while Elizabeth, Heinz's only child, was. Maurice was staying with friends. Elizabeth hadn't any friends with whom she could have stayed, had she wanted to, which she wouldn't have, even if she had had friends, for she was an irritatingly clingy child, worryingly so for seven.

Nothing was said, over tea, about Walter and Kate's remarriage. Her parents were in their seventies now. Her mother was beginning to look like a little old lady. John Thomas Thomas's hair and moustache had become as white as fresh snow. Remote behind a book of essays, with his hearing-aid not switched on, he looked like a god. He had mellowed slightly in his old age, and had now removed the photograph of Lloyd George altogether, believing that his brood were old enough not to need Awful Warnings any more. Kate knew that he must be disappointed in her. She felt dry in the mouth. Even three cups of tea couldn't assuage her thirst. She'd never realised before just how deeply she needed her mother's love and her father's approval. 'I'm not really wild,' she wanted to say. 'I'm steadfast. It may be my fourth marriage, but it's only my third husband, after all, and I didn't actually leave Heinz, he left me.' But she felt that her life had been more chaotic than they could fully accept, and that these arguments would have seemed like mitigating circumstances rather than a complete defence, and in any case she was too proud to defend herself at all.

She didn't know what Enid thought. She was very quiet at tea, and Kate felt that she must be jealous again. There was no possibility of Enid ever remarrying, because there was no possibility of her divorcing, because there was no possibility of her marrying in the first place.

There was no reason for Annie to feel jealous, she thought of marriage as a fate worse than death. If anything, she seemed excited at being privileged to sit in the presence of someone who led such an extraordinary life, though she could never admit this, and so she was very quiet also.

It was a quiet evening, therefore, in the cosy dining-cum-sitting-room, with the deep red curtain pulled across the French windows, and the reproduction of the Cézanne over the table. John Thomas Thomas buried himself in his essays. Annie sat on a hard chair with legs and arms spread out wide, the arms because they were wound with great skeins of wool, the legs because those women who have the least worth showing always show the most. The others talked of inconsequential matters while being acutely aware of the consequential matters about which they weren't talking.

No mention was made all weekend of Kate and Walter's remarriage, but there was melon at the beginning of Sunday lunch, and they had never had a starter before. 'Putting on airs,' sniffed Annie when she saw the melon, and Enid flashed her a quick look of resentment. Yes, thought Kate, I can understand how irritating Enid found that remark, but I actually prefer Annie in critical vein to Annie the gushing orphan. And then Annie spoilt it all by saying, 'Not that I should criticise. I'm so lucky to be here at all.'

As he drove away, Walter said, 'You didn't say anything about Dilys, then.'

'No.'

'I was waiting for you to, now that you'd told me.'

'It's all in the past, Walter. It's all over. Is there any point?'

Walter didn't reply.

Their next expedition was to London, to have dinner with Bernard. He was still working with Simms Fordingbridge, and he still had bits of foamy saliva around his teeth. He looked older than his thirty-seven years, but then he had looked about thirty-seven when he was ten. He took them to Schmidt's in Charlotte Street, where they had Wiener schnitzel and hock, and he said, 'In rejecting Churchill after the war the British people have made the most sophisticated decision, possibly the only sophisticated decision, in the history of democracy.' They expected him to say 'I beg your pardon?' but he didn't. 'There are times when a country needs socialism, and this is one of them.'

'I disagree,' said Walter.

'Oh good. I hoped you would. Wouldn't be much fun if you hadn't,' said Bernard, with a grin that, just for a moment, made him look ten years younger.

Poor Bernard, thought Kate, if he sees that as fun. But if you've worked as an accountant with Simms Fordingbridge for fifteen years, and think Wienerschnitzel with hock the apogee of sophistication, and have flecks of foam between your teeth, you probably don't have much fun.

Kate supported Bernard in the argument that followed. 'If we can't create a fairer, more compassionate, better educated, less selfish world after two massive world wars,' she said, 'there really isn't a great deal of hope.'

'I just want to make a decent profit and lead a comfortable life,' said Walter. 'Does that make me a leper?'

'Intellectually, morally, spiritually and politically, yes, I'd say it does,' said Bernard, and again he didn't say 'I beg your pardon?' when it might have been expected. Kate wondered if he'd stopped saying it.

Walter drove Bernard back to his flat in Kensington – as always, he had no problem getting petrol – and Bernard invited them in for a coffee and some schnapps he'd bought in Austria on holiday with Rodber before the war. He had this friend he referred to simply as Rodber, whom Kate had never met. It flashed through her mind that maybe Bernard was homosexual. Bernard adopted a rather posh, affected voice as he said, 'I felt very at home in Vienna, City of the Strausses, but Rodber didn't take to it. There's no music in his soul.'

When Kate needed to visit the smallest room, as she found herself calling it to Bernard, he waved his hands expansively, as if he was being a really generous host in allowing her to use it, and said, 'You know where it is.'

It turned out that he'd been overoptimistic in his assessment of Kate's knowledge of his bachelor flat. She found herself in his bedroom, and its state shocked her deeply. The bed was unmade, the sheets were grey, and the floor was covered in used shirts, crumpled socks and grey underpants with skid marks. No, she realised, Bernard wasn't homosexual, just asexual, which was far less hygienic.

When he saw them to the door, Bernard shook hands with Walter and also with Kate. She was astonished that he didn't kiss her, but rather relieved.

'It's been good to see you,' he said, 'and it's marvellous that you've got together again, I beg your pardon?'

Not long after their visit to London, they went to Farnham, where Oliver lived in an elegant Georgian house, as befitted a successful surgeon. He offered them sherry. No choice. He was as handsome as ever, thought Kate with pride. 'A lady will be joining us,' he said. 'I hope you don't mind.'

Kate was thrilled. Oliver was not a man who was meant to live alone. She longed for him to find someone else, but honesty compelled her to admit to herself that she was a little worried when he added, 'You'll like Bunny.' It's hard to find two major causes for concern in a sentence of three words, but Kate did. She had found that she never liked people whom she was told she would like, because if the people who hoped she would like them had been confident that she would like them they wouldn't have needed to tell her that she would like them. The second cause for concern was the name Bunny. Kate had met two women called Bunny, and she hadn't liked either of them. She hated the name, and had a vision of a fussy little woman with a retroussé nose, an overwhelming maternal instinct and a distressing enthusiasm for lettuce.

The doorbell rang. Oliver's housekeeper, Emily, admitted Bunny to the drawing-room – Walter didn't attempt to call this one the lounge, he knew when he was beaten – and said, in icy tones of fear and jealousy which she was unwise enough to reveal, '*Mrs* Parr-Parkinson.'

Kate had been wrong to expect a fussy little woman with a retrousé nose, an overwhelming maternal instinct and a distressing enthusiasm for lettuce. Bunny Parr-Parkinson was a bossy woman with huge hands, a loud voice, a smoker's cough, hair in her cavernous nostrils and a leathery skin more suited to a Greek fisherman than a Surrey lady. But Kate had been right about one thing. She didn't like her.

Oliver took them to the Prodigal Son at Worpleton St Andrew, where he gave them an excellent dinner accompanied by a fine Pomerol. They talked about love and marriage, without Oliver saying anything to indicate that his intentions towards Bunny Parr-Parkinson were serious. Kate had to admit that Bunny, whose surname was impossible to pronounce without sounding as though you had a slight stutter, was charming and civilised and not unamusing. In later years her gaffes would become legendary, but she only made one small faux pas that night, when she referred to 'we Conservatives'.

'Are there many wee Conservatives?' Kate enquired. 'In my experience most of them are disconcertingly large.'

'No, no,' said Bunny very seriously. 'I meant "we Conservatives" in the sense of "us conservatives". I assume we all are Conservatives.'

'It's dangerous to assume that other people share your particular views,' said Kate. 'For your information, Walter does, I don't.'

'Kate, please, this isn't the time,' said Oliver, and Kate thought this rather disturbingly weak of him, she'd never thought of him as weak.

'I didn't start it,' she said, 'but no, it isn't the time, so I'll stop it.'

'It simply has been an astonishing year for tulips,' said Bunny Parr-Parkinson, revealing an astonishing ability to change the subject dramatically.

'It has. I've never experienced a year like it,' agreed Walter. 'For tulips,' he added.

Kate met his eye. A gleam passed between them. She felt very happy.

'How did our parents accept your remarrying Walter?' Oliver asked, over the coffee, which was vile. 'They are wonderful people, but very narrow,' he told Bunny.

'Mother was deeply shocked but also delighted, though she wouldn't say so in case Father wasn't, said Kate. 'Father thought it too personal a subject for discussion, so we'll never know what he thought.'

Oliver drove them back to their hotel in his Humber Super Snipe, and said, 'I'm so glad you like Bunny,' though neither of them had said that they had.

On their fourth visit to Swansea, in the summer of 1946, Kate and Walter arrived, with Elizabeth, to find the family in a state of high excitement. The petrol ration had been increased by fifty per cent. This was a rare moment of joy in the austere public life of post-war Britain, to whom Victory had been delivered firmly bound with red tape. It was comparable, indeed, with that other moment of excitement, the arrival of the first bananas. Recalling Elizabeth's excitement at the sight of her first banana, Kate felt a stab of pity for modern children. Knowing only plenty, living among surfeits, how could they feel excitement?

The excitement in the Eaton Crescent household was because Bernard now had enough petrol to come by car. With two cars, there was the prospect of a run. It was hard, even for Kate with her sharp memory, to recall just how palpable was the excitement, in those days, of a family without a car, when they had the prospect of a run.

Bernard was late. By the time the clock in the hall struck eleven, both her parents were yawning. She nudged Walter. Quick on the uptake, he said, 'Look, why don't you all go on up? Kate and I'll wait up for Bernard. It could be well past midnight. It's a long haul through Gloucester, unless he gets the Aust ferry, and there'll be long queues for that on a Friday night.'

'No, no. I should stay up to greet him,' said Bronwen.

'Only I thought we might go for a run tomorrow,' said Walter, 'and you want to be fresh for that.'

John Thomas Thomas and Bronwen were persuaded without great trouble. When they had gone, Enid glared at Annie and said, 'I'll stay up. You're visitors. You go on up. You've had a long drive. I insist. I'll be all right. I'll read Jane Austen in my dressing-gown.'

'Well, I think it's time to go up the wooden hill to Bedfordshire,' said Annie, gathering up her wool.

Kate could see that Enid was bursting to talk to her, and she felt a great pride in Walter when he said, 'I'll go on up, I think. Night-night, Enid. Sleep well.'

'He's surprisingly sensitive,' she said to Enid.

'Oh yes, he's wonderful,' said Enid drily.

Kate sighed.

'Oh, Enid,' she said. 'I hope you aren't jealous.'

'Well, no,' said Enid. 'Not really. But it's very hard for me not to think of you gallivanting around, leading such a rich life – and the silly thing is, of course, I wouldn't want your life, I'd hate it – while I stay here and teach and will stay because someone has to look after Mother and Father. I mean, I'm not blaming you, Kate. I'm here because I didn't marry and I didn't marry because I'm so feeble.'

'Oh, Enid!'

'My holiday this year was a guest-house in Llandrindrod Wells. It's not exactly a glamorous life. Kate, I have to get it off my chest about Annie.'

'What about Annie?'

'She's changed. She used to offer to do everything. "I don't mind. I'm so lucky to have been taken in by this family," she'd say.'

'And now you're beginning to think the family's been taken in by her.'

'You see. That's clever. Well, neat anyway. I never say anything neat.'

'Oh, Enid. So doesn't she do her bit any more?'

'She does her bit. Oh yes, always does that. Nothing more. I mean, she could have offered to stay up tonight.'

Kate kissed Enid and said, 'I wish you were happier.'

'Well, this is the silly thing,' said Enid. 'I am happy, really. I quite like my life.' She plucked up her courage, and asked, in a near whisper, as if she didn't want the grandfather clock to hear, 'Do you still hear from Heinz at all?'

'He sends a card every Christmas.'

Kate sighed.

'Do you miss him?' asked Enid.

'No,' said Kate. 'I sighed because I like him. I didn't like falling out of love with him, but no, Enid, no, I wouldn't say that I miss him at all. Not that I need feel sorry for him. He's engaged, and his fiancée's very pretty. He sent me a photograph of her. That was kind of him, wasn't it?'

'Doesn't he want to see Elizabeth?'

'Oh yes, but he knows he can't. She doesn't know he's her father.'

'Will you ever tell her?'

'At the right time, when she's old enough, yes, I think we must. We must give him a chance to see her. He always asks about his little princess, in his card.'

'Perhaps it's best if he doesn't see her, if he thinks of her as a princess.'

Kate almost retorted angrily, but then she thought about how she would feel if she was a spinster and Enid had four children by three different husbands, and she held her tongue.

They set off shortly before eleven, which was good going. The ladies had made a fine picnic in the scullery, and John Thomas Thomas had said hesitantly, 'Er . . . I suppose Tenby would be too far,' and Kate had realised that he was beginning to get just a little childish.

'Aren't you too tired, Bernard?' Kate had asked. He'd looked very tired after the previous evening's journey.

'No, I'm not tired,' he'd said.

'But won't it use up too many coupons?' Kate had asked, offering Bernard a more official excuse to back out.

'No, no. I can just manage it,' he'd insisted. 'I'd love to see Tenby again.'

Bernard led the way, because he was Welsh and Walter wasn't. The two cars sped along the empty August roads, the little Morris 8 in front, the posh Daimler behind, like a dinghy towing a yacht. Walter and Kate took John Thomas Thomas and

Bronwen, while Enid, Annie and Elizabeth went with Bernard. Elizabeth whimpered because she wanted to go with her mother, but Kate said, 'Don't be so pathetic. I'll only be in the car behind.' Enid would have preferred Elizabeth to go in the car behind, but Annie was grateful for her presence, Kate could see, as a lever to use as a warning to Bernard.

As the Daimler slid through the suburbs of Swansea towards Pontardulais, John Thomas Thomas pointed out a hideous, grandiose, gaunt, pebble-dashed chapel, and said, proudly, 'Walter Copson, that chapel was built by my Uncle Emlyn.' Kate thought Walter's reply of 'It's big, isn't it?' uninspired, but it seemed to satisfy John Thomas Thomas. He asked Walter to slow down as they passed a row of low, grey terrace houses, and said, 'See the house with the blue door, Walter Copson? The best fly-half Llanelli ever had was born there.' Kate thought Walter's reply of 'In that very house? Extraordinary!' rather foolish. The man had to have been born in some house, why not this one? But the answer seemed to satisfy John Thomas Thomas.

On the outskirts of Carmarthen, Bernard pulled in to a garage, signalling to Walter to follow.

Walter and Kate got out of the Daimler and walked over to the Morris 8.

'There's a rattle coming from my car,' said Bernard. 'The big end's going.' He said that with total assurance, even though he had no idea what a big end was, or where it went when it was going, and even though he was talking to a leading light in the engineering industry. Big ends were what went in cars in those days, so a big end going it must be.

The mechanic, however, gave the car a test run and came up with a different diagnosis.

'You picnic set's rattling,' he said.

Walter showed no amusement at Bernard's gaffe, and Bernard showed no embarrassment. Kate felt full of love for her surprisingly gentle husband and her earnest bachelor brother.

A few miles beyond Carmarthen, as Bernard approached a sharp bend, Kate saw Annie turn to Elizabeth and speak. She didn't have to be in the car to know what Annie was saying. 'Uncle Bernard's coming to a sharp, narrow bend, Elizabeth. Watch Uncle Bernard slow down quite a lot and keep right in to the left very carefully.'

They picnicked on the North Beach. Seagulls wheeled over the pastel houses of the trim, Georgian town, and they ate bloater-paste sandwiches and hard-boiled eggs and tomatoes and scones and Welsh cakes and bara brith. John Thomas Thomas and Bronwen stared at the sea enraptured, as old people do. An occasional small cloud passed swiftly across the golden sands, as if strange-shaped camels and elephants were flying past the sun, and a brief shadow passed over the conversation when Enid said, 'Gwen Jenkins whose aunt had a seizure in Brecon had bloater-paste sandwiches and was dead within five hours. There was a lot of tragedy in that family.'

When they got back to Swansea, Bernard wasn't feeling very well and went to bed early. 'Maybe it's the bloater-paste sandwiches,' he quipped bravely, but Kate looked into his tired, deep-set eyes and suddenly knew that it wasn't the bloater-paste sandwiches, he was very seriously ill indeed.

The next morning, in chapel, Kate prayed, on the off chance. After the service she remembered the day when Gwyn had come over to speak to her for the first time. She put her arm through Walter's and squeezed his arm and thought herself lucky after all. She hugged Elizabeth to her, and the three of them set off happily for Sunday lunch. No melon this time.

Later that afternoon, when it was time for Kate and Walter and Elizabeth to go home, and the whole family came to the door to wave goodbye, and they set off down Eaton Crescent, Kate felt a surge of certainty that this time she and Walter would live happily together until death did them part.

They might have done, too, but for Red Ron Rafferty, President of the National Union of Piston Makers, Flange Cutters and Scrag-end Offloaders.

Kate might never have met Red Ron Rafferty, but for a Sunday lunch party that she and Walter gave in the early summer of 1948. Well, it was really a family lunch to which Stanley and Jasmine happened to be invited.

Kate had been just a little upset with Walter over the invitation to Stanley.

'I've invited an old chum of yours to lunch on Sunday,' he'd said, over breakfast in the cavernous kitchen one day. 'Stanley Wainwright.'

'Oh heavens. Why?'

'I thought you'd be pleased. I thought I'd show you that my horizons are expanding. The chap's pretty well thought of, apparently.'

'He's internationally famous.'

'Exactly. He's coming to the works on Monday. I thought I might commission a sculpture for the forecourt. I thought you'd be thrilled if I started becoming a patron of the arts. You know him, and he's famous, so he seemed the ideal chap, so I said, "Why not come up early and come for Sunday lunch?"'

Kate paused in the act of scraping the burnt bits off a slice of toast. Even Walter's money hadn't proved enough to buy a toaster that worked.

'You haven't invited him to stay?' she said.

'No. Don't want to get too intimate.'

'Nor do I. He can be extremely lecherous.'

'Well, he'll have his wife with him.'

'I don't imagine that would stop him.'

'She's called Jasmine.'

'Oh Lord, is she? I can see her now. Vaguely oriental and

sweet and utterly, utterly adoring. I think I'm going to be sick, and I haven't even met her yet.'

'Kate!' He was quite stern.

'What?'

'Sometimes you let your cleverness run away with you. It isn't clever to do that. And you are sometimes wrong. You were utterly wrong about Bunny.'

'I wasn't wrong not to like her, though, I mean, not even asking us to the wedding! Not even asking Bernard!'

'We didn't ask them to ours.'

'That's different. We'd been married before. Oh, Walter.'

She walked round the table to kiss him. It was quite a long walk, so the gesture was hardly spontaneous, but she kissed the top of his head several times and noticed that his unruly black hair was just beginning to thin.

'Thank you, Walter. I think it's a great idea about the sculpture and I'm most impressed,' she said.

'I didn't want you to be impressed,' he said. 'I wanted you to be happy.'

The day of the lunch party was delightful, one of the first lovely days of summer, warm and gentle, with a light breeze bringing the smell of new-mown hay. There were eight of them for lunch, Kate and Walter, Stanley and Jasmine, Bernard and the three boys. Boys! Nigel and Timothy were both at university. Elizabeth wasn't there. She'd made a friend at last, and was away, visiting that friend.

Kate remembered having drinks in the garden, but she couldn't recall a thing they talked about. But when they went inside and were seated round the huge dining table, with Kate at one end and Walter at the other, she seemed able to recall every word.

'How are you liking Copson Towers, Jasmine?' Nigel shouted across the table. 'Sorry to shout, but the acoustics are bad in some of the far corners.'

'Yes, yes, Nigel, it's a big room, very amusing,' said Kate, 'but don't shout, darling, please.'

'I think it's all very . . . er . . .' Jasmine had clearly been going to say 'nice' and then had second thoughts, in case Stanley erupted at the anodyne adjective, or hated the house. '. . . very impressive.' Jasmine looked very tiny, in front of the huge belly of the pseudo-medieval brick chimney. She was vaguely oriental and sweet and utterly, utterly adoring. 'It's not really called Copson Towers, is it?'

'No,' said Nigel. 'That's my little joke.'

'And it doesn't get any bigger,' said Timothy.

The food was traditional, as Walter demanded, but excellent – superb rare beef, succulent Yorkshire pudding, home-made horseradish sauce, golden roast potatoes. The Nuits St George was mature and velvet, soft and subtle.

'This is good stuff, Walter,' said Stanley. 'This is wonderful stuff.' Nigel and Timothy began to drink their wine a great deal more carefully. 'How much did this set you back?'

First mention of money, thought Kate.

'One pound six shillings a bottle,' said Walter proudly.

Kate saw Bernard's eyes widen at the thought of spending so much money on a bottle of wine. He tasted the wine very seriously, rolling it round his tongue. She smiled at him lovingly. There were black bags under his eyes, and she didn't like the sallowness of his complexion. There was a suspicious mark around the flies of his dark flannel trousers, and there was the usual saliva around his teeth. She had to admit that he didn't enhance her table, and she could almost – almost – forgive Oliver and Bunny for not inviting him to their wedding.

'You've certainly got some place here, Walter,' said Stanley. 'I'm not surprised Nigel calls it Copson Towers.'

'I have a name for my mother,' piped up Maurice, largely because he thought it was about time that he spoke.

Kate could sense a sudden tension round the great table, as

everybody prepared to be embarrassed by a fourteen-year-old. Maurice went slightly pink and lost the courage to carry on.

'Come on, Maurice,' said Timothy, not unkindly. 'What do you call her?'

'I call her Kate of the Two Settees,' said Maurice, going red. 'Like Anna of the Five Towns.'

Kate felt quite proud of Maurice. It was a lovely description. And yet . . . and yet . . .

For a moment nobody said anything. What Maurice had said wasn't hilarious, so it would be patronising to roar with laughter, but it really was pretty good, and he was going very red now and thought he had a massive flop on his hands.

'That's very good,' Kate said, meaning it. 'I like that,' she added, not meaning it.

She thought that Nigel looked angry, but he smiled and said, 'No, Mother's right, Maurice. That's very good. Far better than my Copson Towers. Mother, from now on you are Kate of the Two Settees.'

Walter poured more wine. Stanley was drinking fast, and so was Timothy. Maurice said, 'Can I have half a glass without water rather than another glass with water. I want to see if I'm mature enough to appreciate it.'

'I don't see why not,' said Kate of the Two Settees. 'I think you've earned it.'

'I saw a mutual friend last week, Kate,' said Stanley. 'Daniel Begelman.'

Kate found herself resenting Stanley's use of the word 'mutual' in connection with Daniel.

'He's very excited about the creation of Israel. He says it's going to be his artistic salvation, and they're going to live there. He's had a terrible time. They wouldn't even use him as a war artist, and they used everybody.'

'I like the concept of war artists,' said Timothy. ' "What did you do in the war, Daddy?" "Joined the Queen's Own Highland

Light Watercolourists, son. First day in the trenches, our captain said, 'Right, chaps. I want you to get over to Gerry's left flank and paint the bastard. Don't let him see you or he'll go all self-conscious. I want the truth. I want real corporals, not acting corporals.' "'

It was inventive and amusing, as Timothy could be when on form, but Kate didn't feel like laughing. She found it impossible to laugh about war. And Nigel, who had been to war, laughed but not, she felt, with his eyes.

'Why wouldn't they use Daniel?' Kate asked.

'They didn't say. He thinks it's because he's too uncompromising. Olga things it's anti-Semitism. I just don't think he's quite good enough, simple as that.'

Kate wondered if Bernard noticed how this remark upset her, because he suddenly changed the subject most abruptly, saying, 'Do you play much sport at the varsity?' in the affected tone she had heard him use once before, about his trip to Vienna with Rodber. It made her want to cry to hear Bernard using this pretentious voice. It made her realise just how insecure he was.

'I know I ought to be sporty, with my physique,' answered Nigel, 'but I'm not very interested, and I don't have a lot of time. You have to work hard when you read science at Oxford. It isn't quite like reading languages at Cambridge.' He looked across at Timothy with loving scorn. Timothy stuck his tongue out at him. I have to remember how young they still are, thought Kate. 'I play mind games. Chess. Bridge. My mother disapproves.'

'Nigel!' said Kate.

'Well, you do.'

'It makes me sound so priggish. I just feel that there's so much unhappiness in the world, so many problems to be solved, so much stupidity, that people with fine minds ought to save them for the real tasks.'

This proved quite a conversation stopper. After a few very silent moments, Bernard, who might have taken her up on it if he'd had more energy, persisted with his sport theme.

'And what about you, Timothy?' he asked. 'Any sport in your life?'

'Hockey,' said Timothy. 'I love hockey. It's an awful game to watch, but a wonderful game to play.'

'Your Uncle Oliver played hockey for Wales,' said Bernard. 'He scored the winning goal in their 4–3 victory over Uruguay in Montevideo.'

'My word. What an achievement to tell your children about,' said Stanley sarcastically.

'Yes, I think it would be. Unfortunately his only child was born dead,' said Bernard.

There was a horrified silence.

'I'm so sorry,' said Bernard. 'I shouldn't have said that.'

'More meat, anybody?' asked Kate.

It seemed that everybody except Jasmine wanted more meat. And everybody except Maurice wanted more wine. Jasmine frowned at Stanley as he allowed his glass to be refilled.

'So, Walter,' said Stanley Wainwright, 'what do you want from me tomorrow? A tribute to the world of the piston?'

'Oh yes,' said Walter. 'It's hilarious, isn't it? Uncultured Midland businessman, let's take the piss.'

'Walter!' said Kate. 'Language! Maurice is fourteen.'

'I do know what piss is,' said Maurice.

'I'm not taking the piss at all,' said Stanley. 'I admire you. Living in a place like this, serving us wine like this. I'm in the wrong business.'

'You certainly are not,' said Walter. 'You charge hundreds for a commission.'

'Supply and demand,' said Stanley Wainwright.

'And that's what mine is,' said Walter.

'I don't think you can compare the two,' said Bernard. 'Stanley deals in works of art. You can't put an exact price on that.'

'You could very easily,' said Walter. 'So much an hour, plus materials.'

'Stanley isn't a jobbing gardener,' said Jasmine. 'He's a great artist.'

'All right,' said Walter, who was slightly flushed from the wine and the heat, 'so his hourly rate will reflect his talent and reputation and be more than the rate claimed by some wanker who displays in the village hall.'

'Walter! Language!' said Kate. 'What's wrong with you today? What sort of example are you setting Maurice?'

'It's all right, Ma,' said Maurice. 'I know what a wanker is.'

'That's why I don't want your father to talk about it,' said Kate.

'I don't resent your making money out of your art,' said Walter. 'I just resent your suggesting that I'm greedier than you. Awful greedy businessman. Wonderful spiritual artist. You're a greedy man trading on your fame and fortune.'

Stanley Wainwright unwound his great body from his chair and Kate was reminded of her first sight of him in the tea shoppe in Penzance.

'Right,' he thundered. 'Right . . .'

'Oh, please sit down, Stanley,' implored Jasmine. 'If you're going to storm out, finish your Nuits St Georges first.'

Stanley glowered at Jasmine, glared at Walter, glanced greedily at his glass, and sat down. Kate wanted to say, 'Jasmine, I underestimated you. That was cleverly done.'

'Stanley's always storming out these days,' said Jasmine. 'It's selfish. I have a sweet tooth and I never get to stay for the dessert.'

'I'm afraid I am rather volatile,' said Stanley complacently, 'but then I'm an artist.'

'I apologise,' said Walter. 'I overstepped the mark. But I don't think artists have the right to lecture businessmen because they make money. I don't look up to the world of art because it's above greed and money. I look up to it because it's clever and inventive and beautiful and life-enhancing and exciting and fun, and I get as angry about businessmen who despise art as I do about artists who despise businessmen. I do have a problem, and I'm going to shock you here. It's with my wife. I love my wife. I've proved it. I haven't just married her once, I've married her twice. She's a wonderful woman. I take her interests seriously, but she doesn't take my work seriously. It's one-way traffic.'

'Walter!' said Kate, shocked. 'I do.'

'Do you buggery!'

'Walter!'

'It's all right, Ma, I know what buggery is.'

'Where do you learn all these things, Maurice?'

'School. Pretty disastrous concept, really, school.'

'I apologise for my language,' said Walter. 'My civilisation's only skin deep, and I want Kate to help me with that. But it can't just be a one-way process. You've never once come to see the works. You've never taken any interest.'

'I haven't wanted to come,' said Kate, 'not because I don't respect what you do, but because I know I wouldn't understand a thing I see. I must say I do question the whole basis of our education, and the way we choose the subjects that suit us and that we find easiest. It's ludicrous, in 1948, in the middle of the century of the machine, that anybody should be allowed to be so ignorant about machines, and physics, and chemistry. I want to come tomorrow morning, Walter. I'll brave my ignorance.'

'I can't do tomorrow morning,' said Walter. 'I've got Stanley coming tomorrow. If he still wants to.'

'Oh yes,' said Stanley, 'and I'll knock ten pounds off my price if you can find another bottle of this Nuits St Georges.'

'Well, there must somebody who could show me round,' said Kate.

'Talking of Nuits St Georges,' said Bernard, 'I can't help feeling sorry for our parents, Kate, denying themselves utterly the pleasures of alcohol, I beg your pardon?'

'I'm glad you said, "I beg your pardon?"' said Kate, 'because it shows that you know that I'm not going to agree. Yes, the Nuits St Georges is wonderful, and there's never been a drop of alcohol in 16 Eaton Crescent, but they've never had as argumentative a meal as this. Who's for treacle tart and who's for apple pie?'

Ron Rafferty was a big-boned Irishman from Cork, with sandy hair, a melting smile and a touch of haughtiness in his carriage. He was in his late thirties. His every movement spoke of his pride in himself and his scorn for . . . not for Kate, he had too much natural courtesy for that, but for the task he'd been landed with that morning, his role of tour guide to the Managing Director's wife.

The vast sheds were throbbing with noise, pulsating with activity. In the foundry the heat was intense, the glimpses of the power of the roaring flames were awe-inspiring, the noise was deafening, the danger was palpable.

Ron took Kate across vast floors between huge, noisy machines and great furnaces with hot breath. He led her up steep ladders on to galleries which looked down on people who were specks dwarfed by technology.

'Ladies first,' he said with a humorous glint in his eye at the bottom of each ladder. She was certain that he looked up her skirt as she climbed, but not certain enough to rebuke him for it. He stopped in the noisiest places to explain the most obscure processes to her. Fifty-one years later she could remember none of the technical terms and suspected that fifty-one days later she wouldn't have remembered them. She only heard isolated phrases on the day itself. '. . . die-cast aluminium . . . machining the lands . . . compression rings . . . connecting rods . . . gudgeon pin . . . maximum piston speed limited by the inertia factor . . . some have hemispherical heads, some have domed . . .' Well, something like that, but it was as much Greek to her as Greek would have been to him. It didn't make sense to her, she wanted it to make sense to her, Ron Rafferty knew that it didn't make sense to her and she suspected that he didn't want it to make sense to her and that he knew that she suspected that he didn't want it to make sense to her.

She could think of no question to ask that wouldn't reveal the depth of her ignorance. Even 'What's that?' was fraught with danger, let alone 'How do the gudgeon pins connect to the compression rods?' She would doubtless ask 'What's that?' about the most obvious thing in the works, or a fire extinguisher, and his scorn would know no bounds.

And so they toured the works, this strong Welsh lady who wanted to be liked, and this strong Irish man who didn't care whether he was liked or not and was therefore the stronger on the day. Kate felt like a bemused minor Royal without the arrogance. She was the visiting socialite who strikes an alien note. She was the little woman. She was an inconvenience in Ron Rafferty's diary.

'Well, now you know all about how it's done,' said Red Ron Rafferty at the end of the tour, smiling with enough blarney to melt a stone.

She smiled too. 'You know perfectly well that I know nothing about how it's done,' she said. Her head was aching, her ears were pounding, she had never known such noise as on that morning. 'I respected what I understood and what I didn't understand. I shall never make the mistake of underestimating the skill, strength and dedication of the people I've seen working here today. Thank you very much for escorting me. I shall tell my husband that you've done it perfectly. Thank you, Ron.'

She held out her hand and, afterwards, felt almost certain that he'd given it a little squeeze. But she was feeling weak, and might have imagined it.

She was wandering along a pavement in West Bromwich,

thinking about Daniel Begelman, and suddenly there he was coming towards her, in this of all places. Not Daniel Begelman. Red Ron Rafferty. The Begelmans were in Spain. She'd received the letter this morning. 'Israel is too new a country and too surrounded a country and too martial a country. They haven't time for art yet. I simply couldn't do good work there. I need space.'

There he was, hunched against the biting wind in a long coat that might have been more appropriate in East Europe than West Bromwich.

'Mrs Copson!'

'We aren't at the works now. Call me Kate.'

'Bit off your beat, aren't you?'

'I'm not a policeman.'

'I suppose bearing in mind the gulf between our social positions, the chasm I might call it, a drink would be out of the question?'

'You know perfectly well, you infuriatingly clever man, that that is the one approach you could possibly use to get me to have a drink with you.'

He led her into the nearest pub. She didn't even notice its name. It had a series of small rooms, with warm fires. Pensioners were playing cards and dominoes. Office workers were eating liver-sausage sandwiches. Irishmen were digesting pickled onions and the *Sporting Chronicle*.

'Pint of Guinness?'

'Don't be ridiculous, Ron. I've never had a pint of Guinness in my life.'

'Never too late to start. Better in Dublin, of course,'

And so she drank her first pint of Guinness. It took her a long time, long enough for Ron to drink four. It was pleasant, it was very slightly raffish, it was life.

'How long is it since that day?' he asked.

'Oh, I don't know.'

'Nearly three years.'

'Really?'

'You were so anxious to be liked. I did like you, but I wasn't letting on.'

'Cruel man.'

'What brings you to this neck of the woods?'

'A bric-a-brac shop called Junk and Disorderly. A friend recommended it.'

She didn't tell him that she was determined to break up the great spaces and heavy furnishings of Copson Towers with little things, sweet things, cheap things, fun things, undistinguished things.

'You aren't comfortable as a magnate's wife, are you, Kate?'

'It's rude to read people's minds without asking if you can borrow them first.'

He grinned. She noticed that he had marvellous teeth. Good though they were, she had seen enough of them for the time being. She needed to wipe the smile off his cheeky face.

'I'm very happy with Walter, I do assure you, and he with me,' she said, with a touch of asperity.

'Oh, sure, sure, I wasn't meaning that. There are limits even to my cheek. I meant, your Role in Society.'

'Oh, my Role in Society. No, well, my son Maurice – he's seventeen now, goodness, almost grown up – he once dubbed me Kate of the Two Settees.'

He laughed. 'There's a title there,' he said. '*A Tale of Two Settees*. Not quite Dickensian. You look surprised. Not because I know Dickens, surely?'

'No. Yes.'

'I love words, Kate. We Irish do.'

'They pour out of us Welsh pretty freely too.'

'So, this meeting of Celts is a serendipitous event.'

She tried very hard not to look surprised again. He talked about Cork, his childhood, fishing trips, trout-tickling, drinking

233

the Ring of Kerry dry. She talked about her family in Swansea, altering the details ever so slightly to make her origins just a little humbler than they'd been.

When they left the pub he shook her hand and said, 'Will you tell your husband about our meeting?'

'Do you think I should?' she asked.

'I think you should. I hope you won't.'

She didn't.

Kate was astounded when he rang her at home.

'Ron who?' she said.

'Ron Rafferty.'

'Oh. Oh!'

'You don't like me ringing you at home?'

'Well, I . . .'

'There's no risk. Your husband's here. I've just seen him. I wondered about lunch tomorrow. A restaurant this time. Your world, not mine.'

'I don't think that would be a very good idea.'

'The same pub as before, then?'

'That wasn't what I meant.'

'No, I know. Twelve o'clock?'

He rang off. Cheeky swine. Arrogant, irritating, handsome man. How did he know she wasn't doing something next day? She often was. It so happened that she wasn't. The luck of the Irish! No, it wasn't lucky for him, because she wouldn't go. Well, not definitely. Well, definitely not. She wouldn't give him the satisfaction. She needed to go to Junk and Disorderly again, though. They'd have new stuff in by now. She'd go to Junk and Disorderly and then decide whether to go to the pub or not. She'd go to Junk and Disorderly and not go to the pub, even though she'd be so close to it. That would show him. Except that it wouldn't, because he wouldn't know she'd been to Junk and Disorderly.

Even as she left the shop she wasn't sure if she would go. To go, to do his bidding, seemed . . . well . . . craven and pathetic. Not to go, on the other hand, would be . . . even more craven and pathetic. It would suggest that she was standing on the dignity of her social position.

So she decided to go, but fifteen minutes late. That would give him a bit of a fright.

To her chagrin, he didn't look as though he had worried a jot. He seemed pleased that she'd come, though, and they had a pleasant time again.

After that, he would phone every six weeks or so. She never asked why he had that particular day off. He always chose days that were convenient for her. The luck of the Irish.

'You're very lucky,' she said once. 'I'm usually very busy.'

'Are you so? I am lucky, then.'

The swine didn't believe her!

They always went to the same pub, she always had a pint of Guinness while he had four. Once they played darts. She felt emancipated! Ridiculous. No harm in it, though, and she went home feeling happier about being Kate of the Two Settees.

Gradually, inevitably, given their interests and differences, a political element crept into their conversations. On their fourth meeting, Ron talked about the modest lives of the workers, the financial difficulties many of them faced. She found herself defending Walter, saying he wasn't really rich, he worked hard, he took risks, he provided work.

'I'm not fanatical,' said Ron. 'I believe you and Walter should have a better life than us.'

Kate raised her eyebrows.

'No. I'm serious. You should have a bigger home. A better car. A nicer bathroom. Better holidays. But you have three nice bathrooms. You shouldn't have two until all your employees have one. You shouldn't have three till all your employees have two. Your status should be modestly superior.'

'It doesn't work like that.'

'No, but it should. Don't you believe that, deep down, Kate of the Three Nice Bathrooms, who was once a communist?'

Kate had to admit that she did. She went home, that time, feeling less happy about being Kate of the Two Settees.

She decided that the next time she saw Ron she would tell him that she wasn't going to see him any more.

She didn't tell him straight out. It wouldn't have been subtle. She talked first about how unhappy she was not to be working. 'I tell myself it's important to be at home when Elizabeth gets back. She's only thirteen. But if I had a teaching job I could get home too.'

'Could you teach?'

'I did. I taught history in Penzance.' She didn't tell him that it had been a private school. 'Sometimes I wonder what happened to all those girls I taught.'

Somehow she didn't get round to ending it all. It wasn't a sexual relationship. There was no harm in it. It would be awfully stiff and conventional to end it all.

They didn't meet for four months after that. She had to cancel one meeting because her father was knocked down by a lorry and broke his leg. She went to Swansea for several weeks then, missed Walter terribly, missed the sex; he came down for weekends, but the sex was never the same in Swansea.

John Thomas Thomas came home from hospital, and said, 'They tell me I'll never walk without a stick again. That gives me something to live for, doesn't it? To prove them wrong.'

In Swansea, in that straight-living house, in chapel on Sundays, Kate knew that, although there was no harm in her relationship with Ron, there was harm in the secrecy of it. She must either tell Walter or end it, and telling Walter would mean ending it anyway.

When she got back home, she began to look for teaching jobs, but she only wanted to teach history, and it would have to be within driving distance of home, and it proved impossible to find a suitable vacancy. When she told Ron this, at their next meeting, the meeting at which she must end it all, he said, 'I bet you were a fine teacher,' and she said, 'I think I was pretty good,' and he said, 'I'd like to have been taught by you, that I would,' and his casual acknowledgement of the gap between their ages gave her pain. She knew, in a flash, how disingenuous she had been in thinking that it wasn't a sexual relationship. She felt confused, adrift, and again he read her mind infuriatingly. He looked her straight in the eyes and said, 'Let's talk of safer subjects, Kate. I don't want danger any more than you. What does your man really think about the unions?'

'Walter would need to feel he was in control,' she said, 'but he does have an innate sense of fairness. Push him too hard, he'll resist. Be reasonable, he'll give.'

She felt uneasy about having said that. Had she gone too far? No, it was what she thought, and she was being sympathetic to the unions without sticking a knife in Walter's back. She was glad, though, that this was to be their last meeting.

He leapt up, said, 'I have to go,' leant across, kissed her for the first time, said, 'Sorry,' and left without giving her a chance to speak.

She stayed for twenty minutes, determined to finish her Guinness and not feel embarrassed on her own. She thought about Ron. Had he been manipulating her? Had he always wanted to kiss her? Had he left so suddenly because he knew she would end their meetings? Why did he want to continue their meetings? When he'd said, 'Sorry,' had he meant 'Sorry I have to rush' or 'Sorry I kissed you'?

She took her empty glass back to the bar, put it on the counter, and said, 'Thanks,' the way she'd seen him do. Then she drove home feeling dismayed at the situation she had got herself into. She was fifty-one, damn it.

That very evening Walter began talking about trouble ahead,

union trouble. The honeymoon of the post-war years was over. The workers had realised that not as much had changed as they thought it had.

'Do you remember that man who showed you round the works?' he asked, as they sipped a drink before dinner – he a whisky, she a gin and tonic.

Kate's blood ran cold.

'Yes, I . . . I remember him.'

'He's trouble.'

Oh Lord. Try not to shake.

'I thought he was nice.'

'He is nice. That's part of the trouble. He's popular, he's nice, but beneath the niceness, beneath that easy Irish charm, there's ruthless ambition. You may not think it means much to be President of the National Union of Piston Makers, Flange Cutters and Scrag-end Offloaders, but it's the culmination of his dreams. He feels flattered to be called Red Ron. He's always wanted to be a big fish in a small pond. He is that now, and he finds it isn't enough. He wants to increase the size of his pond. I don't want him to have a pond at all. All those little unions that we have to deal with, it's ridiculous.'

'What on earth is a scrag-end offloader?'

'Exactly. Nobody knows. It's lost in the prehistory of the industrial revolution. He thinks I'm a greedy, grasping capitalist. He wants too much.'

'Haven't we got too much?' she asked, very gently.

'Is that what you really think?'

'Well, I think we should have a bigger house than the workers. A better car. A nicer bathroom. But we have three nice bathrooms. You shouldn't even have two until all your employees have one. Our status should be modestly superior.'

'Good God, you sound just like him.'

Kate did see Ron one more time. She couldn't bring herself to break it off without telling him face to face. As she sipped her last-ever pint of Guinness, she said, 'You didn't tell me you were the President of the National Union of Piston Makers, Flange Cutters and Scrag-end Offloaders.'

'Didn't I?'

'Why didn't you tell me?'

'No particular reason, except . . . I'm not a boasting man. Has your man been talking about me?'

'Yes. He doesn't even know what a scrag-end offloader is.'

'He isn't interested.'

'What is a scrag-end offloader?'

'Oh, something they used to do in the early days.'

'What?'

'I don't know.' He grinned broadly, but Kate found that his charm wasn't working as well as usual.

'It's all a load of bollocks to you, isn't it?' she said.

'O'oh! Pub language!'

'You're just out to feather your nest.'

'No! All right, I enjoy my power, such as it is, but I care about my members. We'll be putting in a demand soon. Quite a big demand, though I have taken into account what you said about the man. Very valuable. Now what I want you to be is my eyes and ears.'

Kate stared at him. She could feel the blood leaving her face. Her cheeks felt icy.

'It isn't going to be too difficult, Kate,' he said. 'Don't look so alarmed. I don't want a strike. I don't want war. I want meaningful negotiations.'

'Yes, you probably do, Ron, but Walter's my husband. I can't be your eyes and ears.'

He sighed, as if he hadn't wanted it to come to this.

'I think you'll find you can, Kate,' he said, 'because if I told him about us you'd be in big trouble.'

'I feel such a fool,' said Kate. 'How could I not have known that you were using me?'

'Because I didn't know it myself,' said Red Ron Rafferty. 'I didn't follow you to West Bromwich. This thing began by chance and carried on because I liked you and you liked me and I fancied you and you fancied me and that made me feel sad, Kate, because I will never be unfaithful to Eileen and you will never be unfaithful to Walter, so I thought, Well, maybe it's best to end it, but I could never bring myself to, and so I formed my plan, because I saw that you sympathise with our cause. I liked you before I used you, Kate, I promise you that.'

'You won't tell Walter,' said Kate. 'You wouldn't dare.'

'I think you'll find that you have more to lose than I do, Kate.'

'Oh yes, but you have too much to lose too. He'll never negotiate with you if he knows about us. Never. You're clever, Ron, but not clever enough.'

They stared at each other. Kate felt very sad. She thought Ron did too. Behind them, a young man shuffled the dominoes rather noisily for his three pensioner friends.

'I don't know who's winning the dominoes,' said Kate, 'but I think that you and I have played a draw.'

'Fair enough.'

'I shan't finish my Guinness. The joy's gone out of it.'

'I'll see you to your car.'

'No.'

'Yes. I'm ashamed of myself. I'd like to end on a little note of courtesy.'

They walked out of the pub together. Walter was leaning against his new Rolls-Royce Silver Wraith.

'I knew something was up, Kate,' he said. 'I know you too well. I hired a private detective. He's in the pub. Phoned me from it. Said he'll be in there, playing dominoes. I'd best go in and pay him. I hate having debts.'

Kate sat in the rocking chair in the breakfast room where no breakfast was ever served, and rocked herself very gently. Her mother sat in a tall-backed hard chair at the other side of the unused fireplace.

'What about the children?' asked Bronwen, whose eyes were red from crying.

'Walter'll have them during school terms. Well, I say "them". Maurice leaves school next month. It's only Elizabeth really. I'm happy to have her in the holidays and any weekend when she wants to come to London during term time. She's blossoming a bit at last. Making friends. I just hope this doesn't hurt her too much.'

They heard the front door open.

'Here's your father now,' said Bronwen.

Kate gave a sigh and stood up.

'You don't need to be frightened of him, Kate,' said her mother rather severely. 'He's a kind man.'

'I'm not frightened,' said Kate. 'I'm embarrassed.'

John Thomas Thomas came slowly into the breakfast room, his stick in his right hand, Enid supporting his left arm, and looked at Kate gravely. It was fifteen years since he'd retired, but Kate felt like a junior pupil in the headmaster's study.

'Well well,' he said. 'Well well. Here we are again.'

Kate kissed him.

In the morning, after a nostalgic breakfast of laverbread and sausage meat, Kate said she thought she'd go into town, have a look around the shops, go to the Kardomah for a coffee. 'Then I thought after lunch we might go for a run,' she said.

John Thomas Thomas brightened up.

'Where did you have in mind?' he asked.

'Well, how much will your leg stand, Father?'

'Oh that. Don't worry about that. I don't. I'll walk without a stick yet.'

'Well, how about the Black Mountain?'

'The Black Mountain would do very nicely,' said John Thomas Thomas.

'He misses his runs,' said Bronwen. 'We don't get so many of them now Bernard's not been so well and Oliver doesn't come.'

'It's a shame Oliver doesn't come any more.'

'Oliver's been a better son to us than anyone has a right to expect,' said John Thomas Thomas sternly. 'Every year for nearly twenty years he took us for a holiday.'

'He's building a new life,' said Bronwen. 'Surely you don't begrudge him that?'

'Of course not,' said Kate. 'I just wish he wasn't building his new life with someone who looks down on us.'

'For shame, Kate,' said her mother. 'What will your father think?'

'I missed what she said,' said John Thomas Thomas, fiddling with his deaf aid. 'I can't get this contraption to work very well.'

Kate and her mother exchanged looks. Kate was astonished. She had never heard her father tell a lie before. Bronwen was not astonished. She was with him most of the time.

Kate went to the Kardomah and the market and got salty, smelly Swansea into her nostrils. The planners were beginning the task of rebuilding the town. Only Kate herself could rebuild her life. Who'll make the better job of it, she wondered, as she sat in the Kardomah and let the tide of gossip wash around her.

After lunch they got into Kate's Hillman Minx. It was half day at the High School and Enid was able to come too. It was a tremendous squash in the back for Enid and Bronwen and Annie, but they managed it. It was difficult to get John Thomas Thomas into the front, but they managed it.

Kate drove off, up, up and up through Pontardawe and Gwaun-Cae-Gurwen and Brynaman. How proud and neat the little houses were, with decorative patterns of brick round all the windows to soften their severity. These were solid houses, built for God-fearing people, which was just as well, because they were dwarfed by the stern square chapels built at either end of the street for them to fear Him in.

After Brynaman, they climbed up on to the bare, black hill. A frail pied wagtail with its looping flight had no difficulty keeping pace with them.

'This time next week I'll be in Switzerland,' said Annie. 'My first trip abroad. I daresay our hills will seem quite small when I get back.'

'Gwen Jones slipped on the snow outside Grindelwald and hurt her hip,' said Enid.

Well, at least it's not a death this time, thought Kate.

'Doctor Morris thought it was nothing, but it was the beginning of the end,' said Enid. 'She was dead before Christmas.'

At the summit Kate parked. Skylarks were singing and tumbling. She walked over the dung-rich sheep-cropped grass to a modest stone set at the side of the road. It bore the message 'David Davies age 22 of Glynclawdd Farm, Gwynfa was killed on this spot on 21st May 1884. His horse bolted and he fell under the wheel of his cart which was laden with lime.' On the other side was the same message in Welsh. Unlucky David Davies, four years older than Gwyn. Lucky David Davies, though, to be remembered bilingually after sixty-eight years. Not much use to him, though, or to the girl whose loins grew moist at his approach and who is not remembered at all.

As they began to descend, the road turned a corner and there, spread out before them below the bleak mountain, was the astonishing beauty of mid-Wales, the green breasts of her rounded hills, the open welcome of her deep valleys, a land rich and soft and deep and green and steep and smiling. The road was steep too, and they came to a hairpin bend.

'It's sad when children grow up,' said Annie.

John Thomas Thomas frowned. Annie's sentimentality irked him. But Kate understood the thought process behind Annie's remark. She had thought, I'm scared, but I can't say anything. If Elizabeth had still been little, she'd have been here, and I'd have said, 'We're coming to a hairpin bend, Elizabeth. They're the sharpest bends there are. Watch Mummy change gear and go very slowly.'

The road ran beside a mountain stream. The rushing stream reminded Kate of children growing up. You only have one childhood. Don't wish it away. Linger, laughing water. Linger on these hills where you are young and beautiful and clear. Don't hurtle to get lost in the vast, salty, murky anonymity of the ocean.

They had tea in the Cawdor Arms, there's posh. They had toasted teacakes and scones and Welsh cakes and bara brith. What a tea it was. Kate insisted on paying and left a shilling for the waitress.

As they were walking out after their tea, John Thomas Thomas waved away all help with a spasm of irritation. 'I don't need any more than my stick,' he said, 'and one day I won't need that.' Oh proud John Thomas Thomas. You couldn't be seen needing to be helped out of the leading hotel in Llandeilo.

In the otherwise deserted foyer, a seed merchant was trying to sell seed to a customer.

'It's on occasions like this that I really miss Dilys,' said Kate.

Her mother gasped and grabbed hold of her and said, 'Oh, Kate!'

'She'd have enjoyed that tea so much. You're so kind, all of you, but she was my identical twin. She would have helped me so. Why did she have to die?'

Tears ran down her face, and her mother's. Tears ran down Enid's face too. And tears poured down Annie's face, tears privileged to cry with this family. The four women clasped each other in the middle of the foyer of the Cawdor Arms and sobbed and sobbed and sobbed. John Thomas Thomas leant on his stick and watched with astonishment. The seed merchant said, 'We're developing a strain of turnip that is *entirely* resistant to disease of every kind,' but he had lost his audience.

11 Lily

Kate woke to the clanking of the breakfast trolley. Maurice's words, 'pretty disastrous concept, really, school', flashed through her mind, and she thought, Pretty disastrous concept, really, hospital. What do you need least when you're fighting for your life? Rotten food, bleak walls, and the retching, spitting, gobbing, belching, farting, bleeding, screaming and moaning of the seriously ill.

This morning, though, it seemed very quiet in the ward, and she realised why. Hilda had gone home. It seemed impossible that Hilda could ever have made sufficient impression on anything for her absence to cause even a ripple, but Kate did feel a sharp sense of loss for this woman whom she had never seen and only heard. And she suspected that Glenda and Mrs Critchley felt it as well. Glenda was grumbling, of course. 'Why didn't he send me home instead of her? He hasn't a clue. You contribute all your life to the NHS, and what do you get? Sheer incompetence. When I get out of here I'm going to complain all the way to the House of Lords. This nation is going to be sorry for its treatment of Glenda Carrington.' And then Mrs Critchley joined in. 'The York ham at breakfast was so succulent in the old days. The smoked haddock was oak-smoked. Now it's all dyed. Water oozes out of the bacon. Oozes. I'll come with you to the House of Lords.' 'Quite right,' said Glenda. 'The women of this land are on the march.' She began to sing 'Onward Christian Soldiers' in a wavery screech. 'Hush!' said Mrs Critchley softly. 'You'll wake the little one.'

A nurse came to give Kate her morning ablutions. This one seemed gentle and caring but she was a stranger. It was much worse having these dreadful humiliations performed upon her by strangers. Kate summoned up all her will-power and retreated from Ward 3C into pleasant recollections of the marvellous sex she'd enjoyed with Walter. If the nurse could have seen into the mind of the wrinkled old woman, seen her being taken by Walter from the front and from the back and from the side in rooms to the front and back and side of Copson Towers! If the nurse could have known that she was remembering the joy that Kate of the Two Settees had experienced in making love on both settees! Joy, delight, the pleasure of giving, the thrill of the partner's pleasure. Togetherness. Oneness. What could be unnatural or shameful in any of that, between committed lovers, even for a chapel girl?

And that, all that, was what she had thrown away, through the naivety, the vanity, the sheer stupidity of her behaviour with Red Ron Rafferty. If she hadn't been so stupid, Walter and she would never have been divorced, she wouldn't have married Graham, Graham wouldn't have been murdered, she wouldn't be fast approaching the longed-for, dreaded moment when she had to try to discover which of her three dear sons was a murderer. Oh, Kate! If only you could wind back to 1952 and play a different story for the last forty-seven years of your life. Even videos have their limitations.

She tried to get back to sleep, and was on the point of dropping off when she heard a familiar squeaking in the corridor, a squeaking which she had identified, over the days, as being from a hospital stretcher. Surely even the NHS wasn't so poor that it couldn't afford one can of WD40?

She heard the stretcher come into the ward and she heard Helen – thank goodness for a nurse she knew – say, 'Ladies, this is Lily Stannidge. Lily, meet Glenda Carrington, Angela Critchley and Kate Copson. You'll make Lily feel at home here in Ward 3C, won't you? Good. That's good.'

So Mrs Critchely *was* an Angela! Kate had been sure she

would be. It was as it should be. It was redolent of palm courts and legendary muffins.

The surprise was *her* name! Kate Copson! Surely that was wrong? She distinctly remembered being divorced from Walter and marrying again. Marrying some other fellow who . . . who . . . There was something funny about the marriage, she couldn't remember . . . She couldn't remember! There was a fog blowing in off the sea of her life, a fret blocking out all memory. Her brain was going. Oh Lord. She was sinking into the mists that had enveloped Angela Critchley. She was joining the ranks of the insane. Panic swept over her. Droplets of sweat broke out on her neck and thighs. She was so tired.

She slept for most of the rest of the morning, and when she awoke the panic was over, the mists had cleared. But the incident had alarmed her. Maybe she was beginning to lose her wits. She'd better hurry, hurry on to Graham and the murder.

Timothy came. She wished he hadn't. She wanted to be alone. She was the Greta Garbo of the Bedpan.

She couldn't go straight on to her fifth marriage. There was the evening of the private view. Perhaps the vital clue would lie in that amazing evening. If only he'd go. The moment he left, she'd whip off back to the Corncrake Gallery.

She wondered if he was writing his new book as he sat there. *Trouble in the Ward*, the latest saga in the life of his unbelievable hockey-playing policeman with a taste for cassoulet, Bizet and Goya.

If only he'd go. She needed to prepare herself for her visit to the Corncrake Gallery. So many people that she knew would be there. She needed to be at her best.

At last Timothy pressed her hand and said, 'Bye, Mum. Chin up, old girl,' and was gone.

Almost immediately, Doctor Ramgobi came in to do his rounds. Kate tried not to listen to him, but it was impossible.

'Hello, Lily,' he said, 'are we nice and comfortable?'

'I'm not schizophrenic,' said Lily Stannidge, who sounded well-spoken without affectation. 'There's only one of me.'

'Right. Sorry. Jolly good,' said Doctor Ramgobi. He conducted a few low rumbles with the nurse and then moved on. Kate knew that he'd moved on because he said, 'And how is Glenda this evening?'

'You know how Glenda is this evening,' said Glenda. 'Glenda is very well this evening. Glenda is very well every evening. I must go home, Doctor Rambogi. Douglas can't cope.'

'Ramgobi. I spoke to Douglas yesterday. He's coping very well.'

'Room service!' called out Mrs Critchley.

'In a moment, Mrs Critchley,' said Doctor Ramgobi. 'Sorry, Glenda. No, Douglas is coping. He said ironing is like riding a bicycle. It soon comes back. And he'd made himself a *boeuf bourguignon*. Does that suggest he's not coping?'

'Doctor, I don't want to be rude,' said Glenda. 'I'm no racist, but you don't understand the English, even if you do come from Huddersfield. My husband is an Englishman. He doesn't say what he thinks. He doesn't say what he means, you halfwit.'

'Glenda . . .'

'Room service!'

'In a minute, Mrs Critchley. Glenda, Douglas . . .'

'No, I'm sorry if it's rude, Dr Rambogi, but it's the truth and it has to be said. The English are a very advanced form of civilisation. They throw up smokescreens. When my husband says, "I'm coping," he doesn't mean, "I'm coping," you stupid little black man, he means, "Help me, for God's sake." He's English.'

'Well, Glenda,' said Doctor Ramgobi with unremitting courtesy, 'I shall bear that in mind and question him thoroughly.'

'That's more like it. Test him. Try to trick him. Ask him what he puts in his precious *bœuf bourguignon*.'

'Thank you. That's a good tip. I shall do that.'

Doctor Ramgobi moved on. Kate knew that he'd moved on because she heard him say, 'So how's Mrs Critchley this evening?'

'Hungry,' said Mrs Critchley. 'I've been calling room service for hours. Can you fetch them for me?'

'I am room service,' said Doctor Ramgobi, lowering his voice for fear that the rest of the ward would hear him and start ordering things. Kate could still hear him, though. Her hearing was as sharp as ever.

'Well, why didn't you say so?' said Angela Critchley.

'What can I get you?' asked Doctor Ramgobi smoothly.

'What sandwiches do you have?'

'Chicken, ham, prawn, smoked salmon, salad and cheese,' said Doctor Ramgobi without hesitation.

'I'll have smoked salmon, please.'

'On white or brown or granary?'

'On white, please. Granary has bits that get in my false teeth, and everything's brown these days, isn't it? Bread, sugar, staff. It's a fad.'

'One smoked salmon on white,' said Doctor Ramgobi, and he moved on. Kate knew that he'd moved on, because he stopped right by her bed. He mumbled to the nurse, but Kate could still hear every word.

'No great change. Slight improvement if anything. No reason to change any of the medication. She's putting up a magnificent fight, Helen. Magnificent. You know, I wish I could talk to her just once.'

'We all do, doctor,' said Helen. 'Got right under our skin she has, somehow.'

Kate was absurdly grateful to hear that.

'I asked my dad about her,' Helen continued. 'You know, after you told me she was *the* Kate Copson. My dad said he'd forgotten about her, but it brought it all back. She was quite a woman, he said, specially for her age.'

'Yes, yes, she was.'

Doctor Ramgobi and Helen moved on. Kate knew that they had moved on because she heard Lily Stannidge say, in a near whisper, 'May I have a word before you go, doctor?'

'Certainly,' said Doctor Ramgobi. A note of wariness had crept into his voice.

'Something nice. Praise.'

'Ah. Well, we never mind that,' said Doctor Ramgobi.

'I've travelled a lot,' said Lily Stannidge. 'All round the world. I've met people of all colours, white, black, brown, yellow. I just wanted to say, because I heard what that horrid woman over there said, there are good and bad people of all colours and all races.'

'Thank you.'

'But what I really wanted to say was, these new stabilisers are wonderful.'

'Stabilisers?'

'Yes. There's no movement at all. You wouldn't even know you were on a ship.'

12 Daniel

'I'm so worried, Kate,' Olga had confided on the phone. 'I'm so worried that nobody will come to send off my poor Daniel in style.'

In retrospect, of course, this worry seems absurd. Most of you will know what a sensation the exhibition was, how in one evening the reputation of an ignored artist was raised to a pedestal from which it has never slipped. A man who died of pneumonia, in a Spanish hospital, surrounded only by his family, not even awarded an obituary in *The Times*, it's hard to believe it now when the traces of Begelmanmania, or Begelmania, are still so clearly remembered.

'I will come,' Kate had promised. 'I loved Daniel. Oh, not in a sexual way. Not really.'

'He loved you in a sexual way.'

'No. I don't believe it.'

'Oh, I didn't mind, Kate, because I knew it was a futile love, and I think he loved me more.'

'I'm sure he did. Oh yes, Olga, I'll come.'

'Yes, but Kate, not just you. Bring people.'

'Are you sure?'

'Lots of people. Oh, Kate, I'm not religious, but can any of us be absolutely sure that the dead don't see? I couldn't bear for this to be a fiasco. For this I have worked for years. For this I have slaved since my poor man breathed his last in Caceres.' Olga had begun to cry. 'I'm sorry. I'm so sorry, Kate, I didn't mean to cry, but I haven't allowed myself time to grieve, you see. I have been angry instead. My Daniel was worth ten Daphne Stoneyhursts.'

'Well, I agree. I expect she does too.'

'I'll ask her.'

'Olga! You can't do that.'

'I can. I will. She'll be there. And Stanley Wainwright.'

'Oh dear.'

'I know, but Tregarryn was very important to my Daniel. Very loved by him.' Olga began to cry again.

'Olga, please, you'll have me crying in a minute.'

'Good. And when it's over, when the reputation of my Daniel is secure . . .' Olga always referred to him as her Daniel, as if to distinguish him from all Daniels not owned by her. '. . . we will eat together, and drink together, and remember together, and cry together.'

'I can't wait. Olga, I *will* invite people. Lots of people.'

So Kate had. She'd invited Nigel and Timothy and Maurice and Elizabeth, with partners. She'd invited Oliver and Bunny, and Enid and Annie. She'd even invited Walter.

When she'd invited Bernard she'd said, 'Bring Rodber if you like.' There'd been silence at the other end of the line. 'What's wrong, Bernard?' she'd asked. 'I don't see Rodber any more,' he'd said. 'Cancer frightens him. He's cut me out of his life as if *I* was a tumour.'

It was the first time Bernard had been able to bring himself to mention the dreaded word.

Kate knew that she had never looked lovelier than that night, and she also knew that, at fifty-five, she might never look quite as lovely again. She had bought a black Dior dress in the very latest 'A-line' look. The bodice flowed smoothly from narrow shoulder to banded hip and lightly fitted waistline. It was plain, flowing, feminine, chic. She entered the Corncrake Gallery at two minutes past six. Olga had said, 'Come early. Support me, my good friend.'

There were already a few people in that grand, elegant room with its two Georgian chandeliers. The sight of so many of Daniel's pictures stunned her, and no doubt there were many more in the two side galleries. She accepted a glass of white wine and made her way towards Olga, who was standing in the exact centre of the room, wearing a smart but unfeminine business suit, and looking paler than ever. Three men were talking to her. The one in the smoking jacket and bow-tie looked familiar. The one in the dark three-piece suit looked formidable. The one in the blue sports jacket and dark flannels looked so like Daniel that Kate's heart almost stopped. It was, she realised, his son Reuben.

Before she could reach Olga, Kate was waylaid by a man she hadn't invited. Heinz was wearing a green Harris tweed suit and looked as if he had wandered in from a fashionable shooting party. He looked older, of course, but good. He'd kept himself fit and his goatee trimmed.

'This can't be coincidence,' she said.

'It isn't,' he said. 'I don't believe in coincidence. I told a friend only yesterday, as it happens, "There is no such thing as coincidence."'

'That's incredible. Yesterday! So did I.'

'You didn't? What a . . . oh, Kate, I nearly fell for that.' He examined her, as if she were one of the exhibits. His own private view, before the crowds came. 'Kate, you look fabulous. As good as ever.'

'Thank you. It just takes me longer to get ready.'

He hugged and kissed her.

'You've worn well too, Heinz.'

'Thank you. I came here to see you,' he said.

'Well, thank you.'

'I heard that you and Walter had separated.'

'Oh? How?'

'You forget I worked for him. I have contacts. I also hear news of my princess.'

'She's coming tonight.'

'Here? My princess?'

'Yes.'

'My soup runneth over, as you say. My Inge died, you know.'

'Your wife?'

'Oh yes. A very beautiful woman.'

'Yes. You sent me a photo.'

'So I think to myself, If I do not go and see Kate I will kick myself into touch for ever. Is that right? My English has rusted. So, anyway, here I am.'

'Yes.'

'Are you pleased to see me?'

'Oh yes. Oh yes, Heinz. Of course I am. I . . . we . . . of course I am.'

'Yes, but . . . well . . .'

'I must have at least a peep at the pictures, Heinz, before the crowds come.'

Kate had a very quick look at the pictures. She'd known that Daniel was good, but, seeing them all together like this, she realised that he'd been even better than she'd thought. The next day she came back and looked at them properly. He'd been dissatisfied with his work at every stage of his life, and his life had seemed to move from one phase to another in a most arbitrary way, yet here was a diverse but unified body of work, work of consistent excellence and frequent inspiration, work that could not have been created without Daniel's knowledge of cubism, impressionism, vorticism and surrealism, but which was nevertheless firmly outside these movements and utterly original. Severe, gaunt, eloquent of suffering, masterful in execution, his paintings were a record of a complete yet fractured vision, clear yet distorted, specifically Jewish but also universal. They told a tale of exile, of banishment, of wilder-nesses, and yet of hope; of starkness, cruelty, chaos and yet of beauty. People were like rocks, landscapes were like people, cities were like fields, rivers were like streets, the Negev was like Salamanca, Delphi was like Daphne Stoneyhurst. Yet all his subjects were clearly differentiated and clearly themselves. Kate would have called it a conjuring trick, had that not carried suggestions of deception and guile.

That analysis was for tomorrow, and it was Kate's and maybe hers alone. Now, at the private view of the great Daniel Begelman retrospective exhibition, Kate grieved for the absent genius. Her heart sank to her elegant, high-heeled shoes as she tripped majestically across a room filled with the absence of the slight, quirky, quizzical figure in smock and flat cap, his secular yarmulke. She shook her head, to rid herself of the vision, put on a smiling social face, and prepared herself for the delights of a crowded evening.

She strode up to Olga. Olga had thickened out and no longer looked frail. She looked like the formidable fighter that she was.

'Kate!' she enthused. 'Oh, Kate! Thank you for coming. You know Reuben, of course.'

She introduced the other two men as 'Vincent Anstey, Director of the Corncrake' and 'Oswald Philliskirk, art critic and legend'.

Oswald Philliskirk bowed, flattered by the description.

'We've met before,' he said.

'I know,' said Kate. 'Nobody could forget you.'

He bowed again, taking this as a compliment. Kate thought he looked effete, self-indulgent and smug.

'I'm afraid I destroyed your husband's reputation, with your help,' he said.

Kate was determined not to be apologetic on this night.

'It had to be done,' she said. 'He was a fake. Olga, I don't know what the critics will say, but I think the pictures are magnificent.'

'This critic will say that,' said Oswald Philliskirk.

'I anticipate a huge success,' said Vincent Anstey. His eyes were like cash registers, and his cuff-links were excessive.

'Not much use to my father,' said Reuben.

'To you that is naturally sad,' said Oswald Philliskirk. How smug his bow-tie looked. 'In the history of art it is of little consequence. Your father's name will live, Reuben. That's what matters. Ah well. Duty and deadlines call.'

He moved off, to examine the pictures. Soon Vincent Anstey and Reuben moved off as well.

'I hardly needed to invite my friends,' said Kate, looking at the people pouring in.

'I didn't know,' said Olga. 'I really didn't know. Oh, Kate, why couldn't it happen when he was still alive?'

They talked briefly of Daniel's later years, the travelling, the poverty, the occasional teaching jobs, the impossible hopes, the inevitable disappointments, the unsung end. Then Kate saw Bernard standing in front of one of the pictures, talking to a man who looked as though he wanted to escape. She made her excuses to Olga and hurried over to her younger brother. He looked so ill, he'd lost weight, his hair was thinning, his eyes were set deep in his face, there was a lump on the side of his neck, and he was sounding off about the pictures, pretentiously but not unintelligently, in a voice similar to the one he'd used at Kate and Walter's lunch party, but subtly different, this was his gallery voice. She hugged him, and the man to whom he'd been talking made his escape. Just behind them, but sounding miles away, a man with a stutter said, 'You know these p . p . p . pictures are terrib . . . b . b . . . terrib . . . b . b . . . terribly good.'

Bernard was as pleased to see Kate as she was shocked to see him. They were incoherent in their love and grief.

'Oh, Bernard,' she said at last.

'I know,' he said. 'I know, but the prognosis is much more hopeful.'

Elizabeth arrived, seventeen and clueless, with her best friend Sylvie, seventeen and shapeless.

Kate hurried up to Heinz, to tell him. He was with two good-looking, smartly dressed men.

'Ah,' he said. 'My ex-wife. I'd like you to meet two very good German friends of mine, Graf Von Seemen . . .'

'I'm delighted to meet you, your grafship.'

'No, No. We do not say this. Just call me Wolfgang.'

'. . . and Ernest Halle. He's in the toy business with me.'

'Ah, you're back in toys!'

'I should say he is,' said Graf Wolfgang Von Seemen. 'He is a big man. And now he goes into politics. He is a good man, is Heinz Wasserhof.'

'Oh, I know that,' said Kate.

'If I can play a little part, so that things that happened that shouldn't have happened can never happen again, I am content,' said Heinz.

'Heinz, Elizabeth's here. Sorry, gentlemen, to . . . er . . . but . . .'

'Elizabeth is our daughter,' said Heinz in a low voice.

Kate led Heinz away and pointed Elizabeth out.

'I wouldn't have recognised her.'

'Your English rose has greenfly.'

'Kate! That's cruel.'

'Just my way with words. I love Elizabeth, and she'll make some man a lovely wife.'

'Oh God.'

'Well, she will. But she isn't a princess.'

'No. No, she isn't a princess.'

'Shall I introduce you to her? Begin the process whereby she might one day be told who you are?'

'I suppose so.'

'That sounds very half-hearted.'

'How can I be wholehearted? This is heart-rending.'

'Well, shall I?'

'Well, I think you must.'

So Kate led Heinz over to his daughter.

'Elizabeth, dear, this is a friend of mine from Germany, Heinz Wasserhof.'

'How do you do?' said Elizabeth, blushing slightly from shyness.

'It's good to meet you.'

'And this is her friend Sylvie.'

'Hello, Sylvie.'

'Hello.'

'So what do you think of the pictures, Elizabeth?' asked Heinz.

'I haven't really looked at them,' said Elizabeth, 'but they seem nice enough.'

'Nice! That word surprises me,' said Heinz, 'because I think they are many things, but not nice. I think they are great art but not nice art.'

Elizabeth blushed.

'No, no. Don't be upset. I am not being rude,' said her father. 'The great thing about art is that we all see it differently.'

'I haven't really been taught how to look at art,' said Elizabeth.

'No? Well, I will just say this. Two people look at a painting. One is an expert with fifty years' experience. The other comes from the jungle and has never seen a picture before. But they both have two eyes. Yes?'

'I will come and look at the pictures again, I promise,' said Elizabeth.

Kate found it strange that Elizabeth had said, 'I promise,' to the man whom she didn't know to be her father. It was as if she'd sensed that his interest was more than just polite.

'And what do you think about the pictures, Sylvie?' asked Heinz.

'I haven't had time to look at them,' said Sylvie.

'Excuse me. There's Uncle Bernard,' said Elizabeth. She moved on, and Heinz sighed, and Sylvie gave him a funny look and moved on in pursuit of Elizabeth, her anchor.

'Well, there we are,' said Heinz to Kate. 'I have met our daughter again.'

There was a heavy, flat silence between Kate and Heinz then. Things were hotting up behind them. Kate heard a voice cry, 'Daphne!' and the man with the stutter said, 'Isn't that Bunny Parr-Parr-Parr-Parr-Parr-Parr-Parr-Parkinson over there?' and somebody replied, 'She's Bunny Thomas now. She married some Welshman,' and still Heinz was looking at Kate quizzically.

'Your friends seem nice,' said Kate. 'Herr Halle and the Sperm Count.'

'The Sperm Count?'

'Graf Von Seemen.'

'Kate! You're incorrigible.' His tone changed. He became serious, almost pleading. 'Kate?'

'By all means. Phone me tomorrow.'

'What?'

'You were going to ask me to dinner. Good idea. Lots to mull over. Excuse me.'

Kate began to put on a performance then. She went over to Oliver and Bunny. Oliver was still very good-looking. Bunny had been ill advised about her outfit. Expensive it might be, but red made her look bulky.

'Oliver! Bunny!'

They embraced.

'You look wonderful,' said Oliver, and Bunny scowled. 'That's a beautiful dress.'

'Thank you. I bought it with Walter's money. It's odd, I suppose. On our first separation I wouldn't take his money. It seemed soiled by what he'd done. This time, when it's all my fault, I have no such compunction. It eases the pain a little. Let's get some wine.'

They pushed their way through the crowd to the drinks table.

'I thought there was going to be nobody here,' said Oliver. 'It's an absolute scrum.'

'I know,' said Kate. 'It's not as I expected. Have an olive.'

'Oh no, thank you,' said Bunny, so loudly that two people turned round to see what was wrong. 'I detest olives,' she added proudly.

'What do you think of the pictures?' asked Kate.

'I haven't had a chance to look,' said Bunny.

Bunny approached the pictures with a brave, set face, as if crossing terrain studded with land-mines. This was Kate's chance.

'Bernard looks so ill,' she said to Oliver in a low voice.

'I know.'

'He *is* so ill.'

'I know.'

'Couldn't you do more?'

'Use my influence, you mean? I do, Kate. I've made enquiries. The man he's under is well thought of. I keep a close watch. I put pressure on.'

'I'm sure you do everything you can professionally. I meant as a brother. As a friend.'

'I know. I know. But it's difficult.'

'Difficult?'

'He upsets Bunny. She can't handle it.'

'Upsets her? How?'

'Those flecks of foam around his teeth. Can't he do something about that?'

'I don't know, but it's hardly a hanging offence.'

'That lump on his neck. Bunny finds it difficult.'

'I don't expect he finds it a doddle.'

'I know. I know.'

'Oliver! And you a doctor! And you the golden boy.'

'What?'

'Never mind. Where's your compassion, Oliver?'

'I feel for Bernard, Kate, I love him. But he doesn't make things easy for himself, *vis-à-vis* Bunny. He told her an extinct dinosaur had more political nous than her.'

Kate gave a short snort of a laugh.

'It isn't funny, Kate.'

'No, it isn't. It's tragic.'

'Look after Bunny for a while, Kate, keep her occupied, and I'll go and chat to him.'

'Thank you. How will I keep her occupied?'

'Introduce her to people. People take to her, Kate. She's a good mixer. I'll go and . . . what'll I say to him?'

'You've lived in England too long. Just be yourself. Be Welsh. Tell him you love him. Spout away. Tell him you think of him all the time. Open your heart, and his. Come over all emotional and Celtic.'

'Right. Emotional and Celtic. Will do.'

Oliver slid off looking as if he was about to have a particularly sticky interview with his bank manager. Kate joined Bunny in front of a stark, strong, uncompromising painting of the Negev.

'Well?' said Kate.

'I prefer landscapes.'

'That is a landscape, Bunny.'

'No, no. I meant . . . proper landscapes. I'm sorry . . .' She sounded anything but sorry. '. . . but I can't make head or tail of these.' She sounded proud! Anger rose slowly in Kate's gullet, as Bunny waffled on. 'No, I like things I can recognise in paintings. Fields, mountains, lakes . . .'

Anger at Bunny for her complacent stupidity.

'. . . birds, ducks, geese, Peter Scott . . .'

Anger at Oliver for marrying Bunny. Was he so insecure, the former golden boy, that he had to marry double-barrelled women, not that she'd been double-barrelled before she met Peter Parr-Parkinson.

'. . . I like horses too. Munnings, Stubbs . . .'

Anger at Bernard's undeserved lump. Anger at Daniel's unappreciated life.

'. . . and still lifes . . .'

Anger at this wine-sipping, olive-guzzling, overdressed crowd.

'. . . if one can say "still lifes". Or should it be "still lives"? But that sounds wrong. Anyway, I like them . . .'

Anger at the world for recognising Daniel too late, too late.

'. . . flowers, vases of flowers . . .'

All this anger was no use. Kate tried to control it, turned to Bunny, and said, 'You have catholic tastes.'

'Oh no,' said Bunny. 'I hate all that. Madonnas and *bambinos*. All that spirituality and what the babies so obviously need is a good burping.'

'No, I meant . . .' Why do I persist? To give Oliver time with Bernard. 'No, I meant . . . you like a wide variety of paintings.'

'Oh yes. Not fruit, though.'

'Fruit?'

Bunny looked at Kate as at a halfwit.

'You know. Apples, pears, bananas, plums. Fruit. I can't stand paintings of fruit.' A dreadful thought struck Bunny. 'You didn't give us a painting of fruit for a wedding present, did you?'

'No. I wasn't invited, so I didn't give anything.'

'Thank heavens for that. I can be tactless, Kate. I was known for my faux pas, in Harpenden. Oh good. I'm glad you didn't. Two people did. We keep them in the loft.'

Bunny looked round, searching for Oliver.

'Let me introduce you to some people,' said Kate, steering her by the arm through the swelling mob, searching for people to whom it would be safe to introduce Bunny.

Elizabeth and Sylvie would do. They were huddling together, trying to look like a crowd and failing miserably.

'Elizabeth, this is Bunny, Oliver's wife. Bunny, I don't think you've met my daughter.'

'No. We keep meaning to have you over,' said Bunny, 'but the opportunity doesn't seem to arise, you know how it is.'

Elizabeth looked as if she didn't know how it was. Kate had a wild hope that she'd say something like 'No. Your wedding would have been a perfect opportunity, had we been invited', but Elizabeth had more sense than that, though what she actually said didn't show a great deal of sense. She said, 'No. Of course I know Uncle Oliver well. I used to see him a lot.' That would have been all right if she hadn't blushed furiously afterwards. Kate heard herself say, 'Oh, and this is her friend Sylvie,' and Sylvie's voice said 'How do you do?' while her eyes said, 'What do you take me for? A bloody afterthought?' and then Elizabeth said, 'Oh, there's Maurice over there. Excuse me' and slid off with Sylvie in tow.

Kate gave up on the plan to find people to whom it would be safe to introduce Bunny. She decided to find someone to whom it would be unsafe. Daphne Stoneyhurst loomed up at that very moment like a lighthouse in a fog. The gash of her mouth was more scarlet than ever, like a raw wound. Her hair was a grey beehive. Her cigar was slightly wet. 'Daphne,' said Kate, 'this is a very good friend of mine, well, she's married to my brother, Bunny Thomas. You'll like Daphne, Bunny. She's lesbian.'

Kate moved away, leaving them to it, feeling a momentary exhilaration which died away when she saw Enid standing shyly at the entrance to the main gallery. Enid's face was pale and tense. Her make-up and clothes, over which she had laboured and worried, looked desperately provincial. Kate hurried over to her.

'Enid! You came! Says she, stating the obvious.'

She kissed Enid warmly.

'I've been awful,' said Enid. 'We couldn't both come. Mother and Father need looking after now. Annie suggested we toss for it to see who should go. "Annie!" I said. "That'd be tantamount to gambling. Gambling in my father's house? Never! No, Annie," I said, "I'm Kate's sister. You aren't. This one's for me." I'm ashamed of myself.'

'Why? It's true. It's you I wanted.'

'Now I wish I hadn't come.'

'Why?'

'Look at all these people. I never thought there'd be so many people. I won't be able to think of a thing to . . . oh, my goodness me, there's that dreadful lesbian woman.'

'She isn't dreadful. She fancied you. She probably still does.'

'Oh, Kate!'

'Enid, you don't need to talk to a soul. You can just look at the pictures, which are wonderful. After all, that's what we're all supposed to be here for.'

'I won't know what to make of them.'

'Yes, you will, and even if you don't, no one will know unless you tell them. But there are plenty of people to talk to. There's Bernard, looking very ill, he needs you; there's a chance to spot that shy disappearing species, the Oliver, and that rare bird of prey, the Bunny. Maurice is here somewhere, Timothy, Nigel and Elizabeth.'

'We'll all huddle together like a group of frightened immigrants.'

'You don't have to. You can talk to anyone. Just don't mention death.'

'What on earth do you mean?'

'Nothing. Now go on.'

Kate left her sister to it and began a parade of the room. She went up to Maurice and his beautiful blonde girlfriend Clare. Maurice might not be big and strong like Nigel or sensitive and needing to be mothered like Timothy but there was something about him that the girls adored and Kate wasn't surprised that Clare was so beautiful.

'You're beautiful,' she said.

'The second most beautiful woman in the room,' said Maurice boldly.

'I'm a researcher at the BBC,' said Clare.

'Of course you are,' said Kate.

She moved on to Timothy and his fiancée Milly. She couldn't remember now what Milly had looked like.

'Mum, you look stunning,' said Timothy.

'Sorry, I don't want to stun,' said Kate. 'How are things at Brasenose Preparatory School?'

'Excellent. We're very happy.'

'He's started a book,' said Milly. 'A novel.'

'I always told him he should read more,' said Kate.

'No, he's writing one.'

'I'm sorry, Milly, I did realise that. I was trying to be funny. It's a failing of mine. What sort of book?'

'A detective novel.'

'Oh.'

'Don't sound disappointed, Mum. They sell.'

'Oh, I know.'

'What would you rather, a searing exposé of Western civilisation that sells ten copies?'

'Yes, frankly.'

Kate moved on. Nigel had come on his own, as usual. Her eldest boy was thirty years old, and she had still to see any evidence of a girlfriend.

'How are things at Patterson Burns?' she asked.

'Excellent. I've got a two-pound-a-week rise.' He lowered his voice. 'Actually we're working on some very exciting new drugs. They could be marvellous against all kinds of cancer. It's looking very exciting.'

'Well, go and tell Uncle Bernard.'

'Oh, I don't imagine they'll be much use to him. We aren't talking that kind of time-scale.'

'Nigel!'

'I'm sorry, Mother, but we aren't. I'm not being callous. Uncle Bernard needs treatment now. These'll be several years a-testing. Thousands of mice will bravely lay down their lives before . . .'

'Yes, well, we'll have to discuss the ethical implications of animal testing some other time, Nigel. But do go and talk to Uncle Bernard anyway.'

'I will, Mother. I'm very fond of Uncle Bernard. I didn't mean I think he's going to die next week. I just meant, he can't afford to wait years for a treatment to start.'

He gave her a quick kiss and moved off in search of Bernard, and Kate grasped the nettle that was Stanley Wainwright, whose intertwined pistons had caused many a ribald comment among the workers at Boothroyd and Copson. Stanley was also wearing a bow-tie, with a very smart grey suit. No *outré* artistic touches here.

'Well,' she said, 'doesn't this take one back?'

'Not advisable,' said Stanley. 'Never look back.'

'Oh, Stanley, it's one of the great pleasures of life. It's one of the great achievements of the human brain. It's one of the things that distinguish us from animals. Beavers don't wax nostalgic. Badgers don't have old sett reunions.'

'How do you know?'

'I don't. I'm talking nonsense as usual. Oh but, Stanley, I look back on Tregarryn with an excruciating cocktail of pleasure and regret. The pictures are good, aren't they?'

'*Very* good. I always said he was a significant minor talent.'

'You never said anything of the kind and I think he's a major talent.'

'Kate, that is nonsense and you know it. Yes, there's something there, but don't exaggerate it. No, looking back on Tregarryn, as you want me to, one would have to say we didn't do badly. One minor talent, one major talent and one very decent commercial success.'

'Is that how you describe yourself – "a very decent commercial success"?'

'Stop teasing, Kate.'

'Oh! Sorry! Are you the major talent?'

266

'Well, you didn't think it was Daphne, did you?'

'No. No, I didn't.'

'Kate, I have an international reputation. It'd be false modesty to describe myself as anything but a major talent. This exhibition is very interesting, probably be very successful. It's a long time since I went to a private view where anybody looked at the pictures. I wouldn't be surprised if it sold out.'

'Like you, you mean?'

'What?'

'You've sold out.'

'Why are you so offensive to me, Kate?'

'Because you've sold out. I remember your ideals. No wonder you don't want to look back. How's Jasmine?'

'I grew tired of her. Kate, I still have those ideals, but there's more than one way of breaking eggs.' He paused, vaguely aware that that wasn't quite what he meant. 'There's no future in battering at the door. I work from the inside. Take my Mammon I did for that bank. There's a sly, subtle suggestion of greed and self-destruction there.'

'So sly and subtle the bank didn't spot it.'

'Well, quite. They wouldn't have accepted it if they had.'

'The critics didn't spot it.'

'A notoriously dim lot.'

'I didn't spot it.'

'No comment.'

Kate moved on. She felt a surprising desire to talk to Daphne. But on her way she encountered Oliver and Bunny.

'We're leaving,' said Oliver. 'I have an early start tomorrow. Thank you for inviting us.'

'Thank you for coming. How did you get on with Daphne, Bunny?'

'How could you leave me with that dreadful woman? She made a most unpleasant suggestion.'

'Really? What?'

'She asked me to meet her under the clock at Waterloo station at twelve o'clock tomorrow.'

'Oh, is that all? What did you say?'

'Nothing. I rather like the thought of her waiting there. Come on, Oliver.'

'Must you go so soon?'

'To be honest, Kate,' said Oliver, 'I don't want to be part of a little Welsh huddle in the corner. It's so provincial.'

Kate suspected that the real reason for their early departure was that Oliver didn't cut his usual dash in this gathering. The suave, handsome surgeon, well groomed, impeccably turned out, adored by all the nurses, was just a nobody in this seething mass of metropolitan egos and eccentricities.

She kissed him warmly, but felt that she had lost him.

'Kate!'

'Daphne!'

They hugged each other so warmly that several people, knowing Daphne's proclivities, began to reassess Kate's sexuality. But Kate was motivated only by affection, by a depth of affection that astonished her.

'What a waste,' said Daphne.

'That he died before this night, you mean?'

'No, no. Well, yes, yes, but no, I meant us.'

'Us?'

'It's not like you to be so slow. You and me. That is, I believe, the usual meaning of "us". Our bodies are made for each other, and you refuse.'

'I know, it must be awful for you, such beauty and none of it for you.' They laughed, then Kate turned serious. 'Well, what do you think of our Daniel now?'

'Magnificent. Tragic. All this talent, never appreciated in his lifetime. And me, with my little talent, selling steadily. Kate, I can hardly bear the pathos of this night. You're astonished.'

'Yes. I feel like that. I had no idea you did.'

'I'd like to say I always knew how good he was. You did. I'm not sure I did. Kate, that was a most horrendous woman you introduced me to.'

'I thought you liked her. You asked her to meet you under the clock at Waterloo.'

'I wanted to shock her. You don't think there's a chance she'll go? That'd be fun.'

'Not a chance.'

'Pity. She had no sense of humour at all. Said she was Bunny Thomas, previously Bunny Parr-Parkinson, née Loosely. I said, "I have no intention of making an exhibition of myself, that would be an exhibition too far, and how do you neigh loosely, anyway?" and she said, "No, no, that was my maiden name." Horrendous woman.'

'She's married to my brother.'

'Oh, I'm sorry, Kate.'

'Yes, I think he is too. Daniel told me once you tried to seduce him. Climbed into his bed.'

'Yes, I do sometimes fancy men, when I'm on the cusp. I'm on the cusp today. I could happily seduce that man who's just walked in with that gorgeous woman who is almost as attractive as you, and a great deal younger. In fact, I could fancy them both!'

Kate turned and felt her knees almost buckle beneath her.

'That man was my second and fourth husbands,' she said.

'Good God.'

'Daphne, I like you more than I ever dreamt, let's be friends, platonic friends, I hasten to add, but now I must walk boldly over to Walter before he walks boldly over to me.'

She was just in time. They met halfway.

'Kate! You look wonderful!'

'You don't look bad yourself.' He didn't. A little older, of course. A little ravaged. Beginning to look like a cross between Oscar Wilde and Jean Gabin.

'This is Linda, my fiancée.'

Kate smiled, hiding the fact that she suddenly felt sick, and shook hands with Linda, who was petite and curvaceous and at least fifteen years younger than Walter, though perhaps not quite young enough for the dirndl skirt that she was wearing. A little too hard and grasping a face, if one wanted to be bitchy, and Kate did, for the Austrian milkmaid look.

'I've heard a lot about you,' said Linda.

Oh Lord.

'Oh, Walter,' she said, 'that's hardly fair on the girl.'

'You seem to assume that it must all be to your advantage when comparisons are made,' said Walter.

Kate realised that she had, but she continued smiling, boy, how she smiled, and she said, 'I would hardly think so. She's lovely. I hope you'll both be very happy.'

She couldn't stay with Walter and Linda a moment longer, but found herself walking straight towards Heinz. His eyes gleamed at her with compassion spiced with just a little spite.

'The world doesn't stand still ever for you, does it?' he said. 'So, I'll ring you tomorrow and we'll have dinner before I go back.'

'Excellent.'

She blundered on, aware of admiration as she passed, heard someone say, 'She called him the sperm count,' heard everyone laughing, felt grateful but at a distance, as if her ears were blocked at altitude. She caught sight of Enid, a strangely lively, confident Enid, and hurried towards her for protection.

'Are you all right?' asked Enid.

'I feel faint.'

'Let's sit down.'

They sat on a seat in the middle of the main gallery, letting the crowd swirl around them.

'That's better,' said Kate.

'You want to be careful,' said Enid. 'Gilbert Watkins whose

270

mother had a goitre fainted in Neath Municipal Art Gallery and cracked his head on the fire alarm.'

'Died?'

'No. Set off the alarm and caused five fire engines to rush to the gallery. I've been having a good time, Kate.'

'Marvellous.'

'It's been a real eye-opener. The clothes! Mine looked so smart in Marshall and Snelgrove. Here I look provincial.'

'You look very fetching.'

'Well, that's appropriate. I spend a large part of my life fetching.'

'What do you mean?'

'Father's very forgetful. I fetch and carry.'

'Oh, Enid.'

'But it hasn't worried me that I look provincial. I don't care. I love the paintings.'

'You do?'

'Oh yes. And I went up to Daphne and said, "Thank you for fancying me all those years ago."'

'You didn't!!'

'I did. Do you know what she said?'

'I dread to think.'

'She said, "Meet me under the clock at Waterloo Station tomorrow at twelve"!'

'What on earth did you say?'

'I said, "If it was Paddington I just might make it. I'm catching the one o'clock to Swansea."'

'You didn't! Good old you.'

'I felt quite metropolitan.'

'Sometimes I envy you, Enid.'

'What?? You envy me?'

'Your life's useful. You teach, and obviously teach well. You look after Mother and Father. What do I do?'

'You've had four husbands and four children.'

'Yes, but what do I do?'

'You bring sunlight into rooms that need it. You light up people's lives.'

'Oh yes. I lit up Arturo's.'

'It wasn't your fault. It wasn't, Kate, and even if it had been it was almost thirty years ago. Kate, you must be proud of yourself. We're proud of you. You touch our family with glamour. Your adventures thrill poor Annie. Mother's so proud of you.'

'Not Father?'

'Oh, you know, in his way, Father also. You ease his stiffness a little, you bring interest. You keep him alive. Do you know he's almost walking without his stick? I think he will.'

'He's wonderful.'

'Yes, and so are you. I adore you.'

'I thought you were jealous.'

'Oh, of course, sometimes. Not really, though. Not deep down. We live your life with you, Kate, so go on, for us, if not for you. Please, Kate, live it. Live it magnificently.'

'Enid!'

They hugged and cried and didn't care if it ruined their make-up. One or two people, seeing them crying together, averted their eyes out of politeness and embarrassment.

'I'm going to dinner with Bernard,' said Enid. 'Will you come too?'

'Not tonight,' said Kate. 'You two will do just fine together.'

'Please!'

'How can I refuse?'

They knew that the conversation was over. Without realising how, they found themselves walking in opposite directions. Soon Kate was in conversation with Vincent Anstey, Director of the Corncrake.

'You knew him well, didn't you? At Tregarryn in particular.'

'Yes.'

'A great talent.'

'Yes. When did you first come across him?'

Vincent Anstey made a rapid calculation in his head.

'Ten . . . twelve years ago? Olga's been pushing him in our faces for years. Probably did him an enormous disservice.'

'Really?'

'We pride ourselves on our judgement in the art world. We don't like to be told. We like to discover.'

'But you were told?'

'No, I discovered. When Olga first came to me, I already knew he was a major talent.'

'But you didn't mount an exhibition?'

'It wasn't the time, Kate. People weren't ready.'

'But they are now, when he's dead?'

'Exactly. I needed him dead.'

'You don't mean you killed him?'

'Good God, Kate, what do you take me for? Where do you think this is? Chicago? No, but he had very frail health and I hung on. I gambled, if you like.'

'That's dreadful.'

'It seems so to you. It was a commercial judgement. A Begelman exhibition five years ago would have created interest. Sold a bit. Not a lot. He isn't easy art. People would not have been comfortable with his work on their drawing-room walls. It needed to become fashionable. With his death it will. The artist unappreciated in his lifetime. Every now and then we need that story.'

'But poor Daniel!'

'Yes, very sad, if one believes that the truest rewards are in this world.'

'Your rewards, by a remarkable coincidence, just happen to be in this world.'

'That is true. But I have no misgivings. I've achieved a remarkable coup for the Begelman reputation. Single-handed I have catapulted him to fame. I've earned a fortune for Olga.'

'She wasn't in on this?'

'Good Lord, no. Olga is even more naive than you.'

Kate longed to find something devastating to say to this man. On the whole she felt that she could have done better.

'I disliked you from the moment I saw your cuff-links,' she said.

She went up to one of Daniel's paintings and stared at it. Tears were running down her face, and she wasn't really seeing the picture, she was seeing Daniel at Tregarryn, Daniel in the back of a lorry full of onions, Daniel in the Bandalero. Somebody had said that the past is another country. That was a true remark, and yet another remark that contradicted it was also true. That, she had discovered, was the nature of truth, and of remarks. The past is our own country. We live in a country that was formed by the past. We deny it at our peril. Farewell, dear Daniel, I wish I could believe that you were witnessing all this.

Kate wiped her eyes and blew her nose. She was aware that people around her were aware of her and leaving her alone. She was grateful to them. She was even more grateful to Enid, for what she had said. She resolved at that moment to live her individual life to the full, to the best of her ability, without selfishness or self-absorption. She would continue to bring sunlight into rooms, but she would do more. She would do things that needed doing, good things, bold things, beautiful things.

'Penny for them.'

She turned to see a tall man, big-boned but lean, with a long nose, very full lips and blue eyes that gave nothing away. His hair was slicked back, lending great prominence to his long forehead. She guessed that he was a little younger than her, perhaps in his very early fifties.

'Penny for them,' he repeated.

'No, I was just thinking that I must do things with my life,' she said.

'What sort of things?'

Oh dear, this is going to sound . . . no, don't be bashful.

'Bold things, good things, beautiful things.'

'My word! What things exactly? Can you be a bit more specific?'

'No. I haven't a clue.'

They laughed immoderately. She liked his laugh.

'I'm Graham Eldridge,' he said. 'I'm a journalist.'

'Hello, Graham. I'm Kate Copson.'

'Hello, Kate. Bold things, you say?'

'Yes.'

'What, like going out to dinner tonight with a man you don't know and whose intentions for all you know may be completely dishonourable and who may indeed for all you know be a complete fraud and a sham?'

'That sort of thing, yes.'

'Terrific. Where shall we go?'

'Oh, I was giving a hypothetical answer, Graham, to what I thought was a hypothetical question.'

'No. Real question. How about it?'

'I'm afraid that's not possible. I'm going out with my brother and sister. They're over there.'

'Tomorrow, then?'

'Sorry. I'm going out with my third husband tomorrow.'

'Oh, I see.'

'Oh, we're divorced.'

'Ah. I mean, not that I'm pleased. I'm sorry to hear it.'

'I hope you aren't. He's here tonight. The trim chap with the goatee beard looking at that big picture of Salamanca.'

'It seems as though it's been quite an evening for you.'

'More than you think. My second and fourth husbands are here too.' She enjoyed the effect of this on his face.

'Really? Which are they?'

'Not "they". "Him". Great awkward man with wild black hair over there.'

'The one with the tarty woman?'

'I'm getting to like you. Yes.'

'Do you like this picture? I saw you staring at it very intently before.'

'It's difficult to say. It's difficult to be dispassionate about it. It's a portrait of my first husband.'

'Good Lord! Do you have a fifth husband here, by any chance?'

'No.' She laughed.

Can a remark become a lie retrospectively? Kate's 'no' was true at the time. She wouldn't have believed anyone who had told her that Graham Eldridge was going to become her fifth husband.

13 Hilda

Hilda Mandrake's return to Ward 3C could not by any stretch of the imagination be described as a success. For Kate it came at a particularly irritating time. She was feeling completely exhausted that afternoon, the ward was unusually quiet, Glenda was asleep and miraculously not farting, neither Angela Critchley nor Lily Stannidge was causing any disturbance, and it was Elizabeth's turn to sit with her, and she found Elizabeth's visits particularly undemanding. Every now and then Elizabeth would give her hand a little squeeze, and at the end of the visit she would kiss her cheek and say, 'I'm off now, Mummy. Sleep well,' and that would be that.

So, the October afternoon slid gently by, less than three months now to the millennium and all quiet on the Western Front. Kate slipped in and out of sleep. The hubbub of the private view buzzed still in her head, and it was the quintessence of poignancy to drift between that lively and sparkling scene, when she had outshone, even at fifty-five, all the ladies in the room, and this smelly, stuffy little ward where she lay silent and helpless.

Kate was extremely tired that afternoon. She'd been tired on the night itself, after the exhibition, but she was forty-four years older now and the reliving of it had tired her even more than the living of it.

She was tired but also immensely peaceful. That evening in the Corncrake Gallery had been a turning point in her life. It should have been a cause for yet more guilt. She had met Graham that night, and to fall in love with a shadow, to be utterly fooled by a man at the age of fifty-five, it should have been shaming. But dear, long-dead Enid had persuaded her that evening to put away guilt and shame and self-pity for ever. The peace of mind that she had found that evening in the Corncrake Gallery returned to her in Ward 3C that afternoon as a result of her having relived the whole evening that very morning.

And now here was Hilda, intruding, spoiling things. Now that her body was so useless, Kate found that her senses had heightened to compensate. She didn't know who it was standing at the door, but she knew it was a visitor, and she was sure it was a woman.

'Good afternoon, ladies,' said fat Janet with the eating disorder brightly. 'Look who's come all the way to visit us! Aren't we just the luckiest ladies, ladies? It's our old friend, Hilda.'

Kate's heart sank. She knew it would be a fiasco. She could see Hilda in her mind, standing there, hands tense, mouth working anxiously, smiling too broadly, pale, podgy, dumpy – remember, gentle reader, this is Kate's regrettably ungenerous picture of Hilda. She may indeed have looked exactly like that. Sadly, it's more than probable. But we can't be sure.

'Hello, ladies. Well, I just couldn't keep away!' said Hilda in a bright, brittle voice. 'I must have had a good time here, mustn't I? Well, how are we all today?'

Kate heard Glenda give a low moan and a muffled fart like the croaking of a hoarse toad and she heard Hilda say, 'Hello, Glenda dear. I'll let you wake up properly before I come and talk but I've brought you some grapes.'

Kate's heart sank for Hilda's sake, but also for her own. She didn't want to be visited, that afternoon, by those two old friends of hers, compassion and sympathy. She wanted to rest up before the rigours that were approaching. A woman is lying in bed, paralysed, unable to speak, and she has set herself a task that has baffled even Inspector Crouch himself, thoroughness his middle name.

278

'And I've brought some for you, Mrs Critchley, there you are.'

She hadn't set herself this task out of conceit or as an academic exercise, but as a burning necessity, something that she hungered to solve before she died. She realised now that she had never dared to attempt to solve the problem before, because, if she had solved it, she would have had to act upon it. She would have had to have one of her dear sons arrested, tried, imprisoned. Now she could satisfy her natural curiosity and feel the joy of knowing that two of her sons were innocent, and she wouldn't need to do anything about the murderer because she wouldn't be able to. She wasn't proud of her behaviour in the matter, but she felt it to be understandable in a mother.

And now the moment of truth was almost upon her; she'd already met Graham, another night of recollections and he'd already be dead. Tomorrow she would have to begin what it seemed increasingly pretentious to call her investigations. And now, instead of peace and quiet, here was Hilda saying, 'Hello, you won't know me, but I used to be in your bed. The technical term is, I believe, "the previous occupant". Ha ha!'

'I hope you didn't soil it,' said Lily Stannidge.

'What?? Good heavens, no. Good heavens, what a thing to say! It'd have been changed anyway, even if I had. Which I hadn't. And I'm awfully sorry, but I haven't brought you any grapes, because I didn't know you'd be here.'

'Good. I don't like grapes. They give me the pip.'

'Oh, well in that case . . . oh, pip, very good, I was slow there, smack smack, Hilda! Have you met Doctor Ramgobi?'

'Which deck's he on?'

'Well, don't listen to him. He doesn't know his job. He sent me home and I'm not fit, not with my nerves, I just can't manage, you see. Well, it's such a long way to the shops. I mean, what are old people supposed to do these days?'

Lily Stannidge must have rung the bell. Kate heard Janet say,

'Why have you rung your bell, Lily?' (Easy deduction. Harder one tomorrow. Oh Lord!)

'This woman is a stowaway,' said Lily Stannidge.

'Oh good heavens!' exclaimed Hilda.

'She said she was the previous occupant of the bed. How did she get back on board if she hadn't stowed away?'

'Yes, yes, Lily, good point, we'll sort it all out. Hilda, why don't you go and talk to your old friends and not Lily who you don't know, know what I mean?'

'Well, all right, but I was only trying to cheer her up.'

Kate sensed that Hilda was looking at her now, and wondering whether to say anything. Her body tensed, then relaxed as Hilda moved on.

'Hello, Mrs Critchley.'

'Who are you?'

'Who am I? Oh! Ha ha! I'm your old friend, Hilda, from the end bed on the left.' Hilda lowered her voice. 'A very strange woman's there now. I'm not sure if she's quite right.'

'Well, I wouldn't be surprised if she wasn't. This place has gone down. I was speaking to the manager the other day, he's ethnic, well, you aren't allowed to say foreign these days, are you, but he's very nice, and I said, "Is it true they've stopped the tea dances?" and, yes, they have, can you imagine? Who did you say you were?'

'I'm Hilda. You know. Hilda. Hilda Mandrake.'

'Are you one of the Gloucestershire Mandrakes?'

'No, I live in . . . well, it's hard to say whether it's Edgware or Stanmore.'

'Oh. Only I knew some Mandrakes in Gloucestershire.'

'No. That wasn't me.'

'Get away from me!'

'What??'

'You killed my daughter!'

'What?? No!! Oh good heavens. Mrs Critchley, really.'

Mrs Critchley must have rung her bell. Kate heard Janet say, 'Well, well, how our bells are buzzing this afternoon. What's up, Mrs Critchley?'

'This woman's annoying me.'

'Oh Lord. Oh, Hilda, I'm sorry, but . . .' Kate could sense Janet leading Hilda away. Janet continued in a hushed voice. 'Mrs Critchley's a bit funny today, know what I mean? Glenda's all right, though. You have a nice chat to Glenda.'

Kate almost expelled a sigh at Hilda's humiliations. Just in time she realised that a sigh might reveal even to someone as insensitive as Elizabeth that she was understanding a great deal more than she was letting on.

'Hello, Glenda. *You* remember me, don't you?'

'Yes. You were in the next bed. Hilda.'

'That's right! And I thought, I know what I'll do today, I'll go and see my friend Glenda. It's taken me three buses, it's one of those awkward journeys, but never mind, I thought, I'll go and see Glenda.'

'Why don't you just shove off and get three buses back home again?'

Oh no!

'I can't believe what I'm hearing, Glenda. What harm have I ever done to you?'

'I hate you.'

'Glenda!'

'I should have been sent home, not you. What did you do, bribe Doctor Rambogi?'

'Ramgobi. Glenda!'

'Promised to sleep with him, did you?'

Ha! Awful, but you have to laugh. How cruel is comedy!

'Glenda!! I've a good mind to just walk out.'

'First sensible thing you've said.'

'But no, that would be the easy way out. The coward's way. Glenda, I didn't want to get sent home. I've got nothing at

281

home. I had to have the cat put down before I came in. There's virtually nothing on the television. All those trendy people in the media, there was a very interesting article at the hairdresser's . . . and the girl I like has gone, and the new one's hopeless, I said to her, "You just don't understand my hair. What my hair is is sparse." Where was I?'

'God knows.'

'Oh yes. Television. I read they want programmes with street cred. I don't know what street cred is. I live in a grove. I don't know whether there is such a thing as grove cred. They make programmes for young people and what's the point, they're at their clubs taking their drugs. The only decent thing an old lady in her own home can watch is the *Antiques Roadshow*, and I expect quite soon they'll have suggestive jugs on that.'

Glenda must have rung the bell. Kate heard Janet saying, 'My my my. What a plague of bells ringing we have today. What's up, Glenda?'

'This woman's annoying me.'

'Oh dear. Oh dear oh dear. I'm really sorry, Hilda. It's just not been your day, has it?'

Kate felt Hilda stop at the bottom of her bed.

'Who are you? The daughter?' asked Hilda.

'Yes,' said Elizabeth. She was never a great conversationalist but Kate thought she could have done better than that.

'Well, I'll tell you something about your mother,' said Hilda. 'She can't speak, she can't see, she can't hear, she can't move, but she's more fun than the rest of them put together.'

14 Graham

During the long night that followed Hilda's disastrous visit, Kate relived her life with the man she knew as Graham Eldridge.

It had begun quite gently. It hadn't been a whirlwind romance. Kate hadn't felt any overwhelming urge to get married again. She was still recovering from the shock of her separation from Walter. She was still going through a complicated divorce settlement. And there was Heinz. He would have married her again like a shot. 'Really, Heinz,' she said, on the evening when he actually proposed, 'to marry one man twice seems a bit excessive. To marry two men twice would be positively greedy.' In the end, she had to say, 'I like you enormously, Heinz. I just don't love you. I fell out of love with you when I realised that Walter had become a man I could truly love. I love him still.'

He pushed bits of pork round and round his plate, the way he did when he was tense. 'I realised you'd need time,' he said. 'I'm prepared to give you time.'

'I've had time,' she said. 'I've tried, Heinz.'

'Oh God, that sounds awful. I didn't want you to try. I didn't want effort. Is this it, then?'

'Well, I don't know quite what you mean by "it". I hope we can continue to see each other.'

'I'm afraid not,' said Heinz. 'It makes me too sad.'

'Don't you think we should tell Elizabeth who her father is?'

'Is there any point now?'

'Don't you think the truth matters?'

'Only sometimes.'

But Elizabeth didn't get on with Linda. They were jealous of each other. And although Walter didn't exactly take sides, his

283

interests, if not his feelings, lay with Linda. Elizabeth left home in a huff and a taxi. She moved into a bedsit with Sylvie, and enrolled in a secretarial college. Heinz was very upset when Kate told him.

'A secretarial college? Isn't she clever enough for university?'

'She says she thinks she's just clever enough. She says it'd be hell, at university, to be just clever enough, to be hanging on.'

'That's defeatist.'

'Heinz, it was you who decided that she should have a throne. She has every right to prefer a typewriter.'

They decided, now that Elizabeth was disillusioned with Walter, that it was time to tell her. She took it calmly, said she was glad she knew, said she wanted to keep in touch with Heinz. The three of them had a meal together, at L'Etoile, a good, affectionate but rather sad meal, and then Heinz took a taxi out of Kate's life.

Meanwhile, Kate saw Graham for lunches and dinners. They lunched at the Ivy, dined at the Gay Hussar. Graham began to spend the occasional night at Kate's flat. She stayed once or twice in his elegant Georgian terrace house in Trevor Square. It helped that he was rich. She wasn't surprised that he was rich. He was a well-known journalist. He was Graham 'Mr Con-Buster' Eldridge. He took her to Paris for the weekend. They stayed at the Crillon. They ate good food, drank good wine, made good friends. Olga liked Graham. Daphne liked Graham. Stanley didn't like Graham. So they had a very satisfactory social life, and it didn't matter that much if the sex wasn't terribly good. In that department nobody could compare with Walter, so somehow it didn't seem to be an important part of that phase of her life.

'That phase of her life'! The phrase jolted her. She opened her eyes cautiously, moved them the little bit that she could manage. There was nothing to see. The light had long faded from her window on the world. The ward was peaceful in the dim barley-sugar glow of the night-light. She could hear Lily Stannidge's bed creak as she sailed on the Sea of Dreams. Glenda farted, a real rasper. 'That phase of her life'. That was hindsight. It hadn't been a phase at the time.

It was a strange feeling to relive each 'phase of her life', knowing, as of course she hadn't known at the time, how it would end. It was particularly strange in the case of Graham, in the light of what she had found out about him later. Each moment, in the reliving, was subjected to the question, 'Was it real?'

Yes, yes, cried Kate silently in the silent ward. Those heavenly walks arm in arm by the Seine, they happened, they were joyous, that joy could not be wiped out retrospectively. That gondola ride in Venice, hindsight couldn't dim the pleasure she had felt at the time. Graham Eldridge was good company and kind. He never said a cross word to Kate, was always generous with money, as with his friends. Many splendid dinner parties were given in the smart terrace house in Trevor Square, after she'd moved in with him. Graham was always very kind to the family, having no family of his own. During Bernard's last months in London, before he was forced to give up his job with Simms Fordingbridge, nothing was too much trouble for Graham. They took Bernard to plays, to concerts, to dinners, to Graham's beloved Tottenham Hotspur.

Kate would never forget the moment of Graham's arrival in Swansea. As the taxi pulled up outside the house, the door opened and John Thomas Thomas walked out without his stick, slowly, rather bent now, but without his stick.

'I did it, Kate,' he said.

'Well, I've brought another one,' said Kate to Enid, this time without apology.

Annie beamed excitedly. They had kippers for tea. Graham led them to believe that there was nothing in this world better than a kipper for your tea, unless it was a pair of kippers. He gave the impression that, while lobster and caviare might have their devotees, there was nothing in the world to equal Welsh cakes and bara brith.

'Just a moment,' said Kate, as Annie began to clear away the things. 'Leave them a moment. Graham and I have something very important to tell you. We're engaged.'

Annie sank into the chair, threw her thick-ankled, thick-thighed, thick-stockinged, thick support-bandaged bunioned legs into the air and cried out in her excitement. She removed her lace hankie from her stocking top and blew her wide nose vigorously. Enid, too, had watery eyes.

After the meal, Bronwen kissed Kate and Graham. She gave Kate a grave look and said, 'This time I hope it'll be for ever.' To Graham she said, this frail old lady, 'Look after my little girl.'

Graham smiled and said, 'I like that, "Mother", if I may call you that. Kate is the toast of London, but I suppose to you she'll always be your little girl.'

'Aren't you going to ask where Graham proposed?' asked Kate.

'Where did you propose, Graham?' asked Enid dutifully.

'On the train, at the moment when it entered Wales,' said Graham.

Annie gasped and said, 'Oh, there's lovely. There's romantic,' with a sob in her voice.

'I kissed her in the Severn Tunnel,' said Graham.

John Thomas Thomas pretended to be deaf, and made no comment on that one, but he heard well enough when Graham said, 'Would you like a chocolate? I've brought some rather nice ones.'

'Oh yes, please,' said John Thomas Thomas. 'Is there a key?'

'Oh yes,' said Graham.

'Oh good,' said John Thomas Thomas. 'I like it when there's a key.'

He hunted through the box for some time, comparing the

shapes and squiggles of the chocolates in the box with the illustrations in the key.

'I'm sorry,' he said. 'I'm holding you all up. I'm looking for a marzipan one.'

'There's no hurry,' said Graham. 'The world is in too much of a hurry these days.'

There was no incident so small that Graham Eldridge couldn't find a suitable remark with which to decorate it.

'Besides,' he added, for, if ever he saw a lily, he felt compelled to gild it, 'you deserve a marzipan one today of all days.'

'Why?' asked John Thomas Thomas archly, knowing the answer, charmingly vain now as he approached second childhood.

'Because today you threw away your stick as you had said you would and as the world doubted you would.'

How much had Graham meant of what he said, and did it matter? He gave pleasure wherever he went. They took him round the Mumbles and he marvelled at its charm. They took him round Gower and he exclaimed at its beauty.

'Do you like him?' Kate asked her sister and Annie in the breakfast room, on the morning of their departure.

'I think he's lovely,' said Annie, and blushed furiously. Graham had looked at Annie's abysmal photos of Switzerland as if he had never seen better examples of the photographer's art. He had praised her chutney and her jam. She was eating out of his hand.

'I think he's too good to be true,' said Enid, and nothing in her voice suggested that this was anything other than a nicely turned compliment.

'Who's too good to be true?' asked Graham, entering quickly and silently, as he did.

'Why, you of course, darling,' said Kate.

'I am, aren't I?' said Graham. 'It must all be a sham.' He laughed heartily, and pushed the rocking chair gently, to charm and delight his beloved. 'I have this knack of always saying the right thing.' He kissed the top of his fiancée's head. 'But the thing is, I always mean it.'

There was the faintest of faint drizzles on the hydrangea air of Eaton Crescent as they got into the taxi to take them to the station. John Thomas Thomas, minus his stick again, walked boldly down the tiled path to the very edge of the pavement.

'Come again, Graham Eldridge, and bring more marzipan,' he said.

'Try to keep me away,' said Graham Eldridge. 'I love my new Welsh family.'

Graham's work as 'Mr Con-Buster' made him quite a celebrity in his day, though of course it is entirely forgotten now. To a journalist news soon becomes stale. He can't object if he in turn becomes yesterday's news. But the interest created by his revelations was enormous, and many people were surprised that he refused to repeat them on the rapidly expanding television service.

From the outset he encouraged Kate to be his assistant, and she loved the work. She'd not worked for money since her teaching days in Penzance. She loved the monthly pay cheque, the shared routines, the travel. And of course it was emotionally gratifying to expose the world's exploiters and con men.

During the years of their collaboration Kate and Graham worked on uncovering several large-scale confidence tricks.

There was the scheme where you bought a square acre of the Peruvian rain forest for twenty pounds, and received a scroll to inform you of the fact, and a certificate stating that your patch of South America was saved from exploitation for all eternity. The land in question turned out to be desert, where no tree had ever grown.

There was the double-glazing salesman who asked for a pound's deposit and was never seen again. A pound was such a small sum even in those days that very few people complained, but pounds add up, and by the time Graham tracked him down he was a substantially prosperous man.

There was the racing tipster who sent you tips through the post. You paid him five pounds if the horse he tipped won, and nothing if it didn't. This was a brilliant trick. Nobody complained for years, since, if they didn't win, they didn't pay a penny. He tipped every horse in the race, so some people were bound to win, and he was bound to become rich, while hundreds of people wasted good money on dud horses.

The children, products of Kate's marriages to three husbands, had mixed feelings about her marrying yet another. Kate felt that she ought to try to think herself back into her memory of their feelings, since they might be relevant to the identification of the murderer.

She'd never considered Elizabeth as a potential murderer, and she didn't now. There was nothing fantastic in Elizabeth's life. She'd grown into a thoroughly decent, thoroughly reliable, slightly dull woman. She was neither beautiful nor ugly, neither clever nor stupid. In 1957, at the young age of nineteen, she gave up secretarial college and married a rather dull insurance broker named Don. Elizabeth certainly wished that Kate was still with Walter. She hated the idea of Walter marrying Linda. But Graham was in no way to blame for the fact that Kate wasn't with Walter, and Elizabeth's initial attitude to him was one of caution. Gradually, however, he charmed her. For one thing, he seemed to be the only person in the world who found insurance broking riveting. 'People think insurance is boring,' he told Elizabeth one day. 'I simply don't understand that. Don and I have some fascinating chats about how you evaluate risks in different circumstances.'

In 1958 Elizabeth gave birth to twin boys, Mark and Trevor. Graham loved to play with them, and they adored him. It was just too funny, when they were barely three, to hear them solemnly reciting the names of the Tottenham team that won the league and the cup in the 1960–61 season. Mark had a very deep voice, for a child, and Trevor a little piping one. 'Brown,' they would cry, 'Baker, Henry, Blanchflower, Norman, Mackay, Jones, White, Smith, Allen, Dyson.' 'What a forward line,' Graham would tell them. 'The most boringly named forward line in the history of football, but what players!'

No, by 1961 Graham was a firm favourite. Elizabeth could never have murdered anyone, and she certainly had no reason to murder Graham.

Timothy. Timothy was no longer teaching at Brasenose Preparatory School. His novels were earning him enough to live on. Four had been published now. They were called *Trouble at School*, *Trouble at the Mill*, *Trouble at the Double* and *Trouble in Torquay*. They were murder mysteries featuring Inspector Trouble, as unlikely as he was eponymous. They were ingenious, but silly. They weren't serious in the sense in which John Thomas Thomas used the word. They were puzzles created by a man clever enough to have written better books. Kate's puritanical streak prevented her from admiring Timothy's work, and, because she couldn't admire the books, she found it impossible to finish them, and couldn't find it in her to pretend enough to give Timothy the admiration he craved. Other people did give him the admiration, but he didn't crave it from them. Also, his relationship with his mother was made more difficult by his belief that she had expected Milly to leave him, although she had never said anything to that effect. It was bad enough to lose your wife to a pig farmer on the Somerset Levels, without the added humiliation of believing that your mother wasn't surprised.

All in all, Kate didn't feel that Timothy had been in a good frame of mind, initially, to welcome the arrival of yet another father figure. He was at first almost hostile, definitely mistrustful, and was cool and wary in Graham's presence. One day, however, over drinks in the tiny paved garden at Trevor Square,

Graham said, 'Of course I've read your books, Timothy. They have the subtlety and sexuality of a Simenon allied to the raw bite and honed elegance of a Chandler, yet with a seasoning that is uniquely their own,' and Timothy realised for the first time what a great fellow he was.

'Did you really mean what you said to Timothy about his books?' Kate asked Graham that night.

'Almost,' he said. 'I mean I don't think they're *quite* as good as Simenon and Chandler, but I don't need to say that, do I, and they aren't far off. You ought to be very proud of him, darling.'

Kate did try to be proud of Timothy, but she couldn't help thinking that if this physically timid man had been able to bring himself to murder anybody, he'd have been more likely at that time to have murdered her than Graham.

Nigel only met Graham once before the wedding, and not many times afterwards. His career with Muller-Burns was thriving, and he spent much of his time in Glasgow and Cologne. Every year, the firm held a Muller-Burns Burns Night, in Glasgow, and all their top German people were told, 'We have ways of making you eat haggis and bashed neeps.' Pale from this culture shock, the Germans hurried back to Cologne to make ready for the arrival of the top British people for their turn at culture shock in the form of Carnival, where they drank a lot of beer, thumped tables a lot, and listened to several hours of jokes in German, which they understood about as well as the Germans understood the Glasgow jokes. The rest of his year was less hectic socially, but he was involved in high-level research which was emotionally draining and very time-consuming. When he did meet Graham, he seemed to Kate to be somewhat wary, as if he didn't trust him entirely, but when she asked him if he disliked Graham, he denied it vehemently, and made a point of inviting Graham out to lunch. He phoned Kate afterwards and said, 'We've had a very good lunch. I had the artichoke vinaigrette, the *coq au vin* and the cheese.' 'What about Graham?' she asked. 'Oh, he was very fishy,' he said. 'In what way?' she asked, not without a certain amount of trepidation. 'He had the lobster cocktail and the Dover sole.' 'No, I meant, how did you get on?' 'Oh!' He sounded surprised to be asked this, as if it was something he just hadn't thought about. 'Perfectly well. He has an easy surface charm which he uses to hide the fact that deep down he is actually very charming indeed.'

Maurice was more of a problem than the other three children put together. As a rising BBC journalist in his twenties he had, or at least pretended to have, an enormous amount of confidence in his judgement of almost everything, but above all of people. He was also completely lacking in vanity, so when Graham praised his early television appearances, it cut very little ice with him.

He called on his mother one day, when he knew Graham would be out, and said, 'Are you really going to marry Graham?'

'No,' said Kate with unwonted heaviness. 'We're just playing a practical joke on the registrar. Why?'

'I don't trust him.'

'Why not?'

'He's just too perfect. He always says the right thing.'

'He's courteous, well-mannered, thoughtful, sympathetic, intelligent and understanding.'

'Are you worried that he has no relatives?'

'No, it's a relief. We have so much more time to look after my relatives.'

'No, but isn't it all a little bit convenient? Parents killed in a house fire.'

'Convenient?'

'Only child.'

'Oh my God! He must be the only only child in the country. Divorcee in Husband Only Child Shock.'

'Don't be silly, Ma. No aunts or uncles living?'

'He's fifty-six. They'd all have been over eighty.'

'No nephews, no nieces, no cousins?'

'The family is dying out. Families do. It upsets him greatly, actually.'

'Have you checked up on these uncles and aunts?'

'No! What do you expect me to do? Say, "I know what we could do for a holiday, Graham. Have a dead-uncle tour. They're always fun. Check on a few graves, take some photos of crematoria." I mean, I know we Welsh are obsessed with death, but that'd be going too far.'

'Yes, but . . .'

'Maurice, I don't wish to discuss the subject any more.'

He went quite white. His knuckles were white. Kate had never known him so pent up.

'How's your father?' she asked.

He grunted.

'Silly man,' he said.

'What?'

'Getting engaged to bloody Linda. After you! Trying to relive his youth. Can't he see she's only out for all she can get? Shitty little gold-digger.'

'I've never had a row with you, Maurice, never. I've always respected your judgement and maturity. I think your success is beginning to warp your mind. Suddenly nobody's good enough for Walter or me. The truth is, Maurice, you just can't bear to see either of your parents happy. I think you ought to seek professional help for your personality problem.'

'Me?? Me?? Goodbye, Ma.' He stormed to the door, then stopped, and said, 'Oh hell.'

'What?'

'I've caught something of your Welshness. I can't storm out in case I'm killed on the way home.'

'Maurice!'

He came over to her and hugged her. They held each other in silence for at least half a minute.

'Sorry, Ma,' he said, as he left. Looking back on it now, of course, she realised that she should have been apologising to him. She had closed her mind to a possibility that she just couldn't face.

The decision to marry in private was an easy one. Graham had already said, 'I'm going to feel embarrassed having no family on the great day,' and it was clear that the day would have been an ordeal for Bernard, who was now too ill to work and had gone back to Swansea to die, like a sick animal crawling into a hedge. It would also have been a decision of appalling difficulty for John Thomas Thomas, who loved his daughter but thought that divorce was wicked, and Bronwen would have stood by John Thomas Thomas's decision, however much it broke her heart. And Oliver? In his retirement in Surrey he remained semi-detached from the family. The family, for their part, believed that Bunny despised Wales. John Thomas Thomas and Bronwen were invited to Surrey for a long weekend every year, and so were Enid and Annie, but Oliver and Bunny were never seen in Wales except at funerals. Only Enid and Annie, therefore, regretted the private nature of the ceremony, and even they felt a degree of relief at being spared the agony of deciding what to wear.

They honeymooned in the Seychelles, and Kate had to pinch herself that she was really there, on those exquisite beaches, eating that delicious seafood. The only trouble with that kind of holiday is that there is nothing to talk about afterwards. Once you'd said, 'It was perfect,' and 'It was bliss,' you'd exhausted the conversational possibilities. Perhaps for this reason, as conversation was so important to Kate, the memory of the honeymoon didn't linger with her as vividly as she would have wished. Now, lying in this fetid ward in the middle of the night, she tried to conjure up the full majesty of those tree-fringed beaches, but they hadn't any more reality for her now than photographs in a brochure.

But the shrill noise of the phone in the house in Trevor Square as they walked in after the honeymoon rang in her head as if it was only yesterday. Of course at the time she hadn't found it particularly shrill. In bad films, people anticipate events in an unrealistic way. If a destructive blob from outer space lumbers up the drive and rings the bell, they leap up, gaze at each other in horror and say, 'My God! Who can that be?' when they have no reason to think that it's anything more dramatic than a neighbour asking if they have any self-raising flour. Kate didn't think, 'Oh my God, who's phoning so dramatically at the very moment when I walk in from my honeymoon? It's odds on that my bliss will be utterly destroyed in a trice.' She lifted the phone extremely casually, and said, 'Kate speaking,' and Walter said, 'Hello, Kate, it's me,' and her knees buckled beneath her and luckily there was a little chair handy to collapse into, and Graham raised an eyebrow and waited for her to speak to the caller by name, but she didn't.

'I got your number from Elizabeth,' he said. 'I hope you don't mind.'

'No, not at all. Why should I?'

'Good. How are you?'

'Very well. How are you?'

'Yes, very well.'

'Good.'

Graham was making 'Who is it?' gestures. She wasn't going to tell him.

'Kate, I've got some news.'

'Oh?'

'I've broken it off with Linda.'

'Oh!'

Oh!!

Oh!!!

Oh!!!!

'Well, is that all you can say – "Oh!"?'

'Well, what am I supposed to say? I suppose I could say, though it's none of my business, "Why?"'

'It's all of your business, and you know why.'

'Do I?'

'It was all the most dreadful mistake. I don't agree with Maurice that she's a shitty little gold-digger. I think she's a sweet person. But shallow, Kate, and, because shallow, Kate, not remotely as beautiful as you.'

'Walter . . .'

'Don't speak. Let me say what I have to say.'

Now Graham had to sit down as well.

'Walter . . .'

'No. I must say it. I was a fool to throw you out. It was just that . . . I worshipped you so much that it was an unbearable disappointment at the time.'

'I never wanted to be worshipped.'

'Kate, come back to me.'

'Didn't Elizabeth tell you?'

'Tell me what? She didn't tell me anything. I just asked for your number and she said, "She's away" – typical Elizabeth – and I said, "That doesn't stop you giving me her number. She won't be away for ever," and she said, "No, but it's downstairs and I'm tidying the loft." She did give it in the end but it was such a saga that there was no time for conversation, she wasn't interested, she doesn't speculate, she doesn't even know about me and Linda being over. What is all this?'

'This is Graham's house, Walter.'

'Who's Graham when he's at home?'

'He's at home now and he's my husband.'

'Oh no. Oh, Kate!'

'We were just walking in from our honeymoon when you rang.'

'I see. Well, that's typical of you, isn't it?'

'What?'

'This happening at the very moment you walk in from your honeymoon. You always were a drama queen.'

'That's the most monstrous thing I've ever heard, Walter. You're phoning me!'

'Oh, Kate! Kate! I love you.'

'Walter, I'm really sorry if you only broke if off with Linda because of me, but I suspect you were right to do so anyway.'

'I'd better go now,' said Walter. 'I hope you'll both be very happy.'

Graham came over and kissed her very tenderly.

'No regrets?' he asked.

Kate felt stifled by regret. Her legs ached with regret. When she tried to walk she felt that her feet were stuck in a morass of regret. The Welsh chapel girl who had once promised never to tell a lie smiled a radiant, loving smile and revealed to her new husband a secret talent that until that moment she'd kept from everyone except her sister Enid. She did an extremely good impression of Edith Piaf. She sang the song right through, brilliantly, smiling outside, aching inside. When she'd finished Graham gave her a round of applause.

For more than a year, Kate and Graham led what was to all intents and purposes a happy married life. From the moment she began her Edith Piaf impression, Kate allowed herself not the tiniest flicker of self-pity. She set out to make a success, both public and private, of her marriage. Early in the marriage, she had a dream in which she discovered Graham dead in bed and she cried, 'I'm free. I'm free.' She woke up bathed in sweat and there was Graham alive beside her and as caring as ever.

'What is it, my darling?'

'I had a dream.'

'A nightmare?'

She couldn't tell him that it had not been a nightmare.

'I dreamt you were dead.'

'Oh, my darling. My poor poor darling.'

'Yes.'

'How did I die?'

'Peacefully, in bed. I found you here.'

'Well, I'm here, and I'm not dead. In fact, Kate, I'm very much alive.'

And he began . . . oh Lord, he began . . . and it wasn't a very common event and it wasn't always a great success, but on this occasion . . . oh Lord . . . he was fervent and eager and he came with a great spurt of joy while Kate faked, faked, faked, and hoped that she was doing it more convincingly than she had with Heinz.

It was not the last time Kate had the dream, and it wasn't the first time that she became frightened to go to sleep because of a dream, but even now she felt no guilt about the dream, she couldn't control her subconscious but by God she would control her conscious self, and she did. The dream soon ceased. Kate no longer needed to fake her orgasms and her only regret was that they were not more frequent. She willed herself to be happy with Graham, and to forget Walter, and she did. For the last three years of their married life, after the sad day of her mother's funeral, she hardly thought about Walter at all. She had come to love, truly and fully, a man who was a complete fake. Irony again, she thought, looking back on it from her hospital bed. Oh, Kate, what ironies you have endured.

Happy times, gentle reader, are like that honeymoon in the Seychelles. There's not much to say about them. But, since I have made no attempt to hide how the marriage will end, I think I must assure you that, apart from her visits to Swansea, the rest of Kate's marriage to Graham was truly happy. More good meals, a splendid weekend in Amsterdam, a motoring holiday on the glorious west coast of Scotland, with a bit of work thrown in – an elaborate hoax involving a diesel-powered Loch Ness

Monster constructed by ingenious French students and financed by local hoteliers.

'Apart from her visits to Swansea'. Sadly, these were mainly for funerals during this period. Oh, those Welsh funerals. The sky was the colour of slate, a cold wind blew straight from the subconscious, and old men who had once been dapper stood unaware that there were dewdrops on the ends of their noses.

The first to go was Bronwen. They came in their black finery, on a black day, to send off this old lady who had never in her life had an evil or an ungenerous thought. From Sketty and the Mumbles, from the valleys and the hills, from Cockett and Tycoch and Pontardulais and Ystradgynlais, from Carmarthen and Cardigan they came in their best black. Relatives and friends emerged from all the nooks and crannies of south and mid-Wales. Men in the streets of Swansea took off their hats for the cortège. Bronwen Thomas would have been amazed to have seen how much the world had loved her. The sermon was in Welsh and English, and there were two hymns in each language. There were little men with big voices. There were ugly men with beautiful voices. There were dark, handsome men with dark, handsome voices. How they all sang their farewell to Bronwen Thomas, who had never in her life had an evil or an ungenerous thought, a fact so extraordinary that it is worth saying twice. What an incredible noise is the sound of Welsh voices singing from the heart. Trying hard not to give way to her tears, Kate reflected on the similarity of south Wales to Italy. Dark men. Dark, vibrant, self-satisfied singing. Beautiful girls. Endless talk. Devious politicians. Subjugated women. Less than in the past, of course, but it would still be a long time before Wales became the land of our mothers. But these thoughts couldn't keep the tears at bay for long. Kate's tears flowed and she became at one with all the women who were sniffling all over the bursting chapel. Kate looked round, and saw, through her tears, rows of red eyes. Rows of tonsils. Enid weeping. Annie weeping. Bernard singing and weeping. Oliver trying hard not to weep. Herbert Herbert Cricket singing, Herbert Herbert Politics singing, Mrs Herbert Herbert Cricket weeping, Mrs Herbert Herbert Politics weeping. Bunny with a set face, perhaps wondering how many people there would be at her funeral. John Thomas Thomas, white-haired, staring at his God with a resolute face and dry eyes.

They crowded into the parlour afterwards, and Kate and Enid and Annie and Elizabeth dispensed sandwiches and scones and Welsh cakes and bara brith. Elizabeth and her rather dull husband Don were good at funerals, they might have been made for them. Maurice and his pretty fiancée Clare were doing sterling work, they were always good mixers. Nigel and Timothy were doing their best, but Kate thought they looked rather forlorn, as if feeling the need of a good woman to console them in their grief. Both had come on their own. Nigel always seemed to be on his own, and Timothy was still in shock after Milly's departure. And Graham? He struck, as always, exactly the right note. Kate stood and watched him for a moment. How could you suspect a man for always doing the right thing? Graham did the right thing because he was a good man. Every day, since Walter's phone call, she had tried to love him. Now, in deep grief for her mother, watching him working the room so diligently, she felt that, yes, at last she did truly love him 'till death us do part', which was not very far away, as we know and they didn't.

A tide of talk warmed the cold, unused room. Oh, the price of fish is something shocking, and we should have beaten the French, oh what a summer, what's happening to the climate, we shan't see her like again, do you think cockles have the taste they had when we were young, don't talk to me about the younger generation, mind you, fair play, there's good ones too, have some more bara brith, she always hated waste, how's your hernia, Herbert Herbert?

Kate found it good to be so busy, serving cups of tea and coffee and slicing more bara brith. 'It's going like hot cakes,' said Annie with wonder. 'Grief makes people hungry,' said Kate.

John Thomas Thomas sat in a hard chair, better for his back and more dignified for his grief, and was spoken to by everyone in turn. He showed no sign of emotion. His appetite was excellent. He had three pieces of bara brith. Not a tear came to mist his clear eyes. Not a moment of weakness did he show.

In fact, John Thomas Thomas only ever gave one indication of grief, but it was a powerful one. He died a fortnight later, in order to join his Bronwen.

The same people all came again. It was all very dignified and heartfelt but not quite as emotional. He wouldn't have wanted it to be. He's happy to be with her. The price of kippers is something shocking, isn't it? It's the end of an era. This bara brith is lovely, where did you get it? What'll you do with the house? Too soon, quite right. They don't make them like John Thomas Thomas any more. How's your prostate, Herbert Herbert?

Now Bernard was free to give up the unequal struggle. It would have broken his parents' hearts if he'd died before them. Dilys, Myfanwy, awful, but to have lost one of the boys would have been unbearable.

Kate went back to Swansea to be at his bedside. He had the master bedroom now, so as to be spared the second flight of stairs. It was a large, airy room with a bay window and a huge shining mahogany wardrobe. It rustled with memories of Bronwen's knickers and John Thomas Thomas's long coms. Kate took it in turns with Enid. Annie refused to sit with him. 'He wants his true family now,' she said. 'I've been privileged to be part of the family, but when you're dying you want your true family with you.' Was she sincere, or was it that she couldn't cope? Kate didn't know, didn't care. It served. It was appropriate. By their actions judge them, not their motives.

'Comfy?' Kate asked, one long grey afternoon. 'Anything I can do to make you comfier?'

Bernard's reply was completely unexpected. 'I expect you think of me as a sad man,' he said.

'Why, what a thing to say!'

'Well, never married, never had . . . conjugal relations. Lived in a dark, dirty flat. Worked for one firm all my life. Never even learnt to boil an egg. Deserted by his only close friend. Funny, though, it doesn't seem sad to me. I've loved my life, Kate. I've loved accountancy, my car, my games of bridge, my rugby, my Wales, my mother, my father, my dear brothers and sisters. I've seen Vienna and Verona and Venice. Read Shakespeare and P. G. Wodehouse. Heard Brahms. Eaten lobster and crabs and pheasant and sewin and roast beef and Welsh cakes and bara brith. I've had the best family a man could have. I regard myself as very fortunate. I've loved you as much as anything or anyone, Kate dear. I've lived your life with you. It's been quite exciting.'

He slept then. He slept most of the day now.

The next day, he said, 'Mother and Father never realised quite how ill I was, did they, Kate?'

'No, darling, they didn't.'

'I was brave at the end, wasn't I?'

'You were very brave.'

The next day Bernard was weaker still. Kate and Enid were with him together all day. At half past four he tried to speak. Kate and Enid leant forward to hear his feeble voice.

You read about famous last words. Kate had read about many. She had invented some at parties, and people had laughed. She only, in her long life, heard one person's last words, and he wasn't famous at all. His words moved her almost beyond endurance.

'I don't believe there is an afterlife, I beg your pardon?' said Bernard.

And so they all came again, except for Nigel. He was in

Germany, at a vital meeting, and simply couldn't get away. But he wrote his mother a wonderful letter.

Dear Mother,

I was so sorry not to be able to be at Uncle Bernard's funeral. I went to work in black, and I left the meeting for half an hour. I sat in my laboratory, motionless. I closed my eyes and I pictured Uncle Bernard as he was before his illness got him. I told him that I loved him, and I cried. I don't often cry, I don't find it easy to cry, but, Mother, I cried.

In the months that followed, Graham and Kate went down to Swansea several times to help sort through her parents' and Bernard's effects. There was sadness, yes, but there were rich consolations in the closeness of their companionship as they did these things together and read out loud happy extracts from her father's diaries – his steadfast faith, the simple pleasure that he took from his holidays in Llandrindrod Wells and Llandudno and Eastbourne. Every bus ride he'd ever taken had been a voyage of discovery for John Thomas Thomas. Every animal and bird that he had seen had been a little adventure. There was joy, too, in the closeness of her relationship with Enid. Enid had retired now, and had been ready for it. She had begun to find the children hard work.

The house had been left to Enid, but on condition that Annie could stay as long as she wanted. Annie had been left a small annuity. These arrangements seemed to Kate unwise. They could lead to trouble. But, for the moment, nothing was said, and Annie and Enid were left to clatter around the old house and breathe such life into it as they could.

Life in Trevor Square, meanwhile, was happy. Good food, good wine, rewarding work, heart-warming letters from the victims of confidence tricks. It was very pleasant to be part of the London scene as the nation climbed towards prosperity. It was pleasant to walk in the parks, to see the films of Fellini and Antonioni, to sit in the Albert Hall listening to the subtleties of her beloved *Enigma Variations*, and being thrilled to her patriotic core by the music of Vaughan Williams. They had seen several plays together, most of which she had forgotten, but she still recalled the excitement of seeing *Look Back in Anger* at the Royal Court theatre, and suddenly realising that plays could be about real life.

They had an extremely enjoyable visit to Copenhagen, to investigate the mysterious little-known Danish island of Sudsø. The whole island was a nature reserve, which was said to care for injured seals and whales. An advertisement in the *Daily Telegraph* had helped the scheme enormously through a misprint which seemed too inspired to be accidental. Instead of the phrase, 'Please give generously for a very special purpose,' the paper had printed, 'Please give generously for a very special porpoise.' It turned out that the island of Sudsø was little known for a very good reason. It didn't exist. But money had poured into an address in Copenhagen, much of it sent by children to feed the very special porpoise. The scheme was run with flair. There was a box to tick if you didn't want them to spend money on an acknowledgement. Most people ticked this box, but those who didn't always got a reply. Kate liked the Danes, and had a good time in Copenhagen, so she was quite pleased when the perpetrator of the scheme turned out to come from Spalding.

Kate and Graham only spent three nights apart in the whole of their married life. Kate had flu, and couldn't accompany Graham on a trip to Copenhagen to see Timothy collect the Danish Detective Writers' Award for his novel, *Trouble in the Skagerrak*. Maurice flew in from Moscow, Nigel from Cologne, and they all had a happy reunion without her, after which Graham stayed on to sort out some loose ends in the Sudsø affair. Kate couldn't remember when she had last been ill, and she vowed never to be ill again.

Maurice charged round the world, sometimes in Russia, sometimes reporting happily on the independence celebrations of nation after nation, but he always managed to see them, even if only briefly, with his attractive fiancée Clare, between assignments. Elizabeth and her rather dull husband Don came every now and then with the twins, although they really preferred Leatherhead to London. 'A man who is tired of Leatherhead is tired of life, as Doctor Johnson never said,' said Kate on one occasion, and Elizabeth, missing the point as usual, said, 'It isn't Leatherhead particularly that we like, it's its position. It's so handy for London and the south coast.'

The one puzzling incident occurred at a publishers' party for the publication of Timothy's sixth book, *Trouble at the Hockey Festival*, a gripping yarn about the murder of a complete Spanish hockey team, all murdered so that nobody would be able to work out which of them was the intended victim. Nobody except Inspector Trouble, that is. The critics were beginning to ignore Timothy now, at just the moment when readers were beginning to turn to him.

Graham was in a very solemn mood at the party, Kate remembered, almost as if he suspected that he was going to be murdered.

'You're very solemn tonight,' Kate said.

'I'm on to something big,' he said.

'A con?'

'A con against the whole human race.'

'Good Lord, is that all? Well, aren't you going to tell me any more?'

'Not at this stage. I want to be sure of my ground first.' He saw the disappointment on her face. They were partners, after all. 'I'll tell you soon,' he said. 'Don't I always? S'ssh! Timothy.'

Timothy approached them, kissed his mother, shook hands with Graham, waved to one corner of the room, nodded to another corner, and made eye contact with a pretty young lady, all in one movement, very much the pumped-up celebrity of the night.

'I can't wait to read your book,' said Graham.

'Like fuck you can't,' said Timothy, and he turned away and stormed off.

Kate chased after him.

'What was all that about?' she demanded.

'Ask Graham.'

She did.

'I haven't a clue,' said Graham.

Two days later he was dead. Kate had been shopping in Harrods' Food Hall, which was just across the road. Venison. She remembered to this day what she had bought. Venison, which she would marinade in red wine and a little cinnamon. That was for tomorrow. For tonight there was sea-bass. They had only recently discovered sea-bass, which in those days was still not farmed, and tasted of . . . well, of sea-bass. They would have that tonight, grilled with fennel. She put both shopping bags in her left hand, unlocked the door with her right hand, entered the house, closed the door, walked across the hall, called out, 'Are you home, darling?', got no reply, assumed he wasn't home, went into the kitchen, unloaded, opened the bottle of wine that she'd bought for the marinade because all the wine he'd bought would be too good for a marinade, got the cinnamon, marinaded the venison, made herself a cup of strong black coffee, and only then went into the sitting-room and saw him.

He was sitting in his usual chair, and there was blood all down his shirt. Kate couldn't see where the blood had come from, because his face was covered by a yellow page from *Yellow Pages*. She didn't stop to think about evidence or fingerprints, she whipped the page off and let it flutter to the floor.

Graham was staring at her with a look of deep surprise and shock frozen on his face. There was a single bullet hole in the centre of his forehead.

Kate didn't shout, 'I'm free! I'm free!' She screamed and collapsed in a faint, hitting her head on the edge of something sharp, so that when she came to she was bleeding quite badly, and there was blood on a huge wooden board, with two thick wooden legs, which was lying on the carpet. On the board, was a single word, in huge letters, LENINGRAD.

Kate held her head back and pressed a handkerchief to it to staunch the flow of blood. It was a silk handkerchief initialled KE, given to her by Graham. She lifted the phone, dialled 999, and saw a single sheet of paper lying beside the phone. Neatly typed in capital letters, right in the middle of the page, were just two words: 'Sorry, Ma'.

15 Barry

Well, she'd got there. At last, in the early hours of her ninth day in hospital, the deed had been done. Graham was dead. Her investigations could begin.

Ward 3C still slept, even if the sleep was not exactly peaceful, interrupted as it was by farts, burps, snores, moans, groans and the occasional cry from Angela Critchley.

Kate opened her eyes cautiously, moved them to the right just a little. She really did feel that there was a little more movement in them. She tried to move her fingers and toes. They seemed an awfully long way away, but there did seem to be a little more movement there too. She was improving. She was on the mend. Nothing dramatic yet, but, yes, she really did feel hopeful.

The sky lightened imperceptibly. She tried hard to catch it at its dawn games, but it was too wily for her. You watch a dark sky, you never see it get any lighter, you concentrate as hard as you can, there is never a particular moment in which the light increases, and yet suddenly it is morning. That was how it was that day. Kate found herself staring at a mottled, streaked October sky.

'Rodney! Really! Not in the billiard room!' Angela Critchley was waking up. It sometimes seemed to Kate that there was more consistency in Angela Critchley's night-time world than in her waking one. She wondered if, because the waking moments of the insane were disordered, frightening and surreal, their dreams would reorder the disorder and so become sane and sensible. Maybe they dreamt of going shopping and getting all the groceries, or making pots of tea.

Then there was a staccato fart. Dawn had broken, and so had

Glenda's wind. Kate recognised this as the waking-up fart. Soon they'd be in the throes of the day, she'd be back in the effluent society, listening to the enema variations, her only music now. There'd be the taking of temperatures, pulses and blood pressure, the enquiries about the movement of bowels, there'd be breakfast and lunch and visits by well-meaning clergymen. Kate closed her eyes, too tired for all that, and fell into a sound sleep.

When she awoke it was early afternoon, and Timothy was with her. She still felt tired. Well, it wasn't surprising. She'd spent a disturbed night, living with a man who was about to be murdered, going into their elegant sitting-room and seeing him there, staring at her, with a bullet hole in his forehead. It was enough to tire somebody a lot younger than ninety-nine.

She wished that Timothy would go. She had so much thinking to do. At last he did go, and she wanted to cry, 'Come back! Come back!' She was too tired to think. She realised that she'd been picturing herself, as she played back the story of her life, as the beautiful woman she'd been. She was a shrunken collection of bones and creases. Her face was covered in fine lines, she was like stretched parchment, she'd looked old and frail before the stroke, what must she look like now? She recalled the story of the old woman who goes berserk and runs naked through an old people's home. Two old ladies see her streak past. 'What was that woman wearing?' asks one. 'I don't know,' says the other, 'but whatever it was it needed ironing.' The immensity of her task, the absurdity of her ambition over-whelmed her. She was delighted when Nigel arrived and gave her another excuse not to think.

She found herself thinking, in spite of herself, about some-thing that Nigel had said, here, in this ward, that might be very significant. It hovered, just out of reach of her consciousness. It tormented her. She gave up.

And then Nigel left and she was on her own and she knew that she must start. The beginning was always the hardest thing. With each book it had been so, and it was now. Where to begin?

Then there was another visitor in the ward. She heard the clank of bottles, a stifled laugh, a man talking, Lily replying, and she welcomed the interruption, any interruption.

A few minutes later, Lily had to go to the lavatory. The excitement of visitors often brought this on. The nurse – yet another nurse new to Kate, she hated it when the nurses were new – led Lily away.

The moment she had gone, the man addressed the ward.

'Good evening, ladies,' he said. 'While we're on our own, there's something I'd like to say. My name is Barry Stannidge, by the way. I'm Lily's son. I was in France, unfortunately, in Sarlat-la-Canéda, well, I think they just call it Sarlat really, and I keep in touch with the warden at my mother's sheltered flat, he's very good, he phoned me after she'd collapsed, I was with a friend, I left her and got the TGV back home and here I am. Erm . . . I know that you're going to make my mother very happy here.'

'We'll certainly try,' said Glenda, and Kate felt grateful.

'We certainly will,' said Angela Critchley. 'It's not her fault there's been a mess-up with the bookings.'

Barry lowered his voice. 'My mother led a good life,' he said. 'In the later years she and my father went on cruises. Cruises to places like Greece and Italy and Turkey. My mother loved ruins, and now, sadly, she's one herself. In recent times, since my father died, my mother has not been able to afford cruises. She has sailed only on the Sea of Gin. She has called in, occasionally, to those fine Italian ports, Campari, Cinzano and Martini. In France she has dallied a while in Noilly Prat.'

Kate wanted to applaud. He sounded kind and she liked his style. But of course she couldn't let her guard slip. What a burden is a guard.

'My point is that I have here bottles,' said kindly, stylish

Barry. 'They do not contain water. I hope I can rely on your discretion, and I hope that my mother won't be a nuisance.'

' "Gin", did you say?' asked Angela Critchley.

'Would you like one?'

'Er . . . I would. I'd like that very much, but I haven't any money on me at the moment. In the old days, in Luigi's day, I could have things on tick, as I think it was called. Not any more. The personal touch has gone.'

'I'll buy you this round,' said Barry.

'Oh, thank you, thank you. Bless you, you kind man,' said Angela Critchley.

Kate could have quite fancied a nice gin herself. Plymouth, of course.

'Is it Plymouth?' asked Angela Critchley, and Kate felt a little frisson of shock.

'I'm afraid not.'

'No matter.'

'Just hang on a moment,' said Barry. 'I hear the nurse returning. Our little secret, eh?'

Kate sensed a conspiratorial thrill run through the ward.

The nurse returned with Lily, and it took a while to get her into bed. At last the nurse had gone, and Kate heard the delightful sound of gin being poured. Curlews trilling, streams burbling, gin being poured – just three of this rich old world's delightful sounds.

'Cheers,' said Angela Critchley.

'Cheers.' This was Barry.

'Cheers.' Lily.

'Idle talk costs lives,' said Glenda.

'I beg your pardon?' said Barry.

'One careless word can bring the whole edifice tumbling down,' said Glenda.

'Would you like a drink?'

'Oh! Well . . . I hope you don't think I was hinting! . . . No, but yes, I would if I could,' said Glenda. 'I don't see that it can do any harm. I'm not ill, though the doctor thinks I am, and I'm hardly likely to see anyone I know here, except Douglas, and he won't mind. Besides, the sun has gone down over the yard-arm. Yes, I think a *weak* gin and tonic would be very acceptable. Not *too* weak, of course.'

Kate heard another gin being poured.

'What about her?'

'No, she's paralysed, poor thing.'

So paralysed Kate, poor thing, had to listen to the swigging of gin and she thought of her dear parents, sweet gentle Bronwen, dear stern John Thomas, and she thought, Mother darling, dearest Father, I'm so glad you can't see into my soul now and realise how much I crave a tumbler of gin at this moment.

Her body screamed for gin. How could she ever embark on her investigations without it? How can you think without fuel?

'I'm hiding the bottles now, Mum,' said Barry to his mother, and to the ward he said, 'She gets confused about a lot of things, but never about her gin. It's sad, but it's her *raison d'être*.'

Shortly after Barry had hidden the bottles, Doctor Ramgobi arrived on his evening rounds.

As Lily had a visitor he began with Kate. Kate thought his checks were becoming slightly more perfunctory. She was beginning to be taken for granted. In no time at all he'd moved on to Angela Critchley.

'And how's Mrs Critchley this evening?' he enquired.

'In the pink, doctor,' said Angela Critchley.

'Ah!' said Doctor Ramgobi. 'You know I'm a doctor, then.'

'Well, of course I do,' said Angela Critchley. 'What else would you be?'

'Well, the other day you thought I was room service,' said Doctor Ramgobi.

'We've had room service,' said Angela Critchley. 'I had a gin and tonic.'

'I hope you had lemon with it,' said Doctor Ramgobi jocularly.

'I certainly did,' said Angela Critchley. 'It wasn't Plymouth, and there was no ice, but it was just the strength I like.'

'Jolly good,' said Doctor Ramgobi.

'We've all had gin and tonics, doctor,' said Lily Stannidge.

'Of course you have,' said Doctor Ramgobi. 'You've all had gin and tonics just the strength you like.'

The doctor cut short his evening visit. Kate could just picture the scene, the patients happy and smiling, Doctor Ramgobi beaming with delight as he humoured them and then beetling off while the going was good, as fast as his little legs would carry him. (She pictured him as having little legs. She hoped he had little legs.)

Soon after that, Barry left, and soon after that the ward was being settled down for the night.

As the long hospital night began, Kate realised why she was experiencing such difficulty in starting her investigations. She was starting too soon. Many extraordinary things were said to her, in the days after Graham's death. She needed to sift through all those. Inspector Crouch interviewed her several times (well, he would, thoroughness being his middle name). She needed to go through those interviews with a fine-tooth comb. Tomorrow would provide an awesome challenge. But tonight, tonight she could enjoy herself. Tonight she could wallow in another chapter in the saga of her life, and – imagine this – it was a chapter with a happy ending! She felt exhilarated, as if *she*'d had a gin and tonic.

16 Michael

'Please don't sit there,' said Kate. 'That's the chair in which he was murdered.'

'Oh, that's all right,' said Inspector Crouch, sinking into the chair with a weary sigh. 'Its pathological evidence has been exhausted.'

'I meant,' said Kate sharply, 'that it's offensive to me.'

'I'm so sorry,' said Inspector Crouch. He stood up rapidly. He was a man of medium height with a wide face and very bushy eyebrows below straggly dark hair very carefully arranged to hide his spreading baldness. He was wearing a pale grey suit that showed every mark and fitted him atrociously, being far too tight around his bulky backside. 'So sorry. The wife always says that tact is my Achilles heel. Where do you want me to sit?'

'Nowhere, frankly. I'm in deep shock, inspector, and when I recover from the shock I shall be shattered by grief.'

'Of course. Of course. Daresay I'd be pretty shocked if I went in our lounge and there was the wife murdered. Might I sit here?'

He indicated a Hepplewhite chair that Kate felt to be far too delicate for anyone who used that odious term, 'the wife'.

'I suppose so.'

'Thank you.'

He plonked himself in it. She flinched, but the chair stood up to it. Kate of the One Settee settled herself on her one settee.

He smiled. She preferred it when he didn't smile.

'I don't know if you are familiar with murder inquiries,' he said.

'Only from my son's books, and I can't finish them.'

'I never read detective fiction. It makes my blood boil. It's so unlike my dull life. Madam, I have to tell you that everything you say will be taken down and may be used in evidence against you.'

'Am I a suspect?'

'Oh no, madam. Not as such.'

'What do you mean – "as such"?'

'I have no reason to assume that you murdered your husband, but everyone is presumed guilty until found innocent.'

'I thought it was the other way round.'

'That bit comes later.'

An attractive young lady with muscular calves came in, sat on the matching Hepplewhite chair, and took notes. The inspector led Kate through the whole story of her relationship with Graham from their first meeting to the discovery of the body. When she hesitated, he probed.

'Now come on, Mrs Eldridge. You're prevaricating. Please tell me everything. I shall find out in the end, thoroughness is my middle name. So it'll save your time as well as mine.'

She sighed.

'All right. My youngest son, Maurice, didn't take to Graham.'

'In what way?'

'Graham had no living relatives. I think that led Maurice to fear . . .'

'Yes, madam?'

'. . . that my husband was not . . . as he seemed.'

Kate hated saying such things about Graham. She could hardly get the words out.

'Did your other children take to Mr Eldridge?'

She hesitated.

'Now, now, Mrs Eldridge. We're prevaricating again.'

Kate shuddered in her bed at the memory of Inspector Crouch calling her 'we', anticipating the curse of the hospital by thirty-eight years.

She told him, reluctantly, of the inexplicable incident at the book launch, when Graham had said how much he was looking forward to reading Timothy's new book, and Timothy had said, 'Like fuck you are!' and stormed off.

'What did you make of that, Mrs Eldridge?'

'I didn't know what to make of it.' She felt that she sounded like a character in one of Timothy's novels. Perhaps you had to, when you were being questioned about a murder. Perhaps his books weren't so bad after all! She felt the whole thing to be unreal. She found it unreal that she should be referred to as Mrs Eldridge.

'You didn't know what to make of it?' prompted Inspector Crouch. 'You're an intelligent woman. What did you make of it?'

'I assumed that Timothy also had his suspicions about Graham's integrity.'

'You didn't ask him?'

'No.'

'Why not?'

'I might not have liked his answer.'

After he'd dealt with the feelings of Kate's children towards Graham, Inspector Crouch said, 'I need to go briefly into the parentage of your children. Shall I come back later or do you wish to get all this over with?'

'Will it ever be over with?'

'Who's to say?'

'Well, let's get as much done as I can stand now.'

She told him, very briefly, about her marriages. He remained utterly impassive throughout. When she'd finished, he said, 'H'm. Quite a story.'

'Except that it isn't a story.'

'Mrs Eldridge, can you see any significance in the list of double-glazing salesmen?'

Kate hesitated.

'I can't see how it can have any relevance,' she said.

'Let me be the judge of that.'

She told him that one of the names on the list was that of the man who had done their windows, and she told him about the double-glazing con that she had helped Graham to investigate. When he pressed her for details, she told him that he'd be able to find Graham's article and his notes. 'He filed everything. He was a very meticulous person.'

'Good,' said Inspector Crouch with a sigh, looking hopeful and exhausted at the same time. 'Can you suggest any significance in the railway station sign for Leningrad?'

Again Kate hesitated.

'Please, madam.' Inspector Crouch's voice was gentle but insistent.

'Well, you'll find out anyway. My son Maurice visits Russia regularly. He's a reporter for the BBC News.'

'Thank you. Did any of your children call you "Ma"?'

'Yes.'

'All of them?'

'No.'

'Which of them?'

'Maurice.'

'Thank you.'

Of course they had to have an inquest. Kate had to go through the ordeal of describing how she'd found him. The verdict, 'murder by person or persons unknown', was a formality.

The funeral. Suffice it to say that Inspector Crouch was there, sniffing around, and that all three of Kate's sons looked extremely tense. Maurice was accompanied by his charming fiancée Clare, Timothy by his pretty new girlfriend Emily. Nigel had nobody to comfort him.

On the day after the funeral, Timothy called to see Kate. He looked extremely unhappy. She offered him a glass of Sancerre and took one herself. 'Before you say anything,' she said, 'yes, I am drinking too much, but I will stop. Timothy, I liked Emily.'

'Yes, so did I,' he said glumly.

'What on earth do you mean?'

'She left me this morning.'

'Oh, Timothy! But yesterday you seemed so . . . well, not happy, obviously . . . devoted.'

'She was going to leave me on the day Graham was killed. I said, "Emily, please see me through the funeral." I just couldn't bear to let her go. Every hour she stayed was a bonus. I thought . . . I thought when she saw my suffering she might change her mind. She didn't. She ran headlong from my suffering.'

'Oh, Timothy! That never works, my darling.'

She went over to sit with him on the *chaise longue*. She hugged him. His whole body stiffened, as if he was in one of his books.

'What's wrong, Timothy?'

'I don't think I can cope with sympathy just now. What is it about me and women?' He was such a boy still, even at thirty-four. He stood up, disentangling himself from his mother's embrace tactfully but firmly. He towered above her and cleared his throat, indicating a massive gear change. He was trying to look masterful. He was failing. 'Oh God, I hate this,' he said. 'I don't want to tell you this, but I've told the police, so I think I have to tell you.'

Kate remembered thinking how badly the conversation matched the elegant Georgian drawing-room, whose double glazing muffled the roar of the Knightsbridge traffic.

'It's about Maurice,' Timothy managed to say at last. 'Oh God, I sound like a sneak ratting on his brother, but I don't mean it that way. At least nobody can say I've got an axe to grind over Maurice because I'm envious. Incidentally, I've never had the feeling that he envies me. I suppose he doesn't really need to, he's quite successful in his own way, but . . . oh Lord, I'm not getting on with it, am I?'

'No. Please do, darling. I can't bear this.'

'Sorry. Sorry.' He began to pace the room. His hands worked as if searching for a hat and cane to twirl nervously. 'Mother, I think Maurice knows something about Graham. Well, in fact I know he knows something.'

'Oh Lord. Do I want to know this something?'

'I don't know. I can't tell you anyway, because I don't know what Maurice knows. But I know that before he knew what I know he knows now, he said that if what he thought was what he thought, he'd . . .' He hesitated.

'Yes?'

'He'd kill Graham.'

'Oh, Timothy, did he really? It sounds like something out of a bad detective novel.'

'Like one of mine, you mean?'

'Oh, Timothy, don't be so touchy.'

The next day it was Maurice's turn to sit in the elegant drawing-room, twisting a glass of Morgon nervously in his powerful hands, sunburnt and freckled and already beginning to go bald, looking brave and determined, as if talking not to his mother but to a group of rebel tribesmen who might kill him if he failed to eat their offering of sixteen sheeps' eyes in yak-cheese sauce with sufficient evidence of enjoyment.

He had kissed her, hugged her, let her cry on his shoulder, told her how much he loved her, sent the love of his charming fiancée Clare, and gradually approached the meat of the matter, once she was softened up. Even in her tearful state she could recognise, wryly, the technique that led corrupt politicians the world over to say more to Maurice than they had intended.

Now he was ready. She braced herself.

'Ma . . .' He hesitated. Did he know of the message, "Sorry, Ma"?

'Get on with it, darling, please. I can't bear much more of this.'

'Sorry, Ma. Ma, the awful thing is . . . I found out something about Graham. You know I never . . .'

'Trusted him, yes.'

'It wasn't a question of trust, exactly. I just never believed in him. I was puzzled by the fact that he refused to go on television, and I thought of a possible reason. He didn't want too many people to see his face, in case someone recognised him from another life.' He paused. 'Oh, Ma!'

'What?'

'I've done Timothy's prose style an injustice. You've gone very silent. I thought people only did that in his books. Anyway, I took Graham's photo with me everywhere I went, and showed it to people and asked them if they recognised him. I didn't say he was my mother's fifth husband. And I didn't feel there was any harm in it, because if he had nothing to hide no harm would be done by it. Anyway, eventually, someone did recognise him. His name was Stephen Harris and he was from Otago in New Zealand.'

Kate remained very silent.

'There's more, I'm afraid. He . . . er . . . he had a wife. No children. He was in some kind of vague shady financial racket, this chap thought. You know, getting old ladies to invest in non-existent companies, that kind of thing. This chap didn't know what exactly. Anyway, he left Otago under a cloud.'

'Well, I heard it's a pretty wet climate.'

She wished that she hadn't said this. She could see that her feeble attempt at light-heartedness had moved him deeply, and made it even more difficult for him to continue.

'He . . . er . . . he seems to have just abandoned his wife. He . . . er . . .'

He was a bigamist. Somehow, it didn't come as a complete surprise, but it was still a savage blow. 'It's strange, you know. I knew that you didn't trust Graham. Enid once said he was too good to be true, and he was. And yet, I found that I did trust him. In a curious way it was myself I didn't believe in. I never really quite believed I *was* Mrs. Eldridge. And I suppose legally I wasn't. It's funny, isn't it?'

She didn't look as though she thought it at all funny, and neither did Maurice. He came over to his mother and kissed her and they hugged each other and cried together.

Her numbness was wearing off. A great wave of loss swept over her and almost cracked her heart. She had felt more affection than love for Graham while he lived, but now, when she was being told of his deceit, she felt a huge hopeless surge of love for him. Oh Graham, come back, she implored, so that I can put these points to you in person.

She poured Maurice another glass of wine, and he said, 'Thank you. I'm afraid there's more.'

'Oh dear. Can I take any more?'

'Well, I think you can. I've always thought of you as immensely brave. It's about Timothy.'

'Oh Lord.'

'Well, I hate doing this. I mean, like it or not, I am a national figure on television, and it's difficult not to feel protective towards poor Timothy. I suppose really he's perfectly all right. He thinks he's a great novelist and . . . oh, sorry, Ma, you don't think he is, do you?'

'Sadly, no.'

'Good. Well, I mean not good exactly, but . . . well, you know. Anyway, it seems awful to be saying this but it is a police investigation and I think things always come out if you try to conceal them. Mind you, they do in Timothy's books so they probably don't in real life. Anyway, it seems that a friend of Timothy's, a so-called friend, a journalist, was also a friend, a so-called friend, of Graham, and Graham sent him a letter in which he said, "On the plane I often read my stepson's books. I find it difficult to sleep on planes, and it's the perfect solution," and he told somebody, who told somebody else, and it got back to Timothy.'

Well, at least that explained Timothy's mysterious eruption at the book launch.

'And Timothy said to me,' continued Maurice, 'I mean, I don't expect it's got any significance, people say things like that and they don't mean them, but I thought I ought to tell the police in case they find out because it was in the Cheshire Cheese in Fleet Street and several hundred journalists might have heard him say it, and a few of them might even have been sober.'

'You haven't told me what he said. As if I didn't know.'

'Oh. Sorry. He said, "The bastard keeps telling me how wonderful he thinks my books are. If he says it once more . . ."'

Kate joined in and said it with Maurice.

' "I'll kill him." '

The following day Nigel called. Kate wondered now if they'd been keeping a rota, making sure that one of them called each day, as they did at the hospital. It hadn't even occurred to her at the time. She'd just accepted it as natural.

He sank into the Chesterfield, crossed his legs, sniffed his glass of Beaune, rolled it round his glass, sniffed it again, and held it to the light to examine its colour, irritating her so much that she said, 'How are your haemorrhoids, by the way?'

'Mother!'

'I'm sorry. I just wondered if you were going on looking at your glass for ever.'

'It's what's known as a displacement activity, Mother. I'm very nervous.' He took a sip. 'Pretty ghastly, to be honest.'

'Oh dear. Mr Trench said it was rather special.'

'Not the wine. My haemorrhoids.'

'Oh dear.'

'Well, that's life. No, the wine's terrific.' He took another sip and put the glass down, very carefully, on a charming early Victorian coffee table. 'Mother, there's something I have to tell you.'

'Of course there is.'

'Mother, not very long before his death I met Graham in Copenhagen.'

'I know. At Timothy's presentation.'

'Yes, but I stayed an extra day because I wanted to talk to Graham, and, with you not there, this was my chance. We had dinner together. We went to Krogs fish restaurant. I had the herring platter, the turbot and the *rødgrød med fløde*.'

'The red fruit jelly with cream.'

'You know everything, don't you? Except what I said to Graham.'

'Oh no. I know that too. You said you'd kill him.'

Nigel went white. His sinews stiffened.

'How do you know that?' he gasped.

'A lucky guess. Seriously, Nigel, a lucky guess. No, it's just that people are queuing up to tell me about people who said they'd kill Graham.'

'It's not surprising, really.'

'Nigel! I loved him. I love him still.'

'Mother!'

'I'm sorry, Nigel, but I do. He was a fraud, yes, I know that now, but I don't believe he was a fraud with me.'

Nigel gave her a pitying look.

'Yes, yes, Nigel. Pitying look. Bit old for the menopause, but my mother's gone funny. Sad.'

Nigel came over and gave her a quick, awkward kiss, still embarrassed by physical manifestations of affection, then he settled back to business, with relief.

'Well, anyway, Maurice had told me what he'd discovered about Graham.'

'I see. Family conference behind my back.'

'Only because we love you.'

Kate poured him another glass.

'So, what exactly happened in Krogs?' she asked.

'I said to him, "Graham, I know that you're a fraud. I know that you're a bigamist."'

'What did he say?'

'He went very silent. I'd always thought people only went very silent in Timothy's books. But he went very silent. I said, "Graham, I'm warning you. If you ever do anything to hurt my mother, I'll kill you." I didn't, of course.'

'Well, he didn't do anything to hurt me.'

'Exactly. I would have killed him, you know. I'm capable of killing, for a good reason. Anyway, I thought I'd better tell you because I've told the inspector.'

'Why have you told him?'

'In case he found out. Graham and I had a heated exchange. Somebody in the restaurant might have remembered. Nothing good comes of hiding things from the police. I've learnt that if I've learnt nothing else from Timothy's books.'

Kate dreaded Inspector Crouch's visits more and more as time passed. To be forced to suspect that one of your sons had killed your husband added horror to the nightmare of loss. She hated his every question. She loathed his every revelation.

'Please! Not there!' she cried, as he began to lower his ample backside towards one of the Hepplewhites, on his next visit. 'They're delicate chairs. You'd be more suitable on the settee.'

'I prefer a hard chair, madam, when I'm on duty.'

'The settee!'

The inspector perched uneasily on the edge of the settee, and accepted a cup of tea.

'The cup that cheers,' he said fatuously. 'Ah, well. Now, Mrs . . . er . . . I'm afraid I have some unwelcome news about your husband. There's no way to break this gently. I'm afraid he was . . . I'm afraid Graham Eldridge wasn't his real name.'

'It's all right, inspector. Maurice told me.'

'His real name is . . .'

'Stephen Harris. I know.'

'Michael Thompson.'

'Michael Thompson?'

'I'm afraid so. He was born on a council estate in Runcorn.'

'Runcorn! He told me he went to school at Winchester.'

'Not quite, madam. He . . . er . . . he seems to have been involved in petty crime. He absconded with quite a lot of money, leaving behind quite a lot of debts and . . . and . . . er . . . a wife.'

'I don't believe I'm going through all this. I was told he left a wife in Otago.'

'So I'm led to believe. Very remiss of him.'

'He was a trigamist!'

'I beg your pardon?'

'Well, I'm not sure if the word exists. It ought to. Bigamist comes, as you're no doubt aware, Inspector, from the Greek.'

'Of course I wasn't aware. I'm not a fictional detective. I'm Mr Plod.'

'Well, it comes from "bi" meaning twice and "gamos" meaning marriage.'

'Er . . . no doubt, not having had the advantage of a classical education, Mrs . . . er . . . my verbal gymnastics won't be accurate, but . . . no, he wasn't a trigamist. He was a . . . quadgamist?'

'Quadragamist would perhaps be more elegant. Oh no, he wasn't, was he?'

'I'm afraid so. There is a certain Mrs . . .'

'Please. Spare me the names.'

'Yes. Of course. Let's just say there are wronged women in Runcorn, Otago and Oklahoma City.'

'Not to mention Knightsbridge.'

'No, I wasn't going to mention that. There is also, I have to say, Mrs . . . er . . . I really don't know whether I should call you Mrs Eldridge or not . . . a certain irony attendant on the career of . . . your husband. He seems to have become quite a rich man, this man who ended up as Graham "Mr Con-Buster" Eldridge. He made all his money . . .'

'As a con man.'

'You knew!'

'No. You said there was a certain irony. I made a deduction.'

'You ought to be in the police force, madam!'

'I hope you didn't intend that as a compliment.'

'He made his biggest killing out of the farmers of the Central American corn belt. He sold millions of bags of dyed plain flour mixed with earth and grated maggots as a new form of highly expensive fertiliser. He was lucky. The crops were exceptionally good that year due to the weather. He'd disappeared off the face of the earth long before the deception was discovered, leaving behind in Oklahoma City a distraught . . .'

'Yes, yes.'

'Sorry. That tact again.'

In the months that followed, Inspector Crouch, thoroughness his middle name, called on Kate on more than one occasion. He asked her if she believed any of her sons capable of murder. She said that she hoped with all her heart that none of them was. What would any mother say? He asked her if she thought all three of her sons could have conspired to free her from Graham Eldridge. She told him that he'd been reading too many detective stories. He reminded her that he didn't read detective stories. Would she please answer the question? She told him that even in her worst nightmares she was incapable of imagining that her three sons would collaborate in a murder even to free her from somebody from whom she wanted to be free, and they knew she hadn't wanted to be free from Graham Eldridge. She told him, in no uncertain terms, that he was obsessed with her sons because somebody had typed the words 'Sorry, Ma'. Anybody could have done that. He asked her if she was aware that 'Sorry, Ma' were the last two words of

Timothy's fourth novel, *Trouble in Torquay*. She told him that she hadn't known this as she'd been unable to get beyond page three of *Trouble in Torquay*. She asked him how he knew if he never read detective stories. He told her that Nigel had told him.

That evening she wrote to Timothy and said, 'I sometimes wonder if somebody is trying to frame you by using your words "Sorry, Ma".' In his reply, Timothy wrote, 'I was so relieved to read your comment about "Sorry, Ma". Since you didn't mention it, I'd begun to worry that you weren't able to finish the book, and as you know it's my favourite.'

On his next visit, Inspector Crouch assured Kate that the police were leaving no stone unturned in their search for Graham Eldridge's killer. They'd already interviewed thirty-eight double-glazing salesmen, sixty-six farmers in Kansas and Oklahoma, twenty-three aggrieved investors in New Zealand, and those three wronged women, Jean in Runcorn, Joan in Otago and Evelyn in Oklahoma City.

'I asked you to spare me the names,' wailed Kate.

'I'm so sorry,' said Inspector Crouch. 'The wife'll kill me when I tell her I did that.'

'You don't discuss this with your wife!'

'I have no secrets from the wife. She's very useful. She has a nose for it. Many's the criminal she's helped me bring to book.'

'Not in this case, though.'

'Not so far. I haven't finished yet. Thoroughness . . .'

'. . . is your middle name.'

'Oh, I told you. This is a particularly difficult case to bring to a swift conclusion, Mrs Eldridge. Your husband was a ruthless, evil criminal who wrought havoc, resentment and hatred in his destructive trail through three continents.'

'I loved him, inspector.'

'Oh shit. There goes that tact again. Your sons, Mrs Eldridge, do not seem, in my judgement or the wife's, to have a motive strong enough for murder. Many other people in three continents do.'

Kate knew now that she had never really believed in all that three continents business, but who can blame a mother for welcoming it at the time and persuading herself that there was nothing more that she could usefully do?

She gave a little dinner party for her birthday that year, in her favourite restaurant, the Gay Hussar. Nigel had the freshwater crayfish and the smoked goose breast paprikash. There were just the nine of them round the table, and it was a jolly family occasion. They all knew each other, except for Timothy's new girlfriend Anne, a very tall, thin pale girl with thick lips and a long, classical nose, and she seemed to fit in right from the start. Tokay, Bull's Blood and laughter flowed freely. Kate showed no sign of grief, although, at sixty-three, she was developing deeper lines on her face. In fact she was on sparkling form. She told Anne that Timothy's ex-wife Milly had wanted to be a musician, but had been too shy to say 'oboe' to a Goossens. She described her old school friend Caitlin Price-Evans as a tease who only revealed her true character in drink. On the surface she was full of love and sexuality, but after a few drinks she was nobody's. She upset Don by telling him that he had a lifestyle 'so boring that you have room for your car in your garage'. Nobody at the surrounding tables could have guessed that, less than six months before, this lady had come home to find her fifth husband (or her fourth if you took the view that it was impossible for one man to be two husbands, or not a husband at all in view of the fact that the marriage was bigamous) murdered.

But Kate had not forgotten Graham, and, at the end of the meal, she astonished everyone by ordering two bottles of champagne and nine glasses. Most of them knew her views on champagne. She'd said of it once, 'Its charms fade with the day. It's exciting before breakfast, exquisite with breakfast, rather marvellous after breakfast, very pleasant before lunch, fairly pleasant during lunch, perfectly acceptable before dinner, disagreeable during dinner and vile after dinner.'

'Yes, I know,' she said, as she poured the champagne into the nine glasses. 'This isn't the time for champagne, but I want you to drink a very solemn toast to the man I knew as Graham Eldridge.'

They looked at her in astonishment.

'I know that Graham was a fraud,' she said. 'I know that right to the end he was saying the right thing and not always meaning it. I happen to believe that he'd become a new man in more senses than just his name. I believe that there was a new seriousness in him. I believe that his activities as "Mr Con-Buster" were undertaken partly at least in penance for his past sins. I believe he loved me truly. He may also have loved his previous wives truly. He probably only left them because he had to, in order to escape the law. I don't believe that he would ever have left me. He wouldn't have needed to. But even if I'm wrong, and Graham was fooling me, I had more than four years of travel, of comfort, of respect, of laughter and, above all, of fun. They cannot be taken away retrospectively. I want to say a big thank-you to Graham Eldridge, for the life he gave me. I hope you'll all stand and join me in a toast.'

Most of the guests stood up straight away, although Timothy did so with evident reluctance. Anne didn't stand until she saw that Timothy had. Maurice's buxom fiancée Clare gave him a look, and she stood too. Finally, reluctantly, with an expression that suggested that he was reporting on the discovery of a massacre of nomads in some God-forsaken corner of the globe, Maurice stood too.

'To Graham,' said Kate.

'To Graham,' said her eight companions.

They sat down and sipped their champagne. Then Don stood up again. 'We have to go,' he said, 'or we'll miss the last train to Leatherhead.'

'We have schnapps and another toast to come yet,' said Kate.

'Not for us, I'm afraid,' said Elizabeth. 'We really do have to go.'

'Can't you get a taxi?'

'To Leatherhead? It'd cost a fortune.'

'Stay overnight.'

'We have a babysitter.'

'If I say to you that it's important to me that you stay, what will you say?' asked Kate.

'I'll say that we leave with regret, and with disapproval of the railway timetable,' said Don.

'If you blame us for being boring, when it's British Rail that's boring, I'll be very upset,' said Elizabeth.

'No, no,' said Kate. 'I do understand.'

She kissed them goodbye, and as soon as they'd gone she ordered the schnapps and seven glasses.

'I feel rather drunk,' she said, after the schnapps had arrived. 'It's just as well my dear parents can't see me. I have an announcement to make. I don't expect it to cause much of a ripple. It's something you've heard so often, after all. I'm getting married.'

Things happened then that Kate thought only happened in Timothy's books. Heads jerked upward in astonishment. Jaws dropped open. Hands were frozen in the act of raising glasses.

'Another toast,' said Kate. 'To my fiancé.'

She stood. Nigel, Timothy and Anne, Maurice and Clare leapt up enthusiastically.

'To the darling man I'm going to marry,' said Kate.

The six of them raised their glasses towards her fiancé, all smiling broadly.

Walter looked like a labrador that has just discovered the Sunday joint.

17 Glenda

Kate judged, from Glenda's fart, that it was a quarter to four in the morning. Really, the regularity of these nocturnal eruptions was extraordinary. How shamed she would have been if she'd known. She often complained that there was a cabbagy smell in the ward of a morning. How mortified she would have felt if she had known that she was its creator. There are moments when ignorance truly is bliss.

Kate realised that she'd allowed herself to be diverted, during her exploration of the events that had followed Graham's murder, by her memories of that extraordinarily pleasant evening in the Gay Hussar, when she'd paid her final tribute to her fifth husband (or her fourth or not a husband at all) and announced her engagement to her sixth (or her fifth or her second for the third time). She steeled herself to begin her great task at last, and fell asleep straight away.

She was awakened by a particularly explosive fart, followed by a moan and a gasp, and then silence, utter silence. Then there was a cry from the direction of Angela Critchley's bed, a soft moan from the direction of Lily's bed, nothing from the direction of Glenda's bed. Kate was alarmed. Her heightened senses told her that one less woman was sleeping in the ward. She wanted to ring the bell and summon help, but that would destroy, at a vital moment, the fiction that her brain had gone. Then she realised that even to clasp her emergency bell and press it was probably beyond her feeble fingers. This was a great relief. There was nothing that she could do. But she couldn't help worrying about Glenda. Caring had been instilled into her. It wasn't easy to give it up.

Her overdeveloped sense of irony was at it again. How ironic that she should be pretending to have lost her mind in a ward in which half the patients had lost their minds and didn't know it. How ironic if what she suspected had actually happened, and poor genteel Glenda had farted herself to death.

No more delay. It was time to begin. But to begin was frightening. It wasn't as frightening as it would have been when she might have had to face the choice of having one of her sons arrested or shielding a murderer, but it was still frightening.

But how to begin?

She would begin, in the obvious way, by compiling a list of facts. Graham had been shot. His face had been covered by a list of double-glazing firms. One of the double-glazing firms had done the double-glazing in the room in which he was shot. Graham had exposed a con, what people now would call a scam, by a double-glazing firm not on the list – a very low-key con, not one of his major coups.

A nurse came in at last, a nurse whose footsteps Kate didn't recognise. The nurse hurried out again almost immediately.

Also in the room was a name board for Leningrad railway station, and there had been a single sheet of paper on which there had been typed just two words: 'Sorry, Ma'.

The words 'Sorry, Ma' were also the last two words – the typically sentimental words, she suspected – of Timothy's fourth book *Trouble in Torquay*.

The only person who ever called her Ma was Maurice.

The nurse returned with Doctor Ramgobi. By that time Kate could recognise the footsteps of all the regular visitors to the ward. It was amazing how the deprivation of some senses led to the increased sensitivity of others. She could hear the sheet being pulled up over Glenda's face.

'Is that woman dead?' asked Angela Critchley.

'I'm afraid so,' said Doctor Ramgobi.

'I suppose it'd be selfish under the circumstances to ask

what's happened to my breakfast,' said Angela Critchley.

'It's on its way,' said Doctor Ramgobi.

Only Maurice among her three sons had been to Leningrad as far as she knew.

If Maurice had murdered Graham it would be absurd of him to point to the fact by leaving a name board for Leningrad station and a note saying 'Sorry, Ma'. Unless it was a double bluff. Rather a dangerous double bluff, though. And Maurice was a very direct kind of person. If he murdered, he'd murder out of love and fury, a passionate hot-blooded murder, unless . . . oh Lord, there were always these unlesses . . . unless he was taking care to make it look like a very un–Maurice-like murder. But would he? Could he? She was going round in circles. It all felt very unreal, as if she was using futile mind games to explore other people's mind games. She began to get the same feeling of ennui that she got from attempting to read Timothy's books.

She was in the mood to welcome any interruption and was delighted when yet another new nurse caused an eruption by asking Angela Critchley, 'Have you moved your bowels yet today?'

'How dare you?' thundered Angela Critchley. 'I have been coming to this hotel for twenty-seven years, and I have never been asked such a question. What business can it possibly be of yours? Or does your computer system set aside special rooms for the constipated?'

'This isn't a hotel,' said the nurse. 'It's a hospital. You're a sick old lady.'

'A hospital! I see. I wonder why nobody told me. I'm sorry, dear, what was the question again?'

'Have you moved your bowels this morning?'

'Yes, dear. Definitely.'

'Good. Well done.'

'Or was it yesterday? I'm sorry, dear. I don't remember.'

'It doesn't matter,' said the nurse wearily, but of course it did.

By their bowel movements shall we judge them.

Maybe, thought Kate, turning back to the daunting task that she had set herself, it was all meant to seem like one of Timothy's novels. Did Timothy have the nerve to murder anyone, let alone his mother's husband? If he did murder someone, would he do it in the manner of one of his books, like someone playing 'in the manner of the word'? Certainly he had also used the words 'Sorry Ma'. Was he capable of committing a murder in the style of one of his books, with the addition of touches intended to implicate Maurice? Would he not realise that these touches would be more likely to exonerate Maurice?

Kate's antennae were even more sensitive than usual that day. She knew that Douglas was there even before she heard him mumbling, 'Can I see her?' She heard the sheet being pulled back. The silence of his look was deafening. She could picture the love on the face of this old man whom she had never seen, neatly dressed, she imagined, trying to keep up standards, perhaps an MCC tie, with just a touch of egg on it. His gravely whispered 'Thank you' seemed to be not a whisper at all, but a roar of rage. She heard the sheet being pulled back again. When Douglas cleared his throat it was like the rumbling of a volcano, and Kate realised to her horror that he was about to address the ward.

'Ladies,' he said, his voice on the verge of breaking, 'I want to thank you for making my Glenda's last days on earth as happy and peaceful as you could.'

I did nothing, thought Kate. Angela Critchley had wanted her out of what she believed to be a single room. Lily Stannidge had called her a ghastly woman. Only Hilda had been friendly to her, and only Hilda wasn't there to hear Douglas's little speech of thanks. More irony.

Kate felt a sudden sharp pain. Perhaps she needed to move her bowels. She felt so helpless. The pain grew worse. Maybe she was dying. She couldn't press a button or raise her arm or shout. How could she even think of solving a murder when she was so helpless and pathetic?

Think. Take your mind off the pain, Kate Copson.

Why would Timothy murder Graham? Because Graham had praised one of his novels insincerely? Kate had met a few novelists in her later years, in her literary days, in her famous times. One of them had refused to talk to a critic who'd described his work as meretricious. There had been an awkward dinner party to which two feuding novelists had been invited by a hostess who didn't know that they were feuding. It was still possible, for someone with eagle eyes, to see where the fish cake had landed. But the most violent statement she had ever heard from a writer had been from a notoriously thirsty poet who had said, 'I could murder a pint.' Critics, plagiarists, agents, editors, publishers, publicists, publicans, interviewers, adaptors, book-shop owners and authors of best sellers, she had heard them all reviled by authors. But to murder a member of the public because his praise of your work was insincere, surely not?

Did Timothy know that Graham was a fraud? Could he have murdered him because of that, to save his mother who didn't want to be saved?

Could Maurice have murdered for that? Had he known even worse things about Graham, things that had never come out?

The pain did pass. Probably just wind. Something she'd eaten had disagreed with her. Correction. Something she hadn't eaten had disagreed with her.

Maurice and Timothy. The words 'Sorry, Ma' seemed to implicate them both. The name board for Leningrad railway station could be said to implicate them both, Maurice through his connections with Leningrad, Timothy because it was just the sort of meaningless touch he'd use in one of his books.

Who would be keen to implicate Timothy and Maurice? Nigel? Who had no suspicious fingers of evidence pointing at him? Nigel.

A trolley was being wheeled into the ward. Squeak squeak.

Forget the trolley, Kate. Think. Not easy when a woman has just died and a squeaky trolley reminds you that soon it will be your turn. I hope I'm not a vain woman, thought Kate, but there has been a lot of richness and a certain amount of dignity in my life and I really think I deserve a trolley that doesn't squeak. Have you one last wish? Yes. Please oil my trolley.

It was in that thought that Kate accepted fully for the first time that she was dying, not some time in the future, but soon, here in Ward 3C. She realised in a flash that, at her present rate of progress, she would be about 116 before she could speak and 142 before she could walk. Did she want to recover? Was death so frightening? Could it not be a peaceful thing? She'd spoken of this on her television programme. Surely she had the integrity and honesty to apply it to herself?

This wasn't getting the matter in hand sorted out and if she was going to die it was important to get it sorted out quickly.

Where had she got to? Nigel. The lack of evidence implicating him. Something he had said, though, in this ward a few days ago. She hadn't been listening particularly carefully. It had been impossible to listen carefully all the time.

The trolley was being wheeled out again squeak squeak. Glenda's dead body was on that trolley squeak squeak. Glenda's cold body, soon to rot squeak squeak. Glenda could feel nothing. Douglas had his memories and his *bœuf bourguignon*. Was death so terrible squeak squeak?

Nigel. Sitting there, talking to . . . to whom? Something about . . . about . . . it hovered, oh how tantalisingly it hovered just out of reach. A great wave of claustrophobia crashed through her paralysed body. Inside her, where she wasn't paralysed, there was movement, there was a scream that started at her toes and spread through her whole body. It was as if a great wave was rolling in on to Rhossili beach but inside one of the rocks, it couldn't break, it could never break, it stood petrified at the moment before breaking, for ever, because, if it broke, Kate would die. Nigel's remark hovering, and her brain cloudy, and her insides rolling rolling rolling towards Rhossili beach, that precious vastness, gulls wailing, how that wailing had irritated her, what wouldn't she give to hear the wailing of the herring gulls now? And then it passed, this dreadful moment, the tension eased, not because of anything she had thought, she was helpless in the grip of these hallucinations. Yes. Hallucinations. She was going on a trip. No LSD. No Ecstasy. Just old age. She was sailing over Rhossili beach. Whee-hee. So this is what it's like to be a herring gull. No. A kittiwake. Much more elegant. Kate the Kittiwake. Kittikate. No, that sounded like a pet food. And with the thought of a tin of pet food the trip ended, reality returned, she was in bed in Ward 3C again, thoroughly exhausted, extremely uncomfortable, utterly frustrated. Nigel said . . . what?

Oh heavens. She could sense the approach of Angela Critchley, en route for the lavvy. And then she heard her saying, 'I don't know why I have to go down the corridor to the lavvy. I'm sure I booked a room with facilities.' And then, oh horror, she stopped at the bottom of Kate's bed. Wait for it. 'Oh,' said Angela Critchley, in her talking-to-baby voice. 'Oh, isn't he cute? Oh, who's a cutey-wutey duddly-diddums? You are! Yes, you are!'

Forget Angela Critchley. Concentrate. Nigel said . . . what?

It wasn't an easy day for concentration on Ward 3C. Now things were happening to Glenda's bed, and Glenda's bedside table. There was the hissing of nozzles. Serious cleaning was in progress. Fumigation, even, possibly. Removal of all traces of dead Glenda. Now that is not a nice thing to listen to when you are soon to die in the same ward. Removal of all traces of dead Kate. No! Think of Nigel, saying . . . saying . . . you can do it . . . saying . . .

'I compile crosswords to keep my mind fit.'

Yes.

Yes yes yes.

No. No. Not Nigel. A man who compiled crosswords would undoubtedly be capable of a murder of this kind. Let it not be Nigel. Except . . . except I don't want it to be Timothy either. And certainly not Maurice.

He'd never told her about the crosswords. She'd have disapproved. It's a perverted use of brain power when you should be attempting to solve the problems of the world if you're that clever.

Perverted to use it to kill Graham and to implicate your two brothers in that ingenious but childish way. 'Poor old Parsifal was shown the door long ago.' Parsifal. That still rang a bell. Idly, Kate tried to make anagrams out of Parsifal, trying to get into the mind of the crossword compiler. Pal. That left RSIFA. Royal Society for the Improvement of Farm Animals. Fairs. Pal fairs. Friend goes round amusements with classical results. Parsifal. Easy. Nigel. Glein? Gelin? Nelig. Elgin. Mixed–up man loses his marbles. Oh, this is child's play. Nigel Rand. Rend Glain. Lend grain. She had to admit that at last she could see the attraction of these mind games. They would at least ease the pain of lying here in hospital, and they were a bit easier than trying to solve a murder.

Angela Critchley paused at the bottom of the bed again, on her way back from the lavvy.

'You recognise me, don't you?' she said in her baby voice. 'Yes! You do! Oh, little diddums.'

At last Angela Critchley moved on.

Where was I? Lend grain. Could that be something to do with the Midwest farmers? Hard to see now. Nigel Rand lends grain. Nigel Rand lends grain to Leningrad. The shock went through her body like a wave of ice.

Leningrad was an anagram of Nigel Rand! Oh, Nigel, Nigel, your arrogance has betrayed you. I always suspected that there was a degree of arrogance somewhere in that secretive persona of yours. But to sign your murder like that! Probably fairly safe, actually. Nobody knew you compiled crosswords. Real-life policemen didn't go round trying to make anagrams out of the evidence. Where would you stop? 'Sorry Ma' was an anagram of 'Marry so', an extremely feeble anagram, admittedly, but was it a concealed criticism of her for marrying so often? You've been a sorry ma to marry so. Had Nigel harboured deep-seated resentment of her husbands? She wouldn't have known if he had.

Oh, Nigel, why did you murder Graham? Why why why? Oh, the sadness that Kate felt. She'd thought that she would feel a great sense of relief in discovering that two of her sons were innocent. It wasn't so. Yes, there was relief over Timothy and Maurice, but the pain of the knowledge was more . . .

She had no knowledge! The discovery of the anagram pointed at least as clearly to Nigel's innocence as to his guilt. Timothy and Maurice knew about his crosswords. The subject had been broached here in the ward when all four of her children were together.

'Sorry, Ma' had seemed to implicate both Maurice and Timothy. The name board from Leningrad railway station seemed to implicate them both too. It could be assumed that the fact of there being an anagram at all implicated Nigel, and the fact that it was an anagram of his name implicated him even further. Maybe the station name board was meant to implicate Maurice and Nigel, and the second implication of Timothy came from the nature of the whole murder, which, she understood, was very like the murders in his books. For the significance of the list of double-glazing salesmen had just dawned on Kate. It signified a double framing. That was all. Each brother was framed twice, and each piece of evidence framed two brothers.

But no. That didn't work. You didn't have double frames in double glazing. You had double panes.

Her brain was whizzing now. Memories were crowding in. She could hear Maurice's words as clearly as if they were being said at that very moment. 'They're technically inept. Most of his clues are just slightly wrong.' So, the list of double-glazing firms had been a piece of literary parody! Did that eliminate Timothy? Had he the self-knowledge to know that about his clues? She so wanted him to be eliminated, but she also hoped that he had had the self-knowledge, because if she was able to eliminate him, she would be a great step nearer to solving the murder, and she realised now that she just didn't want to know, she never had wanted to know, which was one more reason why she had never tried to work things out before, and this deathbed conversion to detection had been a bad mistake.

Poor Inspector Crouch, wading through all the double-glazing firms and Midwest farmers and attempting the impossible task of conducting inquiries in Leningrad. All the details of the murder were pure decoration. The answer was to be found much nearer home, and she was more convinced than ever that one of her sons was the murderer.

She didn't entirely blame Inspector Crouch. The poor man had been bombarded with evidence, too much evidence. Lying in her bed she had no evidence whatsoever and no means of finding any. This made her task very much easier.

Too much evidence. Why was there too much evidence? Because the murderer had planted it.

The nature of the murder was fantastic, absurd, convoluted, yet childish. Why?

Kate felt that there could only be one answer. The murder hadn't been fantastic or absurd or convoluted or childish.

She felt extremely tired. All her thinking, which she had believed to be so brilliant, had got her precisely nowhere. She was no better than Inspector Crouch.

There was no chance of her solving the murder and she didn't think she wanted to. She wanted to sleep. And, after she'd slept, it would be rather enjoyable to linger a while in recollection of her third marriage to Walter. She deserved that much, she felt.

18 Enid

She had received his letter only three days after the murder.

My dear dear Kate,

I've just seen the terrible news on the television. I'm so used to seeing Maurice reporting some sad disaster, hearing those solemn words, 'Maurice Copson, BBC News, Dien Bien Phu,' and I assumed that he was speaking from the scene of some ghastly outrage, and suddenly I realised he was standing outside your house, talking about the murder of your husband. I was absolutely shattered. Kate, I could never have wished that you would lose Graham in such a way.

Kate admired his use of 'in such a way'. It was more subtle than she would have expected of him.

I would very much like to attend the funeral, and will unless you tell me that you don't want me there. I won't speak to you unless you want me to, and I certainly won't come back to the house or anything like that. But I would like to feel that, by my mere presence, given the depth of my feelings for you, I will be able to give you some moral support at least.

I should love to meet you again as soon as you feel that you want to, we could have a nice quiet dinner together.

I'm in good health. You'll no doubt be surprised to learn that I've sold the firm. My father died last year. I couldn't do it before that. It would have upset him. But Maurice obviously has no desire to give up a glittering career and become an engineer, and there are very sticky times ahead for manufacturing in this country, so I decided to get out while the going is good. You may not believe this, but the pleasure went out of it for me when you left. I realised, without being sentimental, I hope, that while I could never share your romantic ideal of my workers, they were, on the whole, at least as good a set of people as my shareholders. 'There's progress,' I can hear you saying, with that faint Welsh lilt!

I have no regular partner/companion/lover, whatever you care to call it, so I have a lot of time on my hands. If I can spend any of that time being any kind of comfort to you, it would be a privilege.

I still love you, Kate, but it's a love that expects nothing in return. I worshipped you once. I felt inferior to you. What I did to you on the night of Maurice's birth gave me an inalienable right to feel inferior to you. I never made love with another woman from that day until our second marriage, or rather, until we made love prior to our second wedding! I felt that if there was even a small chance of winning back your love I must pursue it. I like to feel that the strength I showed in those years freed me for ever from the need to feel inferior to you.

After our second split I had no such feelings, hence Linda, who I'm glad to say has found another sugar-daddy.

I think that my behaviour in pursuing you with a private detective was justified, but I wish I hadn't done it. I also wish that I hadn't taken quite such a serious view of what he found. You were extremely foolish and, if I may say so, naive, but not wicked. It was that damned puritan guilt of yours, which you couldn't help, it being bred in you. (Luckily for me you took the guilt off with your clothes! Might a psychiatrist say that this was because you never saw any of your puritan relatives, your dear adored puritan relatives, naked? Such memories I have of your nakedness, my darling!) But I do hate puritanism. I might not hate it so much if puritans didn't always home in on enjoyment, rather than the real villains of the piece – cruelty, meanness, falseness, selfishness, corruption etc. etc. ad infinitum!

I could see afterwards that in your involvement with Red Ron, vague and sketchy though I realise it was, you were being unfaithful not to me but to my money. I shouldn't have been quite so worried about my wallet being cuckolded. Different if it had been my prick. It was my two settees that should have felt wounded, not my two balls.

Well, well, well! I set out to write a conventional letter of sympathy, and I've opened my heart. I sat down all decorous and now I have a hard-on. I made it a rule in business to hold over any really controversial letters until the next morning, to read them again and see if I still wanted to send them. But this is no business letter, and I know that if I hold it over I won't send it, because it's in such extraordinary bad taste under the circumstances, so I'm sending it straight away.

With all my love,
Walter

They met in a pub called the Swan with Two Necks. Walter chose it. It turned out to be a rather run-down hostelry on the fringes of Soho. The stuffing was coming out of the leather seats, and there were cigarette burns on the table tops.

Kate arrived five minutes late, so as not to be the first. She had chosen what to wear that evening very carefully. She always dressed with simple elegance, but the sixties were beginning to swing, dresses were being worn shorter and shorter, youthful fashions were bursting on to the scene and that raised problems if you were sixty-two and didn't want to look old-fashioned. Kate's solution was a stylish short black-and-white dress which she called 'Mary Quant meets Norman Hartnell' and which revealed enough of her legs to show Walter that time had barely touched them.

And there he was, sitting at a large wooden table, in an open-necked check shirt, with no jacket, sipping a pint of Guinness, craggier than ever, hair a bit thinner and streaked with grey, looking five years older and fifteen years younger than on the day on which they parted.

'I hope you haven't been here long,' she said.

'I got here five minutes early, so you wouldn't be the first,' he said, leaping to his feet and smiling broadly; what a rip-roaring, delightful, unselfconscious smile it was, her heart did a handstand at the sight of it.

They kissed, demurely.

'You look very informal. I feel overdressed.'

'You look wonderful. Pint of Guinness?'

'Of course not. That's what I drank with Ron.'

'I know.'

'You horrible man.'

'Indubitably. Dry white wine?'

'Please.'

The wine was Hirondelle. Kate sipped it gravely.

'M'm,' she said. 'One swallow doesn't make a summer.'

'Oh, I've missed your wit.'

'Only my wit?'

Kate felt that Walter almost said something rude, but didn't quite dare.

She found that she was telling him all about Graham, and the discovery of his other wives. She told it without shame, without seeking sympathy.

They had another drink and he talked about his decision to sell. 'I've sold Copson Towers too,' he said. 'You'd never need to be Kate of the Two Settees again.' He closed his eyes in brief dismay at the unspoken 'if we tried again', and Kate thought, Poor Walter, he thinks it's much too early to say that, but I don't mind a bit.

'What happened to Red Ron Rafferty?' she asked, on the basis that, since the subject would have to be discussed some time, it was best to get rid of it quickly.

'Gave up on ambition. He's got a pub in Cork.'

'Good. Ambition didn't suit him.'

'I thought we'd go to a Chinese restaurant in Gerrard Street,' he said. 'Chosen at random. I want food we can enjoy without concentration. We're the point of the evening, not the food.'

'I didn't think you liked Chinese food. What's happened to the roast beef and two veg?'

He smiled a little shyly, hesitated, almost didn't say any more, then decided that he would.

'Linda opened my eyes to a few things.'

'Good Lord! I'm mortified.'

'What?'

'That ghastly little bitch succeeding where I failed. She's dragged you into the modern world.'

He was angry, very angry.

'Nobody liked Linda,' he said. 'She looked rough, she had a voice like a circular saw, and she committed the unpardonable sin of being almost twenty years younger than me. She loved me. We split up because I didn't love her, not because she was after my money.'

'You said yourself she's found another sugar-daddy.'

'She's been hurt. She might go for the jugular next time. But that's a term I'm allowed to use about her, and you aren't. It ill behoves you to call her a ghastly little bitch, you who profess to hate snobbery so much.'

Kate blushed. It was many, many years since she had blushed.

'Apologise to me for calling her that,' he said.

'Are you serious?'

'Never more so. We need never mention her again, after tonight, but if you continue to believe that she's a ghastly little bitch there'll be a cloud between us for ever.'

'Walter! You've changed.'

'Apologise.'

'I'm really sorry, Walter, that I called Linda a ghastly little bitch.'

'Do you now believe that she isn't a ghastly little bitch?'

'Well, no, of course I don't, not just like that. Not entirely. And I never will if we don't talk about her. So let's not sweep her under the carpet.'

'Fair enough.'

'It's sexual jealousy, Walter, that's all, and a rueful admission that she succeeded at something I never attempted – modernising you.' She put her hand on his and looked straight into his eyes. They were more bloodshot than of old. 'I said it because I love you.'

They wandered through the dirty streets of Soho, rubbish blowing, paper bags shuddering in the wind, refuse smelling, greasy men leering, smart tourists looking bemused. They found exactly the restaurant they wanted, and ordered Set Menu A, because it sounded slightly more boring than Set Menu B.

They discussed the theatre and cinema and music. Walter enjoyed showing off his familiarity with these things. 'I'm not an intellectual and never will be,' he said, 'but I've found that I get a lot of enjoyment from art of every kind.'

'Oh, Walter, my love, that's wonderful,' she said, 'and don't worry about the intellectuals. They try to make art obscure so that they can keep it for themselves, but really it's for everyone.'

She told him about the deaths and funerals of Bronwen and John Thomas Thomas and Bernard. He was sad to hear about them, and she cried as she told him. As she blew her nose, the waiter came up and said, 'Food too spicy for the lady?' and Walter said, 'No, the food's fine. There have been three deaths in her family,' and the waiter said, 'So sorry, sir,' and Walter said, 'It wasn't your fault,' and the waiter retreated in confusion, and they laughed, and the waiter turned and gave them a hurt look, and they were sorry.

346

Kate asked Walter if there had been any other women in his life apart from Linda.

'I've had sex with four,' he said. 'A researcher who asked me which brand of washing powder I used, and I said that my sheets were very clean and would she like to see them, and she said 'yes'. An American psychiatrist who was even more guilt-ridden than you. A one-eyed Lithuanian zoo designer. And a very attractive Danish yachtswoman who kept saying "I'm going" when she meant "I'm coming", so the sex was hopeless, I didn't know whether I was coming or going. One of those four was made up.'

'The zoo designer. It has to be.'

'No! She was very real. Passionate about animal welfare and the need to improve zoos. Had her eye gouged out by a tiger. Refused to blame the tiger, blamed the poor design of the zoo.'

'So which one was made up? The researcher?'

'No. That happened, if not quite in the quick way I described it.'

'Not the Dane? I liked her.'

'No, not her. The American psychiatrist. I did meet a psychiatrist, but she was English, and she invited me for dinner, and she answered the door on all fours because she was seeing what it was like to be a dog that day, which gave a literal meaning to the phrase "barking mad". Oh, I've bought a Begelman, by the way.'

'You haven't!'

'I have. I like it.'

'Walter!'

'Exactly. I have changed.'

'That wasn't Linda's influence, was it?'

'No, that wasn't.'

'Good.'

They had toffee apples to finish. Walter leant across with a mouth full of toffee apple, looked at her very solemnly, swallowed his mouthful, and said, 'Is it too soon to ask you to try again?'

'Much too soon. It'd be in appalling taste, with Graham barely cold. But bad taste never bothered you, so you could try.'

'Will you marry me?'

'Yes.'

'Good Lord.'

'Yes.'

'We started the evening in the Swan with Two Necks. Now I feel like a dog with two dicks.'

'Did you choose the pub so you could say that?'

'Yes.'

'Good Lord.'

'Yes.'

'You must have been pretty confident.'

'I suppose I was.'

'From what I remember, one dick will be enough.'

It was. They were very happy. At first they were also very discreet. They waited a few months before breaking the news in the Gay Hussar. Shortly after that they drove down to Swansea in Walter's Jaguar, and breathed brief life into the sad old house with the happy memories.

'Well, here we are again,' said Kate. 'Another husband, but the same man.'

Enid looked awkward.

'What's the matter, Enid?' asked Kate.

'We never have drink in the house. It seems somehow unfair to their memory.'

'I completely agree,' said Walter.

Enid glowed with relief.

When she was alone with Enid in the dark old breakfast room, Kate sank into the rocking chair with a gasp of happiness and sadness, of pain and pleasure, of poignancy too great to be exquisite. Ghosts peopled the room. Bronwen, it seemed, must come smiling from the scullery, bearing Welsh cakes. John Thomas Thomas must come in, a book of essays under his arm. Myfanwy and Dilys, Bernard and Oliver, they would come bursting through chatting and laughing. But no. There was silence, save for the ticking of the old grandfather clock, and Kate saying, 'How are you and Annie getting on?'

'She won't leave the house. I tell her it's too large. I don't mind sharing a flat. I'd rather have two flats, but . . . Annie's all right, but she's clinging to the past, Kate, and you can't do that, even if you've no future to go to. Clinging to the past is like leaning on a shadow.'

Kate kissed her sister and felt a great surge of affection. Of that warm cocooning family of hers, only Oliver and Enid were still alive, and Oliver was almost lost to her.

Kate invited Oliver and Bunny to stay, but Bunny said, 'It's a bit of a problem, Kate, over the dog,' and Kate didn't press the matter. 'But do come over and see us,' Bunny added. 'Come and have a drink and we'll go to the local pub for lunch.'

Oliver and Bunny lived in a modern bungalow, convenient and functional, near Abinger Hammer. 'We know it's not got much character,' said Oliver apologetically, 'but you have to think about your old age.' He'd retired, even though he was only fifty-seven, but it seemed to Kate that he thought about old age so much that he was embracing it prematurely. He was very friendly and kissed her warmly, and they drank moderate sherry, and reminisced about old family jokes, and laughed a lot. Bunny was very pleasant but not in a very personal way. She didn't seem to have aged as much as Oliver, but, as Kate said afterwards, she hadn't had as much ageing to do.

'I'm sorry about the pub,' said Bunny, 'but I don't cook. Oliver cooks for us, but he can't manage visitors.'

'The pub'll be fine.'

The pub was fine, although the landlord and landlady didn't

seem particularly friendly. This may have been because, as they arrived, Bunny said, in a loud voice, 'It has some rather regrettable people in in the evenings, but it's fine at lunch-time.'

'We want to be married very quietly,' Kate told the registrar. 'There'll just be eleven of us there.'

'Fine. Fine. We'll use the smaller room.'

'There'll be my fiancé and I . . .'

'Good. I'm glad you'll be there,' said the registrar, who fancied himself as a bit of a wag.

'My sister and cousin from Wales. My two boys, by my first marriage, one of whom will probably bring his girlfriend.'

'Excellent. If we impress him, he may bring us his business.'

'If only. My boy from the first time I married my fiancé, plus his fiancé, but don't hold out too many hopes, they've been engaged for years.'

'You've been married to your husband once before?'

'No. Twice before. And then there'll be my daughter from my third marriage, and her husband. And we won't have any photos. We're doing it very discreetly, because it's not very long since my fifth husband died.'

'I see. Well . . . fine,' said the registrar. His eyes met hers. There was a dry gleam in them. 'I . . . er . . . I usually give a little talk on . . . er . . . the meaning of marriage, and the seriousness and . . . er . . . the permanence of the enormous step you're taking. I think under the circumstances I might skip that. You'll have been told it several times already.'

It was almost as Kate had predicted. Nigel did come alone. Elizabeth did bring her rather dull husband Don. Maurice did bring his comfortable fiancée Clare. Timothy did bring his new lady friend Felicity. Annie, however, refused to come. 'She went bright red and said she thought it was disgraceful, with Graham barely cold,' Enid told Kate. 'She loved Graham, you know. He praised her chutney. She told me I shouldn't go either. I told her

I loved you and it was none of her business and she'd once been grateful for living with the family, as she'd never ceased to tell us, and if she didn't like my way of carrying on she should shove off to a home.'

'You didn't!'

'Wasn't I awful?'

'No! You were wonderful.'

There were still eleven people in the smaller of the register office's rooms, despite Annie's absence.

'Is this any of your business?' Kate asked the uninvited guest.

'It's very much my business,' said Inspector Crouch. 'At least five of you are, potentially at any rate, murder suspects. Besides, I'm beside myself with joy at seeing you recover from the trauma of your loss so quickly. I said to the wife this morning, "I'd hate to miss it." "Well, be very tactful," she said. "Just don't let thoughts of arrest and imprisonment cast any kind of shadow on the joyous ceremony."'

That was the last Kate ever heard from Inspector Crouch. She thought of him occasionally, pursuing his enquiries, a lonely figure in the American corn belt, his umbrella raised against the rains of Otago, battling against red tape in huge drab offices off the Nevsky Prospect, interfering with the selling of double glazing.

Kate and Walter bought a cottage near Marlow. It was a cottage too beautiful to be true. It had thick, well-kept thatch. Honeysuckle twisted round the front door. There were geraniums and wallflowers in profusion. Daffodils bloomed each spring in the rough bank down to the orchard. Kate called her happy years here 'The Biscuit Tin Years' and when Daphne Stoneyhurst first visited Rhossili Cottage (Walter had grown to love Rhossili and was happy with the choice of name) she said, 'Darlings, this is a painting too clichéd even for me.' 'I know,' said Kate. 'It's really embarrassing, but we love it.'

Walter and Kate enjoyed many happy years together,

travelled a great deal, but neither of them was entirely happy with a life of endless idleness, and they threw themselves into other activities. Walter did charity work, collecting clothes and money and seeking his son's advice as to which was the worthiest trouble spot to target. Kate started to work for the Samaritans. The amount of unhappiness in the world never ceased to shock her. She also took up photography as a hobby.

They also threw themselves into the oldest activity of all, not with the frequency or the abandon of their earlier years, but with more vigour than the young would believe. 'It used to be the positions that were varied. Now, as arthritis strikes, it's the locations,' commented Kate post-coitally one night, after they'd made love to the sound and rhythm of the Tasman Sea. They experienced coitus interruptus on the Orient Express and coitus Intercity on the Inverness sleeper. They travelled by Aer Lingus for cunnilingus in Cork (where they almost visited Red Ron Rafferty's pub, but sanity prevailed). They enjoyed fells and fellatio in the Lake District.

They invited Enid to go to Spain with them, and she accepted. 'Annie grumbled, "Why haven't they invited me?"' she told them. 'I told her it was because she disapproved of you. She's got a month on her own to regret being so narrow. She said, "It'll be horrid in this great house all on my own." I said, "Try a month in a home and see how you like it." She said, "I'll be all right."'

The three of them toured the great cities of Spain – Seville, Cordoba, Granada, Salamanca, Toledo, Segovia and Madrid. Enid enjoyed every moment and went pink when Walter pressed Rioja on her. He told her that sangria wasn't alcoholic and she chose to believe him.

The beauty of the cities filled Kate with fury about what was being done to British cities in the sixties. In her beloved Swansea, in particular, the planners were finishing what the Luftwaffe had begun, the destruction of a town's history. In

Eastern Europe they rebuilt their cities stone by stone and brick by brick and the West mocked. But the public preferred history to the kind of architecture dumped on them by ignorant planners, arrogant architects and good architects who found themselves hamstrung by planners and budgets. The public preferred Warsaw and Gdansk to Plymouth and Coventry. We ruined our towns and cities with brutal office blocks and shoddy shopping malls and had the insolence to criticise the Italians for being bad custodians of their art treasures. It was Enid's suggestion that Kate turn all this anger into a book.

'I couldn't write a book,' she protested.

'You can do anything you want,' said Enid.

Kate shook her head at her sister's simple faith, but in fact *The Bad Building Book*, illustrated with her own photographs, did better than she had dared to hope.

Nigel rose to a position of considerable eminence in Takimoto Burns. He had homes in Cologne, Islington, Loch Lomond and Tokyo. He always seemed to be alone and he always seemed to be somewhere else. Kate once asked him, 'Do you ever meet yourself going in the opposite direction?' and he said, 'I don't know. I'm too busy reading my documents to look up and see me.'

Timothy continued to produce the Trouble novels – *Trouble in Malta* (no holiday was ever wasted), *Trouble in the Balearics*, of which Kate said, 'It sounds painful,' and Walter said, 'Shame on you, Kate Copson. Respect your children.' Timothy married Felicity, and they had a little girl called Roberta. Kate almost dared to hope that at last he would be happy.

Elizabeth at that time certainly wasn't happy. When Don abandoned her and the children in Leatherhead and began a new life in Buenos Aires, the possibility dawned on Kate and Walter that he might not be quite as dull as they had supposed. If he had been, it was unlikely that the daughter of an Argentinian polo player would have married him and stayed with him happily until his death twenty-two years later. Kate had to face the possibility that he had become dull through proximity to Elizabeth.

Maurice continued to visit the world's trouble spots. As his fame grew, the mere sight of him boarding a plane was enough to send the stock market tumbling in the country he was visiting. His intense, freckled face, beneath a steadily decreasing head of hair, was seen looking grave and depressed in a wide variety of places. 'Maurice Copson, BBC News, Gaza.' 'Maurice Copson, BBC News, Saigon.' 'Maurice Copson, BBC News, Salisbury, Rhodesia.' 'Maurice Copson, BBC News, Rawmarsh Main Colliery.' 'Maurice Copson, BBC News, Londonderry.'

Kate phoned him once and said, 'Walter's dying.' He said, 'You're joking!' She said, 'Yes, wasn't that an awful thing to say, but I thought if we had a crisis here we might see you here. I long to hear you say, "Maurice Copson, BBC News, Rhossili Cottage".' He did visit a bit more often after that, in the company of his charming fiancée Clare, and Clare took to visiting sometimes on her own. There were rumours, of course, that Maurice had a girl in every airport. Clare never asked him about it, as far as Kate knew, and never had a fling herself, as far as Kate knew, and she seemed happy to have a share of her magnetic, vibrant, journalist fiancé, who was never in one place for long enough to marry her. Sometimes, though, in the garden of Rhossili Cottage, or in the village pub, Kate thought that Clare's smiles looked brave.

Timothy's smiles were not so brave when Felicity left him and took Roberta with her.

Kate's second book had the rather ambitious title, *The Causes of Unhappiness*. It was written as a result of her experiences with the Samaritans. Unhappy people found it helpful. Happy people didn't read it. It sold extremely well from its publication in March 1969 until November of that year, when the build-up to Christmas began and nobody could admit that such a thing as unhappiness existed.

354

Kate heard that Inspector Crouch had retired. The murder of the man she'd known as Graham Eldridge remained unsolved.

Walter gave up modern cars and bought an old 1934 Wolseley, which he tended lovingly. Every two or three months they drove down to Swansea and took Enid and Annie for a run. Annie was all over Walter now, for fear that she'd be left behind.

Enid was desperate to get a flat, but Annie continued to cling on. Once, before a drive to Saundersfoot, Annie said to Walter, 'You will drive slowly, won't you, Walter. Only Enid's a nervous passenger. She'll never admit it, but she is.' Walter told Kate and Enid, and, on the way home, Enid said, 'Can't you go a bit faster, Walter? I want to get to the shop before it runs out of Welsh cakes.' Kate adored this more mischievous Enid but felt sad for the life that she might have led.

Kate and Walter took great pleasure in entertaining visitors to Rhossili Cottage. It was their greatest joy to share its peace and beauty with friends and family.

Sometimes the friends caused surprises. Daphne arrived one day in 1971 with a companion, named Jenny Carter. At seventy-three Daphne was still a strong woman, handsome in her way, with a thick crop of formidable grey hair. She was at peace with her lesbianism now, all cusps forgotten. Jenny Carter was at peace with her lesbianism too. The two of them were living together, happily and prosperously, in a flat near Sloane Square. Daphne was still painting what was basically the same painting, and still selling it, mainly to people who'd bought it several times already.

Kate gave them a delicious meal, smoked salmon mousse followed by a creamy, garlicky *bourride*, and a bottle of golden Mersault. She did this even though when she and Walter had visited Daphne, in the days before Jenny, Daphne had given them sandwiches and said, 'It's not the food that matters. It's the people.' Kate had said, 'You only say that because you can't cook. Those macaroni cheeses of yours were disgusting.'

Daphne had thrown back her head and laughed and said, 'They were, weren't they? Oh God.'

Daphne enjoyed the succulent *bourride* as much as anybody. It was strange how people who expressed no interest in food when they were hosts often managed to dredge up enormous enthusiasm when they were guests.

As they ate, Jenny Carter said to Daphne, 'Well, she hasn't.'

'Hasn't what?' asked Kate.

'Recognised me.'

'Oh Lord. Should I have?'

'Maths.'

'Maths?'

'I taught maths.'

'At Penzance?'

'Yes. I was walking out with an insurance salesman. I didn't even know there were lesbians let alone that I was one. I just knew I didn't like kissing insurance salesmen very much.'

'You came to my first wedding!'

'I looked at your sister's face and I thought, "What a sad, grey, cloudy face. How beautiful her face would be if the sun ever came out."'

'Enid.'

'Yes. I suppose, though I didn't recognise it at the time, it was a lesbian thought. Is she still alive?'

'Oh yes.'

'That's the one I fancied, isn't it?' said Daphne.

'Yes.'

'Did the sun ever come out?' asked Jenny Carter.

'It peeps out once or twice,' said Walter, 'but it never quite has the confidence to stay out.'

'It was at that wedding that Jenny and I first met,' said Daphne. 'Though it was forty more years before we met properly.'

'Or improperly, as most people would say,' said Jenny Carter.

'It was in the Plaza Real in Salamanca.' She blushed so much that Kate wondered what else had happened in Salamanca.

Olga visited from time to time, sometimes staying for a few days. Once Stanley Wainwright called round when Olga was there, and they all had a huge *salade niçoise* in the garden, liberally washed down by a marvellously well-balanced white Châteauneuf-du-Pape. Olga talked about her favourite subject, Daniel, and Stanley talked about his favourite subject, Stanley. He was in his mid-seventies now but still a big, energetic man. Olga was beginning to look frail again, though there was still a rod of steel in there somewhere. Kate couldn't believe it when she witnessed their first eye contact. Olga and Stanley, both in their seventies. Yet it happened. Within two months they were living together, and they stayed together, with rows and reconciliations, and walk-outs from Stanley, and abashed returns, and Olga patient but remorseless. Kate saw it all in that first look.

Her third book, *The Headless Chicken*, came out in 1973. It was a passionate attack on factory farming and animal feedstuffs and chemical fertilisers. It anticipated mad cow disease and genetic engineering. Kate went on television and said that we cannot pretend to be a nation of animal lovers while one battery chicken is produced legally, let alone millions. A local chicken farmer hurled a brick through a window of Rhossili Cottage. Several mass producers of battery chickens, firms with names like Orchard Poultry and Happy Hens, threatened to sue. Kate threatened to expose their methods in greater detail. Large numbers of people bought the book, and many of them continued to buy battery chickens as well. Kate's television appearance caused a stir. She was a natural. Conservative government ministers described the book as 'pathetic'. Labour shadow ministers described it as 'prophetic'. When Labour came into power in 1974, reaction to the book changed. A Labour cabinet minister described it as 'unrealistic', a Conservative shadow minister described it as 'unforgettable'.

Kate decided that only oppositions had consciences.

One morning, just before lunch, Kate came from her study to find Nigel sitting under a parasol on the lawn, doing a crossword. Walter was out collecting blankets for earthquake victims.

'Do it with me, Mother,' he said.

'You know what I think about crosswords. A waste of time. A waste of fine minds.'

'Well, here we are together, mother and son, each with a fine mind. What's the harm in our minds sharing a bit of fun?'

So she submitted, and tackled a crossword for the first and last time in her life. She got just one clue. 'Army and firm surround graduates, with spicy results.' Answer – Tabasco. He had done brilliantly.

'This Parsifal chap's pretty good,' he said. She'd forgotten about that! Lying in bed in hospital she marvelled at his cheek. Of course he'd done brilliantly. She thought now that he'd longed to tell her that he was Parsifal, but hadn't dared to. That hadn't been all, though. He had gone on. She said, 'Crossword compilers must have funny minds.' He said, 'I daresay they're very ordinary.' She said, 'I wonder what this Parsifal chap is doing at this very moment.' 'Having a crap, probably,' he said. 'Nigel,' she said, shocked. 'Oh, Mother,' he said, 'you've never been able to reconcile yourself to the inevitability of lavatories, have you?' 'I find them boring precisely because they're inevitable,' she said. 'Tolstoy never mentioned them. Jane Austen never mentioned them. Their characters didn't explode from severe constipation, so we may assume that they went to the lavatory. They just didn't think it interesting enough to mention, and nor do I. Now there are lavatories in everything. Is that progress?' She saw him trying not to laugh. 'Oh Lord,' she said. 'You've been winding me up and I've fallen for it.'

Maurice's occasional visits were snatched between wars and coups. His mother always wanted to talk to him about world affairs, but he always refused, preferring to go down to one of the village's two pubs with his homely fiancée Clare, and play dominoes and darts and cribbage with the locals. 'I have to unwind between jobs,' he said once. 'It's the way I cope. Sorry, Ma.'

Timothy was the only one who ever stayed for any length of time, and that only once. He and Daniella had decided to live apart for three months to get what he called 'a perspective on things'. He'd had writer's block in the Majorcan winter. 'I need to get back to my roots,' he said. Kate lent him her study, and that was almost the only time that she had a serious argument with Walter during their third marriage. 'Your writing's ten times more valuable than his,' he said. 'Let him use his bedroom.'

'He has writer's block,' she said. 'I haven't.'

Anyway, Timothy's writing block was swiftly cleared. Fans of the good Inspector Trouble should be eternally grateful to Kate. (In Timothy's books it was impossible to be merely grateful, you had to be eternally grateful; it was his second most favourite adverb, beaten to Adverb of the Decade only by preternaturally, of which he was preternaturally fond.) It was Kate's sacrifice of her study that made it possible for them to enjoy that classic tale of evil among the wallflowers, *Trouble With Dancers*. (The one in which a complete team of Morris dancers is poisoned, so that nobody will ever know which of them was the murderer's real target, but that was reckoning without Inspector Trouble – who had, of course, the advantage of having been faced with this particular plot already, in *Trouble at the Hockey Festival*. Timothy was flattered to find *Trouble With Dancers* reviewed in the *Financial Times*, not realising that the critic only reviewed it because it gave him the chance to sound off about his *bête noire*. 'How can anybody be imprisoned for murdering Morris dancers?' he wrote. 'He should have been decorated.')

It was a great surprise to Kate when Elizabeth married again. 'It's brave of you after what happened,' she said.

'Well, I'm hardly likely to meet two Dons, am I?' said Elizabeth.

There was no risk of Terence becoming dull through association with Elizabeth. He was already dull when she met him.

Kate felt rather guilty that she had difficulty in finding things to discuss with Elizabeth. Elizabeth was a very good mother. The twins had shown no obvious ill effects from the sudden total loss of their father, who never even sent Christmas cards, and now they showed no obvious ill effects from the arrival of a stepfather. At school Trevor was academic and Mark sporty. They weren't particularly close, not in the way that Kate and Dilys would have been close, but they both loved visiting Kate and Walter and playing in their delightful garden with so many trees to climb.

Kate knew that Heinz sent Elizabeth little presents for the children every Christmas. He had married again, and had sent Elizabeth (but not Kate) a photograph of his wedding day. Kate asked Elizabeth what Anke was like and she said, 'Very pretty. Just as pretty as Inge,' but she didn't give any details and she didn't show any emotion and when Kate said that she'd like to see the photo, Elizabeth said, 'Oh, I threw it away. There didn't seem to be a lot of point. Sorry.'

When Elizabeth wasn't there, she seemed to Kate to be a rather shadowy figure, but, every time she saw her, it struck her that she wasn't shadowy at all, but sensible and straightforward and very very solid. She had thick golfer's calves and bought most of her clothes from Jaeger.

Kate could never imagine Terence and Elizabeth getting up to high jinks in bed. One evening, however, at Rhossili Cottage, with the wind and the owls in mournful chorus, Terence suddenly looked almost roguish and said, 'What about going to bed, old girl?' but Elizabeth, missing the point as usual, said, 'You go on up. I'm not tired.'

Annie moved in to a home at last, and Enid was able to buy a small flat in a windy block in Sketty, with a distant view of the sea. Now that Annie was in a home, and Enid no longer needed a break from her, the two of them came to Rhossili Cottage for a week. 'You wouldn't know anybody if you came to Swansea now,' Enid told them. 'Gladys Morgan that had the florist's is gone, Mansel Morris that dyed his hair that had the grocer's shop hasn't any hair to dye any more and the grocer's is a building society. Herbert Herbert Politics has had a heart attack, and Herbert Herbert Cricket emigrated to the Algarve because of Mrs Herbert Herbert Cricket's arthritis, and he died of a broken heart, because there isn't any cricket on the Algarve. You wouldn't recognise Swansea, it's all foreign restaurants and such nonsense. Even the Kardomah's gone. The market's still the market, and that's about all there is. Even laver bread's posh now.'

While Enid and Annie were there, Stanley and Olga arrived unexpectedly for the weekend, Stanley rather drunk and very argumentative, Olga spreading her hands as if to say that it wasn't her fault, and saying, 'I only told him that he hadn't Daniel's instinct for colour. I mean, surely that isn't an insult to a sculptor? But I forgot that Stanley is so conceited that he believes that if he could have demeaned himself to become a painter he'd have been a better painter than my Daniel.'

Enid and Annie were astonished by this stormy and drunken invasion of their peace by people who hadn't even been invited. Enid hadn't seen Stanley or Olga since the retrospective. Annie threw her bunioned legs in the air and said, 'Oh my. Oh my.'

The next morning they all went for a camel ride down the bridle path to Nether Fletchfield. They came to a barn, and Kate and Walter went in and took all their clothes off and made love on camel-back. The camel tried to throw them off. It writhed and jerked and Kate writhed and Walter jerked and the Morris dancers cheered and waved their phallic symbols, and Walter was enormous inside her, and she was . . . awake in Ward 3C, and she realised that she'd been dreaming. Oh, such dreams to have three nights before your hundredth birthday.

It was a little disappointing to return from such a dream to the reality of that weekend with Enid and Annie and Stanley and Olga. The six of them had gone to Cookham for lunch, in Stanley's Rolls. When Stanley suggested going to Cookham, Olga said, 'Not Cookham, surely, Stanley? Won't you get upset to know that not only aren't you the best artist there, you aren't even the best artist called Stanley there.' She turned to Enid and Annie and said, 'Stanley Spencer lived in Cookham.' Enid already knew this, and Annie had never heard of Stanley Spencer and remained mystified.

Annie, who had once sniffed at melon and said, 'Putting on airs,' said, 'Oh! A Rolls-Royce,' and even her goitre blushed with excitement. As Stanley approached a corner rather fast, Annie said desperately, in the absence of children, 'I imagine the insurance on a Rolls-Royce must be astronomical.' Stanley said, 'You're right, Annie. Let's crash it and prove I don't care as much about money as everyone says I do.' Stanley accelerated, Annie almost fainted, Enid screamed, and Stanley just managed to keep control of the car. As he straightened out after the corner, Enid said, 'Glynis Hodges whose father kept ferrets was thrown through the window of a post-bus on the Great St Bernard pass. They didn't find her body for four days,' and Kate said, 'For shame, Enid. Stanley'll think we only talk about death in Wales.'

They lunched in a riverside pub, alone in the spacious restaurant, just conscious of the hubbub in the crowded bar. Annie made no comment when they all ordered starters, but she went as red as a Pomerol when Stanley tried to make her have a glass of wine. Enid came over all sophisticated and said, 'This wine's lovely. It's a little less full-bodied than a Rioja.'

Walter told Olga that he thought that inside Daniel's social realism there had been a surrealist trying to get out, and the dynamism caused by the conflict had been the central thrust of his creative magnetism. Stanley stared at him and said, 'I didn't know our piston manufacturer claimed to know anything about art,' and Kate said proudly, 'Walter looks at art with an engineer's eye, and it always works,' and Annie said, 'I'm listening to an artistic conversation! Aren't I just the luckiest person alive?'

Once a year, Kate and Walter visited Oliver and Bunny in their labour-saving bungalow. They had a sherry there, and then went to the pub. Bunny was getting deaf now, and talked even more loudly. Every year she made at least one faux pas.

In 1973, as they entered the bar, she yelled, 'Their food's not very good, no presentation at all, but I've never heard of anyone actually being poisoned.' In 1974, she boomed, 'They aren't very friendly, but the car park's very difficult at the other place.' In 1975, she didn't say anything as they entered, but, just before they left, a stunningly beautiful West Indian girl with a magnificent Rastafarian hairdo came in to empty the fruit machine. Kate wanted to cry to think of such a gorgeous creature having to do such a mundane job. Bunny screeched, 'What on earth has that black girl got on the top of her head?'

They didn't go to the pub in 1976. They didn't need to. Bunny had committed her greatest faux pas of all. She'd taken a wrong turning and driven her car into Chichester harbour and drowned. Oliver invited them to stay for weekends after that, saying, 'I can do this now. Poor Bunny just didn't like visitors. She liked people, she was a good mixer. But not visitors.' Oliver cooked lasagne and steak pie and gammon and eggs, and they didn't go to the pub once.

Irony never seemed far away from Kate's life. It stalked her happiness like an obsessed lover. That dark night in hospital had been lit by happy memories of her life with Walter. Seventeen years of happiness they had that night. Now, just as a sky as grey

363

and sallow as Oliver's skin began to pale in Kate's window on the world, her memories came to the point where Walter began to fade. Stronger grew the October morning. Weaker grew Walter. The great bulk shrank. The skin hung loose. The eyes tried to hide from the world, hollow dark sensitive orbs above increasingly black bags. Death came to Walter Copson slowly but remorselessly. He retained his humour to the end. Kate admired and loved him more and more, and they were very kind at the hospice when she could look after him no longer. He was always good-humoured except on the final Tuesday, when he didn't recognise her, but on the Wednesday, his final day of life, his clarity had returned, and he whispered, as she squeezed his hand, 'I've been so lucky.'

Kate was eighty-one when Walter died. Her face at the funeral was set and stern. She wore bright red because it had been his wish. She was criticised for it, and didn't bother to defend herself. She told herself again and again that she'd been lucky to know Walter at all, let alone marry him three times. She told herself that she had been so much luckier than Enid or Annie, neither of whom had ever felt a man inside her. She told herself that she had been so much more fortunate than Oliver and his double dose of double barrel, than Bernard who had died a virgin, than Myfanwy who had died so long ago that she was almost forgotten, and than Dilys, who had never had a proper life at all. She told herself that she could have been born a toad, and been squashed to death by a Volvo on the A303. She told herself that she was fortunate to have a daughter who, if not the princess of her hopes, was a thoroughly nice person, and had produced two fine twin boys. She told herself that she had been enriched by the production of three sons, only one of whom was a murderer. And, because she was such a very determined woman, she found great consolation in these thoughts.

They had a small funeral tea at Rhossili Cottage, and Kate was dignity itself. Enid handed round Welsh cakes and bara brith that she had brought from Swansea. She kissed Kate impulsively in the kitchen and said, 'I shall never know sadness like you are feeling, so I suppose that in our very different ways we've both been very lucky people.'

Heinz and his second wife Anke had come over from Niederlander-ob-der-Kummel, both in their eighties, both more erect than they had any right to be.

'How's the Sperm Count?' asked Kate.

'Kate, you are outrageous,' said Heinz.

'I hadn't meant to be. It's how I think of him,' said Kate.

Heinz explained the joke to Anke, who smiled without comprehension and said, 'Graf Von Seemen is a sad, lonely old man. He is very sorry for himself.'

'Ah. That I will never be,' said Kate.

'And nor will I,' said Enid.

19 Delilah

Walter was dead. The hospital was awake. Kate slept. She awoke to find thin Janet performing, as gently as she could, those necessary tasks on which we have decided not to dwell. Suffice it to say that for a proud woman the humiliation didn't lessen as day succeeded day.

Not thin Janet. Janet was the fat one. This one was . . . thin . . . it had gone. Kate felt the mists swirling in her head. As she awoke more fully she remembered the task that she'd set herself. The murder. Go through the alphabet. Thin Alison? Thin Andrea? It seemed a much more fearsome thing, the murder, now that all the decorative trimmings had been ripped away. Someone, almost certainly one of her three sons, had murdered Graham for a very serious reason.

Thin . . . Brenda? Carrie? (There's tension in Timothy, I can tell. I wasn't wrong about Carrie.) Thin Clare? (Poor Clare. Matronly now. He'll never marry her now.) Thin Constance? Thin Daphne? (Oh, Daphne, I do miss you. Imagine that!) Thin Deirdre? Thin Denise?

To be reduced to this!

She remembered that she'd decided that she didn't want to continue with her investigations.

Thin What's-her-name was speaking.

'Ladies,' said thin What's-her-name, 'we're going to have a new friend coming in for you in a minute. Delilah.'

Thin Delilah? Thin Edith?

'Delilah's had a nasty little attack, and she's heavily sedated, but when she comes round I want you to be really friendly to her.'

'I'll be friendly, of course,' said Angela Critchley. 'I'm absolutely fed up with all these stray women being dumped in my room, and I shall sort it out with the management, but in the meantime I shall be hospitality itself. There is such a thing as style.'

'Good,' said thin . . . Elizabeth? (Was she right to eliminate Elizabeth from suspicion?')

'I've never been the complaining type,' said Lily Stannidge. 'I've met women who are and I can't abide them. But if I find that someone called Delilah has been invited to the captain's cocktail party and I haven't, there'll be ructions. I promise you, there'll be ructions.'

Thin Fanny? (Sounds inconvenient.) Thin Felicity? (Wonder what happened to Felicity.)

Why did people murder? Possible motives for murder – envy, jealousy, hatred . . .

Thin Gaynor? Thin Gertie?

. . . sadism, masochism (kill the people you really love in order to make yourself miserable), madness . . .

Gloria? Hannah? Hettie?

. . . greed, lust, love, sexual pleasure (sado–eroticism?) . . .

Hilda? Isobel? Jane?

. . . self-defence, self-righteousness, moral crusade (insanity?) . . .

Gone too far. Begins with H. Sure of it. Trust your judgement. Thin Henrietta? Thin Hayley?

Mist. Blankness. Oh, Kate, oh, Kate, how can you hope to solve a murder when you can't even remember thin Helen's name?

Thin Helen! Oh, the relief. Oh, the blessed relief. And her instinct had been right. And her instinct also told her that she'd left out one possible cause for murder, and that the one she had left out would be the . . .

Why was she continuing to think about the murder? She'd decided not to.

Surely her sons would need a better motive for murder – or did she mean a worse motive – than envy or jealousy or hatred? They weren't men made for murder. They would have to be driven to it.

Stop it, Kate. Stop thinking about it.

Squeak squeak. Delilah was arriving. I'd pop home myself and get a can of WD40, if only I could. Squeak bloody squeak.

None of them was mad. None of them would murder for sexual pleasure or out of some kind of twisted moral feeling. Surely not?

What about self-defence? It was hard to see how that was relevant, but . . .

Her brain was refusing to switch off. It had a mind of its own! It wasn't under her control. This thought terrified her. But what was she thinking this thought with? Her brain. Her brain was telling her that her brain was independent of her. She didn't have to believe it, though. But where would her disbelief come from? Her brain!

This way lay madness. She began to consider her sons as potential murderers in order to stop thinking about her brain.

She accepted, in that moment, that she had to continue with her investigation, now that she had come this far.

She'd known her sons as foetuses and infants and children and adolescents and young men and middle-aged men and now as men who were becoming old. This was the great advantage she had over Inspector Crouch.

She'd known them and not known them. She didn't know them well enough to rule any of them out with utter certainty, and that was even more frightening than your brain declaring independence.

'Where the fuck am I?'

Delilah! She'd forgotten all about Delilah!

'Bleedin' 'ell-fire. What's going on?'

'You're in the Spa Hotel, Buxton,' said Angela Critchley,

'and you're in my room, and I'll thank you to mind your language.'

'Spa Hotel, Buxton? What the fuck am I doing in the Spa Hotel, Buxton?'

'You aren't.' Lily Stannidge must have been leaning across towards Delilah's bed. Her whisper was so low that she hoped Angela Critchley wouldn't hear it. Kate could hear it, but then her hearing was remarkable, and she was nearer to Lily. 'She's a loony. She thinks she's in the Spa Hotel, Buxton.'

'Bleedin' 'ell.'

'I should run along to the purser if you're not satisfied.'

'The purser?'

'Yes. His office is on B Deck.'

'Jesus Christ!' exclaimed Delilah. 'I'm in a fucking funny farm.'

'Language, please!' implored Angela Critchley.

'Yes, I really don't like your language, I have to say,' agreed Lily Stannidge.

'Is she a loony too, over there?'

'She's exhausted,' said Angela Critchley. 'It was a difficult birth. Not to worry, though. Mother and child are doing well.'

'Birth! She looks a hundred!'

There's no need to exaggerate, thought Kate. After all, I'm still two days short of a hundred, if my calculations are correct.

'She's ga-ga,' said Lily. 'She just lies there. Never goes on any of the shore excursions. Can't see the point of coming on a cruise, really.'

'I'm not having this,' said Delilah. 'How do I get out of here?'

'There's a bell for room service,' said Angela Critchley.

'Room service! Christ!'

Why don't they all shut up? Don't they know I have urgent work to do?

Could any of her sons have killed Graham for her sake? And what would you call such a motive? Mercy? Release? To release one, for example, from abuse. Maybe she'd missed out all sorts of categories of motive.

'Yes?' said thin Helen. (I can still remember her name! Good.) 'You rang your bell?'

'Yeah,' said Delilah. 'Where am I?'

'You're in hospital.'

'Jesus! Have I had one of me turns?'

'You've had a heart attack.'

'I haven't, have I? Oh shit. When can I go home?'

'Doctor Ramgobi will see you as soon as he can. He's very busy.'

'Oh, Jesus wept. What a fucking carry-on.'

'Please, Delilah,' said thin Helen. 'They don't like bad language in Ward 3C.'

'Oh!' said Delilah. 'Oh! "They don't like bad language in Ward 3C", don't they?'

Nigel. She'd gone round and round in circles, thinking about him. Maurice, too. Round she went now, again and again. Then a new thought struck her about Timothy.

Timothy would know how to commit a murder, from having invented so many. The blurring of the boundaries between reality and fantasy was a well-known phenomenon of the electronic age. Some people thought that other people killed because they saw so much crime on TV and were able to kill in fantasy in video games and . . . what was it called? . . . interactive television. Surely it wasn't improbable that impressionable people did blur the boundaries? Maybe there was a special risk factor for the writers of detective stories. Timothy in the dock, his lawyer arguing on a defence of diminished responsibility. 'He thought he was in one of his books.' That might be going too far, but to invent murders might diminish the horror and make the reality more possible, that wasn't entirely unconvincing. But, please, let it not be Timothy.

Perhaps, after all, it had been an unbalanced American corn

farmer or a ruined investor in Otago or a wronged wife. She didn't know how they would have been able to frame the three brothers so accurately, but it might have been possible. She couldn't really blame Inspector Crouch for having been so thorough. Oh, how she wished it were so. Damn that instinct of hers, which said it was one of her sons.

'I was a dancer.'

Out of the blue, Delilah began to talk. Kate welcomed the interruption.

'You wouldn't believe it now. Me legs are like pillars of Stilton now. Horrid, they are. Liked me grub too much. But once they was admired by all the leading figures in Dewsbury. Chamber of Commerce. Round Table. Inner wheel. Bankers, wankers, we had them all in the Barcelona.'

Delilah gave a great sigh and returned, Kate hoped, to happier times. She found Delilah's effect on the gentility of the ward delightful. She wished she'd been there in Hilda's day. That would have been a pantomime.

Of course. There was another motive for murder. Well, there might be lots more but this was the one she'd been seeking. This was the one. Her instinct told her so.

It took Kate a long time, hour after hour of careful, often agonising thinking. All three sons came, in turn, to visit her, held her hand, utterly unconscious of what was going through her brain. It was bizarre. She applied this motive, which her instinct told her was the one, to all three. Was there any possible scenario that could cause each of them to murder Graham for this reason? It was laborious work, broken occasionally by Delilah.

'All of them came to the Barcelona, and they all said, "Show us your tits, Delilah."'

'Oh, how vulgar!' exclaimed Angela Critchley. 'I hope you sent them packing with a flea in their ear.'

'No, I showed them me tits.'

'Really, Delilah,' said Lily Stannidge. 'What do you think this is? The *Oriana*? This is Swan Hellenic.'

'I wouldn't show you me tits now. You wouldn't thank me.'

'I certainly wouldn't.'

Fat Janet hurried in. It seemed that both Lily Stannidge and Angela Critchley had rung their bells. Fat Janet remonstrated with Delilah.

'We don't like too much talk in the afternoons in Ward 3C, Delilah,' she said.

'Oh! Oh! "We don't like too much talk in the afternoons in Ward 3C", don't we?' mocked Delilah.

Over those long hours Kate found all sorts of possible reasons why her sons might have murdered the man known as Graham Eldridge. Most of them were far-fetched. Most of them she dismissed. They just weren't urgent enough, big enough, awful enough, to lead a man to murder.

One scenario was, though. It seemed far-fetched too, but it was big enough, and, boy, it was awful enough. She didn't want to think about it, so awful was it.

Some time during the long afternoon she had the idea of looking at the murder from the point of view of her perspective on Graham. She knew that she was bound to have to face unpleasant truths about one of her sons, but what did she want to find out about Graham? There was one thing that she longed to find out, one important factor that, if found to be true, would give her great pleasure. So she decided to hypothesise on the basis that it was true.

Again, it wasn't difficult to think of possible scenarios that fulfilled the condition. Again, one of them seemed to carry that bit more conviction than the others. It certainly was weighty enough to murder for.

It was the one that she didn't want to think about. It was too dreadful to contemplate. And yet, one read about such things.

The mists weren't far away, the primordial slime was all about her, she was dying, she didn't want to think about anything so terrible, but she had to. You can't unknow what you know. You can't unthink what you have thought.

Even Delilah seemed a long way away now, as though under water, saying, 'You probably think I'm as rough as a bear's arse, but in my day I was considered a stunner by men that was particular. Have you any idea what the Barcelona Club in Dewsbury was like?'

Marginally better than the Dewsbury Club in Barcelona, thought Kate, hard though she was trying not to listen and get involved, now that she was on the trail.

'Classy. Glamorous. I mean, not every venue I played was of that standard. The Mona Lisa Club in Newport was a dump. If you'd called the Nefertiti in Droitwich a dump, the manager'd have kissed you. It was a shite-hole.'

'Oh, really!'

'Yes, really. You may be outraged, but if you'd gone to the Nefertiti yourself, you'd have said, "This place is a shite-hole."'

'I can assure you that I'd never go near it, let alone in it.'

'You're not a bad judge.'

'But if I had I would never have said . . . those words.'

The more Kate tested the hypothesis, the more it seemed to fit the bill. It fitted in with something Nigel had said, in response to something Maurice had said, here, at her bedside, only a few days ago. It fitted in with a long silence that Kate had been reluctant to break, as she realised now. It fitted in with an absence that had puzzled her only slightly, but which seemed highly significant now. It fitted in with something that she hadn't found. It fitted in with something Graham hadn't told her. It fitted in with so many negatives that in the end it became a screaming positive.

Doctor Ramgobi was screaming too. 'This woman should have been taken to intensive care, nurse. She could have died.'

'Oh fuck.'

'Quiet, madam. Don't excite yourself. We'll get you there. Heads will roll over this, nurse. Heads will roll.'

She could never prove it, of course, lying there in a hospital bed. She could never tell anybody about it, having lost the power of speech. She could never write about it, being paralysed. That, after all, was why it had at last been safe for her to pursue the matter.

But even if she hadn't been paralysed, and had been able to speak, and had been a policeman with all his powers of search, all his scientific aids, she might not have been able to prove it. Maybe she had misjudged Inspector Crouch. Maybe he had guessed it, but hadn't been able to prove it. In any case, she realised that she hadn't told him any of the significant facts, because she hadn't realised that they were significant, although she might not have told him even if she had. No, she couldn't take too much credit for being so much quicker than Inspector Crouch (if she was right).

Squeak squeak. Removal of Delilah to intensive care. Squeak squeak.

'I'll be off now.'

It was him! It was the murderer (if she was right). The shock swept through her body, like high-speed pins and needles. There just might be a way of finding out, but did she want to, after all? Quick. Decide. Yes. She had to, now that she had come this far. She had just one chance. The look in her eyes would have to be extremely eloquent.

She opened her eyes very suddenly, opened them wide, stared straight into his soul. She hoped that he could see the accusation in her eyes, the contempt, the anger, the intelligence, the triumph. She hoped that it was a look that would allow no other interpretation, except her knowledge of his guilt.

She held her eyes on his astonished face. His jaw dropped open as jaws did in the books. A flush ran up across his neck and right across his face. For a moment he was paralysed with shock, and they stared at each other, mother and son, both paralysed. She saw guilt in his eyes, shame in his eyes, pleading in his eyes, misery in his eyes.

She tried to wipe the accusation from her eyes, now that it had done its job. She tried to wipe the contempt and anger from her eyes, now that they had hit their target. She tried to show him the love she still felt for him.

He turned abruptly, and walked away. She would never know if he had seen the love.

20 Norman

The job was done, and Kate felt completely drained. She felt flat. She'd thought that she might feel at peace, but the enormity of the crime had shocked her, and she wanted to get away from it all, from the memory of the murderer's face, from her horror at the depth of his shame.

On, on with your life, Kate Copson. You were a mere eighty-one when we left you. Eighteen years to go.

During the first of those years she kept the memory of Walter alive by writing a book about him. It was a simple tale, a story of three marriages and one great love. What a joy it was to relive her years with Walter, to bring him back to life in the little study overlooking the patio with the fig tree. How many cups of camomile tea he had placed gently on her old Georgian desk during the biscuit-tin years. It was a story about happiness, but it was also a story with a moral. How could it not be, for it was written by John Thomas Thomas's daughter? It was a story about a man who changed, who grew. It was a rebuke to all those who say, 'I can't help the way I am.' Kate called it *The Smile Tycoon* and subtitled it 'The Story of a Good Man'.

The title referred to a phrase Walter had used at Rhossili Cottage, when he'd come home exhausted after distributing second-hand toys to children's homes.

'I hope you aren't doing any of this as a penance,' she had said.

'I do it for my own joy,' Walter had replied. 'I create smiles where there were none. I'm a smile tycoon.'

The Smile Tycoon was largely ignored by the critics, but very popular with older readers, especially after Kate's appearance on the *Roly McTavish Show*.

'There's a lot of sex in your book,' the laconic Scottish chat-show host pointed out.

'Of course,' said the eighty-three-year-old author, to the delight of the studio audience. 'There was a lot of sex in our life.'

'You come from a very puritanical background,' said Roly McTavish. 'What do you think your parents would have thought of all the sex in your book?'

'The world is full of such bad sex, Roly – rape, child abuse, sado-masochistic violence, stalking, harassment, increasing sexual freedom was supposed to make us more mature about sex, ha ha – that I hope I'd have been able to persuade them that good sex between people who love each other isn't too disgraceful a subject to discuss.'

'Nevertheless, you do seem to be obsessed by sex.'

'Oh no, Roly. There's art in my book, travel in my book, lots of food and drink in my book, lots of portraits of people in my book, there are lots of jokes in my book. But this is television, and you're scared stiff people might get bored and switch off, so you go on and on about sex. It's you, I'm afraid, Roly, who's obsessed with sex.'

Despite the success of the book, it was the last that Kate wrote for many years. Because she was tired, at eighty-three years of age? Not at all, gentle reader. She simply didn't have the time. She was too busy with her television series and her toyboy.

Now, at ninety-nine, Kate really did feel tired. The mental rigours of her detective work had exhausted her. The emotional implications of her discovery had exhausted her even more. She had accepted that she was dying. It was time.

Not quite! Not yet! She really did want to finish her review of her life, now that she had got this far.

She was anxious to die before midnight, in two days' time, thus escaping a card from the Queen, a cake with a hundred candles, the singing of 'Happy birthday to you' and, even worse, the song that was so incorrect for those interested in sexual politics, 'For she's a jolly good fellow'. She felt, therefore, that she couldn't linger too much on her years with Norman.

She drifted in and out of sleep that night, and in and out of memory. The video played all night. Sometimes she watched it, and sometimes she slept.

Snapshots, then, from her years of fame.

With Timothy in Majorca, still fit enough to take gentle walks through the unspoilt mountains of the north, admiring the glory of the flowers that no pesticides had poisoned, listening to the distant ringing of the bells on the necks of the goats, eating lovely fresh fish simply prepared by Lucy. She really liked Lucy, and was sad when they announced their trial separation. She had wondered, once or twice, on those sun-shrivelled hills, if she was walking with a murderer. Well, now she knew.

Trips with Maurice. Two days in Luxor with him and Clare before he flew off to Kabul. She could see the three of them now, under the hot November sun, dwarfed by the majestic pillars of the Temple of Karnak, stunned by the scale and grandeur, but also by the delicacy and intricacy of the decorations, and Kate wondering, could Maurice, who loved beauty almost as much as he loved truth and justice, be a murderer? Well, now she knew.

Great meals with Nigel. The Auberge de l'Ill at Illhaeusern. He had had the *filets de carpe et perche aux haricots cocos blancs*. She remembered wondering, as he ate his dead fish, whether she was dining with a murderer. Well, now she knew.

The kindness of Elizabeth and Terence. Twice they gave up golfing holidays to take her to the great cities of Spain and Italy. They admired these cities, but they didn't respond to them as she did. She was overwhelmed by them, lost in them, moved to floods of tears in the Piazza Del Campo in Siena. Sometimes, on grey days in Britain, she would think, It's there now, at this very moment the lovers and the pigeons are strutting, the tourists are gawping, the waiters are smiling under the awnings. It made the grey days easier to bear, knowing that it was there, waiting for her.

378

Later she had the exquisite joy of introducing Norman to Salamanca, and seeing his astonished face as he entered the Plaza Mayor for the first time. She'd been ninety at the time, and he her toyboy of eighty-seven.

She thought back, in her bed that night, to the heady days of *Granny Copson's Corner*. Her own television series at the age of eighty-four! It had been Tony Bream's idea, and he'd confessed to her later that his motivation in putting it forward had been to infuriate Rob Walsall. Tony had seen the interview on the *Roly McTavish Show*, and had realised that she was a natural. She'd fought against the title. It had sounded cute and patronising, but Tony had insisted, saying that Rob hated it. It irritated her when people assumed that Maurice's influence had helped her get the series. He would never have deigned to use influence.

Maurice did keep her well informed about the politics behind the scenes, though. He told her that Rob Walsall was demanding programmes with street cred, programmes that were street raw, programmes that showed Britain as she was. He told her that Tony Bream argued that Granny Copson was just as much Britain as she was as were unemployed black youths in Brixton. He didn't tell her till years later that Rob Walsall had only agreed to the programme because he was convinced it would destroy Tony Bream's reputation. It was of course, a huge success, and made Tony Bream's reputation, which infuriated Rob Walsall.

Kate, more and more outspoken now, didn't exactly thrill Rob Walsall when she told him, 'You're obsessed with street cred because you've only ever seen a street from the back of a taxi.'

Ironically, though . . . 'Oh, not another irony,' I hear you cry. Well, yes, another irony, I'm afraid . . . despite her confrontation with Rob Walsall, despite the title of her programme, Kate refused to become a TV cross between the Women's Institute and an old people's home. She refused to confine herself to wise old saws, to interviews with eccentrics and naturalists and naturists and herbalists. She insisted on being, in her own way, at the cutting edge.

She upset church leaders with her programme on religious intolerance. Her fury at the bigotry, hatred and cruelty that mankind is capable of in the name of religion got the better of her. She managed to offend the Church of England, the Catholic Church, the Greek Orthodox Church, the United Reform Church, the Pentecostal Church, the Jehovah's Witnesses, the Mormons, the Muslims, the Buddhists, the supporters of Islam and the Scientologists. Good going in twenty-seven minutes. The Archbishop of Canterbury described her remark that 'Jesus would be turning in his grave if He hadn't ascended from it' as flippant. 'Well, thank goodness for flippancy,' she said. 'Nobody ever killed or persecuted or went to war out of flippancy.'

She upset church leaders again, and many senior figures in our great political parties, such champions of family values except in their own lives, when she introduced Norman as her boyfriend and asked him, 'Do you enjoy sleeping with me?'

'Not much,' he said.

She was genuinely shocked for a moment. Everyone assumed that the exchange had been rehearsed, but it hadn't.

'I like being awake in bed with you, though,' he continued. 'Not that I'm capable of a great deal of activity at my great age.'

'What did Enid and Annie and Oliver think of that?' I hear you exclaim. You're very vocal today. Well, I wasn't going to mention it, we've been to so many funerals together, you and I, but Annie and Oliver had died. Enid was still very much alive, though, and Kate had solved the problem of her inevitable outrage by inviting her to be in the studio audience for that edition of the programme. If she'd watched it in Swansea she'd have died of shock, and would never have dared show her face in the Uplands again. Being part of it, in London, made her feel really quite bold.

'Of course, I only have rather a vague idea of what people do in bed,' she said in the hospitality room afterwards, to the astonishment of the researchers, 'but, please, Kate dear, Norman dear, don't exert yourselves too much. Iris Johns's husband died in the act in the very hotel in Madeira in which they'd honeymooned thirty years earlier, and he was a fit man, he'd sung in the Pontardulais Male Voice Choir, and they had an awful job getting his body home.'

Kate, of course, made a programme about death. Many of you may have seen it. She ended the programme with these words, spoken direct to the camera with an intensity to make the hairs stand up on the back of your neck: 'We are all born once. We all die once. That is the end of the equality meted out by this world. Let us not fear this thing. We cannot avoid the fear of painful illness, but we must not fear death itself. It is not only inevitable, but desirable. Eternal life would be appalling. The value of life lies in its brevity. Relish the miracle of life every day. Make the most of it, both for yourselves and for others. If you live as long as I have, and are lucky enough to have as rich a social life as I have had, you'll go to many funerals. Don't fear them. Don't fear other people's death. Hard though it is, don't grieve for your loss, but think of their peace and give thanks for their life which lives on in you. Nothing ends with your death, except unimportant little you. Life is a relay race. Pass the baton. Good-night.'

Rob Walsall got his revenge in the end, of course. He had ways of seeing the advance schedules of all the other companies, and so he was able to schedule *Granny Copson's Corner* against major blockbuster shows. He denied it, of course, but Kate knew that it couldn't be coincidence that she found herself scheduled against David Jason four times. Rob Walsall axed *Granny Copson's Corner* to howls of fury from Middle England. 'It simply wasn't getting the ratings any more,' he said.

She didn't miss the fame. She'd never taken it seriously, and it had been a two-edged sword. She did miss the power, though. What a joy it was to be able to go on television and sound off about what you perceived as the evils of the world. She wanted life to consist of more than just retirement, waiting to die. She began to write another book. The idea crystallised when she found that someone had crashed into her car, and hadn't left a note. Her book was called *Responsibility*. It was an analysis of the need to take responsibility, both privately, for our own actions, and also publicly, for the actions of all the groups to which one belonged, from family to village to nation to species. Every time we opt out, she suggested, we die a little. Every time we avoid responsibility, we lose a little bit of self-esteem. In the end, we are the losers. It's hardly necessary to state that she found the book impossible to get published. It wasn't an exciting message. It wasn't a message for the nineties.

Norman! He'd been visiting friends in the village and they met in the pub. Kate liked him the moment he walked in. He seemed an untroubled man, a simple man in the best sense. Tall, silver-haired, with just the slightest stoop, dignified, courteous, charming. Impeccable manners. Oh Lord, Kate thought, what do those manners conceal? But she never did find any skeletons in his cupboard. He loved his beer and his walking, his food and his conversation, but above all he loved Kate.

They went on cruises and they toured the world. They gave lunch and dinner parties. They went to theatres and exhibitions. He took her book seriously, was proud of her, and was disappointed for her when she couldn't get it published.

Norman had been a pilot with BOAC. Every summer he'd spent a week of his holidays picking strawberries in Kent. 'It was the exact opposite of what I did for the rest of the year,' he explained, unnecessarily. 'My wife thought I was mad.'

'I don't think you were mad.'

'Why didn't I meet you before?'

'Tut-tut, Norman. Be grateful we met at all.'

The very last trip they made was to Swansea and Cornwall. She showed him the house in Eaton Crescent. It was still in good repair. She didn't knock on the door and ask to see inside. It would have seemed too alien.

Penzance seemed alien too. Around the harbour there were one or two new buildings that made her blood boil. They weren't modern enough to be New-Brutalist. They had to be Post-Neo-Brutalist. Post-Neo-Brutalism, in Penzance!

They went to one or two old haunts in south Cornwall, around the Helford river, that seemed as beautiful as ever, but the centre of Cornwall seemed a bleak and desolate place to Kate now, with its mournful wind farms and pylons and abandoned mines. Tregarryn was all holiday homes now, except for the house itself, which was uninhabited and beginning to decay. In Tintagel everything was the King Arthur this or the Merlin that. There was even a watering hole called the Excali-bar. All the magic, all the atmosphere of antiquity, had long been trampled away beneath the tourist armies. We ruin the thing we go to see.

That night, in their hotel, they held each other very tight and listened to the wind, and Norman soothed Kate's anger.

Nothing made Norman angry, and that was the only thing about him that ever made Kate angry. She sounded off about her pet hates and he smiled his 'There goes my darling Kate, sounding off again' smile, and she got even angrier. 'Don't you care?' she shouted once. 'Can't do anything about it, old girl.' She couldn't remember, now, what that one had been about.

He died, in his bed, in his sleep. So did Enid, that lifelong narrator of violent death. Ironic, really.

21 Angela

It was a bad morning in Ward 3C. Angela Critchley started shouting just as Delilah was squeaked back in.

'Rodney!' she shouted. 'Rodney! My waters are breaking. Rodney, I've started.'

'Oh fuck, I'm back,' said Delilah.

'Rodney! Quick!' A nurse rushed to her, and she began screaming and weeping. 'I don't want another child. Look what happened to the last one. Haven't seen him for thirty years.'

Was that part of her madness or a dreadful moment of truth? Kate couldn't cope with all this. She'd had enough. Can you blame her, as Angela Critchley started screaming again, for retiring into fantasy?

She opened a small secret door in her head, which nobody knew was there. It led into the panelled library of her brain. There were books from floor to ceiling in the panelled library of her brain, and further doors led to long corridors, off which there were large numbers of brain cells, also lined with books. It was extremely peaceful in Kate's brain that morning.

'Come in, gentlemen,' she said.

Her three sons entered her brain gravely. Soon two of them would learn who had murdered Graham. One of them already knew.

'Pull up a comfortable thought, and sit on it,' she said.

They sat down. Far away she heard Doctor Ramgobi saying, 'Why has this woman been removed from intensive care?' and thin Helen saying, 'They've an emergency,' and Doctor Ramgobi saying, 'So what? This woman is an emergency.' But that was in another world.

'Now I've assembled you here, in the library,' said Kate, 'because I know which of you killed Graham.'

'Good God!' gasped Maurice.

'Well, it wasn't me,' spluttered Timothy.

'Careful, Timothy,' warned Kate. 'If this was one of your books that would almost certainly mean that it was you. In fact, when I began to consider the murder it soon dawned on me that there were a whole series of preposterous clues, as if it was in one of Timothy's books.'

'I know you don't like them,' complained Timothy, 'but must you rub it in?'

'Quiet,' contributed Nigel. 'I want to know who did it.'

'Oh, do you?' crowed Timothy. 'That means it was probably you.'

'Shut up, Timothy,' commanded Kate. 'I don't want a peep out of any of you. Now I wasted a lot of time on all those clues, and poor old Inspector Crouch wasted months. They were, I admit, ingenious clues, if rather childish. But eventually I realised that they had a purpose that wasn't childish at all. They were designed to make investigators concentrate on the question "How?" and the question "Who?" and ignore the vital question "Why?" And the very fact that they were so decorative led me to think that they were a smokescreen for something that wasn't decorative at all, something that wasn't childish at all, something that was unadorned and adult. They were little boys' mind games, such as Nigel and Timothy might be expected to indulge in, but which seemed out of character for Maurice. I felt certain that Maurice could kill . . .'

'Ma!'

'Don't protest, Maurice. I felt that Maurice could kill, but only for reasons of conscience or perhaps of misplaced altruism. However, I felt that Maurice was clever enough to create these absurd little puzzles as a smokescreen.

'All three of you said you'd like to kill Graham, if certain things happened. They were all pretty far-fetched reasons for killing, and I didn't believe any of them.

'I examined all sorts of potential motives for murder, and I decided that none of you could murder for petty reasons or for sexual reasons or because you were mad.'

'Big of you!'

'Do be quiet, Nigel. I also looked at the whole thing from the point of view of what I wanted to find out about Graham. He'd said that he was investigating what he called "a huge con against the whole human race". He wouldn't tell me anything about it, at that stage. I must admit that after I'd discovered that he had a false name, a history of crime and three abandoned wives I concluded that he'd probably been lying about this huge con. But if I found he hadn't been lying it would go some way towards enabling me to believe that he'd changed for the better, as people can, especially under my influence, let's have no false modesty. Supposing Graham had been speaking the truth. Supposing the reason why he wouldn't tell me was that it implicated one of my beloved sons. I'd still have to face the discovery that one of my sons was a murderer, but at least I would learn something good about Graham.'

Far away, in the ward, Angela Critchley screamed and screamed.

'What on earth's that?' asked Maurice.

'A woman's dying,' explained Kate. 'She thinks she's giving birth, but she's dying. It's very sad, but there's nothing we can do about it, so don't even think about it.'

The screaming grew weaker, and stopped. It was very quiet, then, in Kate's brain, until she resumed her tale.

'Now after Graham's death, when I sorted through his papers, I didn't find anything that could even remotely be described as a con against the whole human race. I wasn't surprised. As I say, I was doubting his integrity at the time. But supposing there was evidence, and whoever killed him removed the evidence. I believe that Graham had something on some-body, something so serious that he had to be killed. There were only two possible motives for the murder that I could accept, knowing you as I do – misplaced altruism saving me from Graham, or desperate self-preservation.

'So I began to try to think of possibilities in the lives of all three of you that could be so serious as to necessitate killing Graham with all the risks that entailed. I had difficulty with Timothy. It was difficult to conceive of anything important enough in his life.'

'Thank you so much.'

'Do be quiet, Timothy. I'm explaining why you aren't a murderer. Surely that can't offend even your touchy per-sonality? I don't think I ever really believed you capable of murder.'

'Mum!'

'I'm sorry if you find the inability to commit a murder an insult, but I'm afraid you'll have to accept that you're out of the frame. Now I do believe both Maurice and Nigel capable of murder.'

'Ma!'

'Mother!'

'Oh yes. I was certain Maurice could kill Graham to save me, but I think that presupposed that he knew something about Graham that had never come out, and I didn't want that to be the case, naturally, since I loved Graham, so I decided to assume, for the moment, that that was not the reason. So, I asked myself, could Graham have enough on Maurice to lead Maurice to need to kill him? We all know he's had affairs all over the place.'

'Ma!'

'But Clare knows it too . . .'

'Ma!'

'Of course she does. The knowledge never leaves her eyes.'

'Oh God, is that true?'

Squeak squeak. Removal of dead Angela. Don't listen. Talk.

'Of course it's true, Maurice. You think more about every poor refugee in Africa and the Balkans than about poor Clare. The plight of gypsies in the Danube Basin keeps you awake but you wouldn't notice a crack in your bathroom basin. It's the way you are, but are you a murderer? What could you have done that was so awful that you would need to kill to save your skin? I couldn't immediately think of anything, so I moved on to Nigel.

'Now in connection with Nigel I thought long and hard about all sorts of things. I remembered an exchange at my bedside between Nigel and Maurice. Maurice said that he couldn't get more than ten pages into Timothy's books.'

'Oh, Maurice!'

'Sorry, Timothy. I have tried. I did actually read one right through.'

'Yes,' said Kate, 'but the significant thing was that when you said that you couldn't finish them, Nigel said, "Oh God, can't you?" and when you asked him why he was so horrified Nigel said Timothy was his brother and we should all like his books, or something like that. That was pretty limp.'

'You remember all that?'

'Yes. I haven't lost my brain power at all! I've been fooling you.'

'Good God!'

'Yes. And a possible explanation came to me for Nigel's horror and his lame explanation of it. The last words of *Trouble in Torquay* are "Sorry, Ma". Nigel's instinctive thought was that if you hadn't finished the book, Maurice, people might realise that you couldn't have been the one that typed "Sorry, Ma" to frame Timothy. It was therefore likely that they'd realise that Nigel was the murderer. I always thought him the most likely candidate.'

'Mother!'

'Nigel, you can hardly complain about my thinking you a possible murderer since you are an actual murderer.'

Nobody spoke. The silence in the library in Kate's brain was so intense that Kate felt she could have reached out and touched it.

'Of course, at first,' continued Kate at last, 'I thought that, because Nigel was the most likely, it probably wouldn't be him, but I was forgetting that this is real life and not a detective story. Now what could Graham have had on Nigel that was so serious that Nigel would need to kill him to save his skin?

'Well, almost immediately I thought of the thing I waited to hear from Nigel. I waited for years and years and years, and for some reason I didn't dare to ask you about it, and I suppose eventually I half forgot about it. You made no further mention of the promising progress on a cure for cancer that you were making.'

She paused. Nobody spoke.

'You've gone very silent, Nigel.'

'You see!' Timothy sounded quite triumphant. 'People do go very silent.'

Kate ignored this.

'I suppose I assumed that you would tell me if you had good news,' continued Kate. 'Or maybe my subconscious warned me off the subject. Now we all know that drugs companies make huge profits, but it does seem to me that you are even richer, Nigel, than one might expect, so I wondered, did you take a huge bribe to conceal the progress you had made and abort this particular research, so that a wider range of drugs could continue to be sold, at greater profit?'

'It's just a theory, a preposterous theory.'

'Well, that's what I thought, but it was the only theory I had, so I thought I'd better put it to the test. And I found that it did explain one or two things that had puzzled me slightly. It explained why you didn't come to your Uncle Bernard's funeral.

You couldn't have borne the guilt. It explains why you didn't tell me at the time about your dinner with Graham in Krogs in Copenhagen, where, I suggest, you had not only the herring platter, the turbot and the *rødgrød med fløde*, but also the shock of your life. *He* was on to *you*. *He* was going to expose *you*. There was a row, but it was the other way around.'

You could have heard an aitch drop in the panelled library. Maurice went over to the rows of old books and pretended to read their titles. Nigel strolled to the window and looked out at . . . what?

'This is all sheer speculation,' he mumbled without turning round.

'I know. There's a lot I don't know. I don't know whether it was your own firm or a rival firm that was paying you. I don't know how you got the name board for Leningrad station or whether it was a fake. I don't know about the gun or fingerprints or whether you did steal a file on you from Trevor Square. I don't need to. I'm not bringing you to court, except the court of your conscience. But I know I'm right. Your face told me so when I opened my eyes and looked at you.'

'You can't prove any of it.'

'Of course not. I'm an old woman in a hospital bed. I'm very sorry it was you, Nigel. You were my first-born and very special to me. But I'd have been no less sorry if it had been Timothy or Maurice. It's an appalling crime against the human race, but why should that be a surprise to me after the times I've lived through. I'm deeply shocked and saddened, less by the murder – after all, I've long known that one of my sons was a murderer – than by what Graham found out and what led you to murder. How could a man capable of being so greedy and immoral have come out between my legs? To think of all the beautiful things that came out between my legs – Timothy, Maurice, Elizabeth – and all the beautiful things that went in and out between my legs . . .'

'Mum!'

'Ma!'

'Mother!'

'Sorry, kids, but I can be as outrageous as I like. I'm almost a hundred. I daresay I seem quite a bold person to you, but consider this. For the first forty years of my life I was scared to admit to myself that Dilys was dead and for the last forty I've been scared to investigate Graham's murder. Bit sad, really. Timothy, Maurice, my deepest apologies, my darlings, for ever having suspected you. Off you all go now. Close the library door behind you. I want my brain to myself now. I want peace. It's over. It's all over.'

Kate heard their footsteps recede. She heard the secret door in her head close very gently. She had her head to herself again and felt desolate. She heard more footsteps, and she recognised them. Thin Helen was approaching.

'Well, well, Kate, and how are you?' asked thin Helen. 'A bit better. That's good. What a day we've had. Lily more confused than ever, Delilah back and fore like a piston, and poor Angela Critchley dead. Kate! You've been dribbling all down your nice nightshirt! What have you been thinking about?'

22 Charlie

It was going to the funeral in Germany that did for her. It was cold in the church and graveyard in Niederlander-ob-der-Kummel, and she went down with bronchitis on the journey home. The illness lasted for several weeks, and it turned her into an old woman at last.

Even now, lying in bed, covered in bed sores, living through what she hoped would be her last night of life, she didn't regret going.

Elizabeth had driven her there. Elizabeth wanted to see her father buried, even though she had hardly known him.

The little church in the picturesque village with its smiling half-timbered houses was crowded for the funeral of this good and upright man. Afterwards, they met his only son. The Sperm Count's son was also there, but death had claimed Graf Von Seemen several years before.

Kate smiled as she remembered telling Heinz's son how difficult she'd found the German language. 'And you can say that,' he exclaimed, 'and you a Welsh lady? I bought a Welsh scrabble set in Llandudno. It had twelve "l"s, ten "y"s, ten "w"s, eight "d"s, and only two "e"s. I am yoking. Do you not remember how my father loved to yoke?'

And it had all flooded over her, memories of Heinz and with them memories of Arturo and Walter and Graham and Norman and Gwyn, whose beauty she could sometimes scarcely remember. There, in that rather austere house on the edge of the tumbling village she briefly gave way to all the weaknesses she claimed to have conquered – self-pity, a sense of loss, nostalgia almost unbearable in its intensity. And now, at two in the morning, in a long hospital night, she felt . . . oh Lord . . . she felt all those human emotions all over again, for the middle of the night is the weakest time for the strongest of us, and Kate was very weak now even at the strongest times.

It was Maurice who took her to the retirement home. The Golden Glade Retirement Home. Big, early Victorian house. Slightly gloomy. Large garden with fine roses, wonderful in summer, horribly bare in winter, all sodden earth and thorns. She surprised him by showing a touch of worldly pride as she introduced him to the other residents with the words, 'This is my son Maurice, whom you may have seen on television, and this is his fiancée Clare.'

They led her along the corridor to a room which seemed desperately small and bare to Maurice and Clare. The radiator was flaking, and the commode was badly scratched.

'Well well,' she said, smiling. 'It's funny to think that six weeks ago I was driving down the Rhine with Elizabeth. From *Zimmer frei* to zimmer frame in thirty-six days. Look, I shall get the evening sun. I've asked for a little rack for my wines. I shall be happy here.'

She had outlived all her generation. Daphne Stoneyhurst, Jenny Carter, Olga Begelman, Stanley Wainwright, all gone now. It's what happens if you're lucky enough to live for a very long time. No point in getting upset about it.

None of the family, to do them justice, had wanted her to go into a home.

Timothy had said, 'I'd have you, but you'd not like living in Majorca, so far away from your friends.'

What friends? They're dead. She had thought it, but hadn't said it. He was right, anyway. She wouldn't have liked living in Majorca.

'And things are a bit frail between me and Paula at present,' he'd said, 'but surely one of the others would have you?'

Maurice had said, 'I just can't have you, Ma. I'm away for

weeks on end. Clare would get the . . . well, not the burden exactly. But it wouldn't be fair on her.'

What a time to be thoughtful about Clare at last, she had thought, but she hadn't said anything. Best not.

Nigel had said, 'You said yourself I'm never there. I'm never anywhere long enough. I hate it, but that's my life. I always seem to be opening up unused houses.'

Poor you, Kate had thought. What miseries those of us with only one home are spared. But she hadn't said anything. No point.

Elizabeth had said, 'I'd have you like a shot, but it's Terence. He's a creature of habit. And there's *his* mother. If you, why not her? And you two'd never get on. She drops her aitches.'

Kate was ninety-five when she entered the home. She was walking quite slowly now, with the aid of a stick. Her balance was bad, and her eyesight wasn't too good any more. Only her superb hearing remained unimpaired. A casual observer might have expected that her relationships with men might be over. Maurice certainly thought so.

We know her rather better, you and I, don't we?

She saw Charlie the moment she entered the residents' lounge on the first evening. She dreaded entering the room, with its rows of huge, droopy armchairs which dwarfed the bony old people who were sitting in them. Kate Copson, she told herself, what you have lived through and still you find it an ordeal to enter this room! So she shrugged, told herself, 'Come on, woman. This is your life now,' and entered, and there he was, at the far end of the room, under the huge salmon in a glass case which was all that remained from Colonel Pride-Aitcheson's days. He was a short, slim, weather-beaten old man with skin like an old bag. She sensed a twinkle in his eyes as he sized her up. She held his gaze for a moment and then sat, discreetly, near the round table covered in magazines almost as old as the residents.

It had only been a brief look, but a woman two chairs away,

394

whom Kate would later discover to be called Martha Kitchen, said, in her know-all's voice, just loud enough to be heard, 'Aye, aye, here's competition. Betty Beveridge had better look to her laurels.'

It didn't take Charlie long to start chatting Kate up, and she offered him no discouragement. Why should she? The other women resented her, and not only Betty Beveridge. What had she got that they hadn't? A real interest in Charlie, that's what. A response to the twinkle in his eyes. An interest in the pain behind the twinkle. Such pain there.

Marjorie Ellingham was quite friendly, despite Charlie, and Isobel Hutton wasn't too bad, but the rest of them!

Charlie had known one of them since he was a child. Margaret Duckworthy. 'Look at her now,' he said. 'Look at that sad, ugly, apathetic, mean-spirited, stupid old hag. It's hard to believe that seventy years ago she was a sad, ugly, apathetic, mean-spirited, stupid young schoolgirl.' He twinkled. Behind the twinkle, such pain. He'd made his money out of scrap. He was shrewd. He tried to teach Kate chess. She resisted at first, the old puritanism. In the end she gave in, and enjoyed it. At first Charlie beat her easily. By the end she beat him more often than he beat her, but it was never easy.

All the children visited her regularly, and she went to stay with Nigel, Maurice and Elizabeth for a week every year, though she stopped going to Majorca in 1997, when she found the flight too difficult.

On her ninety-sixth birthday, in October 1995, they all came to see her, and took her out to lunch to a place round the corner, a pub with a restaurant, called the Speckled Hen. It wasn't bad, and there weren't any steps. Nigel had the fish cakes with light Thai dressing and the calves' liver on a bed of rocket. Even Potters Bar was trendy now.

They raised their glasses to her, and wished her a happy birthday, and drank to her.

'Thank you,' she said. 'Do you know that in Korea there is no word for old people's home? The concept just isn't known.'

They looked at her in horror.

'Did you know,' she continued, 'that in Sri Lanka the very young, the young, the middle-aged, the old and the very old all live and eat and talk and laugh together?'

None of her three sons knew what to say. Elizabeth, to do her credit, rallied first, but then she was a woman.

'But we thought you were happy here,' she said.

Kate smiled. 'I don't want to live with any of you,' she said. 'This isn't Korea. This isn't Sri Lanka. This is Britain in the 1990s. I've had a lot of guilt in my life. Now I'm free of guilt, and you are the guilty ones. It's your turn. Thank you.'

She could see them wondering if she was developing a nasty streak, if she was beginning to go funny. Well, she felt that she had earned the right to have a little sport at their expense.

'I wouldn't have come to any of you if you'd offered,' she said. 'And you'd all have felt so generous and virtuous. It's a shame for you that you didn't invite me. I'll tell you what. After you've dropped me off, this afternoon, have a conference, come back, say you've decided you'll all have me for three months of the year. The rotation of the corpse. I'm practically a corpse now.'

'Mum, this is terrible,' said Timothy.

'Sorry. Aren't I allowed to be just a little bit mischievous? And it's all right. If you did that I still wouldn't come. I am happy, in my way. I have the sun in the evening. I have two glasses of wine every evening, and a third if the sun's shining, to celebrate my good fortune. And I have Charlie. I couldn't leave Charlie.'

'Mother!' said Nigel.

'I might marry him.'

'But he was in scrap!'

'Elizabeth! That is so snobbish. I will marry him, I think.'

She didn't marry Charlie, though, and for a very good reason. He didn't ask her.

On Charlie's hundredth birthday, there were flags and a banner stating '100 not out'. There was a tele-message from the Queen. There was cake and jelly and they all sang 'Happy birthday to you' and 'For he's a jolly good fellow'.

'I find all this very tasteless and schmaltzy,' said Betty Beveridge. 'I hope they don't do it for me.'

'They won't, don't you worry,' said Caroline Upshott.

'You haven't seen anything yet,' said Martha Kitchen, the know-all. 'You wait.'

Kate was keeping a low profile and didn't say anything. It wasn't her day. It was his.

Miss Murchison stepped forward, in her dowdy, baggy clothes, smiling broadly.

'Charlie,' she said, 'we have a little surprise for you. The French ambassador will explain.'

Martha Kitchen smiled smugly.

The French ambassador was tall and elegant and impeccably dressed. How frumpish Miss Murchison looked beside him. He smiled at Charlie, sitting there in his wheelchair, and said, 'Charlie Fletcher, you are a very brave man and a credit to your country. You did sterling service for France in the Great War, and France does not forget her friends. It is with great pleasure and pride that I present you with the *Légion d'honneur*.'

Charlie's jaw dropped open. It was happening all the time! He was moved to tears. He bent his head forward and the French ambassador leant down and decorated him, then kissed him on both cheeks. Dorothy Whatmore muttered, 'Disgusting!' and somebody else said, 'S'ssh!' Kate led the applause. When it died down somebody, probably that know-all Martha Kitchen, shouted, 'Speech.'

'Oh no,' said Charlie. 'I'm not a speaking man. *Je ne suis pas . . . un* speaking man. Thank you very much. *Merci beaucoup*.'

There was more applause. In all the excitement Delia Raddlestone stepped on a balloon, there was a bang, and Charlie flinched, Kate saw him flinch, seventy-eight years since the end of the war, and still he flinched.

The French ambassador was politeness personified, and stayed for a drink. Kate felt so sorry for him and so ashamed of the lack of sophistication in the place that she went up to him and talked to him in fluent French about Paris, the Crillon, her love of Aix-en-Provence. She didn't think twice about it. Afterwards she heard Janet Brighouse say, 'Upstaging everyone as usual,' and somebody said, 'Stealing his thunder,' and that know-all Martha Kitchen said, 'She's ashamed of us.' Even Charlie seemed a bit hurt, and that was terrible. And she'd been so anxious to keep a low profile.

So that was the explanation of the pain behind the twinkle. Several times Kate asked Charlie what he'd done, and he refused to talk. One day, a cold, sullen afternoon, with a sky the colour of death, an afternoon that had never become properly light, he did talk, over a cup of tea under the prize salmon.

'Just did what I was paid to do. Fought. Killed people. Saved people.'

'Where did the French come in?'

'1915. I led a . . . I dunno . . . decoy, I suppose. Like a diversion. Got the Gerry fire on to us, these French blokes could retreat safely, kind of thing. S'pose that was what it was.'

'Brave.'

'What we was there for. So many died then, so many've died later, they've got these medals, they've no one to give 'em to. Giving 'em away, they are.'

'But you didn't die.'

'No. Got invalided out first day of the Battle of the Somme. Lucky.'

'How did you get injured?'

'Went back to save a bloke. Young bloke lying injured, can't have been more than eighteen but he looked older, grown up, seen so much already. I never forgot that look.'

398

Kate's heart was racing. She hardly dared ask, but she had to. 'What was his name?'

'Dunno. We was never properly introduced.'

'Charlie, what did he look like?'

Charlie looked at her, wondering. She didn't want to tell him anything. There was no point now, and he didn't ask.

'I didn't exactly stop to take an identikit picture,' he said. 'I dunno. He had dark hair. I think. Good-looking lad. He looked into my eye, said, "I'm not dying, am I?" I said, "Course you aren't, mate." But he was. There was gunfire everywhere, shells exploding. I saw a leg just lying there on its own. Barbed wire. Bloke impaled on the barbed wire, screaming. I think the leg might have been his. I reckon that lad I tried to save was the lucky one. He never had to see all that again. I've seen it every day for eighty-one years, Kate.'

'Oh, Charlie.'

'Stupid to go back, s'pose, and get a bullet through me leg for it. Dunno, though. Helped him to die nicely.'

Well, there was no point in thinking about it. She'd never know. Hundreds of good-looking men with dark hair and the knowledge of hell in their eyes must have died that day. No, there was no point in thinking about it. But, damn it, she began to cry, and Charlie began to cry too. They clutched each other beneath the salmon, that dark afternoon, and cried and cried and cried.

'Look at those two disgusting love-birds,' said Betty Beveridge who was stuck with her jigsaw.

'Oh, shut up, you dried-up old cunt,' said Charlie.

And Kate laughed. Oh, Kate, how far you have travelled from 16 Eaton Crescent.

Kate recalled now, as the dawn of her 36,449th day approached, the last visit paid by each of her children to the Golden Glade Retirement Home.

Timothy's last visit had been several weeks before her stroke. She remembered sitting on the seat just inside the front door, all dolled up in a bright red two-piece suit.

'Visitors again! My word,' Ellie Smithson had said. She'd stepped into the roll of chief sneerer when Betty Beveridge died.

Kate wanted to say, 'You might have more visitors if you weren't so miserable,' but she didn't, she said, 'One of my sons, and his new lady friend.'

'Have a look at the old school on your way to the Speckled Hen,' said Martha Kitchen, the know-all. 'They're making it ready for Kosovan refugees.'

And then Timothy was there. Seeing her son in his early seventies with a white beard make Kate feel absurdly old. He bent to kiss her and she knew that he was thinking how much she had shrunk.

It was a struggle down the path with her zimmer frame. Her body was seizing up as if the blood was freezing like diesel in winter.

'Carrie's in the car,' he said. 'You'll like her.'

'Let's hope so. How's Roberta?'

Timothy sighed deeply, but said, 'Doing very well. It's agonisingly slow, though.'

Timothy's daughter Roberta was in a drug rehabilitation clinic.

At last the painful journey to the car was over. Carrie got out to welcome Kate. The poor woman was shaking. What had Timothy said about her?

Kate shook hands with Carrie and smiled broadly. Carrie had a wide, friendly, freckled face. She was wearing shorts that might have been described as sensible if they'd been on somebody else. She was tall and brown and flat. She was wearing open-toed sandals. She didn't have the toes for them.

It was agony for Kate, getting into the car, getting out of the car, hanging on to the car while Timothy retrieved the zimmer frame from the boot, struggling into the restaurant, dropping gingerly into a chair in the bar.

The waiter said, 'And for you, madam?' in his best 'Does She Take Sugar?' voice, and Kate said, very firmly, 'A kir royale, please, but very light on the cassis.'

After she'd ordered her rum and coke, Carrie said, 'Excuse me. Gotta go and point Penelope at the porcelain.' When she'd gone, Timothy said, 'You wouldn't think she was fifty-three, would you?' and Kate didn't say, 'No, I'd got her down for sixty-one.' 'At last I've found somebody suitable,' said Timothy. 'Why on earth didn't I meet her years ago?' Kate said nothing. 'Oh God,' said Timothy, 'you don't like her. I think you're jealous. I don't think you'd like any woman I loved.' Kate smiled sadly and hoped fervently that that wasn't true. 'I do like her,' she lied, this old lady who had long abandoned the cruelty of truth. 'I do like her. I hope she is right for you. I hope you'll be very happy. But hush, here she comes, she's finished pointing Penelope at the porcelain.'

It was the same agonising journey a few weeks later, on Maurice's last visit, with his portly fiancée Clare. Maurice was totally bald now, and Clare was unrecognisable as the beautiful young thing who had once charmed the facts out of the BBC library. Kate had the same seat in the bar, chose a kir royale again, and sat in the same seat in the restaurant, at the table that was easiest for her to reach.

They talked about Charlie. She admitted to missing him, and to missing their chess.

'There are only three men in the place now,' she said, 'and poor things all three. At last it can be said that your mother is finished with men, Maurice.'

They discussed the Kosovan refugees. Maurice didn't want to, he was off duty, but Kate had to get it off her chest. 'Lots of the women think we shouldn't have taken them,' she said. 'Ellie

Smithson said, "They're practically gypsies. What do we want with them?" I often feel ashamed to be British these days. I ought to have died long ago. I haven't the energy to fight them.'

'Why should you fight them? What good would it do?'

'That's defeatist. I was never defeatist before.'

When Clare went to the smallest room, Kate said, 'I don't suppose you'll ever marry her now, will you?' 'I suppose not,' said her youngest son, who was sixty-six years old. 'I suppose not. I suppose I'm frightened it might change everything.' 'After thirty-nine years!' she exclaimed, and he shrugged.

Elizabeth and Terence brought the full family gathering, Trevor with his boyfriend Richard, Mark with his wife Sarah and their sixteen-year-old son Ben and their five-year-old daughter Victoria, who came along when hope had been abandoned.

Victoria went down the path ahead of Kate, removing obstructions so that the zimmer frame would have a smooth passage. Everybody said there was more of Kate in Victoria than of her grandmother or her mother. Everyone said she looked just like the photographs of Kate at five.

Kate had been shocked to learn that as a university lecturer Trevor got £30,000 a year, and as the sales manager of a firm making plastic bags Mark got £50,000 a year plus a car, but this wasn't the time for serious economic debate.

She sometimes wondered if Trevor felt envious of Mark and Sarah for having a bigger house, a better car, better holidays, and Ben and Victoria. That day, from a look she caught in Trevor's eye, she got her answer. He pitied them.

'You're very quiet, Great-granny,' said Victoria.

'Thinking.'

'I think sometimes too.'

'Good.'

They had to put two tables together this time, but they didn't mind. They were always very obliging at the Speckled Hen.

Kate made them laugh about the Kosovan refugees, when she told them how she had turned on Ellie Smithson and said that the world had to unite against ethnic cleansing, and Ellie Smithson, missing the point as usual, said, 'We wouldn't get any cleansing if we didn't employ ethnics. The British just don't want to do it.'

'There are people like that who always miss the point,' said Elizabeth. 'They're terribly irritating. I don't know how you can put up with them. Don't you really think now that you should come and live with us?'

'We've discussed it,' said Terence. 'We both want you to.'

'We'd be happy to have you for holidays,' said Trevor, 'if you could stand Richard's snoring.'

'Bitch!' mouthed Richard, so that Victoria wouldn't hear.

'Same in this quarter,' was Mark's slightly less than ringing echo.

They must be calculating that I'll die quite soon, so I won't be a burden for long, thought Kate.

'When I'm very old like you, Great-granny,' piped up Victoria, 'I want to live with people I know who love me.'

'Please come, Gran,' mumbled Ben after glares had been directed towards him. He looked sulky. Oh, how he reminded her of Gwyn. But the world had led him to expect so much more than Gwyn (he could hardly end up with less) and he had a spoilt, wilful look.

'You're all very kind,' said Kate. 'Very kind. I want to cry. But I made my decision, and it's too late now.'

Nigel came less than two weeks before her stroke. 'I've just been to the Speckled Hen,' he said. 'I had the venison terrine and the brill.'

'Why didn't you take me?'

'It's too difficult for you now.'

'The others have all taken me.'

'Have they? Well, in my judgement, and I hope you feel I'm old enough to have earned the right to have a certain amount of judgement, in my judgement, as I say, it has now become too great a burden for you to undertake the journey.'

'Couldn't I have made the decision?'

'I don't think so. You will never admit defeat.'

'Do you mean that next time I leave this place I'll leave feet first?'

'No, of course not.'

But she did.

In the end, she just had to explode. It had been building up for so long. One Sunday, in October, when she saw them standing around the entrance hall with their zimmer frames, waiting for their lunch like a flock of vultures, she could hold it in no longer. Old people have difficulty holding things in, and she was glad that in her case it was anger rather than urine.

'Don't you care about anything except yourselves any more?' she yelled at them. 'Don't you think of other people at all? Stuff your faces, move your bowels, make sure you have the best seat in the lounge. There are hundreds of thousands of us with our zimmer frames, looking at our soap-watching, material-sodden society and doing sod all about it. Can't we even talk about it? What about the morality of saturation bombing? What about the drug culture? What about the increasing gap between rich and poor? What about corruption in high places? What about corruption in low places? What about cover-ups, not about sex – who really cares what people do in private – but about foods that poison the animals we eat and so poison us, and all the hormones and poisons and pesticides that are found in mothers' milk, and cruelty to civets by the perfume industry, and cruelty to badgers by almost everybody? Don't you want to do anything about this land where a sense of responsibility, a sense of decency, a sense of pride and a sense of shame are becoming as rare as skylarks and lapwings, a land where we don't dare rebuke people for dropping plastic burger boxes for fear they'll beat us up, a land of road rage and air rage and now zimmer-frame rage? I've known so much irony in my life but here you are living out the greatest irony of all. Can't you see, you fools, that by being so obsessed with avoiding the death you fear so much you're bringing on the very thing you fear? Stop thinking of yourselves and you'll live longer, I tell you. Oh, can't you see it?'

'Hush, dear. You'll give yourself a stroke,' said Martha Kitchen.

Know-alls! Who needs them?

23 Victoria

Kate closed her eyes, and slept, and woke, and slept, and half-woke, and half-slept. There was pain in her head this morning. Several times she drifted off and woke up in a different place. In Majorca, with Carrie saying, 'Have you moved your bowels this morning, Mrs Critchley?' In Tregarryn, with Arturo, but Arturo was old and bent, and his private parts were deformed, and Stanley was looking at them and saying, 'You see. I do get them right. That's what they look like.' In Swansea, in bed with Gwyn, she tried to see his young face, she couldn't move, she was paralysed, and she remembered. Just for a moment, then, she had seen Gwyn as he had been, she had been able to recall every tiny bit of his beauty, and then it was gone.

They brought Delilah back.

'Oh fuck, it's back to the funny farm,' she said.

'Yes, well, we don't really want you either,' said the nurse, a new one. 'But there's no room in intensive care.'

Doctor Ramgobi was furious.

'She needs twenty-four-hour monitoring,' he said.

'Could she be transferred to Gravesend?' asked the nurse.

'The journey might be too much. I wouldn't risk it,' said Doctor Ramgobi.

'I'm not fucking deaf,' said Delilah. 'I don't like being talked about as if I was a parcel.'

'You aren't a parcel,' said Doctor Ramgobi. 'You're a quandary.'

'I've eaten better men than you for breakfast,' said Delilah.

Kate slipped away from it all, slipped away to Walter's arms. It was nice in Walter's arms. In the distance she could still hear the noises of the ward – 'Have you ever been to the Mona Lisa, doctor?' 'In the Louvre? Yes. It was much smaller than I expected. I do think he might have painted it bigger if it was going to be so well known. Why?' No, no, I don't know about no Louvre. The Mona Lisa Club in Newport. I did a novelty dance there. I shoved a snake up me bum.'

Unlucky bum, thought Kate, and even unluckier snake. Switch off, damn it. Don't get dragged into the affairs of Ward 3C. Surf the net of your mind while it's still there, Kate Copson.

She felt the nurse's hand on her pulse. She couldn't tell which nurse it was. The nurse seemed very far away. She was sinking, drifting, floating, disintegrating. There was another hand on her pulse now. Doctor Rambogi's. Ramgobi's. Obviously he must be concerned. Why should anyone be concerned? It simply wasn't proportionate, the amount of effort involved in keeping old people alive. But then nothing was proportionate. Winning eight million on the lottery while the people next door starved wasn't proportionate, life was enough of a lottery without a lottery. It wasn't proportionate to divert a trunk road to save the habitat of the rare gunge-leaf hairy spider while keeping twelve million chickens in little concentration camps all over the countryside. Don't get angry, Kate. Don't think any more. Don't you understand? It's over.

Shortly after lunch – she could only dimly hear the noises of the last lunch of her life, she felt as if she was cocooned in cotton wool, was this death, no, not yet – the visitors began.

Elizabeth was the first to arrive, with Kate's great-grand-daughter Victoria.

'Hello, Great-granny,' came a piping little voice.

'She can't hear you, darling,' said Elizabeth. 'I told you.' To Kate, Elizabeth said, 'I didn't want to bring her, but she insisted. She loves you.'

'Why do you talk to her, Granny, if she can't hear you?' asked Victoria, thoroughly justifiably, Kate thought.

'Well, we can't be certain she can't,' said Elizabeth.

'I know she can,' said Victoria. Kate could feel Victoria's innocent breath close to her ear. 'You're a hundred tomorrow, Great-granny,' she whispered. 'There'll be a cake, and jelly, and buns. There'll be a hundred candles on the cake. It'll have to be a big cake. I baked a cake but it wasn't big enough for a hundred candles. I ate it too. It was horrid. I know you're only pretending, cos I like pretending too and Mummy says I'm like you.'

'Hush, Victoria, that's enough,' said Elizabeth.

Kate could just feel Victoria's little hand in hers, several hundred miles away across hills and valleys though it was.

What times you will live through, Victoria. In your lifetime you will know whether this civilisation will become the first civilisation not to die. You will know whether this civilisation will destroy not only itself but also the planet, so that there can never be any civilisation again. In your lifetime man will either master the machines he has created or be mastered by them. What changes I have lived through, but they will be as nothing compared to the changes you will live through, for that is the nature of change. I don't know whether I envy you your youth or pity you for it, but I know this, enjoy it to the full, live life to the full, and remain as lovely to other people as you are now. Bye-bye, Victoria. I pass the baton.

'Squeeze my hand if you can hear me, Great-granny,' piped Victoria.

Kate squeezed Victoria's hand.

'She squeezed my hand, Granny,' said Victoria excitedly.

'Don't be silly, Victoria. You're being silly now.'

'I aren't. She did.'

' "I'm not. She did." '

'There you are. I told you she did.'

'She's crying. You've made her cry, you naughty girl.'

Oh Lord, Elizabeth, don't be so crass. Why do you always have to be so crass?

When Elizabeth bent down to kiss her goodbye, and held Kate's hand, Kate squeezed it, as hard as she could, which wasn't very hard. She heard Elizabeth gasp. Then Elizabeth squeezed her hand.

'Come on, darling,' Elizabeth said to Victoria. 'Let's buy you a treat.'

'Aren't I naughty any more?' piped Victoria.

'No, darling. You aren't naughty any more.'

Kate heard mumbling. It was Delilah and Lily Stannidge talking to each other. She couldn't make out the words any more, they were so far away.

Squeak squeak. A new arrival, a woman about whom Kate would never know anything. Forget all that. It's over.

She was just conscious of the arrival of her sons. What was Nigel thinking, she wondered, now that he knew that she knew? Was he dreading that her eyes would open to accuse him again? They wouldn't, of course. She hadn't the energy any more. Her eyes would never open again.

Something was worrying her. What was it? Oh yes. They were having a party for her hundredth birthday tomorrow. She'd get a card from the Queen. 'Who's a lucky girl, then? We are, aren't we? Who's got a cake with a hundred candles that says "100 not out"? We have. Oh, we are a lucky girl.' Have to escape all that. She could hear music. Was the party beginning already? No, it was Morris dancers. She could hear them dancing. She could hear them slapping their sides. She wished they'd go away. She couldn't think why they were there, slap slap, jump jump, jig jig, twit twit. She hadn't enough bed. Dilys never left her enough bed. She wanted to be cross with Dilys, but she wasn't allowed to be. There was something wrong with Dilys. She was faulty. Kate could hear clicking noises in her head. Why were there clicking noises in her . . . what's-it? Must do something about that birthday party. Must avoid all that. One last big effort, Kate, you can do it. 'Happy birthday to you.'

Couldn't bear it. 'Happy birthday, dear . . . dear . . . Dear who? She'd forgotten her . . . her . . . the thing they called you by. Words were running out. She found herself thinking, how do you think without words? How do animals think? How . . . how . . . who . . . what . . . and that was the last thing she ever thought.

Epilogue

She didn't die just then. It isn't as easy as that, dying.

Doctor Ramgobi had alerted Nigel, and they had all come prepared for a long evening and night. 'Who's a lucky lady to have such loving children? We are.'

Nigel, Timothy, Maurice and Elizabeth sat round their mother's bed and listened to the clicking noises in her head and talked in whispers.

Clare and Terence sat in the day room, so as not to make the ward too crowded. They did a jigsaw to pass the time. It was a jigsaw of that great ocean liner, the *Queen Mary*. Nothing about Whetstone General Hospital was too modern. They found, to their great disappointment, that a piece of the sky was missing. It had been eaten, did they but know it, by a deranged chiropodist from Lewes, who had later complained that the canapés were wooden.

There was only one unseemly moment. Thin Helen asked Delilah if she wanted some Horlicks, and Delilah said, 'No, ta, darling, this whore doesn't lick any more,' and roared with laughter, and then stopped in horror and said, 'Oops. She's dying, isn't she? Sorry. It slipped me fucking mind.'

'That's all right,' said Nigel stiffly. He did seem stiff and uneasy in his mother's presence that night. We know why, you and I, but it might have been a bit puzzling to Timothy, Maurice and Elizabeth.

The barley-sugar night-light came on, and they sat round the bed in its strange glow. The clicking in Kate's head stopped. The ward became very silent, as if to justify Timothy's prose style.

At about twenty to twelve Kate's breathing began to get slower and fainter.

'Only twenty minutes to go,' whispered Timothy. 'You can do it.'

It's doubtful if any of them could have said why it was still important for their mother to live to be a hundred. Maybe they would frame the death certificate.

Her breathing grew slower and slower, fainter and fainter, and just stopped. There was no death rattle, just silence. The lines on her face seemed to have melted away. She looked almost young again. Maurice it was who put his hand over his mother's mouth and said, 'I think she's left us.'

It was two minutes to twelve. They stood round the bed, her four children, silent and shocked. It shouldn't have been a surprise, but it was. They shouldn't have been shocked, but they were.

They had thought that all the women in the ward were sleeping, but it was not so.

Lily Stannidge, who had no idea that the person who had just died was her old history teacher, who had aroused in her, when she was Lily Gardner, the historical passion that had taken her to so many ancient sites with Swan Hellenic, said, in a hushed voice, 'I'm sorry she died, of course, but it is rather exciting. I've never seen a burial at sea before.'

Delilah said, 'I once saw a man die of excitement in the Cleopatra Club in Dudley.'

At midnight the nurse pulled a sheet over Kate's head.

'I must say I'm surprised,' said Timothy. 'I really felt the old girl's will-power would see her through.'